THE FIFTH WARD

FRIENDLY FIRE

Praise for
THE FIFTH WARD:

"Fans of diverse cityscapes, mismatched buddy cops, and high adventure will relish this fantasy series launch"

Library Journal

"An entertaining story...A real page-turner"

RT Book Reviews

"Great fun...A thoroughly splendid debut"

The Eloquent Page

"I could have read this story for eternity, the characters and world building are that good...Every scene is brought to life with blazing imagery that is tied to constant movement. The characterization is superb and continues to surprise as events unfold"

Koeur's Book Reviews

"Dale Lucas tells a rambunctious tale that sends the two watchmen into the worst parts of Yenara, fighting orcs and dealing with elves...I can't wait for the next case"

University City Review

By Dale Lucas

The Fifth Ward

First Watch
Friendly Fire

THE FIFTH WARD

FRIENDLY FIRE

DALE LUCAS

www.orbitbooks.net

ORBIT

First published in Great Britain in 2018 by Orbit

1 3 5 7 9 10 8 6 4 2

Copyright © 2018 by Dale Lucas

Excerpt from *The Thousand Deaths of Ardor Benn* by Tyler Whitesides
Copyright © 2018 by Tyler Whitesides

The moral right of the author has been asserted.

A CIP catalogue record for this book
is available from the British Library.

ISBN 978-0-356-50938-9

Printed and bound in Great Britain by CPI Group (UK) Ltd, Croydon CR0 4YY

Papers used by Orbit are from well-managed forests
and other responsible sources.

Orbit
An imprint of
Little, Brown Book Group
Carmelite House
50 Victoria Embankment
London EC4Y 0DZ

An Hachette UK Company
www.hachette.co.uk

www.orbitbooks.net

For Doug.
My friend, my family.

CHAPTER ONE

"Wardwatch!" the piss-monger shouted. "That bastard's gone afoot with my slop jars!"

Rem struggled to regain himself—to wipe the mud from his eyes, to draw breath, to stand—despite pains both broad and acute from head to toe. He heard the raucous clip-clopping of the bulky draft horse's shod hooves galloping along Fishmonger's Row, the speeding cart rumbling rowdily behind it.

"Are you just going to lay there?" the piss-monger brayed, his oafish son at his elbow. "That thieving swine's getting away!"

I know, Rem wanted to say. *That's why I was in the mud, you plank. Did you not see me on the cart's running board? Trying to clamber on? Narrowly avoiding those enormous wheels as I fell?*

But he knew it would do no good. Thus Rem ignored the malodorous nightman, found his feet, and reeled out into the middle of the wide, cobbled street. His quarry raced into the distance, heading east. If the fleeing rogue kept the cart on cobbled streets—to keep from bogging in the mud—his path would have to loop back toward the river and follow it for a short length before he could finally wend eastward again, toward the city gate. If he reached the gates with enough speed behind him, not even the city guards could hinder his escape. Rem knew for a fact that the lazy bastards were in the habit of guarding the city gates at night—but rarely closing them.

Rem leapt into a desperate sprint in the cart's wake, his mind formulating something like a plan, fuzzy though it might be. Ahead, beyond the rattling pisswain, something caught his eye.

A short, stocky form trotted out of a side alley a block on from the rushing wagon. It was his partner, the dwarf Torval, hurrying back onto the main drag from the side street he'd been searching.

And he was rushing right into the cart's path!

Rem had time to shout Torval's name once—just once—before the hurtling cart ran over his stocky dwarven partner, losing no momentum as it jounced down the length of Fishmonger's Row.

Rem screamed something that was no longer Torval's name—just a howl of disbelief, terror, unbridled rage. He sprinted in the wake of the cart while the thief whipped the draft horse hard, opening the distance between them second by second. Something in Rem relented. There was no way he could catch that cart, but at any moment—any horrible, soon-to-arrive moment—he'd see Torval's crushed and twisted dwarven corpse come rolling out from underneath the damned thing.

Any moment now.

Any moment . . .

Losing speed, Rem squinted, trying to get a good look at the cart in the dim moon- and starlight supplemented by the few lit post lamps lining the boulevard. He blinked. Did his eyes deceive him? Could it be?

There was Torval, still very much alive, clinging to the axle assembly on the underside of the cart. The whole bloody thing must have passed right over the old stump, the horse's hooves somehow missing him in its headlong dash.

Rem slowed to a trot, knowing that he could not catch the cart, no matter how fast he ran...and curious as to just what his seemingly unkillable partner was up to.

In a series of quick, jerky movements, Torval worked his way to the rear of the cart. Eager to get up off the cobbled street, he clawed for purchase. As the cart rolled on, Torval dragged himself, hand over hand—precariously, laboriously—into the open rear bed of the cart as it jounced over the cobbles on Fishmonger's Row.

"You've got to be fucking kidding," Rem muttered as he jogged.

But there was no jest to be found. He saw clearly in the dim glow of the post lamps and windows lining the street that Torval had clawed his way up onto the cart bed and now sought a clear path forward among the stout, sloshing jars of piss and shit that stood between him and the thief on the driver's bench. Thus far the thief hadn't looked over his shoulder even once. He just sat there, hunched on the driver's bench, whipping the horse on, keen to leave Rem well in his wake.

Rem gave up. He had to take a moment—just a moment—to regain himself. He fell to his knees and drank in the night air like sweet, cool water in the midst of a vast desert. His lungs burned. His legs felt like warmed-over beef fat.

Get up, a voice inside him said. *Your partner needs you.*

Rem raised his eyes. The cart was just veering right, out of sight, bending southerly now at the beginning of that long loop that would take it back toward the river on cobbled streets before it turned once more eastward, onto a long, straight course toward the city gate.

Rem considered where he was, where the cart was headed, what pathways were available to him...and then realized that there was a route capable of leading him straight into the path of the cart's flight. If he hurried. If he could only find...

He saw what he required not a hundred yards from him: a livery stable, all closed up for the night.

"Aemon wept," he cursed, then struggled to his feet and ran a little farther.

He managed to bridle his chosen mount quickly, but couldn't waste time on a saddle...nor on making the stabler aware that one of his stock had been commandeered by a desperate watchwarden.

Before the present mess with the piss cart, the evening had been lovely: deep into the month of Haniss, creeping toward the solstice, the nights in Yenara utterly devoid of the fog that so often shrouded the city in a choking diaphanous haze. No, that night had been like many of late: keen and crisp, clear as glass, the heavens strewn with a million tiny pinpricks of firelight winking like diamonds thrown carelessly upon a jeweler's black velvet counting cloth, the moon fat as a silver pie, not a cloud to mar the majestic, vertiginous view.

Rem and Torval had been on patrol along Fishmonger's Row, the long, wide boulevard that bisected the little harborside peninsula known as Gaunt's Point. When they heard the hue and cry, the two set aside their heated exchange—an in-depth debate on which bird tasted best from a brazier of coals, pigeon or gull—and broke into a dead run toward the disturbance.

The cries led them from the main thoroughfare into a maze of side streets nearer the waterfront and to a boxy dwelling tucked away between a tavern and a seamen's hostel. It was a home for the orphaned or abandoned children of mariners and fishermen, run by a kindly middle-aged widow named Dorma. Smoke and flames poured from its opened lower windows while local fire brigade volunteers shuttled in water to try to douse it. A few dozen people milled at the edges of the courtyard, coughing smoke from their lungs, most of them women and children. Their injuries seemed superficial for the most part—bruises, scrapes, some soot stains, and a lot of coughing— but there were two or three little ones struggling mightily for breath. The sight immediately turned Rem's stomach.

Dorma stood in the middle of the street, soot streaked, graying hair a tangled mess, banging two cookpots together and shouting.

"Here we are," Torval spat. "Hang that racket."

Dorma stopped beating the pots together, dropped them, and stepped forward. To Rem's great surprise, she laid hands on Torval, a move that—had she been a man—would probably have earned her broken fingers or a sprained wrist.

"They've taken her! There's no time to lose!"

"Taken who?" Rem asked, as softly as he could.

"Iesta!" the woman said, as if it were the clearest fact in all the world. "Recover her, I beg you! No reward shall be too great if you can return her!"

Torval gently shrugged off the woman's grip. "Who's this Iesta? One of the children? Is she kidnapped?"

"No," Rem said, still not sure why Dorma was in such a twist, "Iesta's one of the goddesses of the Panoply. Empress of the Abandoned. Patron of beggars, orphans, and mendicants, correct?"

"Precisely!" the woman said. "And she's gone! They've taken her!"

"Hold on," Torval said. "You're telling me your home is

burning and you've got hurt children all about and you're in a twist about a bloody idol from your house shrine?"

"The idol's hollow!" Dorma shouted, then bent close to add, "All our savings are inside it. Without that coin—"

Ah, there it was. The fire was not just some accidental blaze, but a distraction to cover a thief's flight.

Rem nodded and clapped Torval on the shoulder; time to go to work. "See to the children," he told Dorma. "We'll have Iesta back by sunrise."

She gave them a hurried description of the idol—a heavy, awkward sculpture of half-wrought old jewelry and tinkers' castoffs, about the size of a well-fed toddler—and then the two were off.

"Stealing a household god," Rem huffed as they ran, the cold night air burning his lungs. "Shameful. Who purloins a god, anyway?"

Torval took a sudden left down a dark, narrow alley, and Rem very nearly overshot and lost him altogether. Torval barked back over his shoulder, "Where there's need, there's no decency," he said.

They broke out of the alleyway onto Fishmonger's Row, the only cobbled street in all of Gaunt's Point, running nearly its length. Torval scrambled to a halt and scanned the area. Rem skidded to a stop beside Torval and struggled to catch his breath. Between the late hour and the bitter cold, foot traffic was light, but there were a few shadowy figures scattered along the avenue, reeling their way home from a drink or trudging off to a midnight shift in some warehouse or mill on the riverbank.

"What are we looking for?" Rem asked between great gulps of air.

"Consider the idol," Torval said. "An awkward size and shape. Probably heavy, too. To move such a thing, our thief would have to go by horseback or cart sooner or later."

"Simple enough," Rem huffed. "Carts and horses are forbidden on the streets from dusk 'til dawn. He'd stick out like a sore thumb. He could just be holed up, waiting for morning—"

"Not likely," Torval said. "He had to know that if they raised an alarm, there'd be watchwardens swarming the Point in no time. His only hope for escape is speed and distance. And if he's going to gain ground, he needs hooves or wheels, and fast."

"It's a fool's move," Rem pressed. "Knowing that he'd be caught so easily, on a horse or a wagon, out in the open, when there are none about—"

Torval turned to Rem and eyed him askance. "Except for...?"

Rem suddenly realized what Torval was getting at. "Honeywagons," Rem said.

"Honeywagons," Torval repeated, proud that his protégé had followed his lead.

The only beast-drawn carts allowed to move through the streets at night were those of the nightmen, known colloquially as gong farmers, slop-brokers, or piss-mongers—men who contracted with the wards and their neighborhood councils to collect urine and excrement from the waste barrels that haunted the darkest downstairs corners of most tenements and boardinghouses. They'd crawl slowly up and down the side streets of Yenara all night long in their horse- or ox-drawn slop wains, hauling out those stinking barrels wherein Yenara's good citizens emptied their chamber pots, transferring all that stewing egesta into great clay jars that were then delivered to the city's tanneries for use in industrial leather curing, or beyond the walls to be used as fertilizer for nearby farms. Once or twice Rem and Torval had broken up brawls between competing slop-mongers, as one might try to horn in on another's contracted routes to illicitly top off his jars. Tanners and farmers paid good money for all that piss and shit, after all, and very few people lined up for the dubious honor of collecting it. Generally, though, the wardwatch were aware of the progress of the honeywagons only peripherally, the sight, sound, and smell of them a barely noticed but prosaic element of Yenara's everyday life—best ignored, if not forgotten.

"So, split up?" Rem asked. "I'll head west, you east."

Torval nodded. "Just so. Check any haul you find. Make any piss-mongers you meet aware of who and what we're looking for. Could be, if they're on their guard, our thief won't manage to so easily overtake them."

They split up then. Three blocks along, down a side alley, Rem found just what he sought: two human silhouettes beside a large horse-drawn wain parked in the lee of a three-story tenement. Rem set off down the length of the dark side street, the cart only a short block beyond the main road.

"You there!" Rem cried. "Step away from that cart and stand where you are! Wardwatch!"

The two silhouettes froze and seemed to study him. The shorter of the two clapped the larger one on the shoulder. The tall one bent to his labors again, while the other advanced toward Rem.

"I said stand where you are!" Rem shouted. "Throw up your hands!" Slowing now, he drew his sword, the blade hissing as it slid from its scabbard, keen edges glinting a little in the dim lamplight of the gloomy street. So armed, he slowed his approach just ten feet from the cart and its reeking contents, face-to-face with the big liver-colored draft horse hitched to the wain's traces. The shorter and thicker of the two men stepped between Rem and the cart, then raised something: a wooden ax handle with an improvised lumpy iron crown.

"My permits are paid," the fellow spat, shaking his bludgeon. "If you're from Toomey's camp, trying to jack this load, you'll find my boy and me hard contests, indeed!"

The lug at the rear of the cart lifted his head again. "Need help, Da?"

"Bend to your work, boy. I can handle this one."

Rem reached into his greatcoat—standard issue for all watchwardens in these colder months—and drew out his lead badge on its leather string. "I'm wardwatch, sir," Rem said, showing it plainly. "You have my word. We're just looking for—"

"Steady on, old-timer," the broad, muscled boy at the rear of the cart said.

It took Rem a moment to realize that the boy wasn't talking to him, nor to his own father. He was instead addressing a new arrival on the scene—a bent old man with what looked like a horribly hunched back shuffling up the street toward the cart. The old man leaned on a crooked stick to support himself as he made slow, crabwise progress along the muddy street. It seemed that the boy had noticed the old fellow's struggling, shuffling gait, for he now moved toward him, eager to help him along.

"Myrick," the father said over his shoulder, never taking his eyes off Rem, "get back on those slop jars!"

"Just a moment, Da," the boy said. "This old duffer just about stumbled right over them."

The old man suddenly swatted the young man's shins with his walking stick. The young piss collector bent, crying out. The walking stick rose in the air, then thumped him hard on his melon head. Down the lad went into the mud, moaning. The piss-monger turned to see what troubled his boy.

Rem stared for a moment, trying to puzzle it out: Why thump the boy like that? He'd only been trying to help.

Then something strange happened. The bent old man stood upright, spun round—putting his back to the cart—and yanked at a knot on his tunic. Something heavy—the very hump on his back—dropped with a thud into the cart bed. Suddenly Rem understood.

This was their thief. That hump on his back had been the idol itself, tied beneath his cloak. Now the thief had dumped his cargo and was climbing into the honeywagon.

Rem shot forward as the thief scurried up the length of the cart toward the driver's bench. Just as Rem reached the middle of the wagon and leapt awkwardly onto the running board, planning to clamber over the cart's plank frame in a clumsy effort to cut off his suspect, the thief danced nimbly past him, thumped down onto the sprung driver's bench, and snatched up the reins of the draft horse. There was a snap. The horse jerked in its traces, and the cart was under way.

Rem clung to the side, one boot on the running board, another flailing through space. He had one good handgrip on the rail of the cart bed, but holding his sword in his other hand meant he could not gain purchase without first dropping his weapon. He was trying to decide what to do about that when the thief rose up in the driver's seat and, without loosing the reins, turned and gave the slop jar nearest the outside rail— nearest Rem—a stout kick. Terrified of getting a face full of piss and excrement, Rem threw himself off the trundling cart.

He fell clear of the wagon and hit the mud with stunning force. Somewhere he heard the shattering of a clay jar, and the world was suddenly rich with the smell of ordure—but none of it, thank all the gods of the ancients and the Panoply, had landed on him.

"Are you just going to lay there?" the piss-monger then brayed from above him, his oafish son at his elbow. "That thieving swine's getting away!"

But that was all behind him now, literally, for Rem was galloping along at a foolhardy pace, bent low over his stolen horse as he squeezed its foaming flanks between aching knees and whipped it with reins gripped in sweating hands. Beast and rider barreled on past drunken laborers reeling out of cellar stairwells, barking house mutts, corner congregations of underfed cats, and at least one stumbling, bleary-eyed molly who stank of witchweed and cheap brandy. Less than a mile due west, in the city center, the Brother of the Watch at the great tower of Aemon began his dutiful tolling of the hourly bell, low and sonorous. Rem's heart beat a syncopated tattoo after each plaintive knell. He counted three.

His lungs burned. His thigh muscles screamed. He'd thought running toward his intended rendezvous would exhaust him, yet keeping himself upright on an unsaddled horse—especially one weaving through narrow streets at such a breakneck pace— was no mean feat. But Torval needed him. If Rem didn't make the bridge he sought in time...

There. Up ahead. He saw two familiar high-rises—each towering a dizzying seven stories in the air above him. Those twin blocks marked the entrance to a steep flight of stairs that would put him on a footbridge that arced over Eastgate, the wide cobbled boulevard that the fleeing thief would eventually careen onto. Rem imagined he heard the rumbling rattle of the cart hurtling nearer even now, but knew that it was probably just his own mount's hooves thumping on the street mud.

Rem reined in the mare and she balked, spinning in the street, screaming in protest. He hated to so mistreat her, but he had no time for niceties. Without bothering to hobble or tie her, he swung himself down from his perch, mounted the stairs that rose between the tenements, and bounded upward toward the apex of the bridge. He'd made good time on horseback. If he could put himself in the center of that bridge as the thief's plunging cart passed beneath him...

He could...*what?* Leap? Try to land in the shit-and-piss-jar-crammed conveyance?

He didn't really have a plan. Probably wouldn't have time to formulate one, either.

Plans? Fah! Torval would've scoffed. *Who needs 'em?*

Rem pounded onto the arcing stone bridge and slowed at its center. He was facing west now, along the gentle curve of Eastgate Street as it bent toward the Embrys River.

There, a thousand yards away and closing, was his quarry. The big horse yoked to the cart galloped flat out now—faster than good sense or safety should allow, hot breath billowing in torrid clouds as steam curled in tendrils off the animal's foam-flecked coat. The clatter of its hooves on the cobbles was cacophonous, rising toward deafening as it rumbled closer and closer to where Rem stood on the bridge.

Rem blinked, trying to get a good look at what was happening on the moving cart.

The driver's bench was empty. Two figures—the thief and Torval—grappled, swayed and jerked about in the cargo bed. Only three of the slop jars remained—the rest casualties of the hand-to-hand struggle, no doubt.

No one was driving the cart, meaning the horse's reins would have fallen into the traces. Thief or no thief, a speeding cart behind an uncontrolled horse could spell disaster, not only for its occupants, but for anyone unlucky enough to stumble into its path.

Cack.

Rem mounted the stone railing. He watched the cart rattle nearer and nearer, making an unholy racket as it did so. More than a few of the residents and business-folk lining Eastgate leaned from their windows or peered cautiously from their doorways in answer to the tumult, staring, calling down into the streets to warn the few early-morning strollers or call for the wardwatch.

The cart was almost beneath him. Every tiny particle of Rem's being screamed that he was making a terrible mistake— but Rem refused to listen. How high was he up here? Twenty feet? Thirty? When he looked straight down at the street below, it could have been a hundred. He said a short, silent prayer to whatever gods still might humor him, then leapt.

For just a moment it felt as if he were going nowhere at all— floating, not falling. Everything he saw became crystal clear and languid. He saw Torval and the thief grappling viciously in the cart bed—his partner's bald pate and the dark-blue tattoos on it clear in the murky light, the thief's own mop of unruly brown hair trailing a single long, tight braid at the base of his skull. It seemed to take such an impossibly long time that Rem feared the rushing cart would pass too quickly beneath him, that he'd miss it entirely.

Then there was a rush of wind, a strange feeling in his neth- ers, and he was on top of them. The three—Rem, Torval, the thief—tumbled backward in a tangle of arms and legs, spittle and curses and rancid breath. For one fleeting moment Rem felt Torval's short, thick legs plant themselves in the cart bed to forestall their group plunge backward. Then the three of them—as a single organism—were thrown out of the cart into empty air.

Torval and the thief hit the cobbles first. Rem landed on top, but their momentum threw them into a wild roll along the street. Rem's world was upended—he on the bottom, they on top, he on top, they on the bottom, and—*Gods, those cobbles hurt!*—they kept on rolling, and—*Blast!* Torval punched him in the flank, thinking his body was the thief's—*Son of a*—then their happy little triptych flew apart and—*Snikt! Did someone just draw a knife?*—thankfully, blessedly, their roll became a played-out wobble. Finally they were at rest. Rem lay sprawled on the cobbles, belly-down, cheek against the cold, filthy paving.

"Ow," he muttered, then lifted his head.

Ahead of them—far ahead of them—the horse drifted toward the sidewalk. The beast's hooves left the cobbles and hit the flagstones. The cart followed, jouncing sideways, then leapt up from the flags onto the lowest of a broad series of steps leading up to the entrance of a great stone building. The steps turned the cart up onto its street-side wheels. The horse bucked against its twisting harness and the uncomfortable shove of the wooden shafts binding it. Then the cart, already half-upended, somersaulted sideways. As Rem watched, the horse's harness and shafts tore loose. The cart vaulted into the street and came to rest, its broken wheels spinning in the air, the open cargo bed smashed against the cobbles. The last three slop jars had shattered, spilling their stinking contents across the breadth of Eastgate, nearby witnesses shrinking from the stench and yanking their tunics up over their noses. The horse kept running, faster and faster now that it was free, on along Eastgate and out of sight.

"Watch it, lad!" Torval shouted, and Rem threw himself

over onto his back just in time to see the thief plunging toward him, a shiny, sharp dagger in his left hand. As the thief bent over him, Rem planted one foot in his would-be assailant's gut and shoved as hard as he could. The thief flew backward, right into Torval's waiting arms. As Rem scurried to his feet, he saw Torval's long, muscular arms curl up beneath the thief's armpits. To Rem's great astonishment, their quarry was a very young man of decidedly ordinary appearance and dress. Had Rem seen him on the street, he wouldn't have pegged him as the sort to lead them on such a wild, wearying chase.

Torval's thick, square hands locked behind the boy's head, and his arms flexed. The boy found himself bent halfway over backward, head shoved forward, arms raised comically at his sides. Torval shook the lad and the dagger clattered to the ground.

Rem needed no invitation and lunged forward to hook his left fist into the young man's belly. The boy groaned and bent double in Torval's grip. The dwarf, seeing his prey tenderized, released his hold, and the young thief hit the ground in a bloody heap. He was gasping for breath, moaning, but he made no attempt to rise.

"Stay down," Rem said. He brandished his sheathed sword so that the bent-double thief could see it. "If you move again, I'll take it as resistance, and I'll run you through without a second thought. Do you understand?"

The thief nodded weakly. He couldn't seem to find any words. Rem, gasping for breath himself, knew exactly how he felt. Studying the boy now, seeing how young he was—fifteen, sixteen at most—Rem almost felt sorry for him...almost regretted having hit him so hard after Torval had him subdued. Then he remembered what they'd just survived and shoved his pity aside. The boy might have daring and a mountain of fight in him, but he didn't have the sense the gods gave a goat.

Torval stood for a moment, huffing and puffing in the cold night air, an angry (if diminutive) bull not quite sure if it should charge or beg off. Finally the dwarf shook all over—a strange gesture, Rem thought, almost as if Torval were trying to wriggle the fury out of himself. Then, seemingly calm, Torval turned to his partner.

Now Rem felt even worse. He'd hit the boy in anger and Torval hadn't. How dare the old stump choose *that* moment to show how much self-control he could exercise!

"Did my eyes not deceive me?" Torval asked, sounding more angry than pleased. "Did you not just leap off that bridge back there into our speeding cart?"

Rem nodded, quite pleased with himself. "I surely did. You're welcome."

Torval, to his great surprise, gave him an angry shove. "You daft twat! You could have killed yourself! Or me!"

Rem blinked. "Well, then, old stump, next time I'll just let the cart man drive away with you! Do you have any idea what I went through just trying to get here and head the two of you off?"

"I had him!" Torval growled. "I was an inch away from subduing him when—"

"He pulled a knife!" Rem shouted back. "I suppose you were ready for that, were you?"

"It was sloppy!" Torval sputtered. "Sloppy and reckless and foolish and—"

"And lifesaving?" Rem offered.

"*Whose* life?" Torval countered. "You could've missed us entirely and cracked your skull like a morning egg! And then where would I be? Another dead partner on my conscience! Never again, boy—do you understand me?"

Rem was about to respond, but Torval gave a disgusted wave

of his arms, spun away, and marched up the street toward the wreckage of the pisswain. He shoved through all the lookie-loos now crowding around the mess, and Rem lost sight of him.

Rem stood beside their sprawled, groaning detainee, feeling both infuriated and humiliated. He'd just been trying to help. Was Torval truly angry with him for that?

The boy thief suddenly tried to skitter to his feet and flee. It was a fast, unexpected move—clearly planned through several minutes of feigned injury. Luckily, Rem managed to snatch at the boy's tunic and throw him back to the ground. Once he had him down, he knelt on his back, snatched a length of double-looped rope from his belt, and tied the boy's hands behind him.

"What part of *stay down* escapes your understanding?" Rem asked as he yanked the knots tight. He stood and surveyed his work. The boy flopped on his belly, but his hands were bound tight behind him now. He wouldn't be rising anytime soon.

Torval trudged back toward them. He carried the stolen idol in his arms, cradled like a baby. It was an ugly thing, vaguely anthropomorphic, with a too-large face and too-short arms and legs and almost no torso, forged from a vast and varied coterie of costume jewels, bangles, torques, rings, and varied metal chains, none of quality, all melted toward viscosity and then pressed together by hammer and tongs into a bizarre and almost laughable approximation of a human figure.

This was what Dorma and her orphans paid their obsequies to and submitted their prayers to in their cramped little hostel. What Rem and Torval had almost died for. Though Rem knew that the idol contained a treasure of great importance—the whole savings of that orphanage, its only bulwark against poverty, dissolution, and destitute despair—it still made his stomach turn a little. Despite the blessing it held within, the idol itself was ugly and absurd.

Torval studied their prize and offered an assessment. "Pitiful, isn't it?"

Rem nodded. He felt a crooked smile creeping onto his sweat-cooled face. "People put their faith in the strangest of things, don't they?"

To his relief a similar bent smile bloomed on Torval's broad, flat mug as well. "They do at that," the dwarf said. His eyes narrowed, but his smile remained. "My children thank you," he said quietly. "I suppose I do, as well."

"For what?" Rem asked, eager to hear him say it.

"For saving my life," Torval said with impatience. "Is that what you wanted to hear, you strutting cockerel?"

"Well, I didn't do it for you," Rem assured him, smile broadening. He pointed at the ugly idol. "It was all for her. She's a goddess, after all. She demands our utmost."

He wasn't sure who started laughing first, but in moments, their laughter—brotherly, raucous, unhindered—was all that anyone on Eastgate Street could hear.

CHAPTER TWO

A few watchwardens of the Third and a pair of city guards appeared in answer to the disturbance. When Rem and Torval explained the situation, their fellows of the watch accepted it readily enough, but looked more than a little peeved at the presence of a stinking overturned piss cart in the middle of what would, in a few hours, be one of the busiest streets in their ward.

"Should we call for some extra hands from the Fifth?" Rem offered, brandishing his brass watchwarden's whistle. "Just to clean things up?"

"Looks like you've done more than enough already," one of the city guards said, wearing a conceited smirk that told Rem all he needed to know about how the fancy bastards in their chain mail and crimson surcoats felt about the wardwatch.

"Just take your prisoner and go," one of the Third Warders said, sounding almost embarrassed, as though he wouldn't risk further humiliation under the city guards' reproachful gazes.

Rem almost argued, if only to deny those two smug city guards the satisfaction of laughing at them unchallenged once they'd turned their backs, but he knew it was pointless. Without another word they left the scene, truculent prisoner in tow.

By the time they reached the watchkeep, the first gray light of morning was seeping into the eastern sky and Yenara was awakening. Hawkers, beggars, and proselytes jostled to claim small plots of the frostbitten turf that formed the heart of Sygar's Square, while the shopkeepers and traders around the big square's perimeter were already hard at work behind their newly lit windows and half-open doors. Opposite the watchkeep the smells of charcoal, burning herbs, and seared meats wafted from the glowering edifice of the Temple of the Gods of the Mount—the telltale sign of morning offerings—as the baker just down the street threw open his windows and doors to flood the crisp morning air with the mouthwatering scent of fresh, buttery bread and the caramelized tang of date buns.

Rem's stomach turned somersaults as all the sights and smells of the square assaulted him. He was tired, cold, and ravenously hungry. He craved warm ale or spiced wine, a roaring fire, and a soft bed, preferably with Indilen beside him to keep him warm. Pure hysteria had kept him strong and focused enough to run down the thief now in their custody, but with their quarry run to ground, all that momentary strength had fled. Suddenly Rem was dead tired.

He and Torval marched their young prisoner—who'd said barely a word on the whole march back—up the steps of the watchkeep, through the blessedly uncrowded vestibule just beyond the main doors, and into the crowded administrative chamber beyond. There the telltale signs of a shift change were in evidence: watchwardens of the night scurrying to get their prisoners recorded and locked away, their fines paid and settled, so that the tired officers could beg off, while early arrivals for the day shift drifted, bright eyed and fresh, among the many desks and workstations, sharing friendly words with their night shift counterparts. Over in a far corner, a bushy-bearded Kosterman from the day shift—whose name escaped Rem at present—arm wrestled with Emacca, a tall, strongly built Tregga swordswoman whom Rem sometimes sparred with to keep his blade work sharp. A knot of both watchwardens and curious prisoners watched the contest and cheered their respective champions. Nearer the center of the room, dark-eyed Horus, from the far, febrile jungles of Maswari, and thick, blustering Blotstaff struggled to subdue a hysterical fellow who kept screaming about worms beneath his skin, mad eyes bulging like ripe blisters in his sweat-streaked face. Everywhere activity, deal making, ad hoc interrogations, and tired-eyed report writing. This was their world—night after night—and something about it gave Rem strange feelings of warmth and familiarity.

They found an empty desk and shoved their prisoner onto a stool. Wordlessly and automatically, each of them took his chosen place—Rem bent over the desk with a scrap of parchment to scribble their report, Torval beside the prisoner to tease out his particulars. Torval dropped the idol of Iesta upon the desk before Rem with a thud. Rem didn't care for the way the blocky, primitive-looking sculpture stared back at him with its unnerving saucerlike eyes.

"Look at the little fish!" someone said.

Rem's head whipped round toward the voice. The speaker stood just a stone's throw from him, at the treasurer's booth, collecting his nightly commissions from old Welkus. It was Djubal, a tall, hard-limbed Maswari watchwarden whose favorite pastime was teasing Rem and Torval about the perceived inferiority or infrequency of their collars. The ebon-skinned watchwarden and his short, pale partner, Klutch, seemed to have decided between them that they'd entered into a contest of sorts with Torval and Rem for the greatest quantity—or at least quality—of arrests.

Klutch pulled a patronizing face—the sort one might wear to remark on a precious baby or adorable kitten. "They're really taking off, aren't they? Any day now they'll be graduating to the city guard, all resplendent in their shiny armor and crimson cloaks—"

"If you knew what we went through to nab this one," Torval began.

Djubal waved his hands. "No explanation required, my friend—we all know it's the small ones that often have the most fight in them."

"Or the smallest of all," Klutch added. "Lad, have you even sprouted curlies on your sack yet?"

The young thief opened his mouth, but Torval smacked him on the back of his skull. "Keep your gob shut," he growled.

"There it is!" Djubal said. "The watchwarden's glare! Or is it the nursemaid's?"

Djubal and Klutch shared a hearty laugh at that. Normally Rem would have managed to laugh with them, but he was too tired at present. Hang them both. If they weren't such good backup in hours of need, he wouldn't let the ongoing cascade of laughs at their expense pass. Still chuckling, Djubal slid aside. Klutch stepped up to Welkus's pay booth, laying his citation receipts and confiscated offerings before the treasurer in his little barred and reinforced booth.

Rem, noting that Torval still seemed to smolder over the teasing, turned back to the task at hand.

It took more coaxing than Rem had hoped, but they had their answers in short order. The boy's name was Kyner. He had no coin or valuables on his person to pay his fines, meaning he'd spend the next few days in the dungeons awaiting trial. The theft of the idol was a minor offense, its secret and valuable contents notwithstanding. The more severe charge would be the hijacking and destruction of that city-chartered pisswain, for its stinking contents represented both a considerable investment on the part of the city administration and a rich reward for the filthy men who nightly made those collections.

Only in Yenara, Rem thought as his quill scratched speedily over the parchment, recounting the incident in the simplest language possible. *This damned idol before me—stuffed full of the modest riches that mean life or death, comfort or poverty, to Dorma's orphaned charges—is still worth less than a cartload of piss and shit.*

"What were you thinking?" Torval asked the boy—and not rhetorically, Rem knew. Torval did not ask rhetorical questions. If he posed a query to one of their prisoners, he did so in search of a serious answer. Woe betide the fool who responded with sarcasm or mute indifference.

"What do you care?" the boy asked, eyes downcast.

"I don't," Torval said. "I'm just curious. You had no idea what you were doing, did you? How much trouble you'd land in?"

Rem paused just long enough to study the boy and await his reply. The young thief raised his eyes to Torval—gaze fierce and completely unrepentant. "It was my buy-in."

"Buy-in?" Rem asked.

Torval shook his head. "Thieves' Guild initiation."

"And they sent you after Iesta here," Rem asked, "without telling you what she contained? How desperate Dorma would be to recover her?"

"Or what a trial it'd be to move her without transport?" Torval added.

The boy scowled, as though insulted. "The idea was *mine*. I used to be one of Dorma's charges, along with my little sister and brother. She threw us out for pickpocketing to supplement the alms we begged for the orphanage."

Torval and Rem exchanged dark glances.

"And you thought it best to repay her—and the rest of her

whelps—by stealing the only savings they had? Leaving them all homeless and subject to pimps and thief-lords and work-house body snatchers?"

"Why not?" the boy spat back. "She did the same to us when she turned us out. How do you think I ended up seeking a buy-in to a guild, anyway? My little sister—thirteen years old—is a step away from ending up like those filthy mollies you drag in here every night."

As he offered that last statement, he nodded toward another nearby desk, where two watchwardens—Sempronia and Firimol—were busy trying to keep a trio of face-painted, giggling, half-gassed whores upright while also shaking them down for brass to pay their fines. Rem had to admit, if seeing his own little sister in such a state had been an issue, he, too, might have sought to steal anything of value that he could think of.

Torval, however, wasn't so moved. He snatched the boy up off his stool and shook him. "Live long enough, boy, and you'll learn—sometimes trying to beg, borrow, or buy your way out of a dead end is worse than just standing tall with your back to the wall."

"Save it," the boy snapped. "If I wanted fatherly advice, I'd go down to the beach and shout at the fishes who ate me drowned da, you half-witted little pickmonkey."

Thank the Panoply, Djubal and Klutch were still close enough to catch the boy's bitter invective and know what would follow. Torval drew the boy up and landed one good punch before Rem dove in and dragged him off. Klutch, meanwhile, yanked the boy out of the dwarf's short reach while Djubal lunged in to help Rem restrain his fierce little partner. To the young thief's credit, he showed no fear, shouting instead for someone to undo his bindings so he could give the belligerent dwarf a good sound thrashing on equal terms.

The hubris of youth. Rem had to admire it.

"Get him out of here, please," Rem said to Djubal as he held Torval back. "We need nothing more from him."

Djubal nodded assent, then released Torval and moved to join his partner. Together the two yanked the struggling young thief to his feet and dragged him toward the stairwell just around the corner in the back corridor that descended to the dungeon levels. The youth bucked and thrashed the whole way.

"Let me at him!" the young man yelled, lip bleeding, eye already starting to swell from the one solid punch Torval landed. "I don't care if he's old as the hills, he's just my size!"

Rem saw Klutch snatch a handful of the boy's hair. "I wouldn't," he hissed at the boy. "I really, truly wouldn't."

Then the three of them—Djubal, Klutch, and struggling young thief—were gone, swallowed by the shadowy corridor. Rem heard the squeal of the hinges on the stairwell door and looked to Torval. His partner drew deep, even breaths, struggling mightily to calm himself, even as his nostrils flared and his muscular frame quaked with rage. In the interest of aiding the dwarf in calming himself, Rem picked up his written report and shoved it into Torval's empty hands.

"There," he said. "Read it over. Tell me if I missed anything."

Torval glared at him. "In a moment—"

"Now," Rem said. To punctuate the command, he drew up a chair and slammed it down before Torval, rudely inviting him to sit. Torval, still glaring, did as Rem bade. He sat, raised the parchment close to his eyes, and slowly began to read, mouth moving as he worked his way through the document.

Rem leaned against the desk, watching. Indilen had been

teaching Torval to read for three or four months, and she constantly hounded Rem about being a good companion and forcing Torval, at least once per shift, to read something. At first Rem had found the role of deputy taskmaster in charge of Torval's literacy a rather uncomfortable one. He was delighted that his unlettered partner was gaining the long-neglected skill, but he'd thought from the start that Torval would accept Indilen's kind but firm brand of instruction better than anything Rem could offer. To his great surprise, though, he'd found that after he made it known to Torval that Indilen herself had assigned the dwarf his homework, and that Rem was just the interim authority appointed to oversee it, the dwarf seemed to accept it. He wouldn't listen to Rem about much of anything else, but when their shifts were done and Rem handed him an arrest report or a Wanted leaflet that included a written description of the outlaw pictured, Torval—with minimal grumbling—almost always acquiesced and got down to it.

He won't do much for me, Rem thought, *but by all the gods, he'll do just about anything for Indilen. I suppose that's one thing we have in common.*

That thought brought a smile to his face.

Torval held out the parchment. "It's fine," he said. "Should we add the bit about the guild buy-in?"

Rem was delighted. Mission accomplished.

"What say you?" Rem asked in response. "Is it worth noting?"

Torval shrugged. "Suppose not." His eyes were still darting about the room—a gaze in search of focus, still agitated and overwhelmed. Rem felt a strange pang of worry then. He'd seen Torval flustered by mouthy arrestees before, but there seemed to be something else on his mind, something deeper than mere provocation or insult.

"Torval, I thought you had no letters," a smooth, purring voice suddenly said at Rem's elbow.

The sudden sound in the midst of his reverie made Rem leap off the desk and onto his feet as surely as if he'd been tapped on the shoulder in what he'd thought was a deserted alleyway. There stood Queydon, the dark-skinned elfmaid who was one of the chief sergeants of the watch and the Fifth's most capable interrogator. Queydon stared at Rem with her now-familiar ever-implacable gaze, honey-colored eyes large and beautiful but unnervingly deep. She seemed puzzled by his affrighted response.

"You did not see me here?" she asked.

Torval's preoccupation had fled. The little bastard snickered now. "He *never* sees you, not 'til you're right up on him."

"Haven't we talked about the skulking?" Rem asked her. "The sudden appearances?"

"I simply approached and spoke," she said.

"Your approach was silent as death," Rem said. "Per usual." He suddenly realized what troubled him about that elvish gaze of hers: she never blinked—at least, he could not remember seeing her do so. To test his theory, he stared intently at her for the next few breaths, waiting for her to blink, even once. She didn't.

Queydon shrugged, a tiny, economical gesture typical of her penchant for understatement. "Perhaps," she began, "it is your blunted senses and limited spatial awareness, Remeck, and not my silent approach, wherein the problems lie?" The question was posed clinically, without any sense of blame or insult attached.

Torval's snicker exploded in a snort, then rolled into unfettered laughter. The dwarf bent double, slapping his knees, his body-rocking guffaws echoing in the spacious administrative chamber. Rem felt all eyes in the room turning toward them—toward *him*—and knew his pale, freckled skin was quickly reddening.

"Would you stop that?" Rem asked his partner.

"Limited spatial awareness!" Torval snorted. "Gods, lad, she got you there!"

Rem had no idea what was so funny, but he supposed there was nothing for it. He waved the report and cocked his head toward Ondego's office. "If you'll excuse me."

As he strode away he heard Queydon once more query Torval. "As I said before—I thought you had no letters, and yet you were just reading."

"Blame that lass he fancies," Torval replied. "She's teaching me to read some. Makes him spot-check me. A taskmaster, that one."

Rem smiled at that, but didn't bother to look back at them. As he approached Ondego's office doorway, he caught a last comment, spoken so quietly by the elfmaid that he almost didn't hear it.

"I truly don't understand," she said. "Am I really so silent as he claims? My presence so unnerving?"

"Don't mind him," Torval replied, and Rem was sure the dwarf was speaking loudly just so Rem would hear him, even at a distance. "He's only human."

Rem shook his head, exasperated. He'd been planning to treat Torval to breakfast as soon as their shifts were done. Now he'd do everything in his power to get the dwarf to pay for their morning meal, *and* a mug or two of ale. It was the least the little bastard owed him after such a tiring night.

CHAPTER THREE

They set out through the cold, sunny streets toward the King's Ass, their preferred haunt when not walking their beats or enjoying quiet evenings in their separate homes. Aarna, the owner and operator, always treated them like family and served them well when they buffed her barstools, which was frequently. No doubt, on a frosty morning like the present one, she'd have every fireplace in the King's Ass crackling and stoked and the cauldrons on the fires behind the bar bubbling with warmed, spiced ale, while the smell of fresh-baked bread and panfried meats wafted from the hidden kitchens. Rem was eager—nay, desperate—for all the comforts of that cozy little taproom as they set out across Sygar's Square, but cursed the fact that it would require a good long walk to get them all the way to the Third Ward, where the King's Ass waited. Oh well, at least the sun was finally up and slanting down into the streets, its welcome presence warming the crisp winter air slightly.

They talked little at first, then not at all. The air bit too shrewdly, after all, and the winds were too stiff to carry on any kind of meaningful conversation. Soon enough Rem's tired mind wandered. After once more imagining how good a hot breakfast at the King's Ass would taste, he summoned images of Indilen in his mind, waiting for him back at his rented room, already undressed and under the covers of his bed. True, he had no reason to expect her there—truth be told, he found her waiting for him so welcomingly on only the rarest of occasions—but a hardworking watchwarden who'd spent his night crisscrossing the city in the wake of pirated pisswains, recovering stolen house gods, and keeping angry dwarves from battering hapless young thieves to bloody jelly could dream, couldn't he?

They broke from a side street onto a wide boulevard that traversed a raised plaza beside a broad, sunken square. A vast, hulking construction project rose at the center of the wide-open square beneath them. This would, in time, be a temple of the Panoply—and, to judge by the dimensions of the foundation and the spread of the buttressed walls slowly rising behind a perpetual screen of skeletal scaffolding, quite a large one. Rem wanted to be pleased about that, for the present Great Panoply of Yenara, in the First Ward, was awe inspiring and sumptuously appointed—but also bustling, crowded, and too far away for him to justify a special journey with any frequency. However, Rem also knew that temples of this sort took decades—if not centuries—to build. Even if he lived the rest of his life in Yenara, it was unlikely he'd ever see the place truly completed.

He turned to Torval to remark upon these idle thoughts and suddenly realized the dwarf was no longer beside him. He stopped, scanned the broad, bustling street, even stretched up on his tiptoes to try to see Torval's head low among the press of taller bodies. He found his missing partner some distance behind him, on the broad stone plaza overlooking the grand square below them. What on earth had drawn the old stump's attention? And why hadn't he bothered to tell Rem that he was stopping?

"Fine way to treat a mate," Rem said as he jogged up beside

his partner and took in the view of the rising temple from the plaza. "I turned to say something and you were gone."

Torval looked to Rem, gave a grunt—an affirmation, an apology, who knew?—then swung his gaze back toward the half-constructed temple complex. Instead of pressing the issue, Rem decided to give it a look of his own. He scanned the site, noting the preponderance of hewn cyclopean stones still awaiting placement, the larger piles of stones mounded here and there like strange old burial cairns on a grassless, rocky tundra, and the many little camps and workstations distributed throughout the site, where workers congregated, bent to their labors, or studied enormous hand-drawn plans of the building they were raising. After a moment's survey, Rem noted something unusual about the workers.

"All dwarves?" he asked aloud.

Torval grunted again. "Every last one," his partner confirmed. "The only tall folk I see are a few Panoply priests and administrators, overseeing or approving the work. See there? And over there?"

Rem followed Torval's fingers as they pointed. It was true. He saw a handful of priests in their color-coded robes—scarlet and saffron, gold and green, scintillating silver, robin's-egg blue, and pearlescent white—most of them speaking with what Rem assumed to be the crew leaders, referring to the plans laid out before them or sawing the air with their hands, suggesting the shape of the walls or the towers yet to be built. But despite the presence of that small knot of human overseers, the greater share of bodies moving steady and ant-like about that work site were short, muscular, and broad shouldered, just like Torval.

"Perhaps I'm wrong," Rem said, "but isn't that a bit strange? Dwarves raising a temple to human gods?"

Torval only grunted again. Rem stole a glance at him. His partner seemed quite intent upon something—or someone— in the laboring crowd of dwarves. Rem turned his gaze back to the bustling work site and tried to tease out who or what might be holding Torval's attentions so steadily. It was no good, though. All he saw were dwarves at work. Perhaps not such a strange thing, all in all, but certainly not a common sight in Yenara. The dwarven quarter itself was nearby, true, but everyone knew the dwarves who occupied it rarely undertook work beyond their enclave's unmarked borders. To see so many of them at work here, now, and on a house of divinity, no less...

"Is something troubling you, Torval?" Rem asked. "I could be wrong, but you've seemed preoccupied all night."

"Bah," Torval said. "It's nothing." He turned from the stone railing and set off again. Rem, more than a little perturbed at the dwarf's reticence but knowing that he had neither the strength nor the patience to press the issue, fell in behind his partner and quickened his pace. Like it or not, Rem supposed Torval would make his thoughts known in his own time, and not a moment sooner.

Soon enough they were deep into the Third Ward, rounding a corner to espy the familiar image on the shingle of the King's Ass: a fat, besotted king grinning foolishly atop a frowning, sway-backed donkey. In milder weather—the sort Yenara boasted for most of the year—the doors would be wide-open during business hours, but they were presently shut against the cold. Quickening his pace, Rem made the entryway first, yanked open one of the heavy oak doors, then held it as Torval stepped inside. Upon stepping over the threshold, Rem was enrobed in the tavern's comforting warmth, his senses teased by its sights, sounds, and smells: the gaudy colors of a set of newly installed stained-glass windows off to his left; the pleasant, rumbling murmur of dozens of conversations; the woodsy, bucolic tang of the fresh rushes and sawdust that littered the floors; and the mouthwatering aromas of roasting meats, baked bread, and spices mulling in hot ale and wine. Gods, his whole miserable, exhausting night now seemed worth it if this was where it had all led!

He fell in behind Torval, who was already halfway to the bar, and they slid onto the first stools that presented themselves. The place was lively this morning, but not crowded. Aarna was busy farther down the bar, delivering plates of fried eggs, thick-sliced ham, and kippered herrings to a trio of muscular bruisers who didn't have an unbroken nose among them. Tavern bouncers, Rem guessed, or some other night workers valued more for their rough appearance and brusque manners than their delicacy. Ah well...took all types, didn't it? No doubt this lot were just getting off their own night shifts, like Torval and Rem, and sought nothing more than a good breakfast and a long sleep.

Two stout mugs filled to the brim with a steaming, frothy brew appeared on the bar before them. They'd been delivered by young Davijo, one of Joedoc the Brewer's boys. Though only thirteen, he was already tall and sprouting some whiskers on his face.

"Good morning, sirs," Davijo said, his boyish voice having dropped since the last time Rem had seen him—which was only a few weeks before. "Anything to fortify the ales?"

Rem suggested the bruisers farther down the bar. "What they're having. And throw in some of that old, veiny cheese and a loaf of fresh bread."

The boy nodded deferentially and hurried into the back.

"Growing fast, that one," Rem said to Torval.

"They do that," the dwarf said, almost wistfully. His eyes

were downcast, his mouth set in a stoic frown. Suddenly he spat out, "I've a favor to ask."

"Anything," Rem said.

"If this offer offends you, please, make it known to me immediately—"

"Torval," Rem said, crossing his arms on the bar in front of him, "there is nothing you can ask for that would offend me. We're partners, and I'd like to think we're friends. Go on, make your request."

Torval nodded. What on earth had him so worried?

"Four nights from now," the dwarf said, "on the solstice, is the Fhrystomein—a solemn feast of remembrance and reparation among my people. We keep the rituals at Osma's request, because she wants the children to understand where they came from, what they are part of…"

Torval trailed off, as if his explanation was falling short of some silently held expectation. Rem considered trying to help him along, but kept quiet. He wanted to give Torval the chance to say all that he intended to say without interruption.

"At any rate," Torval said with a sigh, "it is, ideally, a feast to be shared among true family and the closest of friends. It comes in the midst of winter so that we can remember what we've gained and lost in the year past, and petition the gods for good fortune and bounty in the year to come."

"So you won't be in for your shift?" Rem asked, not sure where this was going.

Torval nodded. "Aye, I'll not—and I asked Ondego to release you as well. So that you could join us. With Indilen, if that's your wish."

Rem stared. Blinked. For some reason that he could barely articulate, Torval's request truly moved him. Perhaps it was the fact that Rem had almost forgotten what it was like to share a holiday feast with friends and family. Or perhaps it was the notion that, despite the fact that he and Indilen frequently lingered here, at the King's Ass, with Torval, or had, on occasion, enjoyed a simple picnic lunch with Torval's family, this was the first time that Torval had explicitly invited both Rem and Indilen—together—into his home for a solemn occasion. That simple realization touched Rem deeply.

"We would be honored," Rem said. "I'll admit, it's not a celebration I'm familiar with. Should I bring something or—"

"Just bring yourselves," Torval said, waving one thick, square hand. "Ours is just a family gathering. Earnest, but not overly solemn. Osma and I, we just...we agreed that the two of you have become good friends to us—to our whole family. It is right that you should join us."

Rem clapped Torval on one muscular shoulder. "You never fail to surprise me, old stump. Just when I think you're hard as steel and twice as sharp, you show me what a bed of dandelions you can be."

Torval smiled a little—an awkward, self-effacing smile that Rem found incredibly charming—then shrugged. "Don't embarrass me, lad. You know I've come to rely on you. You've acquitted yourself in this mission—and at my side—admirably." Then he scowled. "Just don't go thinking this means I'll go easier on you! You're still a babe in these woods, after all!"

Rem straightened his posture and squared his shoulders. "Indeed, sir—and so much left to learn." He snatched up his mug and presented it for a toast. "To friends," he said.

"To friends," Torval answered.

Their mugs touched and they drank.

Aarna appeared then. Grinning warmly, the ever-welcoming tavern matron bent over the bar, first planting a heavy kiss on Torval's ruddy cheek, then moving to plant another on Rem's.

"My two favorite head-breakers," she said with a broad smile and genuine affection. "Have you ordered?"

"Indeed we have," Rem said. "And once we've quaffed these ales and scarfed our victuals, we've a mind to turn this place upside down. Slow night on the ward—got to get our head-breaking in somewhere, you know."

"Is that right?" Aarna asked with a knowing cock of her brow.

To Rem's great surprise, Torval played along. "There's been a noted decline in the quality of your patrons," the dwarf said, scanning the room furtively. "I'm inclined to agree with the Bonny Prince here—this taproom's overdue for a good, cleansing brawl."

"Might I remind you," Aarna said, "that the last brawl you two started left me with barely half the furniture I started with? Not to mention a few broken windows."

"We paid for those windows," Torval said. "And look at the stained glass our coin bought!"

"*And* we got you new furniture," Rem added, gesturing around them. "The confiscated contents of the Moon Under Water, just as you asked!"

"And to say we started that brawl—" Torval began.

"Quiet," Aarna broke in. "You win—the both of you. For my new windows and my fine new furniture, I'm forever in your debt."

"Truth be told," Rem said, sipping his warm spiced ale and loving it, "we're probably in *yours*, which is why we spend so much money here."

Aarna smirked. "I feed you for free, Freckles."

Rem raised his mug. "But we pay for the ale," he countered, offering his best crooked smile. "And we drink a lot of it."

Aarna rolled her eyes and raised her arms to the heavens.

"Why? Why were these two miscreants forced upon me? What sin did I commit to earn their attentions?"

"Too friendly," Rem said.

"Too beautiful," Torval added.

Aarna, always game for compliments when they were given in earnest, planted her hands on her hips and raised her chin expectantly. "Don't stop there, boys. Flattery will get you everywhere."

Davijo arrived with their plates: two large platters heaped with eggs fried in pork fat, seared slabs of thick-cut salted ham, smoked kippers lightly warmed beside the fire, two generous plates of pungent, veiny cheese, and, on a third plate between them, a loaf of soft, steaming brown bread fresh from the ovens. When the plates were laid before them, Rem took a long moment to study his own, savoring the sight of it. His stomach growled and curled in the center of him, like a napping puppy slowly stirring toward wakefulness. He took a last long draught of his spiced ale, preparing the way for the feast to come.

"About time," Torval said, then laid into the food before him.

Rem was just about to tear into his own when a new arrival slid onto the stool beside him. Two dainty hands shot into his field of vision, snagged his plate, and pulled it away from him. Rem spun toward the offender, ready to protect his hard-won breakfast, and found a familiar beauty with auburn hair and brown eyes beside him. She was all wrapped up in a simple fur-lined winter coat. A small oblong wooden box of fine make— her personal secretary set—sat on the bar beside her. With only the briefest, sweetest batting of her eyes, she turned from Rem and snatched up a slice of the salted ham.

"Truly," Indilen said, "you're the best mate a girl could have. I'm famished."

"I was going to eat that," Rem said, staring at her, finding it impossible to even feign anger.

"And you still can," Indilen said. "You're just sharing now. Pass the bread, please?"

Rem laid down his table knife and turned to tear off a bit of the hot bread. As he delivered it to her, Indilen purloined his fork right out of his hand. Daintily she began to feed herself. She turned to give Rem a bright, winning smile as she chewed her first bite, and Rem found himself almost disgusted by how besotted he was with her. She was so beautiful, so bright... even when stealing his meals and annoying the living piss out of him.

"Aarna," he said without taking his eyes off Indilen, "could I beg another knife and fork?"

"Can't spare any," Aarna responded, bustling away to see to new customers farther down the bar. "Eat with your hands like the rest of us, Bonny Prince."

Indilen forked up some eggs and kippers and offered them to Rem. "Bite, love?"

He opened his mouth and she fed him. He dared to risk getting his grasping hand forked and reached for a pinch of the cheese, using a soft slice of the bread to pick it up and smash it. He popped the whole bite—bread and cheese—into his mouth and savored it.

"What brings you out so early in the morning?" Rem asked as he and Indilen ate from the same plate, as naturally as a ragged old farmer and his timeworn wife.

"Took a chance I'd find you here," Indilen said, sopping some hot bread in a puddle of runny egg yolk. "And I wasn't lying—I *was* famished."

"Well, now that we're both being fed," Rem said, leaning

closer, "what say we work it off back at my loft when the plates are clean and the ale's run dry?"

"Tempting," Indilen said, throwing Rem a knowing glance. "But I've got more pressing business. And you should come with me."

"Pressing business?" Rem asked.

"I need new quill nibs," Indilen said. "The best I can afford."

"New quill nibs?" Rem repeated, truly puzzled.

"I know, it sounds ridiculous," Indilen said, "but I've been offered a very good job for the Great Library at the university—six weeks guaranteed, premium pay, plus a little extra for materials. I'll be copying out a dozen or so old manuscripts as well as adding multicolor illuminations. If I'm to do work of that detail and magnitude, I need good brushes, quill nibs, and inks. I've got the brushes and inks, but dwarven finesmiths make the best quill nibs, so that's where I'm off to when we've finished here."

Rem was taken aback. That *was* most impressive. "I knew you did scribe-work," he said, "but you never told me you could *illuminate*."

Indilen shrugged as if it were plain as day. "Calligraphy, illustrations, embellishments—I'm a woman of many talents, good sir. Haven't you learned that yet?"

"I was thinking of something less—decorative," Rem said.

Indilen bumped him warmly with her elbow. "Knave," she said with a smile. "Impugning my honor."

"Thief," Rem said, leaning closer, "stealing my heart."

"Mercy!" Torval suddenly cried. "You're making me sick! Stop slinging that treacly pap or I'll yark on my kippers!"

Rem and Indilen shared a conspiratorial laugh over Torval's outburst and fell back to picking at their shared breakfast.

"Well," Rem said, "I'm damned proud of you, and despite my exhaustion I'll be happy to take a stroll through the Warrens with you. Just promise me it won't be the whole day? I do need *some* sleep."

"Vowed and attested," Indilen said with a curt nod. "I know you do. And truth be told, it's not that I need a chaperone—I just wanted to see you. It's so hard, sometimes, our days spent only catching one another in passing, with only one full day together each week."

"You could take some night work," Rem suggested. "Copy manuscripts by candlelight? Sleep through the day at my side?"

"And end up blind before I'm forty," Indilen said. "No, thank you. So long as I'm a working quill-slinger, I'm working *by day*."

"Well, then," Rem said. "Sooner started, sooner finished. Should we go now?"

Indilen shook her head. "This plate's not clean, Bonny Prince. I'm not moving 'til it is. If you're in such a bloody hurry, help me."

Aarna suddenly reappeared and placed a fresh, steaming mug of her spiced ale before Indilen. "There you go, lass. I'll put it on their collective tab."

"Then buy the whole bar a round," Indilen said, sipping the ale. "On them."

"By the gods, lad," Torval suddenly interjected, throwing a warm, knowing smirk at Indilen. "You *are* a salty one, aren't you?"

"Sour, salty, soft, and sweet," Rem said before she could respond. "And all mine."

Indilen smiled at him, took a healthy bite of pork and eggs, then washed it down with a good, stiff draught of the hot ale. Rem couldn't take his eyes off her. And to think: if he hadn't left it all behind—his family, his world, the future that had been decided for him—he never would have met her. The very possibility that he could have lived his whole life without finding this woman, whom he'd come to love so dearly in just a few short months, filled him with a terrible dread, even as the fact of their love and affection warmed him.

"You're staring," Indilen said.

"Should I stop?" Rem asked.

"Oh no," she said sweetly, her gaze meeting his. "Keep staring."

Rem obliged, satisfied that he now had all he needed to fill his belly and his heart for the morning—hot food, warm ale, his best friends, and the woman he loved. He settled in, feeding himself as the warmth and welcome of the King's Ass swaddled him like a newborn babe.

CHAPTER FOUR

It was nigh on eight bells when Torval mounted the stairs to his rented rooms, fished the key from one of the pouches at his belt, and let himself in. He was more than a little ashamed of himself—bright and early in the morning, the rest of the world waking and off to work, and here he was, drunk and ready to collapse. He knew his was a topsy-turvy, nocturnal life—awake and about while most of the city, including his widowed sister and his children, slept—and that his early-morning breakfasts were the equal of most working folks' suppers, but he was still left with a vaguely skeevy feeling about coming home in such a state: reeking of ale, swaying as if he stood on a rolling ship's deck, desiring nothing but a bed and the sweet oblivion of sleep. He'd lingered too long at the King's Ass, even after Rem and Indilen set out for their little shopping sortie in the dwarven quarter. But that wasn't an accident, was it? No, he'd lingered deliberately, until he knew that his sister, Osma, and his daughter, Ammi, would be in the market, at their stall, while little Lokki took his lessons at school. For only then, alone, anaesthetized, could he return home without feeling the ache of Tav's conspicuous absence.

Torval shut the door behind him and studied the front room: fire burnt down to ash and cinders, plates and cups left to dry on a towel beside the emptied washbasin, two bundles—food of some sort, intended for him—wrapped in cloth on the trestle table where they all ate their meals. Though he'd probably missed Osma and the children only by an hour or less, their living space was already cold and empty. Torval preferred it this way of late. When they were all about—Osma cooking or cleaning, Lokki bouncing between Torval and Ammi in search of attention or entertainment—Torval found himself unnerved by the noise, the energy, the scurrying, and the ever-changing half-finished conversations. None of it felt right—felt *complete*—without his eldest son. Oh, certainly Tav dropped in to see them once a week on his appointed day of rest, usually with some special little bauble for Lokki, tales of apprentice-ship trials for Ammi, and all sorts of lively, scripture-themed dissertations for Osma—but even as Torval's son shared such rapport, such warmth and energy, with his siblings and his aunt, he seemed to be at a loss when speaking with Torval. And Torval, admittedly, was at a loss when speaking to him.

Because he chose his people over his father, Torval thought. *He chose* them, *even though he had to know what it would cost* me.

What stung was that Tav had gotten what he wanted, while Torval felt as if he'd lost everything he had. His pride, surely... and maybe, just maybe, some of the affection he'd borne his eldest son.

Even as the thought bloomed in his brain—red, pulsing, like iron hot from the forge—he cursed himself for entertaining it. Tav was the son, Torval was the father. Tav could have no power that Torval did not give him. If it was true that Tav's desires had forced Torval into a horrid, backbreaking capit-ulation that still, weeks later, made Torval feel the drum of his heartbeat quicken and his body shake with rage when he remembered it—then the blame could only lie at Torval's feet.

You mewling, whey-faced little shoat. Why are you still dwelling on this? You are made of scars and bruises and knitted bone and anointed in blood—and here you stand, grieving for the forfeit of your pride. Why should it trouble you so? You're stronger than this, aren't you? Tougher than this?

No. Apparently he was not.

Perhaps it was just his pride that was forfeit—but that pride meant a great deal to him. So far as he could see, it was all that remained in the world that was truly, entirely his.

But now even that was gone, wasn't it?

I remember you, Eldgrim, the dwarven ethnarch, had said.

And Torval remembered him as well. For years he'd sworn that if he ever met any of those who'd beaten and humiliated him all those years ago, he'd have their hides. He'd wear their braids and beards from his belt and he'd flay their skins for new boots. But then, standing before one of those he'd dreamt so long of having his vengeance on, what was he forced to do?

For Tav's sake, he was forced to kneel.

Grunting disgustedly to himself, Torval unbuckled his belt and hung it and his maul on one of the cloak pegs by the door, then lurched across the room toward his bedchamber.

He opened the door to the oversize pantry that served as his own private sanctum, edged past the inward-swung door, then collapsed onto the bed wedged inside. He liked his little room, and his little bed, and it was all because of that narrow door that separated the space from the common room outside. That, and its notable lack of windows. The twin luxuries of privacy and daytime darkness had eluded Torval for years as he shuttled his family from place to place in search of a home, in search of a job—in search of a life that wouldn't be rendered obsolete by deflated labor markets or inflated rents. Hells, they'd been happy enough at their last apartment—the one above the arkwright's, which they'd fled after an attempt on Torval's life—but even there the little cot that Torval slept on by day had occupied the very same room that the boys slept in by night, and the shutters on the windows had never quite shut out the infernal daylight. Torval was proud of the fact that he'd adapted himself to living in a world of vertiginous blue skies, blindingly bright light, and panic-inducing vastness when most of his people chose to live their whole lives in underground cities lit by only firelight and the natural luminescence of strange cave fauna. But if there was ever a time when he most missed the subterranean world that had borne him, it was during the day, when he was trying to sleep.

To sleep well he needed darkness, a darkness so deep it threatened to swallow him. And returning each morning to a home where his eldest son no longer slept, where the boy's terrible absence somehow mocked Torval in both mind and spirit—well, wrestling with those demons required darkness, too. Darkness. Silence. Stillness.

And ale. Lots of ale.

He kicked off one boot without rising, then went to work on the other. The door to the little chamber still stood ajar, so Torval kicked his remaining boot toward it. The heavy boot thumped against the door, slamming it shut, then slid to the floor, acting as a stopper. The room was dark now, the air pleasantly close, the only light a pale thin line beneath the door.

Close, dark, airless—anathema to the tall folk, a blessed comfort to one as accustomed to close, dark spaces as Torval.

And still it seemed too large. Tav's absence had left a hole in their home—a hole in Torval—just as surely as if he'd died or run away. Even here, in this welcoming, warming little closet that served as his bedroom, Torval could not escape that absence, and could not forgive the conditions of it. No matter how cramped the room enclosing him, the hole in the middle of him—the rage within him—seemed as deep and wide as ever.

You're a fool, he thought. *Every son comes of age and makes his own way in the world. Did you really think he'd be here, beside you, on your knee, forever? What a braying, bawling little billy goat you are, Torval.*

He *had* been a fool, should've known the day would come. The boy was forty-two years old now and entering puberty. Torval had known that age—that season—would bring with it restlessness, a desire for Tav to buck against his childhood traces and bolt free like an unbroken colt. That was the way of things, and deep down Torval had expected it.

But he hadn't been ready for Tav's mode of youthful rebellion—not in the slightest.

What'll it be, then? Torval had said when Tav finally spoke directly to him. *Arms, perhaps? We could squire you to a soldier, someone who makes their home here when not on campaign. Or maybe a trade? Leatherwork? Carpentry?*

None of those, Papa, Tav had said. *Truth be told, I don't know what I'd like to be—but if I could, I'd want to learn an art from my own folk . . . from dwarves.*

And Torval had known what that would entail. When a dwarven boy or girl came of age and pursued a trade—accepted their purpose—that was a sacred vow, a dwarf's first true, adult oath. If Tav wanted to rejoin the dwarven collective, then his father—an outcast and exile who'd separated his son from that world—would have to offer reparations of some sort.

And dwarven reparations were seldom only material in nature. Usually they involved a great deal of groveling, coupled with oaths of obedience.

I should have said no, Torval thought, wishing he could just drift off to sleep but finding it impossible. He hadn't been prepared for Tav's willing submission—his actual *desire* for a return to the fold, to the prescribed paths and fixed regimens of dwarven culture.

I know why we left home, Papa, the boy had said during one of their arguments. *But now I'm coming of age and I feel a hole in me—a void I can't fill. It's the home we left behind—the people that we're no longer a part of.*

Holes. Voids. Losses. What did that boy know of such things? Did he remember what it had felt like to lose his mother, sister, and brother to orcish steel? To see his father beaten, shorn, and shamed for challenging the very people who should have abetted his vengeance instead of forbidding it? How silent it had been the day they'd all left their home in Bolmakünde, shunned by their neighbors and clan-kin, denied even good tidings or farewells?

Could the boy even comprehend the hole he'd now left in Torval's heart? How he ached for his son to be back in his life, back in their home, back under his guidance and influence, and not subject to the teachings of the very folk who'd betrayed them and cast them out?

Or that Torval had bought Tav's desires with his own shame?

What did Tav know of losses and the voids they left? Hadn't Torval spent the whole of their lives from Olian's death to the present trying to fill the voids in his children's hearts with the promise of a wider world, where anything was possible? Where hopes and destinies were not limited by foolish rules and the accidents of birth?

You can't hold on to him so tightly, Osma had said, more than once. *Especially since you're not afraid that he'll meet resistance or be cast out, as you were. You're afraid he'll love the place he's found among them. That he'll choose them over you.*

They'll cast him out, Torval said, *or they'll take all the fire out of him. I'd spare him either fate, if he'd just listen to me!*

You can't spare him anything, Osma snapped with some final-ity. *Hold on to him and lose him, or let him go and keep him. Those are your only choices.*

And so, though it galled him—though it pained him to the core—Torval had relented. He'd made his petition. He'd stood, more than once, before the ethnarch's court and answered its questions about his beliefs, his actions, his loyalties, his past transgressions.

I remember you, Eldgrim, the ethnarch, had said with a gri-mace on his face and a malign light in his eyes. Torval remem-bered him as well. He swore he could still feel an itching in the scars on his pate that the ethnarch's sentence had once given him, all those years ago, long before they ever came to Yenara.

Of course they both remembered. Dwarves never forgot, and never forgave. They were vengeful losers and insufferable win-ners. And it was there, before the court, in the final meeting they held before deciding Tav's fate, that the ethnarch had demanded a show of obeisance as a condition of Tav's fostering and edu-cation. Torval had promised many things: coin to pay for Tav's education, training, and board; that he would bring his family to the temple at least twice each week for rites and prayers; and that he would never again speak ill of their people or their cul-ture, nor speak of the price of his own transgressions, paid so long ago. But those promises weren't enough for Eldgrim. The ethnarch, wielding power over this half-forgotten, low-grade sinner who hadn't darkened the doorways of his own people for almost two long decades, had taken the opportunity to demon-strate what cruel and arrogant victors dwarves could be.

One thing remains, he'd said, his sneer almost blooming into a grin.

Torval waited, fearing what would come next.

Kneel, Eldgrim had said. *Kneel and prostrate yourself and beg this tribunal for the forgiveness of your sins, exile. Do this, and the stain on your honor will not mark your son.*

Torval had faced death a hundred times, but no bloody duel to the death nor brush with the hungry void had ever filled him with as much dread, as much fear, as much red-eyed, tooth-grinding rage, as that simple command.

Kneel.

And what did Torval do? What *could* he do? *Hold on to him and lose him, or let him go and keep him*, Osma had said. *Those are your only choices.*

Torval knew she was right, damn her. So he knelt. He laid himself upon an altar—let those bastards in the ethnarch's court all but cut his heart out—and he let Tav go. And damned if he didn't let something else go in himself—something precious that he wasn't sure he could ever recover.

Thendril's tits, Torval thought bitterly. *There are tears on my pillow.*

Fool. Failure.

Coward.

And then, at last, as that last word echoed through his ale-addled, exhausted mind, sleep took Torval, granting a reprieve, however brief, from the ache of that stubborn wound that festered and would not heal.

CHAPTER FIVE

Here they stood: Rem and Indilen, side by side, arms round each other for warmth, gawping like shepherds on their first city sojourn at the wonders of the dwarven quarter. Before them lay a multilevel maze that rose and fell and curled in and out upon itself. Every street was a curious, canopy-covered arcade where the sun's light penetrated only as a diffuse glow through street-spanning awnings of many-colored silks. Rising above those streets were a series of tiered pyramids, hewn of granite, supporting structures and lanes far above street level, rising in a haphazard arrangement throughout the quarter like handmade hills. Everywhere about them were ramps, stairs, switchbacks, and plazas; there were store-lined streets forty feet above their heads, and still more in deeply recessed pathways twenty or thirty feet below where they stood. And, adorning all these manifold pathways, the unique, austere beauty of dwarven architecture, expressed in multiroofed towers, finely wrought pillars of wood or stone, and delicate, soaring pinnacles and spires—a complex, dizzying geometric arrangement that stunned the two of them to awed silence.

"It's as if they missed the mountains," Indilen began.

"So they brought them here," Rem finished. "Amazing, isn't it?"

If one studied it on a map of the city—as Rem had once or twice—Yenara's dwarven quarter seemed rather small. It encom-

passed six or eight city blocks total, with only one major boulevard running through it, diagonally, crisscrossed by a dozen
narrower streets and lanes. But, as Rem had been taught in his
youth, and later learned through experience, maps were entirely
symbolic and could be misleading. What looked smooth and
orderly on parchment was often far more disorienting in the
physical world. Such was the dwarven quarter: dense, labyrinthine, tiered, terraced, and possessed of more narrow alleys and
pinched side streets than any map could ever show. Hence its
evocative nickname: the Warrens.

"What is it they call themselves?" Indilen asked as they
walked, Rem's arm around her shoulder.

"Dwarves collectively?" Rem asked. "They're the *welk*,
which just means 'folk' in their tongue. These dwarves"—he
suggested those bustling around them—"are from the Ironwalls, specifically. They're called the *Hallirwelk*—Hallir's Folk."

"Is Hallir one of their gods?" Indilen asked.

Rem shook his head. Usually she was the one imparting
all sorts of fascinating and disparate knowledge to him—yet
another of the many things he loved about her. For once—
because he'd asked the right questions of Torval—Rem had
something to offer her in return. "No," he continued, "not a
god. The first of their line—"

"Like Edath and Yfrain for humans," Indilen broke in.

"Precisely," Rem said. "Each dwarven tribe has a name of
its own based on the name of its progenitor. The *Hallirwelk*, the
Borthenwelk, the *Kjonderwelk*—"

"Gods," Indilen breathed. "Look at the molding above those
arches!"

Rem followed her gaze and saw what she spoke of. The
dwarves had a proclivity toward a very particular sort of arch
for their doorways—neither boldly rounded, like the arches of

the desert temples in far Magrabar, nor gracefully pointed, like those employed in the Aemonist temples across the mountains in Warengaith, but bent inward and topped with a flat, narrow lintel. Rem had already seen a dozen such portals in the half block they'd so far strolled through. The detailing above the doorway that Indilen now indicated was stunning indeed— a series of intricate, interlaced, unending knots, not curved, but wrought of hard angles, carved into a panel of dark-gray marble veined with green and white. Drawing, painting, or molding such a design would be challenging enough, but the thought of slowly, patiently chiseling it into that stone, drilling holes without shattering the whole thing, slowly sanding the edges to the smooth, delicate roundness they now possessed— it was mind-boggling.

Rem had always known dwarves to be hewers of stone and makers of mighty things, be they princely halls under soaring mountains or sharp axes to cleave orcish skulls—but he'd never realized how their handicrafts could just as often display patience, delicacy, even whimsy. No wonder Indilen had come here in search of the best nibs for her writing quills.

"Have they always been here?" Indilen asked idly as they carried on. They were not the only tall folk on the crowded street, and they and their human fellows towered among the milling bodies of the enclave's residents, none of whom were more than two-thirds the height of the conspicuous outsiders moving among them.

"As Torval tells it," Rem said, "the dwarves first came in large numbers about one hundred and fifty years ago."

"After the elven resurgence," Indilen offered, "and the orcish onslaught from the steppes?"

"Exactly," Rem said. "The Ironwall dwarves lost tens of thousands—men, women, children—and all but expended their food stores and treasure reserves. They were desperate to restock their granaries and replenish their numbers. Meanwhile, Yenara was half-wrecked and in need of quarried stone to rebuild itself—including new, higher city walls. So the two parties made a mutually beneficial arrangement: the dwarves would quarry the great stone blocks needed for Yenara's restoration and transport them overland to the city, and once the stone had been delivered, the Council of Patriarchs would provide them coin and foodstuffs. They even threw in funding for a few mercenary companies to man the mountain passes and give the dwarven populations in the Ironwalls a chance to bury their dead and sow a new generation."

Indilen shook her head in disbelief. Her eyes still danced over the strange world bustling around them. "And how long did that take? Hewing all those rocks and shuttling them from the Ironwalls to the coast? That's more than a hundred miles!" They were passing a pie shop, redolent with the scents of hot buttered pastry, spiced meats, stewing leeks, and sweet candied fruits. Rem was still stuffed to bursting, but he made a mental note of where to find the place; he'd certainly have to find his way back some night when their patrols brought them near here.

"A long time," Rem said, enjoying his role as historian. "A slow, steady parade, the way Torval described it—a constant stream of massive stones being rolled toward the city on hewn logs, sometimes going no farther than a league or two a day. I think he said the great canal was restored after long neglect just to help get some of those stones here.

"Moreover, Yenara's postwar boom was so desperately needed—and so well funded—that the building never stopped. So for decades dwarves poured into the city in great road gangs, hauling their cargo from the foothills, then they'd wait around for months for the stones to be claimed by their customers and payment rendered. Since there was a slow, constant influx of dwarves who ended up making the city their home for months or years at a time, and since those leaving were always replaced by new arrivals, the dwarven merchant guild that oversaw the quarry arrangement started buying up lots in the quarter. Once the collective owned land here, it wasn't long before they started making the place look more like the home they'd left behind."

Rem wasn't entirely sure that the dwarven cities under the Ironwalls looked anything like the strange, muscular, beguiling architecture that surrounded them now, but he knew that what surrounded him was unlike anything he'd ever seen in a human settlement.

The pyramids were the most impressive part, to be sure. They were often half a block wide or more at the base, and rose in gentle slopes toward leveled platforms, upon each of which stood another, smaller flat-topped pyramid, and then another. Shops and houses were crammed along the leveled terraces, all the way up to the flat summit, with switchbacked streets or steep stairways providing passage from one landing to the next. Apparently, living in the shadow of Suicide Hill—the highest point in the Fifth Ward—had inspired the dwarves to create their own vertical topography. And so they built hills of their own and turned them into prime real estate.

Less wondrous but more pleasing than the pyramids were the canopies that covered the streets. When he'd first seen them, Rem thought them merely decorative—they were made of silk, after all, light but strong, in an unending host of rich, vibrant colors: sunny gold, bright vermillion, flashing emerald, and cobalt blue. But Torval had explained their true significance.

"Most dwarves don't like the open sky," he'd offered, almost conspiratorially. "Gives them vertigo. Not to mention the sun's light on a bright day can be blinding to one who's lived underground all their life. Some of us out in the world get used to it, but many more don't—or don't want to. By tying those canopies up over all the streets, the dwarves can go about their daily business, out in the open, and they never have to be troubled by what's above them."

Studying the canopy above them now—a fiery, autumnal orange, rife with strangely knotted geometries—Rem supposed he could understand why someone who'd lived underground might see such an adornment as utilitarian and not merely decorative. Rem simply thought it beautiful and comforting. Wouldn't it be lovely here on a hot summer's day, hidden from the midday sun and its skin-burning tyranny?

"Here, I'll ask this fellow," Indilen suddenly said, and raced away from Rem to inquire at the workbench of a pewtersmith laboring over the tracing on a drinking stein outside the doorway of his little shop. At his elbow stood a dwarven boy, equivalent to a human nine-year-old, perhaps. In the shadows of the shop, another body moved among the merchandise. Rem watched as Indilen spoke to the craftsman, explaining her needs. He was half-afraid the little tinker might rebuff her questions—she didn't have the look or poise of one who did business here regularly, after all, and dwarves could be rather suspicious and insular.

But to his great delight, the bearded tinker smiled brightly, stood up from his workbench, and walked to the center of the street with Indilen, leading her by the hand. There he pointed out several other dealers who might have what she sought. When he'd finished with the gently zigzagging street before them, he started in on directions to other nearby finesmiths, off side streets or up on the tiers of the nearest pyramid. Indilen, beaming and offering a series of very gracious thank-yous, bid the tinker farewell and hurried back to Rem.

"Success?" he asked.

"He told me of a half dozen," she said. "But he told me, very candidly, that if *he* were buying quill nibs, he'd only go to one finesmith: a lady, just around the corner on that next street up ahead. He said she does beautiful work and always asks a fair price."

"Well, then," Rem said. "Lead the way."

They carried on, passing all manner of folk transacting every-day business. There were dwarves trading or haggling with dwarves; an elf or two perusing fine jewelry or browsing the offerings of local bladesmiths; and several humans, most of whom Rem marked as tradesmen—carpenters, stonemasons, wood-carvers and the like—in search of finely wrought tools for their various trades. He saw a few housewives buying bread or pastries, a human female apothecary haggling with a grocer over dried mushrooms, and a fat brewer and his sons filling a hand-cart with hogshead casks of dwarven ale—a very peculiar brew that tended to inspire intense love or virulent hate in most non-dwarves who tasted it. The place was alive and bustling, alien enough to be enchanting, familiar enough to make them feel welcome.

They turned the corner and found themselves in a very dark, narrow side street running along the foot of a pyramid, cold in its shadow. A blue-gray awning billowed restlessly above them, blocking any view they might have had of whatever structures squatted on the landing of the pyramid above their heads. There was only the smooth, sloping stone wall of the pyramid on their right, and another meandering line of close-packed, low-doored shops and taprooms on their left. As welcome as Rem had felt on the boulevard they'd just departed, this street left him feeling just a little lost and out of his depth. The dwarves seemed to stare here, more openly suspicious of their presence—or, perhaps, more eager to exploit it. Rem shot a glance at Indilen, to see if she was similarly afflicted, but she seemed untroubled. Her eager gaze searched the shops they passed, in search of the finesmith she'd been referred to.

They stopped twice when Indilen thought she'd found her destination, only to learn that the woman she sought was still farther along. Rem was about to ask if she might have misunderstood the tinker's directions, since they were nearing the end of the street, a very broad, sunny opening visible just beyond. Sunlight meant no more canopy, indicating that they must have reached the very edge of the dwarven quarter.

"There," Indilen said, pointing. "That's got to be the one."

She hurried toward the little shop, dragging Rem behind her by the hand. He had to duck to fit through the low-linteled doorway.

Inside, the shop was cramped, but tidy. There was a counter on the right, just past the open door, and shelves full of mixed merchandise off to the left—pendants, rings, bracelets and earrings, quill nibs, ceremonial knives, brooches, and cape clasps—all beautifully detailed and finely wrought. Rem wagered that if he stood in the dead center of the little space, he could probably touch both walls. He and Indilen could barely fit inside together. Worse, the ceiling was quite low. Indilen could stand straight with a fingerlength between her head and the roof, but Rem had to bend his head awkwardly to avoid thumping himself on the low-hanging rafters.

The curtain that separated front from back was swept aside, and the finesmith appeared. She was plump, with full, rosy cheeks and deep-brown eyes almost as warm and welcoming as Indilen's. Like many dwarven women, she sported well-trimmed whiskers—a gentle, wispy pair of muttonchops framing her round, friendly face. She swept one strawberry blond lock behind her ears and planted her thick hands on her wide hips.

"Can you hear me up there?" she asked Indilen, bending back a little. "Glory be, I'm surprised you can fit in here, tall thing like you."

Indilen and the finesmith shared a laugh. Rem forced one. His neck hurt.

"I'm in search of quill nibs," Indilen said. "The tinker round the way said you'd be the lady to ask."

"Old Kraki, was it?" the finesmith said. "Widower, that one. Been trying to court me for years. Probably thinks sending me a paying customer's like to win him my sweaty old hand at last."

"Missus," someone said from the back, and another dwarf arrived—a boy this time. His thin face, large nose, and black hair made it clear that he was no relation of Indilen's new friend. When the boy saw Indilen and Rem, he froze, like a rabbit spying a fox among the ferns. "My pardon," he said. "I didn't know you had customers."

"My apprentice," the lady said to Rem and Indilen. "Linger, lad, you might learn something."

"As you say, missus," the boy answered.

"Now, then," the finesmith said, and rubbed her hands together. "Let's talk nibs, shall we?"

Rem tried to be patient, but after some time had passed and Indilen and the finesmith had proceeded no further than the laying out of a vast array of possible nibs on a velvet cloth for close inspection and laborious description, he finally decided to excuse himself. Indilen sent him off with a wave and a smile, deeply involved in her shopping. Rem returned to the shady little side street in the pyramid's shadow and began a slow perambulation of the area, idly perusing all that there was to see: hand-carved woodwork, finely tooled leather, a bookbinder's, and a brownsmith's, the latter hard at work hammering the dents out of a well-worn brass platter.

The bookbinder intrigued him, so he lingered there. He was more than a little disappointed to see that the books being sold were all blank—bound journals, ledgers, diaries, and the like—but the craftsmanship they displayed was nonetheless impressive. The binder had tomes of every shape and size, every thickness and thinness, and had encompassed between the colorful leather- or cloth-bound covers everything from thick parchment to thin paper, of all colors and textures. Rem was tempted to buy something—he loved books, and had always treasured them—but the sort of books that moved him had stories and histories already bound within them, not blank pages awaiting print.

That's when he heard the commotion. It was nearby, just around the corner at the end of the lane, in fact. It sounded like voices raised in declaration, punctuated from time to time by sudden cheers or the boos of a crowd. Turning toward the sound, Rem watched the narrowly framed opening at the end of the street, trying to see if he could determine just what was going on out there. Since he could see nothing from where he stood, he left the bookbinder's and went to investigate.

The covered street opened onto an oblong plaza of sorts—a broad, open area demarcating the edge of the dwarven quarter on one side and the resumption of human habitation on the other. It was the almost-even mix of warm bodies before him that first struck Rem as different from the Warrens themselves, the number of dwarves and humans crammed into this crowded little square being more or less equal, unlike in the streets he'd just been traveling, where humans were a rarity. Dwarven street sellers choked the periphery of the square, hawking everything from pottery to woven cloth, clearly making an appeal to the human passersby.

But it was not the sellers or the buyers that interested Rem so much as a large congregation of humans at the far end of the plaza, all crammed elbow to elbow, surrounding a tall, wide-shouldered man orating from a raised platform. The orator seemed to be shouting at his fellow tall folk as they strolled among the dwarven stalls, idly admiring or keenly inspecting the merchandise.

"—hundreds, nay, thousands of human craftsmen and human vendors, just blocks away! Why, then, do you linger here, haggling with the small folk over their trinkets, while your own kind scrounge or go hungry?"

The crowd about him cheered, supporting the question posed. A few passersby shouted back.

"Better prices!"

"Better work!"

"What are *you* selling?"

"We sell nothing!" a thin, wiry man in the wide-shouldered orator's retinue shouted back. "We're stonemasons by trade, and proud to be so! We're only here now because we've been put out of work, by these same half-pint hammer tossers you're buying from!"

The wide-shouldered man turned to the new speaker and seemed to quietly scold him or try to calm him. It wasn't working, though—the thin man's enmity was already permeating the crowd around them in the form of murmured assents and nodding heads.

A dwarf stepped forward from a vendor's stall crammed full

of fired clay pots and cookware. He was covered in thick rusty-red hair, and his beard was hoary and unbraided. "I'm a potter, longshanks! Not a stonemason! How on earth am I taking work from you?"

A number of passersby cheered in support of the potter.

The first speaker—the tall, broad-shouldered one—held up his hands as though to beg silence. When the crowd's noise subsided, he spoke. "You speak true," he said, voice booming across the square, "so go back to your stall, sir! We're here to address our people—our folk! This has nothing to do with you!"

"Nothing to do with us?" another dwarven vendor—this one a boot maker—chimed in. "You stand there and say we're stealing work from you lot—that's got *everything* to do with us!"

A man stepped out of the milling throng on the far side of the square, apart from the group gathered in protest. He took up a handful of cold mud from the street and threw it at the dwarven peddler.

"Shut your gob!" he spat. "The man weren't talkin' to you!"

The flung mud escalated things. As Rem watched, a few of the dwarven vendors stepped forward, all scolding the mud flinger at once. One of them scooped up his own handful of mud and flung it. The clod separated and splattered the crowd around the man, barely touching its intended target.

The murmuring of the crowd rose toward a tidal roar. Rem could see, could *feel*, the tension in the square escalating. Fists shook. Eyes bulged in red, angry faces. Teeth were bared and spittle flew. The close-packed crowd rippled like a stormy sea.

Someone touched his arm. Startled, Rem spun and found Indilen at his elbow. She looked shocked, as though she'd just caught him doing something unseemly. Rem glanced back at the crowd, then returned to Indilen. He was torn. Part of him felt he should intervene—at least give his watchwarden's whistle a toot and call someone in to break things up. Another part of him just wanted to grab Indilen's hand and flee the scene, as fast as their feet would take them.

"What is it?" she asked. "What's all the fuss about?"

He was about to explain when he heard something new— the voice of that thin, wiry man again, raised and embittered.

"Do you like to throw things, you stunted bastard?"

As Rem rounded, he saw the thin man—the one who'd identified the angry men as stonemasons—separated now from his companions, stalking toward the dwarven potter's stand. As Rem watched, the man snatched up a big clay pot, then smashed the pot on the ground at his feet. The dwarven potter, enraged that someone would so carelessly wreck his inventory, lunged at the wiry man. A few close-at-hand dwarves dove to stop the lunging potter. Some nearby men hurried to defend the thin pot breaker, forming a sort of cordon around him. As the potter foamed and spat, the thin man smirked and taunted him. Little by little the foul energies swirling between the two aggrieved parties rippled through the crowd. As Rem watched, things happened fast—too fast to be stopped.

Someone threw a punch. Tugged hair. Kicked. A throng surged. Fists began to fly. A peddler's cart was overturned with a crash.

Time to go. Rem shoved Indilen back toward the street they'd come through, stealing glances back over his shoulder as they went, trying to get some picture of what was happening and where it might go. His look back gave him only fleeting glimpses: that tall stonemason raising his hands again, as if to calm his companions; the crowd, surging toward the potter's stall; men snatching up the earthenware and hurling it to the ground; a few dwarves in hasty retreat; others charging to meet the agitators. Mud flew. Someone screamed. A donkey hitched to a cart brayed and bucked in its traces.

"Rem," Indilen said as he hurried her along, "shouldn't you do something?"

Absently Rem nodded, drew out his watchwarden's whistle, and began to blow. The bleating sounded tinny and pale beside the fulsome jostle and roar of the rioting crowd. Even as he blew, Rem did not stop to see if anyone answered his call: his only concern was to get Indilen as far from the violence as possible.

"Oh dear," Indilen breathed, now stealing her own backward glance at the chaotic square, "someone's bleeding and—*Gods*!"

That last exclamation caused Rem to turn and look back. The violence was naked now, men and dwarves laying into each other with any weapons at hand: rocks, broken stall struts, grasping hands, and bare fists. The scene was total chaos. They turned a corner and Rem fell into a trot, dragging Indilen along beside him.

"What started it?" she asked, quickening her pace to keep up with him. "What was it all about?"

"Angry masons or something," Rem answered. "But it's spreading. We need to go, now." He pulled up his whistle again and blew as they ran.

In moments they reached the main street that they'd followed into the quarter. Rem turned right, Indilen in tow, intending to retrace their steps as quickly as possible. As they raced up the crowded street, however, threading a path among the shoppers and strollers, they found their way blocked. Up ahead, dwarves and humans fleeing the riot flooded the street and choked the intersection, desperate for any egress, every path blocked by a press of frightened, confused evacuees. So fraught and tumultuous were the surges and eddies of the confused crowd, Rem and Indilen were unsure which way to flee, pressed and jostled from all sides. Then, without warning, a tight band of dwarves in flight came barreling into the intersection with a pack of human agitators on their heels. The tall folk sowed discord as they went, overturning vendor carts and street-side merchandise indiscriminately. Somewhere in the distance, Rem heard the angry whine of watchwarden whistles, but he saw no sign of intervention. Driven by the new, oncoming threat from the human rioters and the few dwarves that engaged them, the crowd exploded outward in every direction. In the sudden pandemonium, Indilen was torn from Rem's grasp.

She shouted for him, reached for him, but the current of the crowd was too powerful. As Indilen was dragged backward by the fleeing throng, Rem felt himself yanked in the opposite direction. It did not matter than most of the bodies were dwarf-size, and that she and Rem towered above the majority of those caught in the mad dash—the rip was still too strong to resist. In moments Indilen had been swept down a side street, and Rem, driven back, lost sight of her.

Rem cursed, rage and panic rising in him. He began to shove and kick, forcing his way bodily through the crowd. He felt sick with himself for moving so aggressively—so carelessly— but only one thing mattered at that moment: he had to get off this street and find his way back to Indilen. He could not abandon her here—not in the middle of all this violence.

There, off to his right: a narrow alley, barely a breezeway. Rem forced his way out of the rolling throng that shoved and jostled him and dove in, its width barely sufficient to allow him through. Awkwardly he shuffled along the winding little path until it opened onto a parallel street, this one covered by a rippling canopy of canary-yellow silk. All around him he saw

and heard the signs of flight: swirling bodies, boots pounding mud, screams, curses, the names of lost loved ones shouted
above the din. Merchants and tradesmen busily drew in their
merchandise and set to locking up their shops, keenly aware
that the coming storm would sweep over and engulf them in
moments. Rem searched the chaotic scene, desperate for some
sign of Indilen.

Someone suddenly took a handful of his coat's mantle and
yanked. Rem spun, fists up, ready to bare-knuckle it and leave
the fool intent on ambushing him bleeding in the mud.

When Indilen saw his raised fists, she screamed and threw
up her hands.

"Just me!" she cried.

"Fuck all, girl!" he shouted back, then threw his arms
around her and squeezed her hard enough to make her yelp.
"You scared the living piss out of me!"

"We should go," she said in his ear.

"Yes, we should," he agreed, then broke their embrace, took
her hand, and led the way. The noise was behind them now,
while the path ahead looked clear. In just a block or two, they'd
be safely out of the Warrens. He could still hear raised voices,
the approaching cry of watchwardens' whistles, and the vague,
soft sound of wood thumping flesh.

"So what now?" he asked as they went. "Lunch?"

Indilen threw him a glare, the sort that said, *I know you're
joking, but now's not the time.* Rem kept his mouth shut after that.

CHAPTER SIX

"So there we were," Rem said, never breaking stride, always keeping pace with Torval beside him, "suddenly surrounded on all sides by this mess—riot, protest, whatever the sundry hells you'd call it. One minute people are flinging words, then it's mud, then it's fists and blood and screams and everyone's running."

"Huh," Torval said, an emphatic but noncommittal grunt.

"I lost her for a moment, you know. It terrified me." Rem shook his head, shrugged. "Made me sick, losing her in that moment, fearing what might befall her...right down in the center of me."

"Mmm," Torval said.

Rem studied his partner, trying to get a good look at him in the spotty post lamp light as they strolled along on their nightly patrol. The dwarf kept pace, and he seemed to respond at the right intervals to Rem's story, but something was amiss. The old stump wasn't in the moment, that was clear. His mind was somewhere else. The great puzzle for Rem was, where could it be? He'd never known Torval to be so preoccupied or lost in silent contemplation before. Certainly the dwarf had a right to such moments—Rem didn't begrudge him a little brooding—but it was decidedly out of character. As such, it filled Rem with a mix of idle curiosity and brotherly worry.

They were on the west side of the Fifth, near the riverfront but not on it, their patrol taking them past street-level shops and live-aboves interspersed with a few better-than-average trade-class tenements and multiroom boardinghouses. The neighborhood was closely packed, well kept, and lively, even at this late hour, approaching the midnight bells. As they tramped along, Rem saw moving shadows in all the leaded windows of the local taverns and taprooms, and where the drinking houses were too crowded to accommodate all comers, there'd be small knots of citizens in the street outside, usually warming their hands over a fire built in an iron brazier or a clay pot. The night air was bitter, but the ale they quaffed, the fires before them, and their laughter seemed to keep all these street-side revelers amply warm.

"Torval, are you listening to me?" Rem asked.

"You there!" Torval suddenly shouted, addressing a group of drinkers huddled around a crackling brazier outside a brightly lit pub. "Move that firepot farther into the street! You're too close to the eaves and like to set the whole damned place ablaze!"

One of the drinkers rose and stepped toward the oncoming dwarf. "See here, old stump," he said, clearly trying to be friendly, "the lee of the pub's keeping the wind off. We drag that fire into the street, we might as well not have it at all. It's bloody cold out tonight!"

Torval, without breaking stride, hove right up to the brazier and its crackling fire, took hold of its hot edges in his bare hands, and upended the whole thing into the muddy street. The burning wood scraps spilled onto the mud, swirling trails of embers and ash winding down the street under the ministrations of the rushing wind. The drinkers stared, gape mouthed, as their previously roaring fire slowly died on the cold, packed earth of the street.

Torval carried on right past them. Rem scurried around the pile of cinders and ash now in his path in an effort to keep up with his partner. "There you are!" Torval shouted back over his shoulder. "No more fire, no more threat. Huddle under the eaves all you like."

"Casca's tits, that's a fine way to behave!" the man who'd approached Torval shouted. "I'll have your badge, you stunted little bastard!"

Torval gave an annoyed wave of his arms and kept walking. Rem kept pace. Part of him wanted to circle back and apologize for his partner's enraged response, but that would do little good at this point. The more important question was, what in all the sundry hells was eating at the dwarf? Rem had never seen him be so gruff—so unfairly rude—to a citizen who wasn't even breaking the law.

"What was that about?" Rem asked. Was Torval's pace increasing? It was becoming harder to stay abreast of him.

"I warned him," Torval said, almost to himself.

"That's not an answer," Rem said, and hurried forward so he could get in front of Torval. He started walking backward—a risky gambit, true, but he wanted to see his partner's face as he questioned him.

"Tell me what's eating at you," Rem pressed. "You've barely been listening to me all night, and now you're flying into berserker rages without the slightest provocation."

"Berserker rage," Torval huffed. "Did you see that brazier? So close to the walls and the eaves? Fire hazard, plain and simple."

"Enough!" Rem shouted, and did something he'd never expected to do: he laid one hand on Torval's chest and stopped his forward motion. Torval snarled and tried to move round him, but Rem stepped into his path. He was hardly surprised when

Torval suddenly gave him a great shove and tried to advance again. What surprised him more was his own determination to stay on his feet and in Torval's path. He wouldn't let him go so easily.

"I'm warning you," Torval said through gnashing teeth.

"No, old stump, I'm warning you," Rem countered. "You need to talk to me, right now. I'll not take another step until you tell me what's bedeviling you. Was it something I did?"

Torval looked genuinely annoyed at that, but also a little apologetic. He shook his head and waved his hands emphatically—dismissive, flustered. "Nothing, lad. Nothing to do with you at all, just... It's just..."

"What?" Rem asked.

"It's not *for* you," Torval said. "I've got things weighing on my mind and heart, but there's not a damned thing you can do to fix or change them, so there's no use shrugging them off on you. Just let it lie."

"I won't," Rem said, quite proud of his determination, but also secretly hoping Torval didn't decide to wallop him headwise in the next instant. Such a response was not beyond him. "I'm your partner, and I thought I was your friend. If something's troubling you, I'd like to hear about it."

Torval's face seemed to curl in on itself in an expression of pained reticence and severe annoyance. Rem had seen that expression before, but actually took it as a good sign. That was usually the face Torval made just before he was about to relent and undertake an unpleasant task he'd tried to avoid. Finally the sour countenance sagged into a sort of weary indifference. Torval sighed and searched the street. After a moment he found what he sought and waved Rem toward it.

It was a small, cozy inn, crammed between two taller tenements. Its leaded windows were gold with lamplight, and although shadowy forms moved within, it didn't seem terribly boisterous or crowded.

"Come on," Torval said. "Let's talk over something warm."

The inn, known as the Chimney Sweep, was cozy, welcoming, and blessedly calm. The few patrons present were all engaged in quiet pursuits—card games, easy conversations, solitary musings over spiced wine or frothy ale. Torval asked the innkeeper for two ales, but the innkeeper—an old man with well-trimmed gray whiskers and a round, rosy face—was so pleased to have watchwardens in his public room that he insisted on something special, without elaborating on just what "something special" might be. He bustled away and returned moments later with two steaming clay mugs and presented them with bright, beaming eyes and a wide grin.

"Specialty of the house," he said. "Hot buttered apple brandy, with some spices mixed in. Hope you love it, gents."

Torval accepted the two mugs, handed one to Rem, then cocked his head sideward. Apparently he wanted to drink their buttered brandy and talk out back. Rem followed dutifully, stealing a sip of his beverage as they went. It was absolutely stunning—just what he needed on such a cold night.

Torval led him through a narrow back hallway, through the kitchens, and out into a little courtyard formed by the walls of the neighboring tenements and the stable out behind the inn itself. While it was cold out here, the shelter provided by the high neighboring buildings and their proximity to the inn's kitchens seemed to keep the winter wind from biting too aggressively. And, of course, the brandy helped immensely.

Rem sipped, the brew still too hot to guzzle without searing his mouth and tongue. Torval, to his great surprise, gulped down a great mouthful of the stuff as if it were tepid. For a long time they sat in silence. All around them Rem heard the sounds of an ordinary night in a quiet neighborhood: the vague susurration of distant conversations, an intermittent laugh, a called name, dogs barking at passersby, cats mewling as they screwed in dark back alleys. They were comforting sounds—prosaic and familiar—unlike Torval's pensive silence.

"Talk," Rem said, trying to be both forceful and friendly at the same time—to assure Torval that he wanted to hear it, whatever *it* might be.

"It's foolish," Torval said.

"Let me be the judge of that," Rem said, and sipped again. The mug warmed his cupped hands nicely.

Torval took a great deep draught from his own mug, then opened his mouth to speak. Rem waited for the tale to come... but nothing came. A moment later Torval closed his mouth and sniffed the air.

"Do you smell something?" he asked.

Rem leaned forward and breathed deep. He could smell the cinnamon and nutmeg in his brandy, the rich ordure of the nearby stables, and the buttery scents of baking bread and stewing onions from the kitchens at their backs. But there was something else, wasn't there? Something acrid and foul.

"Fire?" Rem asked.

Torval leapt to his feet and hurried back into the inn. Rem followed, gulping down his brandy as they went. They weren't likely to sit here and have a quiet conversation now, and he couldn't let the stuff go to waste.

Torval left his mug on the bar and Rem did the same as he passed. Both of them then crossed the public room and burst out of the front door into the street. They strode right to the center of it and stood, sniffing, scanning the gloomy cityscape around them for some sign of smoke or flames.

Torval was looking back toward the tavern they'd passed earlier. Rem suspected the dwarf thought those street-side drinkers might have rebuilt their fire in its brazier, right under the low-hanging eaves. But there was no sign of trouble in that direction.

Yet the smell was getting stronger, wasn't it?

They scanned the street, the buildings, the sky for any sign. Off in the east, toward Suicide Hill, a column of smoke rose into the night above the rooftops, lit from beneath by an angry orange light.

"There," Rem said, pointing.

Torval was already off and running.

The quiet night was forgotten. Torval's unspoken troubles were forgotten. The silky, spicy taste of that buttered brandy on Rem's tongue was forgotten. The world now rushed past Rem, wind in his ears, heart hammering in his chest. Torval had taken off at a dead run and left him behind, swift little bastard that he was. So, driven and determined, Rem raced on, zigzagging through the labyrinthine streets, dodging curious passersby who stopped to scan the sky and an ever-growing number of frightened townies fleeing westward, toward the river, ahead of the blaze.

As Rem neared the conflagration, the acrid smell of char and ash grew ever more pungent in his nostrils. The streets he traversed grew more thickly enrobed in a tenebrous black fog and falling embers that swirled down like hellish snow. Amid the thickening smoke the crowds teemed and swarmed in a frenzy, the sounds of screaming women, crying children, and the pounding boots of volunteer bucket brigades already growing to a din in Rem's ears.

The stench of smoke and char were acute now, almost sickening, and Rem's eyes watered as the haze thickened. As he hastened on, Rem noted scattered squadrons of looters, sometimes consisting of whole families, using the chaos to smash storefront windows and flee with quickly seized prizes. *Parasites!* If he didn't have more pressing business ahead, Rem would have challenged every single one of them.

At last, just as the crowds thickened and the swirling smoke coaxed deep, hacking coughs from his lungs, Rem rounded a corner and burst from the narrow streets he'd been threading into a broad, open square. He recognized this place, for he'd lost Torval to one of his strange reveries there that very morning: it was the high plaza overlooking the under-construction temple of the Panoply.

And it was that temple—its wooden scaffolds, working lean-tos, pulley systems, swiveling cranes, and ramps—that now burned. The Yenaran night was alight with a fearsome auric glow, something from a prophet's vision of the hellish pits where the damned suffered, screaming, through endless eternities. The affrighted fled. The brave charged in. The perverse stood by and watched.

Rem pounded down into the main square, skirting the edge of the inferno and the chaos surrounding it. He saw bucket brigades already at work, shuttling water from nearby fountains in an effort to quell the blaze. Their efforts were valiant, but barely effective. Every little pail of water tossed at the foot of the rising wall of flames seemed only to tease or enrage the elemental abomination now loosed.

One crew, knotted close to a looming latticework of burning

beams, broke and ran as the trusses above collapsed in flames and came crashing down onto the stone steps surrounding the temple. Moments after the truss collapsed, a half-constructed stone arch formerly supported by those beams disintegrated with a thunderous crash.

Gods, where was Torval? The little bastard had gone rushing off ahead of him, and now Rem wondered if he had joined a bucket brigade or if he was already buried under the burning timber. Rem was eager to join the fight, but his concern for his lost partner kept him from leaping in as he otherwise might have.

"You there!" someone cried out. Rem turned toward the sound of the voice, not sure if the call was meant for him or not.

A tall, fair-haired Kosterman stood just a stone's throw from him, holding a full pail in each of his muscular hands. This was Hildebran, the very same Fifth Ward watchman who had arrested Rem six months earlier and inadvertently landed him in his present vocation.

"That you, Rem?" the barbarian asked, squinting. The bright-orange flames were behind Rem, and must have made his face quite hard to make out.

"Aye, that," Rem said, hurrying closer and snatching one of the water pails.

"I didn't even recognize you," Hildebran said. "Where's our little friend?"

Rem threw his arms wide. "Your guess is as good as mine. When we smelled the smoke and saw the flames, he took off running and I lost him."

Hildebran shrugged. "Probably here already. Bend to it, then."

Rem needed no further prodding. It was going to be a long night.

Time and again Rem scurried back and forth, took water

pails from whoever offered them, tossed the water into the flames with almost no effect, then did the same all over again. He kept at it for some time—minutes, hours, he couldn't say— before an insistent, familiar sound among all the noise and bluster caught his ears.

It was Torval's voice, crying out in the night, again and again. The dwarf seemed to be calling for someone.

"Tavarix."

His son's name, over and over again. "Tavarix. Tavarix."

Rem began to search the manic jostling around him, trying to pick out his partner. There were dwarves, but none of them were Torval. There were youngsters, but none of them were Tavarix. There were fire-brigadesmen, watchwardens, and everyday citizens, but his partner—the one person he desperately sought— was nowhere to be seen.

And yet he could hear him, clearly, calling into the night, screaming even. "Tavarix. Tavarix." Where in the sundry hells was he?

Someone barreled up to Rem and shoved a pair of water pails into his hands. He did not see who, nor did he ask what they wanted of him. This was the routine. Take the water, toss it into the flames, hurry back for more. Rem mounted the temple steps, rushing toward the framework of what would be, in time, one of the lesser chapels of the main sanctuary. He upended one bucket, then the other, then turned to run back down the stairs to fetch more water.

That's when he saw Torval. His partner moved right in the midst of the fire, far off to Rem's right, darting among a jungle of looming support beams and imminent scaffolding, all engulfed in a ferocious blaze. The dwarf was searching the ground as if for someone trapped or wounded. As he went, he kept calling his son's name.

Could the boy be trapped among the fire and falling debris? What might he even be doing here?

But there Torval went, still pushing his way through that garden of smoke and flame, threatened by a hundred louring trusses and support beams, all licked with hungry flame and creaking toward final collapse.

"Tavarix!" Torval cried. "Tavarix!"

Rem heard a series of terrible cracks akin to the sound of oncoming rock slides in the Ironwalls or calving icebergs in the great northern seas. He saw a spiderweb of truss work near Torval buckle and split, spewing swirling embers in a hot golden rain upon his desperate, searching partner.

"Torval!" Rem cried, and sprinted up the temple stairs. He shouted his partner's name all the way, but Torval couldn't hear him.

This is going to get me killed, Rem thought absently. Yet still he ran. The smoke seared his lungs, the flames forced his eyes shut, made his body shrink instinctively from the sweltering heat.

There was Torval, just a short distance away. There were the trusses—shrieking, cracking, toppling, leaning into an inexorable fall. Were people screaming somewhere? Shouting his name? Urging him to get the hell out of there, now?

Rem could no longer hear them. He could hear only the roar of the flames and Torval's insistent cry as he searched for his son. "Tavarix! Tavarix!"

Rem hit Torval at full speed. He tackled the dwarf and put him on his back just as the supports above them toppled and crashed into the space they'd just occupied. For a moment the world was nothing but heat and light, fire and smoke, choked breath and stinging tears. Vaguely Rem heard Torval cursing. Rem hurt all over, but he wasn't burning, and he wasn't dead.

Struggling to see through tears and smoke, Rem rose and tugged at Torval's prone muscular form. The dwarf struggled against him, but they were moving now, inching clear of the collapsed scaffolding, the deep, bright heart of the inferno. Moments later Rem's burden seemed to lighten, and he realized that he was no longer alone. Someone else—someone he could not see—helped him drag Torval clear of the flames.

When they were safely away, out of the inferno's gaping, hungry, red-hot maw, Rem let himself collapse onto the cool mud. He hugged it like a needy lover. Blinking, he searched the murky world around him and saw something like the outline of Torval, bucking against grasping hands, shadows bent over him like surgeons in a field hospital.

"He's here somewhere!" the dwarf cried. "My boy! I know it!"

Rem wanted to assure Torval that he was mad—Tavarix was nowhere nearby. Why would he be? But he didn't have a word left in him.

Then it all went black.

Rem regained consciousness a short time later. Nearby, Torval told those attending him—a few watchwardens and people Rem did not recognize—that he was just peachy and they should get the hell away from him and let him get back to work. Unfortunately, when Torval tried to rise and rush back toward the fire, he fell to his knees, racked by a horrible coughing fit. Rem fell into a fit of his own, his half-seared lungs trying to expel all the smoke and soot they'd absorbed. For a while that's all there was for the two of them: coughing, punctuated by sips of water and prodding by a local barber-surgeon eager to make sure they weren't more profoundly injured. Only after what felt like an eternity of painful hacking and interminable poking did the two of them manage to breathe normally and chase the barber away.

As they sat there, side by side, propped against an empty horse trough, a pair of dwarves went dashing by. They held buckets of sloshing water and were heading right for the flames.

Torval all but leapt at them. "You there! *Hallirwelk!*"

One of the two dwarves skidded to a halt and looked back while his companion kept running. When he saw that it was one of his own kind addressing him, he approached.

"You all right?" the water-carrying dwarf asked.

"Are you one of the temple masons?" Torval asked him in return.

The dwarf nodded.

"Tavarix—one of the apprentices, a fosterling—have you seen him?"

Rem was astounded when something like recognition dawned on the other dwarf's face. "You're the boy's father? The watchwarden?"

Torval leapt to his feet. Rem had never seen him so eager, so helpless. "I am! Where is he? Tell me!"

"Back at the dormitories with the others," the dwarf said. "They were already in for the night when the fire started."

Torval nodded. "My thanks, friend. Truly."

The dwarf looked as if he wasn't sure how to respond. Finally he nodded and backed away. "Don't worry about him," he said, then turned and hurried away.

Rem thought that sounded rather strange. Don't worry about *him*, the dwarf had said. Emphasis on the last word. What was going on here?

Torval turned back to Rem. There were fresh tracks cut through the soot on his face—moisture of some sort. Rem supposed it could be rivulets of sweat, but those tracks looked more like tears.

"We should get back in there," Torval said. "They need all hands."

Rem nodded and rose. Whatever was happening with Tavarix...he'd just have to wait for an explanation. Without further words they hurried back to the blaze.

They bent to it again, shuttling buckets, aiding in the digging of a firebreak, and generally doing whatever was needed as the fire raged through the night. When at last the inferno waned and the first gray light of morning crept into the world, Rem surveyed the scene and noted that almost all of his hundred-odd Fifth Ward comrades were present and accounted for, covered in soot and ash. Even Ondego and Hirk—their prefect and master sergeant—were visible in the milling crowd, just as filthy and exhausted as everyone else. All in all, nearly a thousand Yenarans—watchwardens, the volunteer fire brigade, concerned citizens, and sadistic pleasure seekers—choked the square around the half-finished temple.

A few nearby buildings had succumbed in the course of the night, but the damage was, to Rem's great amazement, largely contained by morning. The temple itself and its great quarried stones survived the blaze intact. A few in-progress arches and vaults collapsed when their wooden supports burned out from under them, but by and large, the structure looked much as it had before the disaster, though now blackened and littered round about by debris. There was only the curious impression that, now littered with ash and smoldering beams and fallen stone, the yet-to-be-completed Panoply resembled not a thing unfinished, but a thing long ruined—ancient and abandoned, racked by the depredations of time and the elements.

Filthy and wasted, Rem and Torval retreated to a nearby

fountain in sight of the ruin. Many of their fellow watchwardens were already there, rinsing away the soot and grime with the icy water, tending wounds acquired in the course of their battle, and slaking their considerable thirsts with the same cold and blackening waters they employed for bathing. Rem wondered if he would ever get the smell of smoke out of his nose, the taste of char and ash off his tongue.

Eriadus, their watch quartermaster, moved among the watchwardens alongside Minniver, one of the healers often employed to tend their most acute injuries. They practiced their separate arts when and where they could, and when they encountered more severe injuries, they made sure those victims were rushed to the Sisters at the Houses of Healing.

Rem studied Torval under the wan light of dawn. His watchwarden's winter coat had been long abandoned in the course of the fight, and every bare inch of skin exposed—his face, his forearms, his bald pate—seemed to have some small measure of bruising, abrasion or blistering upon it. The injuries looked painful, but Rem supposed they were marginal in light of what they'd been through. He wondered how he himself looked.

"Thank you," Torval said suddenly, then dunked his head under the frigid water in the fountain.

Rem waited until Torval came up for air to respond. "You're welcome. What the bloody hell were you doing up there? You could've gotten yourself killed. Or me."

Torval looked more than a little ashamed. He couldn't seem to look Rem in the eye. "I feared Tav was hereabouts somewhere. He's been working here, you see, as an apprentice stonemason. When I saw the fire, I feared the worst."

Well…that explained Torval's curious exchange with that dwarf earlier.

"So," Rem said, "you know he's safe now. Feel better?"

Torval nodded, but it seemed a half-hearted gesture. Maybe the dwarf was just tired. Rem certainly knew he himself was. Nonetheless, he had the vague sense that Torval was still keeping something from him—something deep and worrisome. But they'd had a long night already, hadn't they? No need to push the issue—not now.

Rem slumped against the fountain and turned toward the ruins. He saw members of the Panoply conclave—a tight knot of priests in variously colored robes and vestments, each servant to a different god or goddess—pressing through the crowd toward the disaster site. They were accompanied by a group of soot-covered dwarves—probably the stewards of the masons' guild overseeing the construction, joining their employers for a survey of the destruction. As the intrepid little group of dwarven craftsmen and human priests picked a path through the wreckage, Rem studied them.

There was an old man in scarlet and saffron robes—obviously a priest of Honus, the sun god—accompanied by two women. One of the women was middle-aged, a fact made clear by her time-lined face, while the other was much younger—probably a recently vested priestess just beginning her ascent in the temple hierarchy. The middle-aged woman wore the orange, brown, and yellow vestments of Belenna, goddess of the hearth and home, while her younger companion was swaddled in blue, white, and silver silks, the colors of the lunar and harvest goddess, Yerys. Trailing behind these three clerical aristocrats were a pair of younger men—novice priests or temple acolytes—wearing gray robes indicating that they had made no formal declaration of patronage.

While the dwarves and human clerics stumbled slack-faced among the ruins, the middle-aged priestess of Belenna—

clearly more curious than aggrieved, to Rem's eyes—broke away from the group, mounted the soot-blackened temple steps, and began a slow, methodical perambulation of the scene. From his place on the cold stones beside the fountain, Rem watched her. Someone—he could not say who—handed him a wet rag. Without bothering to search out who had handed him the offering or thank them, Rem merely accepted it and set to scrubbing his face and soot-blackened hair in a vain attempt to make himself feel slightly less like a chimney sweep fresh from his filthy duties. As he did so, he kept his eyes on the mourning clerics and the lone, probing priestess.

"What's she after?" Rem muttered, entirely to himself. Torval grunted beside him and shrugged.

Up among the wreckage, the priestess froze. Her eyes seemed to have locked on something of note. "I need strong hands!" she suddenly called. "A pail of water! And rags!"

A few watchwardens close at hand answered her summons, breaking from the throng about the temple and mounting the steps, pails and rags in hand.

Rem looked to Torval. Torval shrugged again, still at a loss as to just what the woman had been searching for and what she might have found.

"I'll check it out," Rem said, and rose stiffly to do so.

"Not without me," Torval rasped, and struggled to his feet.

The two of them mounted the temple steps, followed by other curious parties, all the while keeping their eyes on the priestess and the impromptu crew now gathering around her. A few of the men worked in concert to cast aside a tangle of blackened beams, clearing a path toward a certain span of stone wall that seemed to have drawn the priestess's attention. Another pair hurried forward. At the priestess's insistence, they emptied their water pails against a half-finished wall. After dousing the wall, they set to scrubbing away the scorching.

Rem and Torval drifted nearer. Even at this distance, Rem could see the puzzled and astonished faces of the cleaners, the grim countenance of the priestess; they had washed away the soot that blackened a certain collection of fitted stones, revealing something of import beneath. The priestess sought out her ecclesiastical peers and waved them nearer.

Rem and Torval began to pick their way through the debris to the section of wall that had drawn the priestess's attention. From the corner of his eye, Rem noted a familiar figure and turned to see who had joined them. It was Ondego, along with a few other officers of the watch and fire brigade leaders—all eager to see what the priestess's probing curiosity had uncovered. Torval drew Rem aside in an effort to both clear the way for officials higher up on the chain of command and get a better angle on what the priestess and the men with the water pails had uncovered.

It was a message, painted onto the temple facade in large white letters. The paint must have dried and clung fast to the stone before the flames had covered it with a film of soot. Now that the black scum had been washed away, the graffito was clear for all to see, painted in tall, sloppy, but legible characters.

I say to you, this is your inheritance, your kingdom, your domain, it said.

The sacred scrolls, Rem immediately realized. The *Scrolls of Derivation, all about the creation of the first man and woman, Edath and Yfrain, and their commission to quell the Maker's other wayward creations.*

Below the words was a strange symbol, also painted in white, but with a giant scar-like swath of red painted over it diagonally.

Rem tried to make sense of the symbol that had been crossed out but was at a loss.

"What *is* that?" Rem asked.

"It's an ancient symbol," Torval said, "a battle standard from the Great Furor, in the time of the Plague of Storms."

"Whose standard?" Rem pressed, not recognizing it.

"My people," Torval said. "Dwarves."

CHAPTER SEVEN

The dayshifters were already gathered when Rem, Torval, and the other night shift watchwardens arrived back at the watchkeep shortly after dawn.

Rem and Torval—and all their fellows on the night shift, for that matter—had very little commerce with the dayshifters, so anytime a long night stretched into the early-morning hours and forced the two teams to cross paths, the world seemed—to Rem anyway—strangely off-kilter. He often forgot that the Fifth Ward was patrolled by anyone while he and his companions slept their days away.

But here they were, a hundred-odd souls—male and female, human, elf, and dwarf—all gathered in the watchkeep administrative chamber for a preshift briefing by their prefect, a hardfaced woman in trousers named Torala. Both shifts were in shock as they mingled, the nightshifters regaling the day shift with tales about the horrors of the fire, their own favored possible causes, and their personal experiences at the fore of fighting it. Rem supposed such tale swapping and self-mythologizing was all part of a watchwarden's life, especially when something so out of the ordinary invaded it.

Sure, I was there during the flood of the Black Autumn! Remember it well . . .

I knew that one—the watchwarden turned outlaw. Always a good mate, from where I sat. But I was never entirely sure about him, either . . .

Fight the fire? Boys, I was right at the forefront! I had to be dragged off before one of those burning scaffolds crushed me! Nearly lost my skin...

Tales were told, lore expounded, near misses and unlikely triumphs added to the well of communal memory. Rem could see, all around the room, how the dayshifters receiving the stories from their nocturnal fellows-in-arms all had one of two looks upon their faces: earnest concern or jealous amazement. Rem, for his part, had no energy left for celebrating his exploits through the night. He wanted nothing more than to be home, in his bed.

And clean. How he would love to be clean!

Torval leaned against a nearby desk, shoulders slumped, lost in thought or just plain tuckered out. Rem edged nearer.

"Are we here for a reason?" he asked. "Or can we call it a night?"

Torval was about to answer when someone else, at Rem's elbow, beat him to it.

"We're to wait," that silky voice said, and Rem felt his whole body stiffen suddenly in shock. He spun and found Queydon once again skulking nearby.

"Would you please stop that!" Rem said, beseeching. "Announce your approach? Ring a bell? Something?"

She gave a deep nod. "My apologies, Watchwarden Remeck. I keep hoping—against hope, apparently—that your awareness finally catches up to my own natural stealth."

Torval clearly wanted to laugh, but didn't have the energy. He simply smiled and shook his head.

Rem decided to change the subject. "So," he said, "is there going to be some sort of announcement?"

Queydon nodded in answer. She opened her mouth as if to reply, but she was interrupted by Ondego's emergence from his office. As he shuffled along, he wiped soot and grime from his face and hair with a cloth that looked as if it had been retrieved from a mine shaft. A similarly filthy Hirk followed, along with Prefect Torala and her own second—a tall, stone-faced fellow with a lantern jaw and ice-blue eyes whose name escaped Rem presently. As they moved en masse toward the center of the room, every conversation in the room ceased.

Ondego cleared his throat. "Prefect Torala's given me kind permission to address you all," he began. "You've heard about the fire at the temple. Before you start asking questions, I'll address the meat of it. Yes, it was as bad as everyone says. Yes, there were injuries—some serious—though thankfully, our watch nor the gentle public hasn't lost anyone yet. And yes, we think it was no accident."

Rem felt a chill worm through him. Injuries, but no deaths... *yet*. That wasn't terribly comforting.

"Who's hurt?" someone asked from the far side of the room.

Ondego lowered his eyes. He then named five of their comrades now nursing wounds of various sorts, from incidental to life-threatening, and promised to offer updates on their progress when he had them. Ondego was a hard man who'd lived a hard life, but Rem knew him well enough now to know that losing any of his charges—or seeing them in mortal danger—shook the prefect deeply. The fact that he reported their compromised states with eyes down, in a droning monotone, told Rem that he was doing his damnedest not to betray the real depth of his emotions to those who'd made it back to the watchkeep unhurt.

"There are rumors," someone else began, "that this wasn't just mischievous vandalism, but a deliberate attack. What's the word on that?" It was Woldor, a russet-haired dwarf who shared the night shift with Rem and Torval. His high, piping voice was unmistakable.

"That is correct," Ondego said, now raising his eyes to the gathered company. "Some evidence at the scene suggested, shall we say, directed enmity. When we've got all the facts, we'll present them. 'Til then, just know that we should be on the lookout for anyone with a proclivity for setting things on fire."

"Or who hates dwarves," Woldor added.

Ondego leveled a sober glare across the room at the diminutive watchwarden. "Let's hold off on that, eh? Until we know more."

Murmurs of assent circled the room. Ondego gave them a moment to do so, then raised his hands once more for silence.

"I know my people have had a long night, and they need to be away from here, quickly, so they can clean up and rest. I've no inkling what you dayshifters are in for. Suffice it to say this is a bitter business indeed, and we best all keep our eyes open wide. We hope it's just a onetime thing..."

He paused, sighed. Rem had never seen his prefect so tired, so bereft of words.

"Just be careful out there," he said finally. "My people are dismissed."

"And mine can hit the streets," Torala added. "Eyes open, fists clenched, backs to the wall."

The meeting broke. The soot-stained nightshifters all said their goodbyes and made for the doors. Rem looked to Torval, eager for the two of them to do the same. His partner stared back at him as though awaiting some wise words or eager questions.

"Ever seen such a thing?" Rem asked him quietly. "Arson? That anti-dwarven stuff?"

Torval shook his head slowly. "Never."

"Well, then," Rem said, "I guess we should do as we've been told and be on our way. I know I need some sleep, desperately."

Torval studied his black-streaked arms and filthy hands. "I'm thinking I might stop by the bathhouse on the way. I can't go home like this. It'd take ten baths in the tin tub to get me clean."

Rem nodded. "Fine idea, old stump. Count me in."

He clapped Torval on the shoulder and the two of them moved to make a straight path for the door and freedom. They'd gone only two steps when they heard their prefect's gravelly voice behind them.

"Torval! Rem! Rein those horses."

Rem froze, as did Torval beside him. They both turned. Ondego waited at the door of his office, looking right at them. He waved them in. "A word before you're on your way, boys."

"So close," Rem whispered as they approached the office.

"This had better be good," Torval grumbled, leading the way.

The office was crowded. Ondego and Prefect Torala both hovered behind the desk, but neither took the single chair there, as though they could not decide who deserved it more. Hirk's and Torala's tall, looming seconds haunted opposite corners on the far wall. Everyone was grim and silent. Rem was set on edge immediately. It felt like a tribunal, not an impromptu meeting in their commander's chamber.

"That fire was on our shift," Ondego said, "so that means we're responsible for investigating it."

Rem and Torval exchanged puzzled glances. Were they supposed to say something?

The lady prefect, Torala, chimed in. "Those scrawlings were religious in nature," she said, lined mouth frowning. She was a hard-faced, tautly muscled woman, probably just past fifty. Though she dressed like a man and wore her hair in a series of tight, utilitarian braids, her stone-hard gaze and regal bearing brought to Rem's mind images of ancient empresses and unconquerable barbarian queens. "Given the anti-dwarven graffito, and the riot in the Warrens yesterday morning that you reported on, Remeck, we're assuming the blaze was set deliberately."

Rem thought back to when he'd started his shift at sundown the night before, how he'd come into this very room and given Ondego a summary of what he'd witnessed in the dwarven quarter with Indilen. Now, just twelve hours later, it wasn't an isolated incident; it was indicative of a coming storm, a possible prelude to acts of terror directed at Torval's kinfolk in the Warrens.

"That doesn't make any sense," Torval broke in. "Your kind and my kind have lived side by side, with barely a hiccup, for almost two hundred years."

"True enough," Ondego said, "but that was a dwarven work site, and whoever marked up those stones and set that blaze clearly didn't care for them. And I don't think we can underestimate the importance of that dust-up yesterday morning."

Torval lowered his eyes. He seemed to take that news personally somehow—though Rem could not guess why. Rem, for own his part, suspected what they were about to hear. He decided he'd try to earn some points with a blurted guess.

"They replaced them, didn't they?" Rem asked. "The dwarves? The human stonemasons were fired and the dwarves hired in their place."

"Just so," Ondego said. "Their contract wasn't renewed and the temple clergy went with Torval's folk instead."

"There you are, then," Torval said. "The dwarves stole a

contract from those stonemasons, and the masons are in a bind over it. Cancel the contract and give the tall folk their jobs back. That should solve the issue."

"You know it's not that simple," Ondego said, and Rem thought he saw real worry and sadness in the prefect's haggard face. As though he, knowing Torval so well, and for so long, could not believe how obtuse and resistant the old stump was now being. Since when did Torval try to avoid a fight, or suggest a compromise in place of hard justice? Truth be told, Rem was a little shocked himself...but knowing that something had been eating at Torval for the past few weeks—something that Rem had only just gotten Torval to relent on the night before—well, that explained a great deal of his untoward behavior, didn't it?

"And why not?" Torval asked, clearly growing impatient. "Ten to one my countrymen undercut those poor sods. Offered twice the work for half the price. That's our advantage, you know. We don't tire the way humans do. We don't need all the little comforts and supports that humans need."

"If their contracts were negotiated fair and square," Torala broke in, "then we can't make anyone do anything. But we don't know what actually happened. The information before us now is just what we've been able to scare up in the last hour. One party out, the other in, the temple burns. There are all sorts of assumptions we *could* make, but we'd like to get some hard facts."

Torval barreled on, grumbling almost to himself, as if the rest of them weren't present. "They should've known that if they took coin out of human pockets and food out of human mouths, they'd cause trouble." His argument was a little too forceful, Rem thought. Torval then raised his eyes and spoke to Ondego. "I'd advise laying the law down on them."

"The law is *exactly* what we're talking about here!" Ondego suddenly shouted. Rem felt his body stiffen in answer to Ondego's raised voice, like a hare in a wood hearing the snarl of a predator. "Assuming there's been no legal malfeasance, those dwarves have a right *by law* to contract with anyone they choose and to work, without threat or coercion. *By law*, setting fires in my ward is a crime, last time I checked. And *by law*, since that fire was on our watch, it's *our* gods-damned job to get to the bottom of it. That's what I'm angling at here, to put not too fine a point on it."

"So where do we fit in?" Rem asked, trying to manage the mounting tensions in the room. The last thing he needed was a steely-eyed squaring off between Torval and the prefects.

"I'm tapping the two of you," Ondego said, all the fury suddenly fleeing from him. No matter how many times Rem saw that sudden change in Ondego's mood—furious to calm, or vice versa, in an instant—it never ceased to unnerve him. "Torala's only dwarven watchwardens are city born or from the far provinces, so we can't send them. No natural rapport with the ethnarch and his people. While Woldor out there is good in a fight, he's not a keen questioner. Too affable. Since both of you were present, saw the blaze and the evidence left in its aftermath, I want you to dig and get to the bottom of it."

"You're telling me that, just because I'm a dwarf, I've got to make nice with Eldgrim's court?" Torval asked.

"Is that a problem?" Ondego asked. His tone made it clear that it shouldn't be, even if it was.

"It well might be," Torval said. "I have history with the ethnarch and his court, sir, and none of it good."

Ondego studied Torval carefully for a moment. He seemed to honestly, fairly weigh those words before offering his own answer to them.

"Be that as it may," Ondego said, "I need you to do this, Torval. A hotheaded little runt you are, to be sure, but you're the only one I trust to speak with this lot—to really study them and tell me *what you think* of their responses. If that ruffles your feathers—fuck all. Care to argue further?"

Torval scowled but said nothing. After a long silence he finally shook his head.

Ondego continued, now addressing the two of them. "Work both angles. Find out how the dwarves got that contract, then talk to the stonemasons and see if they strike you as belligerent or vengeful sorts—at least, vengeful enough to burn a gods-damned temple down. Get copies of the contracts—the one the masons were released from and the present agreement between the dwarves and the Panoply. It could be those human stonemasons have got nothing to do with this, but as of this moment, given their motive and their violent demonstration, they're our prime suspects. I hate to ask it of you, but I'd like you to make your first sortie to the dwarven ethnarch right now, before either of you go home for the day. You can go straight home from there and question the stonemasons this evening—even start your shifts late, to get some extra rest. Nineteen bells, let's say—but I'll expect a full report when you arrive this evening."

Rem looked to Prefect Torala. Her level gaze said it all.

"Understood," Rem said, hoping that Torval would let him talk now and would keep his own mouth shut.

Ondego nodded. "I know it's a shit job and not fair to either of you, considering the night you've had. Here and now, though, that's the way it's got to be. We need facts—stone-hard facts—to get us started, and you're the only ones I trust to get them."

Rem nodded. Torval as well—though barely. For a long time no one said anything.

Ondego broke the persistent silence. "Fuck off, then. I'm tired and you've got work to do."

"Aye, sir," Rem said, eager to end the meeting and be on his way. He turned to go and clapped Torval on the shoulder. "Come on, partner," he said quietly.

Torval sighed, grumbled something under his breath, then turned and left the office. Rem followed dutifully behind him.

CHAPTER EIGHT

Rem let Torval lead the way—across the administrative chamber, through the main vestibule of the watchkeep, down the front steps, out into the cold, sunny morning. He waited until they were nearly all the way across Sygar's Square, the watchkeep far behind and the knotted streets of the ward ready to engulf them, before he finally spoke.

"Tell me, now," Rem said, trying to sound both forceful and casual at the same time. "What's been eating at you? Is it something to do with Tav?"

Torval shrugged diffidently but offered no elaboration. For what felt like a long time, he strode on in silence. They left the square for a shadowy side street that was even colder than the sunlit square. Rem pulled his greatcoat closer around him, shoving his hands in its deep outer pockets.

"Bad blood, that's all," Torval finally said.

"I don't follow," Rem said.

Torval shook his head. "Don't trouble yourself over it, lad. It's my burden to bear."

"It may be," Rem said. "But you're *my* burden to bear, and whatever *this* is, it's making you a damned heavy load. You've told me there's trouble, now tell me what it is."

Torval kept marching. "Tavarix is of an age to be apprenticed. I thought I could place him with a tradesman in the city, but...he wanted to learn his trade among his own kind."

Now they were getting somewhere. Rem knew that Torval had a rather combative history with his own folk—he'd challenged their ironclad caste system and been cast out and exiled for his pains, and probably still bore the psychological wounds of that ostracism.

"So," Rem added, "you've had a rough time with your people. Reason to hate them, even. You can't make amends somehow, for Tav's sake?"

"Oh, I did," Torval said bitterly. "I went to them. I beseeched them not to hold my sins against my boy. They heaped requirements upon me, demanded all sorts of assurances and vows... but they agreed to take him in the end."

Rem waited for some elaboration. None came. Still, he could see on Torval's face a terrible look of bitterness and gall. The muscles of his jaw seemed so taut he might grind his own teeth to dust.

"Well," Rem said. "Mission accomplished, then. Isn't that good?"

Torval suddenly stopped, right there in the middle of the street. "They made me kneel!" he spat. "Stripped my pride and my dignity from me! Right there in that damned court chamber of theirs! All because they knew I loved my boy and I'd refuse him nothing!"

Rem didn't really know if being made to kneel before one's nominal enemies had some special disgraceful connotation in dwarven culture, but he could clearly see the memory of it made Torval quake top to toe, his expression a strange mixture of rage and despair. Rem thought he saw the glint of tears in Torval's eyes, a nakedness to his gaze and aspect. It had to be the long night, their exhaustion. Otherwise, Rem imagined, there was no way in all the sundry hells Torval would consciously be so forthcoming with his deepest feelings—even to Rem.

"So they took him, then?" Rem asked. "They accepted Tav, and he's apprenticed to a dwarven tradesman now?"

"Aye," Torval said. "A stonemason."

Cack. That added a new wrinkle to things.

"That's why you were calling to him in the fire last night?" Rem asked. "That's why you were so panicked?"

Torval nodded. "I found a gang of workers on-site when I arrived, but Tav wasn't among them. When I saw that—that he wasn't with the others—I just lost my mind. I went in among the wreckage, sure I'd find him pinned somewhere."

"But you know he's safe now, Torval," Rem said, remembering the assurance his partner had received from that dwarven mason the night before.

"Aye," Torval said, nodding. He still sounded miserable.

"Look," Rem said, desperate to see his friend comforted, "what say we stop and see him? We're headed to the dwarven quarter now, aren't we? We'll just pop in at his dormitory and—"

"I can't do that," Torval said.

"Why not?" Rem asked.

"Because I'm an outcast!" Torval spat miserably. "That's why they made me work so hard for Tav's acceptance. And I promise you, every boy that Tav is housed with knows where he came from. Who his father is. If I go in there, casting about, I'll look like a fool, and I'll make him hate me even more than he already does."

"Than he already does?" Rem asked. "Torval, that's ridiculous."

"He chose *them*, didn't he?" the dwarf asked. "He chose

them, knowing all too well what it would cost *me*! If it had just been a matter of coin... gods, I would've worked day and night to buy him any mentor he chose. But to go to *them*... to insist that he live and work under the watching eye of Eldgrim and his court, who made me get on my knees and brand myself all but a criminal and heretic..."

Torval hung his head miserably. His shoulders shook as he choked on a sob. Rem wasn't sure how to handle this. Hugging Torval might embarrass the dwarf further. Acting as though it didn't matter would be patronizing. Just standing here left his partner exposed to the glances and gazes of every curious passerby.

At a loss for anything else to do, Rem took Torval gently by the shoulder and led him away from the center of the street. They found a stone horse trough, still filmed over with a thin sheet of ice from the night before, and sat on its wide rim. As Torval sat there, head hung, miserable, Rem cursed himself for not having had this conversation with the dwarf earlier. He'd noted signs of something strange in Torval for weeks— increasingly frequent reveries and asides on the subject of his self-imposed exile, a mood alternating between frustrated rage and weary resignation, a general sense of inwardness that was, for Torval, wholly out of character.

For his own part, Rem had always thought Torval's decision to leave his people and make his own way in the world had been a rather courageous one. After all, Rem had done the same. But he could just as easily understand Tav's impulses. The boy was getting older. Though most youngsters were, in essence, headstrong foals waiting to be saddle broken by the world, it was usually a sense of culture, kinship, and duty that helped them to refine their restless energies and make something of themselves. Even if they were rebellious sorts—and

Tav had never struck Rem as such—they needed traditions to push against, expectations to undermine. Without a culture to embrace or to shrug off, a young person was nothing: lost in a void, not sure what they were or how to relate to anything. Torval's sacrifice of both pride and stature in his son's eyes to fulfill the boy's desires—to give Tav something that Torval had relinquished—was a precious, loving gift. Rem saw that clearly. But all Torval could see was the cost—his crushed honor, separation from his son—and not the possible benefit.

"Wheedling shoat," Torval snarled, pressing his fists against his face. "Mewling, vile little pig."

For just a moment Rem thought Torval might be cursing his own son. But when the dwarf began to knock his own fists against his forehead, he realized that the grunted insults were directed at himself.

"Stop it," Rem said.

"Wengrol, give me strength," Torval muttered through clenched teeth. "Yangrol, take this soft iron and make it steel."

Rem had never heard Torval pray before. Hearing it now—the pain in his partner's voice, the loss and confusion—made him feel like a lost little boy, somehow. The way he felt the first time he'd realized that his father could be wicked and cruel—and was, thus, fallible, not the god-man his child's heart had always made him out to be.

"Torval," Rem said quietly, "there's no shame in what you did."

"Isn't there?" Torval asked.

"You put your son's desires before your own pride," Rem said. "For his sake—and for the sake of your family—you made peace with your enemies. That's not weakness, old stump, that's the very definition of strength. They may think they've broken you, but that's not true. You've *bent*, and you've *endured*.

The dwarf before me now is the same brave soul I've come to know and rely on since my time on the watch began. Don't try to tell me the head-breaker who's got my back is any less than the bravest, ballsiest lump of blood and bone I've ever known."

Torval drew a deep breath, clearly trying to calm himself. "Why do I feel, then, like what I gave away can never be regained? Like Tav might thank me for giving him what he wanted, but still be ashamed for being the son of an outcast? An outcast who came crawling back, begging forgiveness?"

"Only fools and despots never ask for forgiveness," Rem said. "Besides, in your heart, do you really think you were wrong? Ever?"

Torval looked to him. Puzzled.

"You did what you had to do to keep your family together, to give them a new life after the old one was taken from them. And now, to give Tavarix something precious—something *he* needs—you also did what you had to do. There is no dishonor in that. Hold your head high, old stump."

Torval wiped his face. Sniffed. He was calming now...but he wasn't done probing at the wound.

"I imagine all the ways it could go wrong," Torval said. "What if Tav decides that the way of our people is the only way—the *right* way—and that all the decisions I've made for our family are wrong? Or what if all our time living apart from our people, among the men and women of the west and strange elves and the blasted orcs that infest this city, have actually ruined him? What if Tav isn't dwarven *enough* any longer, and he ends up just like me? Cast out? Humiliated?"

"You're overthinking it," Rem said gently. "One of the priests who schooled me—a good man, one of the best I've ever known—told me once that our greatest hopes and deepest fears are seldom realized. Trust Tav to understand and discern on his own. Trust him to be strong when things are hard. And trust that your love for him, all these years, will have planted deeper roots than any fostering or instruction ever could."

"Even so," Torval said, "there's the ethnarch and his court. If they feel they've been wronged, and I cannot promise them vengeance—"

"You'd owe them that?" Rem asked.

"Not as a dwarf, as a watchwarden," Torval said. "Anyway, they're not going to want an investigation. They're going to want names. They'll cry for heads on pikes, and if we don't deliver, our heads may be added to the list."

"That's ridiculous," Rem said. "Surely they can't be so vindictive?"

"Dwarves never forgive," Torval said, "and they never forget."

Rem laid a hand on Torval's shoulder. "As you've demonstrated, some do. Maybe Eldgrim and company will surprise us."

Torval finally seemed fully in control of himself again. He shot to his feet, cocked his head to indicate that Rem should follow, then set off at a hard march. "Come on," he called over his shoulder. "That's enough pissing and moaning for one day."

Rem smiled as he hurried to catch up. It was nice to have the old Torval back, if only for a little while.

CHAPTER NINE

Rem felt strange when they passed into the dwarven quarter. Though he'd just been there yesterday, and had loved the brief hour or so that he and Indilen had spent exploring before the eruption of violence, the crowded streets, colorful awnings, looming pyramids, and diminutive people who lived and worked there had now all taken on a daunting, alien quality. The sense of joy and easy purpose that he'd noted the day before was gone. Every face wore a frown or a resigned grimace; all eyes were downcast, all movement aimless or automatic. Openness had yielded to wariness. Purposeful labor had become oppressive toil. The change in the air was unmistakable.

Torval led Rem deeper through the twisting streets, past open bakeshops, silent saloons, and artisans undertaking their daily business beneath a cloud of melancholy and apprehension. Rem tried to keep his eyes down, to avoid directly engaging with anyone. Suddenly he was unpleasantly aware of his own alienness in the current surroundings. Soon they moved past the area that the riot had swept through the day before, the streets still littered with the gathered-up detritus of the chaos: broken handcarts, shattered pottery and crockery, torn clothing and muddied tapestries, discarded bread and sweetmeats trampled into the mud. Just yesterday all those things had embodied the hopes and labors of the people who called this quarter home—investments, wages, handicrafts wrought with love for sale and barter. Now it was all junk, good for little more than a firepit.

The ruined wares and broken furniture weren't all that had suffered, either. Several of the colorful silks once stretched between the buildings had been torn from their moorings and now trailed into the churned mud, the flayed skins of once-colorful beasts. Windows were broken. Wooden support struts bent, dogleg, while the eaves and roofs they supported sagged. More than a few doors had been torn off their hinges or hung askew in mute testimony to just what sort of damage a furious mob could do. Among the wreckage the locals labored, clearing the entryways to their shops, gathering up their ruined offerings—wasted money and effort now—and making haphazard attempts to restore their homes and places of business to some modicum of structural fidelity. The wreckage, though isolated to just a few intersecting streets, was ugly and unnerving. Rem felt ashamed just passing through, as though he were somehow to blame.

Torval marched on, purposeful, as if he knew where he was going. Little by little, through the occasional gaps between silk awnings and looming pyramids, Rem noted rooftops and houses rising gently in the distance. That meant they were approaching the slopes of Suicide Hill and, presumably, the dwarven ethnarch's citadel. Finally the street opened onto a broad square—the divergence of several streets into an open space complete with one of the city's ubiquitous burbling public fountains. On the far side of that square, their destination waited.

The citadel hunkered in the shadow of the hill behind stout stone walls covered in ivy. Rem saw only a single entryway, a wide wrought iron gate flanked by high hewn-block towers on either side. A pair of dwarven guards in house livery—deep blue-gray and silver chased with copper accents—stood guard at the gate itself, each with a thick-handled halberd in his hand and a sword sheathed at his side.

"Let me do the talking," Torval said over his shoulder, then seemed to lean into his stride toward the gate and the sentries. Rem only gave a curt grunt in reply and kept pace. He was still trying to get a good look at the citadel.

As they drew nearer, Rem was afforded a better view into the compound through the thick iron bars of the closed gate. The grounds were dominated by two structures, each clearly born of the same dwarven architectural imagination but with peculiarities of design and form that denoted their separate, distinct purposes. The structure to the right looked, to Rem, like a castellated manor house, adorned with leaded windows and sporting fine landscaping in its dooryard, but fortified nonetheless—its walls stout, its roof hidden behind battlements and a low crenellated parapet. Its angles were sharp, its lines clean, its thick walls, buttresses, and geometric design suggesting strength, resilience, a robust harmony. Though laden with decorative accents—thorny dwarven runes, intricate multilayered knots, the graven images of squat warriors and thick-legged maidens opposing hoary giants and abominations from the ageless depths of dwarven cavern countries—the structure nonetheless struck Rem as gloomy and severe.

To the left, separated from the great house by a small wooded park crammed with shade trees and stone arches, stood the dwarven temple. The hulking edifice, slate gray and built of hewn blocks as large as a peasant's hovel, sported the same severe angularity, geometric imperiousness, and glowering strength of the great house, but on a far larger scale. Its squat, strong buttresses put Rem in mind of the seeking roots of some long-petrified tree, and the four rising towers of the structure completed that image. Something about the two buildings suggested kinship, as though the temple were the great house's grim and overbearing father.

As Torval approached the great iron gate, the dwarven guards stepped forward. Perfectly in unison, they dipped their halberds to create a barrier against his advance. Up close Rem could better see the details of their uniforms—the intricate, endless knots woven into their surcoats, the square scales of the mail shirts beneath, the beautifully embossed leather bracers and greaves they wore. Clearly the ethnarch spared no expense in the arming and outfitting of his house guard. The one on the left was clearly older, his intricately woven, well-oiled beard a streaky iron gray. Rem assumed the guard on the right, whose beard was shorter and of a rich brown, to be much younger.

"Stand fast there!" barked the older soldier, whom Rem named Gray Beard. "Name yourselves."

Torval studied the sentries. Rem stood silently beside him, trying to look hard faced and undaunted, but only feeling tired and out of his depth.

"Watchwardens of the Fifth," Torval barked back, "under official orders to treat with the ethnarch."

"Regarding what?" the younger guard—whom Rem dubbed Brownie—demanded.

"Regarding wardwatch business fit only for your master," Torval said. "Stand aside."

There was a pause. Gray Beard spoke again. "We'll need more than that."

Torval paused a long while, as if considering his answer

carefully, and that pause made a deep impression on Rem. In six months of working at Torval's side, he could not remember the dwarf ever choosing his words carefully.

"*Adet isyeine tsaffliende,*" Torval said curtly. "*Stammiende dimwa. Naga.*"

Gray Beard and his young partner seemed to chew on those words, whatever they were. For a long time they said nothing.

Rem let his hand hover close to the pommel of his sword, taking special care not to reach for it. He had no idea what Torval was saying to his countrymen, but the hard consonants, broad vowels, and forceful delivery gave no impression of friendliness. The sentries, implacable, stood fast and studied the two of them. Rem saw that there was something like disgust and disapproval on their faces—what little of those faces he could see beneath the crown and cheek guards of their molded helms. Whether it was Rem's presence or Torval's words that troubled them—or both—he could not say.

Then, finally, both slid sideways and drew their halberds up vertically to allow passage.

"*Dza digyornen,*" Gray Beard said to his young partner, who withdrew to the gate and opened it. The intricate lattice of iron filigreed with creeper vine swung on its half-rusted hinges, squealing ominously as the interior of the compound beckoned them. Torval led the way.

As they passed through the gate, Rem heard whispered words between Torval and the guards. Most of those words passed in a flurry of wide vowels and hard consonants, but the last word— spoken with bitter emphasis by Gray Beard—lodged in Rem's awareness like a stone in his boot.

"*Sweppsa.*"

Torval froze for a moment when that word was spoken, raised his head the slightest bit, but did not look back at the guard. From where Rem stood he could not see Torval's face. But he could see Gray Beard's, and he studied it now. The old dwarven guard's frown was bitter and malicious, his gaze wary. Clearly, whatever *sweppsa* meant, it wasn't friendly.

Gods of sea and sky...were they about to get into a fight, right here on the ethnarch's doorstep?

To Rem's great relief, the answer was no. After his moment's hesitation, Torval carried on, clearing the gate and making a path across the gravel-strewn courtyard beyond toward Eldgrim's manse. Rem followed, silent and relieved. Clearly the sentry had thrown an insult at his friend...and Torval, miracle of miracles, had successfully fought the urge to answer that insult with violence.

Who said dwarves couldn't change?

The span between the gate and the manse's main entrance was roughly two hundred yards, traversed by a meandering flagstone path through a cramped garden filled with an array of glowering stone dwarven figures, all carved with the square strength and strident stylization that Rem recognized as unique to dwarven crafts. He had been in sculpture gardens before, but he was intrigued to note that, in this dwarven version, there was really very little garden—just a few stunted well-trimmed evergreen shrubs and some leafless trees spaced as punctuation of a sort between the sculptures, with beds of hibernating wildflowers lying dead nearby. Rem found it rather disconcerting that the sculptures, while possessing the typical features of the dwarven race—the squat build, large feet, thick hands, and elaborate beards—were also larger-than-life, standing nearly eight feet tall, blank stone eyes glaring out of implacable, frowning stone faces. The figures towered over him, filling him with a distinct sense of unease. How much more intimidating must these looming, frowning figures be to Torval's kinsmen, who were so much shorter than they?

Everywhere watched, Rem thought idly. *Everywhere judged. What a dreadful place . . .*

A dwarf in house livery waited at the door. He looked young, his beard barely an inch from his chin, too short to braid. He opened the door for Rem and Torval silently. Sharing the briefest glance, the partners entered the house of the ethnarch.

Another house servant waited within, right in the center of the grand hall just beyond the entry. This dwarf took their names, asked the nature of their business, then disappeared through a door off to their left. Torval stood rooted, eyes darting about the great room, shoulders square, as if ready for a fight. Rem didn't want to wander far, so he drifted a few idle steps from his partner, just enough to get a better look at the size and scale of the grand foyer they now stood in.

It was strange for Rem to stand in such a space—high ceilinged and clearly expansive, but, based on the proportions of his own body, still wrong somehow. Too small to his senses, if not immediately to his eye. The floor was made up of slabs of black and gray marble. A great gaping fireplace stood off to their left. The pillars and mantel of the fireplace were carved in a dynamic, breathtaking frieze of what Rem assumed to be dwarven history: stout heroes, shapely maidens, humpbacked goblins, and many-headed trolls, all interwoven with those ubiquitous endless dwarven knots. A few stately chairs were spaced close around the fire, while a few more—along with a lounge or two—adorned the room's outer walls.

"Now listen," Torval said, voice low. "We're about to step into the ethnarch's court. We'll stand before Eldgrim himself, his wife, Leffi, and all the officials appointed by the home council to oversee operations here: the trade minister, the captain of the house guard, and the four high priests."

"Four?" Rem asked, moving back toward his partner.

"Our clerics have specific roles and responsibilities, and—"

"—And they don't step outside of them," Rem finished. "Got it."

"Only speak if spoken to," Torval said slowly. "Dwarven administrators live for ceremony. They want everything to run smoothly, and for the conversation to follow a prescribed sort of script. If they do happen to address you directly, answer in the simplest possible terms, then keep quiet again. Am I understood?"

"I should think," Rem said, "that I'd know a thing or two about courtly proceedings." Rem suddenly realized what his statement was implying—the truth of his noble blood and upbringing—and quickly decided to amend it. "Being a groom's son. Raised in a noble house and all."

Torval barely seemed to notice. "Not this court, you don't. Just do as I say."

Rem nodded. Torval returned to his silent brooding. Rem finished his perusal of the room.

Directly ahead of them, a line of columns and arches marked a sort of arcade beneath the second-floor balcony, which sheltered an open doorway that probably led deeper into the manse. To their right a long, grand staircase hugged the wall, climbing up to that balcony above the arcade. Save its dwarven accents and its peculiarities of proportion, Rem could have assumed this to be the home of any well-to-do baron from the north.

The hinges on the door to their left squealed. The herald marched through, waved them on, then led them into the chamber beyond. Rem had to duck to get through the door, but the room itself—a fairly typical throne room and audience chamber—was large and spacious. Despite the high ceilings and great length of the room, he still felt like a clumsy giant. How must the everyday, oversized world feel for Torval, then—for any dwarf who lived and moved in a world built for humans? A world full of strange giants and oversize construction that constantly reminded them of their own smallness? Their own *otherness*?

Rem made a quick survey of their surroundings. To their left was an offset space of sorts, dominated by a great oaken table littered with the remnants of a working breakfast—boiled eggs of various sizes and varieties; fresh brown bread, torn and half-eaten; some wedges of strong, ripe cheese; and an assortment of fruit preserves and sausages—all interspersed with untied scrolls, quills, ink pots, and scraps of parchment. Two or three wine goblets and cups holding varying amounts of wine or beer suggested that the meal recently under way had been interrupted by the watchwardens' arrival.

The lord and lady of the house, along with their privy advisers, waited at the far end of the chamber, off to Rem's right, past a broad, open expanse flanked by rows of columns and arches along the outer walls. The ethnarch and his wife were seated on finely wrought thrones of iron metalwork, those thrones standing side by side on a raised stone dais. As he and Torval moved into the center of the great room and approached, Rem tried to study the ethnarch and his court without appearing to stare.

Eldgrim cut a rather impressive figure—of typical dwarven size and shape, but somehow exuding largeness simply by virtue of his rich, heaped-up raiment, all of soft velvet, fine furs, and silks, his long, tightly wound braids, and his elaborately plaited beard. Rem had to admit, that beard was impressive—

long, lustrous, well oiled, and finely knit in a complex array of tight silver-gray braids—the sort of facial weave-work that Rem had always taken for granted as inherently dwarven—before he'd met Torval, anyway. It was Torval who'd explained to Rem that, despite folklore and appearances to the contrary, not all dwarves wore beards, and not all beardless dwarves were criminals or outcasts—like Torval himself. But Rem was still amazed when he saw the time and effort that most bearded dwarves expended upon their facial hair. According to Torval, it was not mere vanity, but a sort of personal narrative. Dwarven beards literally told a story and announced their owner, after a fashion, if one knew the signs and how to read them, as surely as the colors and sigils emblazoned on a lord's battle banners. But even knowing that, Rem still found himself immediately awed by what a beautiful work of art the ethnarch's copious whiskers formed. Were they in a friendlier space, on less purposeful business, Rem might have quietly asked Torval to give him a rundown of just what Eldgrim's beard might "say" to one initiated in the arena of dwarven hair design.

Beside the ethnarch was his bride, Leffi, a stout woman with lively hazel eyes, rosy cheeks strewn with a few light freckles, and a soft mouth that seemed at rest in a slight, welcoming smile. Her hair was truly a wonder to behold—piled atop her head in a dizzying, architecturally breathtaking arrangement that defied gravity before spilling down around her in a storm of tight curls and thick, shining braids. She had no whiskers that Rem could see, and he wondered if that meant that she simply had not grown any, or that she went out of her way to shave them.

There were six others crowded onto a lower tier of the dais off to Eldgrim's left. One of them, a youngish fellow with an aquiline nose and a short blond beard, spent most of his time with eyes downcast on parchment covering a lap desk before him, scratching away with quill and ink—a secretary, no doubt. Beside him was a much older dwarf—face lined, cheeks full and streaked with beer blossoms, nose bulbous with rosacea. Rem had no idea what function he might perform, but his simple, elegant dress suggested some sort of secular minister or adviser.

The other four, however, were clearly priests, for each wore an identical dark-gray robe of heavy cloth and sported some sort of ceremonial headdress. Their priestly duties and offices seemed to be denoted by those headdresses, as well as by the stoles or mantles they wore draped around their shoulders and the embellished trim their otherwise-matching vestments sported. One old, grizzled fellow's robe was edged in a geometric pattern of gold, green, and crimson. Another elder's robes boasted interlaced loops and fringes. The mantle of the one female among them was covered by a pattern of silver, copper, and bright-blue thread that looked alternately like leaves and dragon scales. The priest seated farthest from Eldgrim—much younger than his fellows, looking between thirty and forty in human terms—wore a simple stole of light gray with dwarven runes arranged thereon.

They reached the foot of the dais then, and stopped three or four long strides from it. Torval, to Rem's great surprise, suddenly gave a deep, slow bow from his waist—a deferential gesture that Rem had never seen his partner give before to anyone, man, dwarf, or otherwise. Rem quickly followed suit.

"Good tidings, Lord Eldgrim," Torval said, spitting the words out as if they tasted bitter in his mouth.

Eldgrim studied Torval slowly, carefully. Rem knew that practiced affectation well—that sneering, arrogant pause and perusal. His father had been a champion employer of it, as had a number of the lords he'd known during the course of his youth. Almost without fail, Rem had ended up hating men who looked on others with that particular brand of disdain and dismissal.

"Good tidings, Watchwarden," the ethnarch finally said, though there seemed to be very little that was good in those tidings, offered as they were with a derisive smirk. "Why do you call upon us at such an early hour…and in such a disheveled and disrespectful state?"

Rem and Torval shared the briefest of sideward glances.

"Sincerest apologies," Torval said. "Our prefect sent us, with all haste, to treat with you regarding the upsets in the quarter and last night's fire. Humbly we beg you to hear our petitions and support our endeavors."

Aemon's balls, Rem almost longed to be before Gorn Bonebreaker, the orcish ethnarch. Would all their commerce with this bearded rooster really have to proceed with such officiousness?

"And why were *you* chosen?" Eldgrim asked suddenly. "Why, Torval, Son of Jarvi, should you be the messenger for your prefect? Do you hold some position of special privilege? Some rank of import?"

Torval's lips pressed together as though he fought the urge to answer with a barb. "I am, in my chosen line of work, nothing special," Torval finally said. "Perhaps it is the fact of my kinship, as a member of the *Hallirwelk*, that led my prefect to choose me to treat with you. I can only guess he assumes we share something, and can speak with candor and forthrightness."

Eldgrim seemed to chew on that statement, his lined, leonine face moving through a series of strange, unreadable expressions as he shifted his bulk on his throne. A quick study of all those assembled—from Leffi to the lowly secretary sitting at the farthest corner of the dais, scribbling in a court log—showed that even they—so familiar with Eldgrim's quirks and affectations—seemed impatient with his long pauses and pregnant silences.

"State your business, then," Eldgrim finally said.

Torval nodded curtly. "The violence in the streets yesterday. The fire last night. Have you any ideas about how either began?"

"Out-of-work agitators," the ruddy-faced adviser on the dais said. "They envy us. They envy our industry and our wealth, and they came here to humiliate us."

"Minister Broon, you were not addressed!" the ethnarch snapped.

Rem's eyes slid sideward. His partner's eyes smiled, only the slightest bit. "In truth, good ethnarch, my question was for any and all present."

Eldgrim turned a baleful gaze on Torval. "If you speak, Watchwarden, you speak to *me*."

"Very well, then," Torval countered. "Speak, Lord Eldgrim. I await your reply to my inquiry."

Eldgrim glared at Torval for a long moment. He seemed to be carefully weighing a response, yet unable to find one that would vindicate him. Finally he sighed and reclined on his throne. "I shall let my court offer their own responses," Eldgrim said. "Weigh them as you will."

Without thinking, Rem happened to lock eyes with Leffi, the ethnarch's wife, at the very moment that Eldgrim replied. Unconsciously, Rem felt his own face betray his incredulity.

A moment later, when he realized the terrible mistake he'd made, he was surprised by the Lady Leffi's silent response: a single raised eyebrow, a quick glance at her husband, and a subtle, devilish curling at the corner of her lip.

How do you think I feel? that look seemed to say. *I have to live with him.*

It took every ounce of Rem's strength to keep from laughing. He counted himself lucky. Who knew what the ethnarch might have done if he'd caught that furtive glance between a human watchwarden and his wife? A look shared that testified to Eldgrim's own haughty ridiculousness?

"I was not present," one of the priests on the dais now said. "But I've heard much talk in the last day and night from our people." As Rem watched, the dwarf leaned forward in his seat, addressing all present. He was the last in the line of four, the young one. His furtive eyes and halting speech suggested that, priestly office or no, he was not at ease among his peers.

"Our people say it started as a speech, of sorts. The men said they were angry because our folk had stolen their work and their wages. When no one listened, or they told them to be quiet or go home, they carried on, working themselves into a fervor."

"The bitter will always talk, Bjalki," said the oldest priest, face a craggy mask of crow's feet and liver spots, beard the color of snow fox fur. "They spew their bile in hopes of planting it, like seeds, so that the world may be overgrown with their enmity."

Broon—the rosy-faced fellow who'd spoken at the outset—chimed in again from his seat on the far side of the royal couple. "They want our gold and our homes, it's that simple!" he said. "They want us out of their city and out of their lives! We have ever been unwanted here! Why should it change now?"

"But clearly," the junior priest, Bjalki, countered, "they have grievances. They tried to articulate them. Even though the violence they incited was unjustified, perhaps some peace could be made—"

"What peace?" a third priest broke in. His beard was rust red, his voice high and piping. "What peace can there be where there is no justice? No honor?"

"Are we impugning the honor of Yenaran justice now?" Leffi said, clearly trying to remind her countrymen that there were watchwardens—outsiders—among them, and that their careless words could have consequences.

"Silence!" Eldgrim suddenly roared, and his council obeyed. They all fell back in their seats and closed their mouths.

Rem threw a worried glance at his partner. Torval's frowning response gave him no confidence.

"It is clear," the ethnarch said, not without venom, "that my council is blind. They have *seen* nothing, *know* nothing. Would they were struck dumb as well, so I would not have to hear their braying."

"And that," the last, long-silent member of the clerical quartet broke in, "is why we are in this predicament." It was the priestess, the one whose mantle reminded Rem of dragon scales. Now that she had spoken, something curious happened.

The others—even Eldgrim—all leaned forward the slightest bit. They listened. This dwarf woman's words carried some weight among them.

She continued. "Auspice Bjalki reports, correctly, that our people have spoken to us since the violence yesterday. They have reported what they saw, what they heard, what they suffered. Elder Hrothwar, our chief sage"—she suggested the old priest with the snow-white beard—"points out that these men were more than likely driven by some bitterness—some wrong they sought redress for. Trade Minister Broon knows well what drives the hearts of men and dwarves—gold—and that it was the gain for one and the loss for the other that may have sown the seeds of this discord. And, sad as I am to agree"—she gestured toward the priest with the red beard and the voice like a flute—"Arbiter Haefred speaks to you, good watchwardens, and gives voice to our greatest fear: that whatever the cause of all this unrest, whoever is wrong, in the end, Yenaran justice cannot be trusted to take our side."

She let her words sink in before continuing. Rem half expected someone to interrupt, but they all remained silent.

"You're all speaking, but none of you are listening," the dwarven priestess said. "Each of you has a piece of it, but none of you know how to put it together. You can only wind the springs and thread the gears if you first *listen* to one another, then seek common ground from which to proceed."

"Do you hear her?" Eldgrim asked, looking right at Rem and Torval. "The Docent Therba speaks to you. I suggest you listen!"

"I speak to *all* of you," Docent Therba said gently. "For *all* of you. Everyone would do well to listen, for that's what we've all failed to do hitherto."

The influence the priestess had among the group was unmistakable. Even Eldgrim, whose downcast eyes and deep frown suggested a great distaste for being corrected by the old woman, could not seem to openly find it in him to dismiss or countermand her.

"Well," Torval said, trying to break the tension in the room by shattering the silence, "that clears things right up."

"I wonder," Eldgrim began, and his bushy gray brows came together over the bridge of his beakish nose, his slate-dark, flint-sharp eyes narrowing suspiciously. "Son of Jarvi, why should your own kind be so clearly wronged, and yet you would make sport of them?"

Torval stared down the scowling ethnarch. "I make no sport, milord."

Eldgrim shot to his feet. "You lie!" he shouted, and his voice filled the hall like the thunder of a falling boulder. "You know well who set that fire, you cur! If you do not, you're even more foolish than I first took you to be."

Torval stiffened beside Rem. Rem took a step closer to his partner. Pity it should come to this, so early and after such a long night.

Leffi rose and moved to Eldgrim's side. "Good watchwardens," she said, "my lord means no offense—"

"I mean what I say!" Eldgrim snapped. The fury in his voice made Leffi retreat from him. She did not look frightened, precisely—more like a kennel keeper giving a slavering hound a wide berth. Eldgrim barreled on. "We are the ones wronged, and yet we are also the first suspected of wrongdoing. And when we try to answer your ridiculous questions, you mock us."

"I suspect you of nothing," Torval said, and Rem tried to control the expression that he knew was now forming on his face: slack-jawed amazement mixed with stunned worry. Simply by using *I* instead of *we*, Torval had just single-handedly made this bizarre little standoff a personal matter, not simply part of an official inquiry. "I was sent by my prefect," Torval continued, "to ask *all of you* if you had any pertinent facts regarding who might have set that fire, or who might want to harm your subjects—*your people*."

"*Our* people," Eldgrim said slowly, "are *your* people, Son of Jarvi."

Torval took a single step forward. Rem laid a hand on his shoulder.

"Business, Torval. Stick to business."

Rem felt the restless energy—the anger, the anxiety, the bottled rage—pulsing beneath Torval's muscular frame. The dwarf drew a deep breath, a clear effort to calm himself. When he spoke again, the chained fury was still evident in his voice. "We are but humble servants of the law, milord . . . We may suspect things, but at this early stage we *know* nothing. We came here for your assistance, and to pledge our own—"

"Your assistance," Eldgrim sneered, as though it were the deepest insult.

"Aye," Torval countered, not backing down. *"Our assistance.* Now I ask again: Have you any enemies?"

Eldgrim snorted derisively. "Who could it be?" he said, now slowly descending the dais. "Who would be so hateful, so spiteful, so envious of our abilities and position that they might slight their own gods in order to humble us?"

As the ethnarch approached, Rem had a terrible premonition of their audience with Eldgrim devolving into open violence.

"That's enough, Husband," Leffi said. "There is no need for this."

"Silence, woman!" he shouted back. "I rule here!"

"Milord," the priestess Therba said, "I would urge you to calm yourself."

Eldgrim did not. He kept advancing toward where Torval and Rem stood.

"Who could it be?" Eldgrim continued. "Who suffered when we gained advantage in contract negotiations? Who brought a riot to our very doorsteps not two days ago? Who calls us unwanted aliens, half men—*pickmonkeys, tonkers*—when we pass in the streets?"

"I'm sure I would not know," Torval said slowly. "Perhaps you could enlighten us all, milord, and be done with all your aspersions—"

"You are a shameful creature," the ethnarch muttered. It was said low, under his breath, but Rem heard it clearly.

"What Lord Eldgrim suggests," Leffi suddenly broke in, clearly trying to ameliorate her husband's rage with diplomacy, "is that the most likely perpetrators are those who might benefit from our calamity. Or, at the very least, assuage their own frustrations by it."

Torval did not acknowledge her statement. Nor did Eldgrim. The two dwarves—watchwarden and ethnarch—stood just three strides from one another, each determined to stare the other down.

Rem could stand the silence no longer. "That is one theory, milady," he interjected hastily. "We were informed of the Panoply building contract and of the, uh, bad blood between your own stoneworkers and the human guild that preceded them."

Eldgrim swiveled his head and its mane of iron-gray hair toward Rem. "You mean those of *your* kind?" he asked, and just for a moment, Rem thought he saw his own imperious father standing before him.

In an effort to draw some heat from Torval, Rem played the fool. "Not my kind," Rem said. "I've never worked stone a day in my life."

"He meant *your kind*," Torval said, not even looking at Rem. "Humans."

The ethnarch snorted derisively. "The prefect mocks our misery by sending two of his densest louts—"

Rem shrugged. "We beg your forgiveness, milord—"

"Shut your mouth, lad," Torval snapped. "Don't waste any more words on this preening badger."

Eldgrim frowned upon hearing that. "Say that again, *sweppsa.*"

Rem looked to the Lady Leffi. It seemed that everyone else in the chamber did the same. As if beseeching her, silently, to put an end to the contest that threatened to unfold. After a long, awkward silence, she managed to speak.

"Perhaps some wine?" she offered. "Or beer? We're well stocked with both, good watchwardens. And by your looks, you're both horribly parched."

"They'll not enjoy a single drop from my bottles or barrels," the ethnarch said, turning and stomping away.

"Wouldn't dream of it," Torval answered.

Rem shook his head deferentially. "We could not so abuse your hospitality, milady. Perhaps we came too early, after all—"

"Or too late," Eldgrim said, dropping onto his throne again.

"Let me be sure I have this in order," Torval said finally. "In answer to our inquiry, you all agree that speaking with that Stonemason's Guild would be pertinent?"

Leffi leaned forward, eager to be the voice of reason. "We would all pray it not prove true, of course, but at this stage, it seems a most likely explanation."

"We are not welcome here," Eldgrim said, pouting almost to himself. "We will *never* be welcome here."

Torval looked to the ethnarch. Rem waited for his partner to say something, to provoke the angry dwarf...but Torval remained silent.

Despite Torval's silence, Eldgrim raised his eyes to meet Torval's own. The last words between them were his.

"*None of us* will ever be welcome here," he said, staring at Torval.

Torval sighed. He drew his gaze from the ethnarch and addressed all present. "You can find us at the Fifth Ward watch-keep. If you should have any more thoughts or questions, send them there. Good day to you all."

For once Rem did not wait for Torval to lead the way. Upon

the last word of Torval's parting message, Rem gave a curt bow, turned, and headed straight for the door. He heard his partner's heavy footfalls on the flagstones behind him.

The ethnarch decided, at that moment, to fire a parting shot.

"Tell your prefect," he shouted, "that I will protect my people, first and foremost. If the city's watchwardens cannot keep them from harm, the Swords of Eld will!"

Rem did not look back. He could not see if Torval had turned to look back. He knew only that he wanted to be through that door, just a few paces away, and out of this room.

They did not speak again until they were outside, well away from the ethnarch's manse, far across the street by the great fountain that stood in the center of the adjacent square. All of the dwarven quarter bustled around them now, and little by little, the feelings of distrust, suspicion, and overt disdain that Rem had known in that house began to melt away.

Torval sat on the fountain's stone lip. The masonry that ringed the big fountain was shiny with a pebbled skin of water droplets, but the wet surface seemed to make no difference to Torval, who just sat, sighed, and clasped his thick-fingered hands in a loose fist between his legs.

"Well," Rem ventured, "I suppose that could have gone far worse."

"Hang his pride," Torval said, then spat into the mud. "We got what we needed."

"Did we?" Rem asked. "Who are these Swords of Eld the ethnarch spoke of?"

Torval made a gesture toward the front gate of the citadel and the two guards who stood there.

"They are," he said. "The house guard. A full company, trained hard and armed to the teeth."

Rem felt a chill move through him. "So...Eldgrim just

threatened to put his house guard on the street, in the dwarven quarter, as armed police?"

Torval stared grimly at Rem and nodded.

Rem whistled. "Aemon's bones... Sounds like a recipe for trouble."

"And no mistake," Torval agreed. "Eldgrim and his court may just be suspicious, and those suspicions wholly unfounded, but their surety that it was the Stonemasons' Guild is telling. Clearly they regard them as enemies."

"Seems too neat, though," Rem said. He sat on the lip of the fountain beside Torval, wet trousers be damned. "If the stonemasons are, in fact, so dead set against these dwarves stealing their building contracts, wouldn't something so blatant and dangerous make targets of them? It seems to me they'd be smarter than that—less direct." He yawned. All of a sudden, the night's strain was catching up to him. He felt drowsy and breathless, as though he could curl up right there and go to sleep.

Torval shrugged, still staring across the square at the citadel. "Who's to say? I know this job sometimes forces us to think like thieves, to peer round corners in our minds and chisel tiny cracks in the stone face of logic. But sometimes, the explanation for a crime really is the simplest one imaginable, undertaken in the boldest and most direct terms."

"So you think the stonemasons fired the temple?" Rem asked.

Torval shot him an impatient look. "I didn't say that. Just that it was possible. Maybe even likely."

At that moment a great commotion rose above the gentle murmur of nondescript streetsong. It was a band of dwarven workers emerging from a nearby stone house with a high-peaked roof with slate shingles, one of several such, huddled together just outside the citadel walls. Rem studied them as they trudged across the square toward where he and Torval sat, a loose column, almost every one of them sporting a leather apron laden with tools round his middle, stout hammers cocked on their broad shoulders. No doubt they were off to the now-ruined temple site to begin the labor of cleaning up and rebuilding.

"What did it mean?" Rem asked idly. "That name the guards called you? *Sweppsa?*"

Torval didn't look up, content to stare at the ground beneath his dangling feet. "There's no real word for it in your tongue. It's sort of like a burden that one can't be rid of. A mongrel dog that keeps licking at your bootheels—but bearing some close, undeniable association. A notorious parent. A reprobate child. Shit on your shoe, I suppose."

Rem was horrified. He stared at his partner, trying to discern if that horrible appellation hurt him at all. Torval, eyes down, remained unreadable. Finally Rem sighed and shook off his desire to somehow fix the situation, since he knew that he could not.

"Should we go see the others now?" he asked. "Our human suspects?"

Torval slid off the lip of the fountain and landed on his feet. "To the sundry hells with that," he growled. "I'm wrought like iron. It's time we both went home."

Rem noted that Torval was suddenly agitated—as though he could not be away from where they sat quickly enough.

"Let's plan to meet them before we start our shifts this evening," he said, already walking away. "How's the sound of eighteen bells strike you?"

Rem rose and nodded. Gods, but his body was stiff and achy! "Eight and ten will do. I like the way you think."

Torval nodded and quickly set off across the square, away

from the fountain and the passing column of dwarven artisans. Rem lingered for a moment, watching the marching line of young dwarven apprentices as they filed by, and a familiar face in the approaching line caught his eye.

It was Tavarix. He marched among other young apprentices about his age, a few even younger. When the young dwarf saw Rem staring at him, he smiled, a wholly delighted, unbidden gesture. The smile was followed by a hand raised in greeting.

Rem waved back. That's when he saw realization settle on Tavarix. If Rem was here, that meant his father must be, too. As the boy marched on in his line, inching ever closer, he began to study the square, seeking his father. When he could not find him, he spoke hastily to one of the boys beside him, then broke from the line and hurried to where Rem stood.

"Is my father here?" he asked.

Rem suggested the far side of the square. "Took off when your column advanced. It's good to see you safe, Tav."

Tav nodded. "Thank you, Rem. It's good to be safe. We'd already been brought back to the guildhall when the fire started. The proctors wouldn't let us out to help fight it."

"Your father will be glad to hear it," Rem said. "He nearly killed himself looking for you in the flames last night."

Tav's face fell, his normally rosy cheeks suddenly paling. "Is he all right?"

"Hale and hearty," Rem said. "Just worried."

A long silence fell between them. Tav looked as if he wanted to speak, but was too ashamed to. Rem tried to work out just what he could say without overstepping his bounds as a friend of the family. One of the older dwarves marching past suddenly barked at the boy.

"Back in line, youngster!" he said. "No time for chitchat!"

"I have to go," Tav said.

"Talk to him," Rem said hastily. "At the first opportunity. Take it from one who knows, when a rift opens between a father and son, you have to work to shore it up. Left alone, it only gets wider."

Tav nodded, seeming to understand, but just as sad for the depth of that understanding. Without another word the boy turned and broke into a run to catch up with the line. Once he'd resumed his place in it, Rem turned toward the square at his back. He searched, hoping to find Torval waiting for him.

There. Standing on the far side of the square, skulking at a corner, barely discernible at this distance. Torval looked as if he were trying to hide from someone, but he was looking back, eyes locked right on Rem.

Rem almost started across the square to meet his partner, but thought better of it. Torval had watched. Torval had seen. He knew Tav was safe, and he could go home secure in that knowledge. Maybe all he needed now was solitude and rest.

So, to release him, Rem simply raised a hand in farewell. A moment later Torval offered the same gesture, then disappeared around the corner.

With a sigh Rem set off. He could already imagine how good it would feel when he reached the public bathhouse and washed the grime from his flesh, how welcoming his bed would be when he knew that he could fall into it clean.

When a rift opens between a father and son, you have to work to shore it up. Left alone, it only gets wider.

Wider than Great Lake, Rem thought solemnly as he walked. *Wider than Hatarau Bay. Wider, even, than the four hundred miles separating Lycos Vale and Yenara . . .*

CHAPTER TEN

Rem was dreaming of fire and crumbling stone when he felt warm, gentle hands on his shoulders. He was shaken, firmly and insistently. Something brushed his ears and cheeks: a pair of soft lips. Slowly the crust of sleep began to crack and slough off him. The flames roiling in his mind's eye dissipated, like smoke before a blast of wind.

"Wakey wakey," a lovely voice purred in his ear.

Rem opened one eye. Indilen knelt beside his bed, hands folded beneath her chin. He thought lazily in that moment that there was nothing better in his life than awakening to that smiling face, those deep-brown eyes. She smiled at him, then reached out a single finger to idly stroke his bare forearm.

"There's my sleepy lad," she said, and leaned in to lay another kiss on his forehead.

"Have you been here all day?" Rem asked. His voice sounded like a hinge in need of oiling.

"I have, in fact," Indilen said, drawing up a little step stool and sitting on it. "All day, when I could have been scouring the city for vice or earning my keep, I've just been sitting here by this bed, watching you slumber, ruminating on your quiet vulnerability."

Rem smiled. No, then. It had probably been a silly question, now that he thought about it. "So you've crept in just now?"

"I thought I'd come to see you before your shift. Your

landlady said you'd left word to be awakened at the sixteenth bell. I said I'd be happy to oblige."

Rem threw off his blankets and forced himself to sit up. His head instantly swam, but he embraced the momentary dis-orientation and gave his face and scalp a vigorous rubbing in an effort to banish the sluggishness of sleep. Though he could already see that the sun was falling outside and knew that he'd slept the day away, he still felt as if his head had barely hit the pillow. Out in the streets, he heard peddlers trying to sell their dregs before slumping homeward, handcarts being broken down and prepared for travel and storage, bootheels marching in mud after a long, laborious day.

Indilen rose and moved to a small table on the wall opposite his bed. A pitcher of fresh water and a pair of cups waited there. She poured him a cup and handed it over. Rem gulped the cool, clear water down thirstily, then held out his cup for an immediate refill.

"Long night?" Indilen asked, and nodded toward a pile in the corner: Rem's soot-covered clothes from the night before.

"Horrid," he said between sips. "There was a fire—"

"Oh, I know," Indilen cut in. "I heard the news on my way to the university this morning. And once I'd heard it, I ran all the way here to make sure you'd made it home safely. Wouldn't leave your landlady alone until she let me peek in and see you sleeping."

"You could've woken me," Rem said.

"No," Indilen said with a curt shake of her head. "Clearly you'd had a long night and deserved the rest. I just needed to make sure you were safe, that's all."

Rem smiled. "Sorry to frighten you—but thank you for let-ting me sleep. After our shift, we had to stop in the dwarven quarter—"

Indilen poured herself some water now. "You had so much fun yesterday you just had to return?"

"Official business," Rem said.

"Related?" Indilen asked, now thoroughly engaged. Sometimes Rem thought Indilen found his job more fascinating than he himself did. "Some link between the riot and the fire?"

"Ondego sent Torval and me to treat with the ethnarch. Didn't go so well. There's bad blood between them. Torval and the ethnarch, that is." He rose from the bed on stiff legs and moved toward his second set of clothes, draped over a chair near the far wall. At present he wore only a simple sleeping tunic. Without hesitation or reservation, he threw off the tunic and began dressing as he spoke. He explained it all to Indilen in the simplest, least exciting terms: the suspicions of the prefects, Torval's unease, the less than warm welcome they'd received in the court of the dwarven ethnarch.

Indilen interrupted his tale. "Slowly," she said, as Rem drew on his breeks and began to lace them up. "I like a show, you know."

Rem threw her a villainous glance over his shoulder. "Temptress. You're lucky I've got places I need to be."

"I wouldn't call that lucky," Indilen said, and then her arms were around him. She had him from behind, her soft hair against his bare back, her arms wrapped around his lower torso, just below his ribs. For a moment Rem stood, enjoying the feeling of being enfolded by her, held by her. After a moment he pried her hands loose, spun in her arms, and swept her into an embrace of his own. They stood like that for a long time, holding one another, his chin resting in her gently waving auburn hair.

"I love this feeling," she said against him. "Here. With you. I know it's just for a moment, before you run off to work and I hurry home, but that's why it's all the more precious. I wish it could be this way all the time."

Rem considered that. "Why can't it be?"

Indilen raised her eyes.

"Honestly," Rem carried on, "why can't it be? It's foolish, maintaining two residences. Why don't we pool our resources?"

Indilen pulled away. Her expression was a puzzled one, part bemused delight, part shocked disbelief. "What are you asking me?"

Rem shrugged. In truth, he'd been considering it for some time—raising the issue, at least. He just hadn't been sure how to do it. Indilen's offhand comment had opened the door.

"I'm asking you to get rooms with me. To build a home with me."

Indilen waited. "And is that all?"

Rem suddenly realized what she was suggesting. Oh dear. He hadn't anticipated the conversation going in that direction. "I hadn't thought of that," he said, eyes widening.

"That's all right," Indilen said, and pulled away from him. "I'd not dream of forcing your hand or making demands—"

Before she could move more than a step or two away from him, Rem reached out, took her hands, and pulled her close again. He met her gaze and hoped that his own was sure, steady. "Listen," he said, feeling a hitch in his voice, "where I'm from, we don't get to choose our partners. Not so often, anyway. Someone's always making that decision for us, for the good of this or the strength of that. And I know it's just been a few months, Indilen, and that maybe asking you this is rude or daft or just plain pointless, but you raised the question and I think that's the answer: let's stop existing separately. Let's stop throwing our money away on these cramped little rooms of ours, and let's stop just seeing each other in passing. I'll still work through the night, and you'll still work through the day, but at least we can each know we're coming home to someone. To something."

"You don't get to choose your partners," Indilen said slowly. "Where you're from."

Rem cocked his head. What was she getting at?

Indilen smiled, but there was some sadness in it. "I did not know that the sons of horse grooms and their wives were subject to the rigors of arranged marriages and alliances."

"Well," Rem said, suddenly realizing what he'd revealed without even trying. Oh bollocks... he was botching this. And here he thought he'd been taking a step in the right direction. "It's just, sometimes... That is—"

Indilen laid a finger on his lips. She met his gaze levelly. "I would love to make a home with you," she said. "I won't even ask that you marry me yet, if that's not where your heart is. We're not in the royal courts or the marches. There are no local priests to shame us, no village gossips to sully our names. Questions of propriety aren't so vital here as they might be were either of us in our homelands, among our families."

"Indilen," Rem said, "I love you. You know that."

She smiled and cupped his face in her hands. "Of course I do, you fool. And I love you, too—but let me finish. I love you, and if you're ready, we can find ourselves a place of our own, a place that can be *ours*, not just yours or mine. But if we're going to do that, I think we need to have a few more talks about... the past."

"The past," Rem said. He should've known that would come up. How couldn't it?

Indilen nodded. "I feel I know so much about you," she said. "But you and I both know that something's missing. There are things you haven't told me"—he started to speak, and she laid her finger on his lips again—"because I've never asked. I assumed we would each give up our secrets in time, as our hearts moved us. But if we're to take this step...I think perhaps some of those secrets need to be aired. Sooner rather than later."

Rem studied her. She did not seem distressed or overeager or insistent. Her voice was perfectly calm, her demeanor easy. But what she asked...that they tell each other everything...

And why shouldn't you? he asked himself. *You just asked her to share a room and a bed with you, you silly sod! Why shouldn't she ask for everything that you've been hiding from her?*

But what if I tell her the truth and she leaves? What if she decides that secret was too weighty to keep from her? Or that she's afraid to get involved with someone like me, for fear of what might come in the future?

Or worse, what if she embraces it? What if the truth leads her to try to get me—get us—to go back there? What if, when she learns of the power and privilege that was once mine, she wants that for herself?

"I see the struggle in you," she said then, and Rem felt his face flush warm and red like a roasted apple. "I'm making no demands, Remeck. I'm just saying...a home can't be built on secrets and lies. If it's going to last, it's got to mean the end of that."

"It's really no great thing," Rem said half-heartedly.

"If it were no great thing," Indilen countered, "you'd have told me by now. Besides, why do you think it's only you?"

Rem's eyes narrowed. He studied her. Indilen raised her chin, a subtle but defiant gesture that made him love her and fear her all at once.

"You're not the only one with secrets," she said, and the challenge in her voice was implicit.

"Well," Rem said, then drew a deep breath and blew it back out. "I suppose the time's come, then—"

"Not now, you fool," Indilen said, shaking her head. "It's getting late. You need to go."

"But I thought—"

"You asked me to live with you. I'm saying I will. But I'm asking you to tell me the things you've been keeping from me, and I'll do the same. But it need not be *now*. Fair enough?"

Rem drew her into his arms and held her.

"I love you," he said.

"I know," she answered.

For those few breaths, it seemed that he couldn't squeeze her tightly enough, couldn't take in enough of her. He held her close, loving the feel of her warmth against him and the faint smells of jasmine and lavender that rose from her hair. Gods, but he wished he could just blow off work tonight and stay right here with her. Lay everything out. Bare all that he'd hidden from her and leave his silly fears and misgivings behind.

But the ward needed him, as did his watch, and—most of all—his partner.

"I won't let you down," Rem said.

"You never have," Indilen said. "I wouldn't expect you to start now. Finish dressing. You need to go."

The onslaught of a bitter wind forced Rem to pull his watch-issued greatcoat closer around him. It was a good garment, modeled on the sort used by whalers and fishermen, sewn from oilcloth, with a high, stiff collar and a broad mantle over the shoulders to keep the rain off—but at present Rem wished he'd been smart enough to wrap himself in a few more woolen layers, or perhaps a nice warm muffler. In another clime Rem might have expected snow; the evening sky was bruised, leaden, the fast-falling sun obscured by clouds, and the air slashed mercilessly, like tiny crystalline daggers, at any inch of exposed skin. But there was no snow in Yenara. Its continental placement and the sea currents that churned Hatarau Bay all ensured that, however cold it seemed to get, it would rarely, if ever, be cold enough to snow. More likely was a wet, stinging rain driven by a bracing wind, preceded or followed by a swirling pall of impenetrable, porridge-thick fog. That was Yenara, the City by the Sea: cold, damp, windy, misty, rainy. Rem made a mental note to buy himself some good gloves— the best he could afford on his salary, anyway. Maybe even a hat—though he knew he'd look a fool in one. When he'd come south from the Vale, it had been at the onset of summer; he hadn't thought to bring winter clothes with him. On some level he probably hadn't expected to still be in Yenara when winter arrived. He'd really had no clue where he was headed, or where his journey would end.

Rem quickened his pace, shrinking into his coat as he advanced against the press of the cold wind, which grew more frigid, more insistent, with each passing moment. After what felt like an eternity, he finally rounded a corner, the narrow lane he'd been walking along spilling onto a wide, uncobbled boulevard that intersected ahead with several other streets. There were a number of grogshops and stew kitchens hereabouts, their separate shingles creaking in the gusts as the soft, warm light within them spilled into the gloomy street. Rem felt a pang of envy. He'd pay good coin to be by any one of those hearths right now, basking in the warmth of a flickering fire, smelling stew meat and broth and warm, soft vegetables, enlivening himself with a tankard of ale or a cup of brandy. Anything but to be out on these cold streets, about to reunite with his partner and question a bunch of chisel jockeys who might or might not be terrorizing the city's dwarven populace.

Up ahead, right in the middle of the great intersection, Torval waited, staunch and unmoving, a statue awaiting a fountain yet to be built. There were numerous people in the streets—laborers done with their laboring, mongers done with their mongering, friends off to sup and carouse with companions—but Torval let them all mill and flow around him, totally oblivious to their passage. As the waters of a stream might part and flow around an immovable boulder, the strollers flowed around Torval. The dwarf wore his own greatcoat, but it flapped in the breeze, wide-open and unbelted. In truth, the frigid air seemed to trouble the dwarf little. Rem wished he had been built so stout and impervious; he'd love to stand out in the elements—on this night in particular—and say that he barely felt anything. Instead he just trudged up to his truculent partner, cursing the wintry winds, numbed hands deep in his coat's pockets.

"I'd just about given up on you," Torval said, then hawked and spat into the cold mud.

"Sorry I'm late, old stump. Indilen woke me and—"

"Say no more, lad," Torval cut in, the barest hint of a smile on his face. "I'm surprised you bothered to meet me at all."

Rem understood immediately. "No. Not that. I only wish…"

Torval must have noted the dejection in his voice. "What's the trouble? There's no quarrel between you two, is there?"

Rem shrugged. He scanned the intersection and located the Stonemason's Guildhall about a hundred yards down a side street. He was sick of the cold. With luck they would perform their interrogations inside. Rem led the way and Torval followed.

"No quarrel, precisely," Rem said as he walked. "Just… questions. About the future."

"Well, you're going to marry her, aren't you?" Torval asked, as though it were a long-settled conclusion agreed to by all.

"Well, of course," Rem said. "I mean, I suppose. Truth be told, I just hadn't thought about it yet."

"I've seen you together. You're besotted, the both of you. Go see the priests and start the baby making."

"Hold on, then!" Rem said. "Who said anything about babies?"

"That's the way of things, isn't it?" Torval asked. "You love someone, you marry them, you breed. What else is there?"

"What about just enjoying one another?" Rem asked. "Taking our time?"

"What time?" Torval asked, and he suddenly swung right into Rem's path. He stood his ground, blocking Rem from going any farther. The guildhall was just a hundred feet away, but Torval didn't seem to care. Rem felt a lecture coming on.

"There is *no* time," Torval said slowly, absolutely earnest. "We always think there is, but there isn't. No promise of it, anyway."

"I'm young, Torval," Rem said. "So is she—"

"Aye, and young people die every day," Torval spat back. "We see it, don't we, lad? Knifed in an alley. Head cracked for a purse full of coin. A bad oyster. Fever. Plague. A runaway horse." The dwarf snapped his fingers. The cracking sound echoed in the largely empty street. "Over. Done. In an instant."

Rem drew a deep breath, then ran his hands through his hair. Were they really discussing this? Didn't they have suspects to interrogate? Work to do? It was too bloody cold out here to be having this conversation now.

"I know, all too well," Torval carried on, "how all the time in the world suddenly turns into no time at all. Only you know your heart, lad, so only you can decide—but remember this as you do: *there is no time*. There is never *any* time. There is only the moment, a miracle unparalleled and unrepeatable."

Rem was always caught off guard by that—how the stout, rough-spun dwarf could offer the deepest wisdom, the most profound insight, and make that bloody poetry wholly native to his cursing, grumbling little mouth. Rem looked into his flinty blue eyes and saw great depths of feeling there—passion, pain, love, loss, hope, despair. The dwarf's gaze was like a sea before a storm: roiling, but not yet surrendered fully to chaos.

"It's not so simple," Rem said. "There are things I haven't told her."

"The same things you haven't told me?" Torval asked.

Rem was taken aback by that. Before he could answer, Torval barreled on.

"You think I don't know you're hiding something?" Torval continued. "Probably running from something? I'm no shoat in the wallow, boy. *I see you.* Even if I don't know the whole truth, I can piece out enough of it to paint a picture."

"Torval, I—"

"Shut your mouth," the dwarf said. "I don't need an explanation. These months we've been walking the ward, I've seen all I need to see. You're brave, you're honorable, you do your duty, and you watch my back. We've supped together, gotten drunk together, faced death together, and laughed it down. You've broken bread at my table and made my children smile. I know all I need to about you, lad. Whoever you are—or were—whatever it is you ran from...I don't care. And I'd be willing to lay coin that Indilen feels the same way."

"It could change things," Rem said.

"Then let it," Torval said. "Tell her the truth and let her decide. If she stays, she's yours forever. If she leaves, she was never yours at all. My coin says she stays."

Rem stood there in the middle of the street for what felt like a long time, mulling over Torval's words. He knew the dwarf was right, damn him. But that didn't make acknowledging the fear he felt when he considered telling Indilen the whole truth any easier. To be honest, it terrified him.

But why should it? he wondered. *Why should it be so frightening?*

The truth, he realized, was this: the prospect of losing her frightened him because he honestly, truly loved her. He *did* want to take her to the priests. He *did* want to call her his wife. He *did* want to have children with her. But even knowing that troubled him somehow. Where did that doubt come from?

Torval suddenly slapped him. It was aimed at his temple, but it took his ear and made it ring. "Raathen's balls!" Rem exclaimed. "What was that for?"

"Get out of that haunted head of yours," Torval said. He gestured toward the waiting guildhall. "We've got work to do."

On they went. Rem's cuffed ear throbbed in the cold night air.

The guildhall was nothing special from the outside: stone-and-mortar walls topped by stucco with an inlaid timber frame, two stories high, brooding beneath its slate-shingled roof and glowering eaves. A matching pair of beautifully wrought iron lanterns on matching iron hooks flanked the entryway, their light dim but welcomingly warm in the cold darkness of the street. Just beneath the lantern to the right of the doorway hung a hand-chiseled plaque of marble, mounted with rusted iron bolts.

Stonemasons' Guildhall, it said. *Sixth Chapter, Fifth Ward. Established 6 Miras 5654 A.R.A.*

Beneath that inscription lay a motto in Horunic: *Out of Chaos, Order.*

"Just over a hundred years old, then," Rem said. "Is that all?"

Torval stepped up to the door. "The Yenaran Stonemasons' Guild, all in all, is over a thousand years old," the dwarf said. "This must be a younger chapter. Established during the Reclamation, as the city was putting itself back together."

A polished brass bell hung beneath the lantern on the left, a thin line of hemp trailing from the unseen clapper within. Torval grabbed the frayed cord and yanked. For such a small bell, the sound was loud and strident in the largely empty street. It made Rem's head hurt.

Torval elbowed him. "Badge," he said. Obeying, Rem went rooting beneath his coat for his lead watchwarden's badge on its cheap, sturdy chain. Torval had his out in an instant and held it before him, not even waiting for someone to answer the door.

After a few interminable moments, a peephole in the door slid open and a pair of eyes peered out. Torval raised his badge to be sure that whoever was on the other side of that door saw it clearly through the little rectangular window.

"Watchwardens," Torval said, as though he were declaiming some ancient monologue upon a stage. "Official inquiry. Open your door, please."

The peephole slid shut. Rem heard locks clanking, a heavy wooden bolt thrown back, then the stout door opened inward. They stood face-to-face with a handsome young roughneck, seventeen or eighteen, trim and muscular, with a short-cropped nest of brown hair and rather limpid-looking blue eyes. At the boy's side stood a big, muscular dog, not pretty, but probably loyal unto death.

From within, Rem heard the low murmur of men's voices in conversation, the scuff of benches on a wooden floor, the distant crackle of a fire and the pop of an exploding pine knot. He smelled roasting meat, then fresh, hot bread. His stomach growled. He'd been in such a hurry to get here and meet Torval that he hadn't eaten since waking. Gods, he wanted to be over that threshold.

"Watchmen," the boy said, studying their badges under the light of the door lanterns. "What can we do for you?"

"You're not in charge," Torval said. It wasn't a question.

"No, sir," the boy answered politely. "I'm just on door duty tonight. If you could state your business—"

"What's this about?" someone said from within. A moment later a second form materialized out of the gloom. Rem studied the newcomer: older than the boy, probably nearing forty or just past it, with the strong shoulders and muscular arms that marked all who worked in stone, but on a more wiry physique—taut, ropy. He had a narrow, hangdog sort of face with shrewd eyes and a wide mouth that seemed to smile knowingly—haughtily, even—as though he were in on some private joke that never ceased to amuse him. Rem had known a hundred careless, arrogant, entitled spawn of lords—jackasses and villains, most of them—who'd lived with similar expressions on their faces. That look made Rem nervous. He could never quite trust a person who smiled like that.

Then Rem realized who he was looking at. It was the fiery speaker from the riot in the dwarven quarter, the very same man who'd broken that first dwarven pot, setting everything off.

As the newcomer studied Rem and Torval, he sipped from the cup in his hand, then installed himself in the doorway, just behind the polite young man. The way he stood, propped against the jamb, wholly unimpressed by their badges of office, told Rem that he didn't give a coal miner's fart for their official business. Though he might not openly fight with them, he certainly wasn't going to make their errand any easier.

The man's cunning eyes set upon Torval and rested there.

"What can we do for you, good officers of the watch?" the man said slowly, silkily.

"We're here on official business," Torval said again. "Questions regarding a fire set in the ward last night at the Panoply temple, not far from here."

"I can assure you," the man said, "neither myself nor my fellows would have any knowledge about such things. That's not our contract, you see."

"No longer, anyway," Rem interjected, just to see if he could ruffle the man.

The stonemason's eyes shifted to Rem. He gave a slight, deferential shrug. "Aye, that's the way of it. We'd laid the foundations and built up the walls, but the clergy did not renew our contracts. Now if you'll excuse us—Come on, Jordi."

He laid a hand on the boy's shoulders and gently drew him back into the dark vestibule. When the elder mason moved to close the door, Torval stepped forward, laying one thick, square foot just over the threshold, making it impossible for the man to shut them out.

"A guild's hall is sacred ground," the man said to Torval, as though explaining something to a child. "I'd suggest you remove your foot, old stump, before I'm forced to remove it for you."

Within, the big watchdog snarled, a low, rumbling sound rising from its thick, muscular throat. Rem's hand emerged from his pocket and drifted toward his sword's pommel. His hand was numb in seconds, but he was determined not to put it back in his pocket again.

"This is official ward business," Torval said. "Therefore official city business. I'm more than happy to honor the sanctity of your guild's hall if you'll do me the honor of answering our questions. Out here or in there, you decide." Torval paused, licked his lips slowly, then added, "I would likewise urge you not to call me 'old stump' again, sir. That moniker's reserved for my dearest of friends, which you most certainly are not."

The man in the doorway smiled wolfishly and appraised Torval. Through the half-closed door Rem saw the boy, Jordi, lurking in the shadows behind the man, trying to calm the agitated dog. The worry on the young man's face was readily visible, as though he expected violence and dreaded it. His eyes were far too easy to read.

"Hrissif!" someone called from within.

The man at the door answered, but never took his eyes off Torval. "Here in the vestibule, chief!"

Heavy, determined footsteps. A moment later two more men crowded into the dark little foyer beyond the door. The first was larger than the smug bastard who'd blocked them—taller, broader, stronger—a wolf to the other man's fox. He looked about the same age as the belligerent doorman—Hrissif, the big man had called him—but gave an immediate impression of greater charisma and nobility, a more substantial presence. Beside the big man stood a much older fellow, bald, bearded, and graying, probably at least ten or twenty years the elder of the other two but still hale, hearty, and built like an ox.

The big man slipped past Hrissif, placing himself right on the threshold, filling the doorframe with his height and his broad, muscular shoulders. As he stepped forward, Torval stepped back, giving him some room. Even the dwarf knew when to show a little respect.

Rem recognized this man from the protest in the quarter as well. As Rem recalled, his words had been diplomatic—apologetic, even—but whatever good they might have done was smashed to bits once the deputy, Hrissif, had opened his mouth.

"Is there a problem?" the big man asked.

"We're from the wardwatch," Torval said, clearly growing impatient. "We're here to ask a few questions. Now, which of you is most likely to cooperate?"

Rem caught movement out of the corner of his eye. He turned his head to scan their surroundings. Their little stand-off at the guildhall door was drawing a crowd. A dozen people were scattered along the street, before them, behind them, across the way. Some were just passersby, but a few had clearly come from the nearby taverns and pubs, for they carried tankards and cups with them. They all watched—probably hoping for things to escalate, praying for some excitement, maybe even fisticuffs. A good bloody row was a fine evening's entertainment, after all.

Rem turned back to the unfolding drama, praying that there would be no show for them.

"I'm the steward," the big man said, crossing his arms over his broad chest. "I'll answer your questions."

"Perhaps we should talk inside?" Rem suggested.

"We're fine here," the steward said. "Talk."

Torval studied the man for a moment—sizing him up, Rem knew, as the dwarf always did. He was a fine reader of folk, Torval, with an eye for detail and keen instincts regarding trustworthiness and motivation. Though Torval himself was the least duplicitous person Rem had ever met, the dwarf still had a knack for sniffing out and exposing the markers of dishonesty in others. And here, now, he seemed to relax a little. Clearly there was something in the stonemason that Torval sensed was honorable—more respectable, at any rate, than the wiry Hrissif.

"What's your name, sir?" Torval asked.

"Valaric Loriksson," the big steward said.

"And these others?"

Valaric stepped through the doorway so that he could better indicate the men crowded in behind him. "Hrissif, my deputy steward. Frendel"—that was the older man, who Rem could now see had his left forearm splinted and tightly wrapped—"our treasurer. And the young lad's Jordi. Now, what crime is it we're accused of?"

Rem took that as an opportunity to intervene. "No crime at all," he said. "We just had some questions to ask. You heard of the fire at the Panoply last night?"

Valaric Loriksson nodded. His stony expression never moved. "I have."

"And it's true that your guild was, until recently, contracted to work at that site?"

The steward blew out a long breath through his nose. It plumed in the lamp-lit air like smoke. "That's true, yes."

Rem cleared his throat. "So it's also true that your guild's contract was not renewed?"

The steward raised his chin a little. He looked down at Rem as if he might reach out, grab him, and snap him in two over his knee. Though this Valaric was only a fingerlength taller than Rem, Rem still guessed he could do it if he chose. But he made no movement. After a long silence, he finally just shrugged. *How much of human communication comes in shrugs?* Rem wondered absently. *What a marvelous, manifold gesture . . .*

"The clergy alleged that we had fallen behind," Valaric said. "And so they did not renew our contract."

"Had you fallen behind?" Torval asked.

Valaric looked down at the dwarf, frowning. "Any and every hindrance to our progress was reported, discussed, and evaluated for our benefactors. When we fell behind, they knew, and why. *Always* why. Raising a temple is not short work, and sensible people know that. Most of us my age, or older, know we'll never live to see that temple completed. It'll be Jordi's children, or their children, who see the first worshippers climb its steps. That's the nature of our work. Slow, steady, but always to a purpose."

"The stump'll be there," Hrissif muttered, staring into his cup. "His sort are long-lived, aren't they?"

Rem almost said something, but, thankfully, Torval gave no indication that he'd heard the man's words. *Stump.* It was a terrible insult to dwarves—perhaps not as insulting as *pickmonkey* or the dread epithet *tonker*, but not far off. *Old stump* could be used only among friends, but *stump*, all by itself…that was an invitation to a bloody duel.

Torval, bless him, seemed to have let it slide by…

"And yet," the dwarf continued, as though Hrissif had said nothing, "they fired the lot of you."

"They did not renew our contracts," Valaric said slowly. "That's not the same thing."

"Hear, hear," someone said. Rem turned toward the voice. It was a single onlooker—one of many now. He stood in the middle of the muddy street, a smoking pipe clamped between his teeth, a mug of something in his hands. There were dozens now, many still hewing close to the places they'd drifted out of—nearby taverns, basement grogshops—and still more haunted the middle of the street. They gathered in a loose, ill-formed semicircle, whispering to themselves or to one another as the watchwarden and the steward stonemason traded barbs. Rem suspected that at least a few of them were laying odds and trading coin, betting on when or if the whole confrontation would turn bloody.

"I should think," Torval countered, and Rem turned his attentions back to his partner and the shop steward, "that the clergy would have wanted to keep the men who laid the temple's foundations, if they were reliable enough."

"I should think, master dwarf," Valaric said, "that you'd be more suited to joining your fellows at the work site than to walking this city's streets and harassing its honest citizens."

Rem saw Torval bristle at that. The dwarf's mouth twisted. His shoulders tensed. "I wouldn't call a few simple questions *harassment*."

"Few," Valaric said, as though the round of questions he'd endured had been anything but *few*. "Are we done yet?"

Rem intervened again. "That fire was no accident," he said, trying to appeal to the man's good sense. "We were sent by our prefect to treat with you because the Panoply clergy told us about your business arrangements and their unpleasant ends."

Valaric shrugged again, a strangely provocative gesture for all its apparent indifference. "There were no unpleasant ends. Our client decided that our good work was too expensive for them, and they released us rather than renew our agreement. We were disappointed, certainly, but we were not bitter. There is no quarrel between us."

"Between you and the clergy, maybe," Torval said. "What about your competition?"

Valaric turned toward Torval. His crossed arms fell to his side. His hands were fists now. "There is no *competition* between us," Valaric said, leaning down into Torval's face. "Our work, our ethic, our honor, all speak for themselves. If the pagans of that temple want to throw their coin to half men while leaving their brethren unemployed and hungry, that is their business. Let them save a few coppers while your kind toil without so much as a fair wage or a day of rest, like slaves. In the end they'll get the temple they deserve. We're done with them."

"I think we should be done with these two, as well," Hrissif said. "Our night's vigil's just begun—"

"I am steward here!" Valaric barked, not even turning to look at his second. "I'll talk for all of us and I'll decide when the talking's done!"

"Let him talk," Rem said, taking an awful chance. "Just like you did the other day, in the Warrens."

Valaric's dark gaze swung toward Rem. "What did you say?"

"I was there," Rem said. "I saw your gathering, your demonstration, whatever it was. I saw that man"—he pointed to Hrissif—"break a potter's wares. If you ask me, that's what set it all off."

"I didn't ask you," Valaric said.

Rem waited for a response to his jabs—some indication of how this man, Valaric, felt about what had happened in the quarter the other day. It was a terrible risk, winding him up, but if it revealed something...

And then, suddenly, Rem discerned a strange sound from within the guildhall. The murmur of voices ceased, then coalesced into something new. The men inside were singing a song—a low, slow, dirgelike recitation that was, to Rem's ears, immediately familiar. Painfully so.

Torval heard it as well. Rem saw it on the dwarf's face—a realization slowly dawning on him in answer to that melancholy canticle, that song for the departed.

Rem looked to Valaric. "You're in mourning?"

Valaric nodded. When he spoke his voice was strangled, with none of the force it had carried only a moment before. "Just a boy. One of our apprentices. His family carried him out to the tombs today, beyond the walls. Now it's our turn. We'll be here all night, saying our farewells."

Rem looked to Torval, suddenly embarrassed. Gods, had they really just interrupted a death vigil? Rem saw that Torval was moved as well. He knew grief—and what it demanded of the grieving—better than anyone. His broad face seemed to be at war with itself, his desire to complete their mission and his desire to respect these men and their loss wrestling with one another.

"Our apologies," Torval said quickly. "We did not know—"

"Didn't you?" Valaric asked. "Your prefect sent you here seeking justice for the Panoply, and justice for your kind, master dwarf—where, then, are the watchwardens seeking justice for our fallen brother? Where are the inquiries into his death? Where is the manhunt for his murderers?"

"Murderers?" Rem asked.

"Aye, for murder it was," Valaric continued. "He was separated from us in the dwarven quarter. There was no one to help him when those little bastards beset him. They beat him within an inch of his life, crushed his hands with their hammers, so that he would never work stone again! But they need not have bothered—his hands were useless, but their beating did the real work. He'll never need those hands again now."

"Was it reported?" Torval asked.

"Would you have cared?" Valaric asked, then turned to Rem. "Any of you, you bloody mercenaries?"

"Are you seeing this?" Hrissif suddenly shouted, addressing the curious onlookers and passersby. "Do you see how peaceful, honest, hardworking men are now harassed by the authorities, just because a few priests have their robes in a bind? Because a few cowardly pickmonkeys decide that the powers that be need to do their fighting for them?"

Murmurs and grumbles of assent moved through the crowd.

Rem looked to Torval to see if *pickmonkey* had reached his ears. By the dwarf's deepening frown and narrowed eyes, he guessed that it had. Clearly Hrissif's verbal thrust had hit and drawn blood. The situation was about to spiral out of control, unless Rem could yank it back on track.

He turned to the crowd. "All of you, on your way! This is ward business—an official inquiry! There's nothing to see here and it's too cold for the lot of you to be crowded into the bloody streets!"

"So you're our nursemaids now?" an old man with a voice like gravel shouted back. "You get to tell us when it's too cold outside? When we need our bloody mufflers?"

Laughter exploded from one contingent among the watchers.

"Move along!" Rem barked in answer. "Any man still standing here sixty seconds from now will be upended and his pockets emptied to pay a heap of obstruction fines! Now move!"

"Bloody catchpoles," someone muttered, off to Rem's left and behind him. "Moneylenders' whores, the lot of them."

Rem fought to ignore that. There were more pressing concerns at hand than a few hurled insults. He looked back to the doorway, where Torval yet stood, staring down Valaric. Hrissif, having stepped out of the doorway when he addressed the crowd, now haunted the space off to Valaric's right, still holding his cup of wine or whatever it was. As Rem rejoined the confrontation, he caught Hrissif staring at him, quietly sizing him up. Though he knew little about the man, he truly disliked him. He seemed the sort of man who'd throw a kitten on a swarming ant pile just to see what would happen.

Torval was still trying to reassure Valaric.

"...For that, we are truly sorry," he was saying. "But that does not change why we've come here. We meant no disrespect, and I believe we've given none, but you must meet us halfway. You seem a good man—do the right thing and talk to us."

"I believe I've said all there is to say," Valaric answered. Rem caught some strange set to his mouth, a sad sort of glint to his eyes. As though he wanted to say something—to offer something—but simply could not. "Please go now. We've a long night ahead of us."

"Fine," Torval relented. "We'll go. But this isn't finished. We'll have to come back. There are still questions to be answered."

"I've said all there is to say," Valaric said.

"The wardwatch decides when all the questions have been answered," Torval responded.

Rem hung his head. *Not now, Torval. Don't insist on having the last word now . . .*

Valaric stared at Torval, trying to read him. The dwarf, surprisingly, did not seem belligerent, but beseeching. "The next time, it might not be the two of us," Torval said. "Whoever comes next might not be so kind."

Valaric took a single step that planted him right in front of Torval. He leaned down, his face just inches from Torval's own. "Look up and down this street, master dwarf. That hostel down on the corner? We laid those foundations and paid for the framing from our chapterhouse coffers. The cellar stew kitchen just behind you? Rebuilt, better than before, after an unexpected fire—our gift to the widow who owns that lot and runs the place. The three-story town house down at the end of the block? A pension gift to the children of one of our own, who died on a work site, crushed by falling scaffolding. Our silver and gold—our labor—built that place, and it's now a boardinghouse whose proceeds keep those children schooled, clothed, and fed, and that will continue to provide for them in the decades to come. This block, and several that surround it, can tell many such stories, stories of loss, or need, or deprivation, all of which were answered and countered by our generosity, our largesse. This whole neighborhood, and nearly everyone in it, owes us one debt or another. Debts we'll never collect on...unless we need to. Unless we need their aid against hostile outsiders intent on painting us as criminals and troublemakers."

Rem laid a hand on Torval's shoulder. "We should go," he said. "We'll get no more from them tonight."

"We're not your enemies," Torval said to Valaric.

Valaric shrugged a little. "Aren't you?"

Torval's eyes remained locked on Valaric's. "I reckon you think you're a good man," the dwarf said. It was an odd statement—part idle observation, part challenge.

"Better than some," Valaric answered.

"And you're their steward," Torval said. "Their leader."

"We're done here," Valaric said, and turned to go back inside.

"Whatever happens to them," Torval shouted as the man left them, "will be upon you! Upon your shoulders! Upon your conscience!"

Valaric, filling the doorway, turned back to Torval. He seemed to study the dwarf for a long time, as though he meant to say something—something barbed and poisonous—then thought better of it. "My conscience is clear," he said finally, and disappeared into the shadows of the guildhall. Hrissif followed, gave Torval and Rem a smug half smile, then yanked the door shut behind him.

Torval bared his teeth. For just a moment Rem thought he might sound one of his great, bellowing battle cries out of simple frustration. But after blowing out a long, pluming breath into the cold night air, the dwarf finally just shook his head and stalked away from the guildhall. Rem hurried after him.

"It's all right, partner," Rem said as they hurried along, side by side. "We did our duty. If Ondego wants more from us, he'll tell us."

"Gods, save us from the depredations of proud men," Torval grumbled.

Rem knew that prayer well. He'd said it himself—or something close enough to it—on hundreds of occasions, usually after an unpleasant confrontation with his father. A very proud man...the sort of man whose pride could wound his loved ones and get his subordinates killed.

"Do you think they had anything to do with it?" Rem asked. "I mean...just based on your first impressions?"

Torval shook his head. Shrugged. Threw his hands in the air again. "I have no idea. I only know I'd like to see all their smug faces pressed into the mud. Slap manacles on the lot of them and give them a nice long walk of shame back to the watchkeep. Let the dungeons soften them up for a few days or a week..."

"You know that won't help," Rem said. "All that cack he threw at us about the largesse of the guild and how much the locals owe them—it might have been tacky, but it was absolutely true. If they're that closely bound to the neighborhood and its people, arresting them just to terrorize them won't help us. Far from it, in fact."

"I know," Torval spat. "Believe me, I know. But oh, how it galls me..."

The dwarf was shaking. A rage had bloomed inside him, but it had nowhere to go. Rem knew it well, for he'd seen it in Torval before. The only cure for it was a brisk walk, some persistent silence, and—if their luck held out—perhaps a crime to foil or a perp to run down before they made it back to the watchkeep.

Such a distraction, right about now, would serve Torval nicely. So Rem shut his mouth, kept his feet moving along at the same quick step that Torval had established, and prayed to all the gods of the Panoply that, somewhere between the Stonemason's Guildhall and the Fifth Ward watchkeep, there was a footpad or purse snatcher on a collision course with the two of them.

CHAPTER ELEVEN

"I see you've turned the library into a hermitage," Therba said.

Bjalki raised his eyes, her voice yanking him out of a waking dream. The old docent had approached without a sound, and now she stood just on the other side of the table from him, bright eyes smiling in her lined, round face, its many creases and liver spots darkened in the dim candlelight.

"Good reading?" she asked, her eyes sweeping over the works arrayed before him.

Bjalki managed a weary smile. "In truth," he said, "ponderous."

He'd been poring over the texts before him for hours—so many hours, he'd lost count. He sat at one of the study tables, walled in behind a great collection of dusty old codices, bound scrolls, and ancient, flat stone tablets, inscribed by chisel in bygone ages, now housed in ornate wooden chests. Two lonely candles burned in the vast darkness of the library, just enough for dwarven eyes to read by; far more comfortable, in fact, than the brighter light a human might require. They were subterranean folk, after all, bred to a sunless world. Night vision was one of their greatest inherent gifts.

"Everyone's been wondering where you disappeared to," Therba said, drawing a chair out from the table. She laid aside her ceremonial stave—mostly used as a walking stick—and sat. "What have you been reading?" The docent sat, silent, clearly awaiting an explanation but too tactful to force it.

Bjalki stared at her for a moment. Though Therba was at least a century and a half older than Bjalki himself, something in her—her sternness, her kindness, her practicality, her hard-won wisdom—yet reminded him of his wife, hundreds of leagues away. Those were the responsibilities of dwarven clerics appointed to an ethnarch's court: to tend to the administrative needs of the local ethnarch and the spiritual needs of the dwarves in residence, without familial distractions to undermine their clerical duties. It was good work—important work—both rewarding and sanctified, with only a single downside: separation from one's family, however temporary it might be.

It had always been thus, those years apart from their families a rite of passage in the lives of many young priests and priestesses working their way up the ecclesiastical hierarchy, reinforcing in both their hearts and the hearts of their families that not only were the needs of their people placed before their own wants and desires, but also that, whether at home or abroad, dwarves could and should always rely on one another, as a great, extended family. Love between spouses mattered, as did the devotion of parents for their children, and children for their parents—but kinship—*dwarfhood*, in its largest sense—was the greatest allegiance any of them could know. Everything else paled beside it.

Bjalki had never questioned the validity of those values. But suddenly, reminded of his wife and children and their distance from him, he felt a pang within—sharp, palpable, like a knife in his gut. He wanted to feel Wettelin's strong arms around him, the warmth of his three daughters as they all jostled and scrambled for a place on his lap. Only they could give him the strength he needed to see to his duties here, to be an asset to his people, to earn his way home.

"Bless me," Therba said, almost to herself. "He's lost the power of speech."

Bjalki smiled in spite of his melancholy. "My apologies," he said. "I came to study and to pray, hoping maybe I could be of use."

Therba cocked her head. "Do you not feel of use, presently?"

He started to answer, but the words evaporated before he'd uttered them. In the end all he could do was raise his hands in a silent question and let his eyes skate over the tomes and texts scattered before him. "As I am the auspice," he said, "Lord Eldgrim told me outright that I should read the signs and portents for him. Tease out the future. Determine a course of action."

"He wants a resolution?" Therba asked.

Bjalki shook his head. "He wants a weapon. He wants...an edge. He wants to know that whatever he decides, he is justified in doing so."

"And you will find such things in these?" Therba asked, suggesting the litter before him.

Bjalki shrugged. "I've always felt that what's to come is already written in what's past. When I study the chronicles and legends, it seems to stir something in me...give me some sense of what to do in the moment, in answer to the crisis of the day."

Docent Therba's mouth twisted at its corners, the barest hint of a smile. Bjalki knew what came next. She was about to question him, to lead him toward a debate with himself that would, with luck, reveal some wisdom that lay still undiscovered, right under his nose. Wettelin often did the same.

"And what," the docent said, "do you see as the crisis of the day? What troubles you, that you'd sequester yourself in here and pore over all these moldy old tomes?"

Bjalki leaned forward, fingers laced before him. "It feels as though we're on the edge of something," he said. "A precipice of sorts. What we do next could yank us back from it, or send us plunging over. I'm simply trying to tease out which action is best—the retreat or the plunge."

"What do you think?" the docent asked, then hastily added, "And stop holding out on me, Bjalki. It's just the two of us. This is not a clerical conclave, nor a privy council meeting with the ethnarch. This is two colleagues talking."

Bless her for saying so. Bjalki had both great affection and great respect for Docent Therba. She was the finest docent—the finest priest or priestess, period—he had ever known. When others feared, she hoped. When others rested, she worked. When others squabbled and separated, she alone undertook the hard work of mediation in search of some accord. Old Hrothwar, the sage, was often too prickly and aloof to treat with meaningfully, while Arbiter Haefred seemed forever in search of a solution, but resistant to first probing and defining the problem. But Docent Therba, she was the best of their ill-matched quartet—the mortar that bound the bricks, the keystone that kept the arch from collapsing. She could even get Eldgrim, their stubborn and quarrelsome ethnarch, to examine his words and change his frequently unchangeable mind. For lesser miracles, dwarves had been deified.

"This business with the temple contract," Bjalki said, "the riot, the fire... it frightens me, Docent. From such humble sparks come terrible conflagrations."

"What remedy do you seek, then?" Therba asked, indicating the books and scrolls and tablets strewn about. "What have the histories and legends told you?"

"They've told me that the price of impatience is often high," he said. "But often the price of hesitation is equally so. The hell of it is in discerning which is called for, and when. Perhaps I'm just inclined to pessimism at the moment, but all I find, time and again as I peruse the annals, are small conflicts that bloomed into ruinous wars, blood feuds that claimed generations of combatants, cycles of vengeance and retribution that were only broken when all offending parties were finally dead, and none left to thirst for more blood."

"But such is the nature of our people," Therba said. "'Let every wrong endured plant the seed of retribution, but pick not the fruit until it is sweet and ripe.'" It was a quote from the *Pillars of Kondela*—their holiest text—specifically from the *Chronicles of Wengrol*, the warrior demigod whose exploits and conquests made him the eternal paragon of dwarven masculinity.

Those words—so cold, so absolute—seemed almost unholy when spoken by one whose heart was as open and understanding as Therba's. And yet...they were holy writ, were they not? From his childhood—from his earliest memory—Bjalki had been taught that vengeance—the righting of wrongs, however slight, however long past—was a holy endeavor, a sanctified mandate. That was the only way that evil was quelled and wickedness punished. For every wrong, *someone* was responsible, and that someone must pay the price in order to restore and redeem the world. It was a given, like the passage of seasons or the strength of stone or the warmth of the sun. Some human gods and sages—the riven and reconciled Aemon, to name but one—taught that forgiveness and reconciliation were not just graceful practices or moral imperatives, but necessary for spiritual and mental health, the only way to strip evil and wrongdoing of their ultimate power over one's life. But most dwarves, even if pressed or engaged in a reasonable debate, could not truly embrace such thinking.

"I fear for our people," Bjalki said finally. "Our place in this world—the world of men—is precarious and risky. We are at their mercy if we do not guard and defend ourselves."

"True," Therba said.

"But must our dealings with men be so...hostile? So guarded and distrustful?"

"I've often asked myself that same question," Therba said, smiling thoughtfully. "I cannot number the times I've urged patience, understanding—even a pause for breath before action—and been ignored."

"Perhaps we're weak," Bjalki said.

"*Who* is weak?" Therba asked.

Bjalki studied her. There was a new light in her eyes now—inquisitive, guarded. *"We,"* he said, as though it were obvious. "You and I. Those like us. The peacemakers. We lack something that our kin have naturally, a combative instinct we must forever go in search of."

"Do you really think that's true?" Therba asked him, leaning forward.

"It must be," Bjalki said. "The scriptures say so. My family and clan always said so. Truth be told, I would not count my openheartedness as a deficiency, but...the world seems to. So I must find a way to be of service with the strengths I *do* possess—knowledge, discernment—and leave better dwarves to lead the way when action is called for."

Therba stared at him. As though urging him to offer more—to better justify himself. Taken by a sudden inspiration, Bjalki plunged on.

"Consider the *Book of Ormunda*," he said, indicating the great dusty pile of parchment and leather before him. "In those days war was endless. Our people suffered so much, they finally tried to put it all behind them. They put away their swords and their axes and their shields and they made a concerted effort to live in peace with the world. And what was their reward? Slaughtered by orcs. Enslaved by elves. Raided and robbed by men. Only Ormunda the Red saw how weak we'd become, how vulnerable. She showed our people the way—"

"She summoned demons from the Fires of the Forge Eternal," Therba said sharply, "and reanimated the dead with those unclean spirits. The blood those monsters spilt has stained the hands of our people for five thousand years."

"But they fulfilled their purpose," Bjalki countered. "They gave our people strength and resolve when they had none. And they enacted the worst punishments—the most terrible depredations—upon our enemies, so that, in the end, we did not have to."

"Do you think that absolved Ormunda?" Therba asked pointedly. "Savior or no, she blighted us. She damned herself. Do not lift her up as a hero, Bjalki. Even in her own tale, she is the villain."

Bjalki shook his head. "Perhaps," he said. "But she made a choice, and that choice saved our people, even if it ultimately damned her."

"Is that what Eldgrim wants?" Therba asked. "An army of *Kothrum*? Foul spirits to do his dirty work for him?" She uttered the old name for those demons of vengeance as though it were a curse just to speak it.

Bjalki said nothing.

Therba took a deep breath, sat back in her chair, then folded her hands in her lap. "I would urge you, Bjalki, to have more faith in yourself—and certainly to have more faith in me."

"Docent, I meant no disrespect," he said. "To call you weak—"

"To call yourself weak!" she said. "It was not the insult that hurt me, but your inability to trust your own heart above words recited by rote and traditions clung to without understanding."

Bjalki stared at her. The docent's words bordered on blasphemy. Trust one's own reason over the scriptures? Trust instinct over received wisdom? "I don't understand," he said, and he truly didn't.

"We are not weak when we ask questions, Bjalki. Nor when we feel compassion, nor when we strive to change things. It is in those moments that we are strongest, for we are pushing against forces set in motion before we ever took our first breath. Each thing has its season—its purpose. If we are endowed by the gods with reason, then that reason must be vital to some part of our existence. If we are blessed by the gods with compassion and understanding, then there must be times when they are not just puzzling eccentricities but cardinal virtues. Remember that Wengrol the Warrior is just *one* of the Givers of the Law, Bjalki—not alone, complete unto himself."

"Even believing so," Bjalki said, "how can I make them listen? I'm the youngest of the Clerical Council. I'm no one."

"Make them listen," Docent Therba said slowly. "They may not take your advice, but do not let them move forward without it. Your silence may be far more damning than your failure to conform to their expectations."

Bjalki shook his head again. He understood why she was arguing—pressing him to both better understand and challenge himself—but it still frustrated him. "Docent, even if I could make them listen, at this moment I know not what to tell them." He fell back in his chair and stared at the great many old books and scrolls arrayed before him—the history of the world through the eyes of his people. The stories were vast and various, some thrilling, some torturous, but all, seemingly, bent toward the same ultimate assurance.

"Tell me, then," Therba said. "Say it to me, just to hear it said."

Bjalki drew a deep breath. Sighed. Swallowed heavily, his throat dry as a creek bed in late summer.

"If the annals are to be believed," Bjalki said, unable to raise his eyes and face the docent, "then we are beasts, one and all. Men, dwarves, elves…we all believe we've left the savage primeval lands of our birth behind. That our gods have taken our hands and lifted us up, even above the others we share this world with. But we haven't ascended far. We still fight over piles of acorns, or a bit of scavenged flesh. The beasts of the primeval past still live in us, and no amount of tall towers or paved streets or finely wrought bric-a-brac seems to placate them."

Therba nodded. "Well said. If you see this—if you believe it—why, then, don't you say as much to the ethnarch when he asks for your advice?"

"Because," Bjalki answered, "though the beast often leads us into temptation, it can also save us when we're threatened or cornered. Who am I to say that now is the time for peace—for understanding—when the beast may be all that is called for? All that will save us?"

Now, hearing those words spoken aloud—speaking them himself, from his own sickened heart—Bjalki was overtaken by a terrible gloom. How long and deep were the oceans of history that they bobbed upon? How many men, dwarves, elves, and orcs had lived and died since the first stirrings? And in all that time, over all those untold eons and through all those uncounted generations—had any of them really improved? Did they fight any less? Succumb to greed with less frequency? Sow charity and compassion and concord instead of discord and hatred and fear and destruction?

It seemed there was no beating the beast. There was only feeding it, keeping it placated, until the time came to unleash it…

He felt Therba's hand on his. When had she bent forward and moved closer to him? How long had her warm, soft hand been resting there, on top of his own? He looked up into the docent's eyes and saw that she stared down at him with a great welling up of pity and understanding. She seemed to despair for him and believe in him all at once.

"At least," she said, "you are still asking questions. In that there is hope."

And then, without another word, she left him. Bjalki sat there, alone in the night-darkened library, for a long time, basking in the silence, contemplating his own restive doubts and fears.

CHAPTER TWELVE

Though Ondego had cleared them for a late arrival—providing they questioned the stonemasons on the way in—Rem and Torval somehow managed to stroll into the administrative chamber of the watchkeep more or less when they normally would have. Expecting the familiar bustle of the closing day shift, the routine grumbling and easy indolence of his fellows on the just-arriving night shift, Rem was most surprised to find the administrative chamber packed to the gills—day- and nightshifters alike—and uncomfortably quiet.

"Wengrol's beard," Torval muttered, "Who died?"

Rem could only shrug. They wended their way through the crowd, searching for one of their closer compatriots to glean some sense of what was unfolding, what everyone was waiting for. In moments they stumbled upon Djubal and Klutch, the partners haunting the desk at the corner of the room that Rem and Torval normally favored as their perch for nightly briefings.

"What's all this?" Rem asked, casting about for an open bit of desk or an empty chair and finding neither.

"Everyone was told to gather and wait," Klutch whispered. "Both shifts. The prefects are still in the office, talking."

"Talking to who?" Torval asked. "About what?"

"Visitors," Djubal said, and nodded toward Ondego's office.

Rem was at a bad angle to see anything clearly through the prefect's open door, but he could just make out a pair of figures milling about in there under Ondego's watchful eye. One was a short, stocky man whose outfit offered a glint of chain mail and a length of crimson-gold-and-black surcoat. The other was massive—nearly a head taller than Rem, and far wider at the shoulders—with skin as smooth and dark as Djubal's own. Rem felt his breath catch. He looked to Djubal and Klutch.

"The city guard," Rem breathed. A moment later he added, "And is that Black Mal?"

Torval nodded, having lifted himself up on his tiptoes to try to get a gander.

"The same," the dwarf said. "And, between you and me, lad, seeing both our wardwatch commander *and* a city guardsman here, in our watchkeep, bodes not well."

Rem had known that instinctively, if not explicitly. As the wardwatch was tasked with keeping order in the streets, the city guard's jurisdiction was the periphery of the city: the gates, the walls and guard towers, the outlying townships and settle-ments that existed under the protection of the Free Republic of Yenara. Rem had seldom interacted with the city guard during his six months in Yenara, speaking to them mostly as he passed in or out of the city gates. But he'd come to recognize—first by instinct, then through the embittered grumblings of his peers on the watch—that a deep and poisonous rivalry existed between every wardwatch in the city and the city guard. Some of it was, no doubt, related to funding and image. The city guardsmen, acting as the closest thing the city had to a standing army, were justly proud—even a little arrogant—about their stature and their impressive customs-funded armor and uni-forms. They received better weaponry and more frequent and rigorous training, operated under a more strict system of command, and naturally drew a greater modicum of respect from casual passersby.

The wardwatch, by contrast, seemed—to the uninitiated—a rather haphazard force composed of all sorts of men, women, elves, dwarves, and ne'er-do-wells, whose professional training could best be described as "hasty" (or simply nonexistent) and whose only uniform consisted of stinking old leather cuirasses that had probably been old and worm-nibbled even before Rem's grandfather was born. To everyday citizens the city guard were knights in armor, shining protectors of the city, the wardwatch just a bunch of smelly, coin-grubbing roughnecks with whistles and sticks. Unless they were needed to bash a burglar or run down a sneak thief—then, miraculously, their disreputable trade and shabby appearance were gentled, if only temporarily, in the public's collective eye.

Never mind that many on the city guard only used their positions as stepping stones to seats on the Grand Council or a stake in a trade delegation. Further discount the ample evidence that city guards bearing witness to crimes unfolding anywhere but right beneath their gatehouses tended to ignore those crimes altogether, usually citing jurisdiction as the reason for their failure to act. No, in the minds and hearts of the people of Yenara, the city guard were resplendent guardians of law and order, swaddled in the city's own proud colors, while the wardwatch were just a bunch of overpaid leg-breakers, probably in the pockets of merchants and thief princes, as prone to rob you as to come to your aid.

So the presence of Torquin, captain of the city guard—for all intents and purposes no friend of the wardwatch—boded not well. That and the presence of Black Mal—the watch's own chief magistrate and commander, who lorded over all the watchwardens of the city—made it clear that something terrible was afoot. Something bound to make all their lives a little more difficult for the foreseeable future.

The six officers now emerged and strode along the edge of the chamber to the middle of the far wall. Hirk kept his eyes down, while Ondego looked like an embarrassed father preparing to watch his children get punished by his liege lord. Torala and her second stood apart, forced to bear witness to the censure about to come, but apparently not implicated in it. Captain Torquin stood, hands clasped behind him, looking down his long, rosacea-swollen nose at everyone in the room. Towering Black Mal scanned the crowd with his one good eye (the left—his right being clouded by a cataract of some sort) and frowned so darkly Rem thought he might spit at them in the next moment.

"I trust these men need no introduction," Ondego said to everyone present. "They'll speak their piece, then be on their way. Hold your questions for after, when it's just the lot of us."

As Ondego stepped back, Black Mal stepped forward. "It is my understanding," he said, voice deep as a mountain chasm, "that there was a riot in the Warrens yesterday afternoon. Some said it was a protest gone awry. Others just an argument that escalated. Whatever its cause, there were injuries—possibly deaths, though we can't seem to get any verification of that."

Rem thought of the elegies being sung at that very moment in the Stonemasons' Guildhall.

Mal threw a sour glare at Ondego, then turned to the room once more. "Your job—collectively—is to keep the people of your ward safe. You see violence, you stop it. You see bloodshed, you end it. You see trouble, you answer it. You cannot handle it, you call for help. You hear that call, you answer. I understand there were watchwardens present yesterday, but that they were unequal to containing what spilled through those streets."

Rem felt a strange flush come over him, making his face hot and his palms sweaty. It was embarrassment. He recalled how he had stood there and watched as things went insane, how all he'd done was blow his whistle and run—completely failing to join the fight, to enter the fray—all because he was more concerned about fleeing with Indilen than keeping the streets of his city safe. He was not exactly sorry . . . yet still, he felt that he'd failed somehow.

"This was not a brawl got out of hand in some winesink," Black Mal continued. "People bled—hundreds. Goods were ruined. Fortunes lost. Businesses wrecked beyond repair. That's not just on the ones who answered the call and couldn't gain control of the situation. It is also on every one of you who *heard* those whistles and did not answer. Or who heard those whistles and failed to blow your own, to spread the call far and wide. And I have not even broached the subject of last night's fire, have I? A fire set right under our noses, when dozens of you were probably wandering on patrol just a street or two away." His voice had risen, its thunder filling the chamber, making Rem feel—probably making them all feel—like a scolded, misbehaving child.

Mal pressed on. "Any failure of law and order in this ward is a failure for you—*the lot of you*. And, by association, *my* failure. And I do not countenance failure."

"He really doesn't," Klutch whispered to Rem. "You should hear some of the stories."

Rem nodded, hoping Klutch would shut up. The last thing he wanted was to be seen whispering while the chief magistrate addressed them.

"So," Black Mal continued, "in light of what a spectacular

clusterfuck you humps made of your own ward over the previous day and night, let me offer a little motivation. Hearing of what's unfolded, the Council of Patriarchs sent Captain Torquin here to speak with me. He has been authorized, at any time, per his own discretion, to deploy his city guardsmen into these streets and maintain order if he thinks my watchwardens—all of you—cannot."

Captain Torquin sneered—quite smugly, Rem thought. Was the man really so eager to send his men into the streets? Or was he just delighted that the wardwatch were covered in mud and humiliated, making his own pack of colorfully liveried ruffians look shinier and more noble by comparison?

"Effective immediately, any failure on the part of this wardwatch to maintain order will be seen as a failure of the entire wardwatch system, and Torquin's boys in their pretty little surcoats *will* step in. Do I need to remind any of you how much the thought of others doing our jobs for us chaps my pimpled ass?"

A few murmurs in answer. *No, sir. Of course not, sir.*

"Do I need to remind any of you," Black Mal barreled on, "that this is one of life's most basic lessons: if you fail to uphold your vows and promises, there is always someone else ready to uphold them for you, and to snatch your pay purse in the bargain?"

More voices now. *No, sir.*

"Then do not fail me again," Black Mal said. He nodded toward Ondego. "Do not fail your prefect again. And do not fail the people of this city again. Am I understood?"

Understood, they all said.

"Fine. We are done here."

Away he went, Torquin marching out in his wake like a conquering hero. Rem was quite amazed at how long the relative silence endured after their departure, as though everyone wanted to be absolutely sure that the sounds of their bootheels moving through the front vestibule and the creak and thud of the front door were heard, that the coast was clear. Finally Ondego stepped forward.

"I'm doing the talking because the shift about to start is mine," Ondego said, eyes sweeping over all those crowded into the room. "But you dayshifters better listen up, because I'm talking to you, too, with Prefect Torala's gracious permission."

The lady prefect nodded her assent. Ondego carried on.

"What you just witnessed was no small thing. Black Mal never comes down here, and no one can remember the last time anyone suggested the wardwatch needed the city guard to do its work for it—"

"Complete shite," one of the dayshifters suddenly spat. Rem recognized the man—hangdog face, icy blue eyes, receding hair—but could not recall his name. "That mess in the Warrens just caught us off guard. It's never happened before and won't happen again—"

"Shut it," Prefect Torala snapped. "Ondego wasn't finished."

"But it's not fair," the man countered.

Prefect Torala took a single step forward and tilted her chin upward. It was the smallest, simplest of gestures, but it worked. Under the weight of her glare, the dayshifter fell silent and raised his hands in surrender.

Ondego resumed. "Leave *fair* for the little ones," he said. "It's our job to hold it all together. If it falls apart, we are the ones to blame—regardless of what's fair."

"Do we know what started it?" someone asked.

Ondego seemed to search the room for a moment. When he found Rem and Torval, over in their far corner, both doing their best to feign invisibility, he speared them with an inquisitive glare, then carried on. "We're working on that," he said, and Rem felt the weight of his prefect's unspoken expectations. "Regardless, Black Mal's order stands: from here on, we maintain the peace. If we fail, it could be the end of us—of our jobs, anyway."

Murmurs and whispered curses circled the room. Rem looked to Torval, Djubal, and Klutch—far more experienced than he, and so better able to put things into perspective. The dark glances shared by the three of them gave Rem no comfort.

"Get out there and earn your andies. See anything or hear anything that may shed light on all this? Come to Hirk or me, no hesitation. Savvy?"

Everyone agreed.

Ondego nodded. "Very well, then. Eyes open, fists clenched, backs to the wall. Now fuck off."

As everyone started to disperse, Ondego and Hirk made for the office. Ondego shouted over his shoulder, without even looking in their direction, "Torval and the Bonny Prince! In my office!"

Djubal and Klutch looked to Rem, faces wearing comedic masks of dread and delight, respectively. Rem rolled his eyes at their theatrics, even as they assailed him.

"Punishments await!" Klutch said, sounding far too happy about it.

"So young, so inexperienced," Djubal said. "A shame he didn't know any better. What are you staring at, Torval?"

"Trying to decide which one of you looks more like my *sluuk*."

Djubal and Klutch burst out laughing, both delighted at the insult.

"You can both go rutting with bugbears," Rem said, shaking his head and making for the prefect's office.

Ondego barely let Rem and Torval make it through the door. "What have you got for me?"

"More codswallop of the sort just witnessed," Torval grumbled.

"I must say," Hirk chimed in from the corner of the room, "I thought it quite kind of them to actually warn us that they're angling to do our jobs for us, instead of just showing up and telling us to sod off."

"Elaborate," Ondego said, ignoring his second's comment. "First, the dwarves."

"Belligerent," Torval said.

"To put it mildly," Rem added.

"That so?" Ondego asked.

Torval nodded. "Eldgrim threatened to put his own house guards in the streets, on patrol, if we couldn't keep his people safe."

"Honus Almighty," Ondego sighed.

"He means it, too," Torval added. "I wouldn't test him on it."

"We were already talking about setting up a swing shift," Hirk offered. "Midday to midnight or some such."

"What good will that do?" Rem asked.

"We increase our presence in the Warrens," Ondego said. "We also provide armed escorts for the dwarves working at the temple site. Get them to and from work safely until we've unraveled all these knots."

"But that's just spreading us thinner," Torval said.

Ondego shook his head and leaned forward, over his desk. "The Grand Council's already cleared us to hire more. Pull back in some retirees. Grab a few trustworthy bouncers and bodyguards who know how we work. We can cover it. The important thing is that the people of the Fifth—especially that gods-damned Eldgrim—see more of us, and know we're watching. What about the stonemasons?"

"Just as bad," Rem said. "Apparently they were holding an all-night vigil for one of their own. A young man. They say he got lost in the Warrens and ended up beaten bloody by a band of angry dwarves."

"Beaten bloody," Ondego repeated. "Now dead."

"So they say," Torval said. "We've no reason to disbelieve them."

"They were hostile to our inquiries," Rem said. "And they made it clear that the whole neighborhood owed them and supported them. All but challenged us to come back in force, to see what would happen."

"Then maybe we should do just that," Hirk said.

"The fuck we should," Ondego snapped. "Aemon's bones, what a rotting shambles. What's your take on them? Dirty? Guilty?"

Rem looked to Torval. He felt unequal to making a judgment on that front. Torval's pinched expression suggested the same.

"It would make the most sense," Rem said, "but that still doesn't make it true. We can't go raiding guildhalls and throwing working men in prison, just based on hunches and inference."

"The Bonny Prince is right," Torval added. "You know I'm keen to bust heads, same as anyone hereabouts, Ondego... but it feels too soon, based on too little."

Ondego nodded. "And yet," he said, "what happens next when someone steps on dwarvish toes? Or butchers some unlucky dwarf who crosses their path? Blood for blood and all that nasty business. Would you haul them in then?"

Torval shrugged. "Maybe."

"Maybe it ends here," Rem said. "The dwarves are on guard, and now these stonemasons know we're onto them. If it *was* them, they'd be wise to stop now, before things get even worse."

Ondego offered a strange expression: an almost-smile that struck Rem as profoundly sad. "Ever the optimist," he said, mordant gaze pinning Rem where he stood. "Tell me, Bonny Prince, you've been here six months now; how much wisdom do you see enacted on those streets every night?"

The only answer, the honest answer, was one Rem didn't care to utter.

CHAPTER THIRTEEN

It was nigh on the wolf's hour, past midnight but still a span before first light, when Valaric's brothers in the guild ran out of songs to sing. They'd already been through "Reconciled and Renewed," "Beyond the River," "In the Maker's Hands," and "Any Port in a Storm." A few of the men had tried to start serenades based on lesser-known hymns or the work of obscure bards, but no one knew those words, and so no one could join in. Schorr sang a few lovely lines as a soloist—he was a husky man, thick and tall and, to any casual passerby, a giant and an oaf—but when he sang he became the mouthpiece of angels. The men liked to hear him, and so, when he would begin a song that no one knew, they would not join in, but they would not stop him, either. In those moments Valaric could feel the palpable grief in the room, the sense of wrongness, of choked-off possibility. Grendan was too young to be dead; it was a plain, simple fact.

When the men grieved, Valaric grieved with them.

But it was in between, in the moments when their anguish gave way to frustration or restlessness, that made him far more uneasy. It was as if someone intermittently stoked the collective fires of their resolve, or whispered wicked words in their various ears. Cups were tossed and broken. Harsh words spewed like venom from the jaws of a spitting snake.

"Someone should make them pay," Valaric heard more than once.

"Bloody half men," Foelker said, during one communal winter of discontent. "What are they doing in our city, anyway? Haven't they got mountains to live beneath? Their own bloody homelands to cultivate and defend?" He was Hrissif's brother—as amiable and untroubling as Hrissif was crafty and dubious. Valaric had never known Foelker to be hateful or aggressive, in any fashion, but he was a good weather vane for the moods of the rest. If something came out of his mouth, it was probably because he'd heard the same words spoken, repeatedly, by those around him.

"The reconciled Aemon shan't let this pass," one older man whispered to his apprentice-age son—the boy a well-known friend of Grendan's, nigh inconsolable since his companion's death. "There shall be justice, lad," the father assured his boy. "That's a fact. Bank on it."

Valaric needed to be away from it all, if only for a moment. Perhaps he should go to the stores and fetch up another cask of ale. The strong stuff, so as to calm them all and urge them to sleep. True, the whole point of their vigil was to avoid just that, but they hadn't stopped drinking, had they? And, truth be told, he had no words left to calm them. His last, best hope to keep them from whipping themselves into a frenzy was to slowly, surely anaesthetize them with drink. So what if they all passed out before morning? At least that would keep them from taking their rage into the streets.

It wasn't a long walk to the dwarven quarter, after all. Not for angry men.

Valaric rose and crossed the room, heading for the back corridor that led to the kitchens and pantry stores. Just as he rounded the corner, leaving the common room behind him, someone started to sing "Weeding the Garden."

Valaric froze where he stood, out of sight, but still capable of hearing the words as the men sung them. "Weeding the Garden" was an old crusader's shanty about the primacy of mankind beside the inhuman otherness of all the other sentient races of the world. It was a marching song from the plague years, and its jaunty tune, well timed for a company of marching men, belied the bitter, hateful nature of its words. Almost every man of Valaric's grandfather's or father's generation knew the song, but Valaric had always half hoped it would die out among the men of his generation, and especially among those younger. Apparently it had not. Hearing it bellowed forth now, strong and vibrant, in the midst of their mourning, gave him no pleasure.

How did we come to this? he wondered. *When we went down there, to the dwarven quarter, it was just to make our cause known. To treat with the people. To be heard. We meant no harm.*

But we did *harm, didn't we?*

Hrissif, did, anyway. Rabble-rousing fool.

But Hrissif didn't beat Grendan, did he? Didn't crush his hands and break his bones and leave him gasping for breath and dying. Maybe we started a bit of a row, but is that any excuse for what happened to the boy? What was the true cost of the upset we caused? A few broken pots? Some torn awnings? Ruffled feathers and shattered windows? Material damage hardly equaled cruelty and murder, did it?

Did it?

Moment by moment, verse by verse, "Weeding the Garden" grew louder. With each repeated chorus, Valaric felt a terrible dread, like a poisonous vine, slowly climbing up the wall of his soul, spreading to engulf his heart, his lungs, his bones, his very being. They were so lost...so angry. What could he do to draw them back? *Could* he draw them back, before someone did something foolish and got themselves hurt?

"You're not singing," someone said beside him. Valaric turned, suddenly ashamed and abashed, like a boy caught in some unnatural act by his mother. It was Hrissif, the smirking fool still holding that damned cup of his—eternally half-full—and staring at Valaric with a bemused disdain that made Valaric want to tear the man limb from limb.

Internecine fighting of that sort would be pointless, though—and disrespectful to boot—so Valaric resisted the urge. He simply let his eyes settle back on the dregs of ale in his own cup. Silently he prayed for Hrissif to leave him be. His deputy steward moved closer anyway. They were all alone in the cramped, dark little corridor.

"This is when they need you the most," Hrissif whispered. "You're their leader, after all. Lead them."

"Lead them to what?" Valaric hissed in answer. He did not want the men to hear the two of them talking like this. "We are grieving, Hrissif. This is a vigil. There is nothing to lead them to 'til dawn, when our vigil's done. Then every man can lead himself to his bed."

Hrissif's smirk widened. He leaned in. It was a conspiratorial gesture—one that suggested a close kinship between the two of them, making Valaric uncomfortable.

"This vigil is for their sadness," he said. "But what about their rage?"

"What about it?" Valaric asked.

"Don't be coy," Hrissif said. "You know exactly what I'm talking about. They want justice. Do you think the wardwatch will give it to them?"

"Won't they?" Valaric asked, but he already knew the

answer to that. He'd said as much, hadn't he, when those two watchwardens had come around earlier?

"Valaric," Hrissif said, and the slow, measured tone of his voice grated on Valaric more than any of Hrissif's snorts or asides or insults ever did. "We have been wronged. These men . . . our entire guild . . . every man, woman, and child of human birth in Yenara. We lost one of our own to the rancor of aliens—outsiders—and we know the authorities will not avenge that boy's death. Should we let that stand? Should we not seek our own justice?"

"We cannot," Valaric said. "We're stonemasons, Hrissif, not assassins or mercenaries."

"The only difference between a civilian and a soldier," Hrissif said, "is a cause."

"Stop it," Valaric said, perhaps too loudly. The men sang on. He hoped they had not heard him. Nonetheless, he could not let Hrissif's provocations go unchallenged.

He tried to continue, forcing himself to remain calm. "That sort of vengeance carries a price, Hrissif. Forgive me if I wager these men and their families are not equal to paying it."

"You underestimate them," Hrissif said. "They set a fire readily enough, didn't they?"

Something snapped in Valaric. He knocked Hrissif's cup away, then snatched his deputy's tunic in both fists and slammed the wiry bastard into the wall.

"You and your brother, you mean," Valaric said. "And don't think I don't hold you fully responsible, even if he was beside you! Foelker wouldn't swat a fly unless you told him to, but we all know that when you give orders, he follows them. Don't try to convince me that half the guild crept in there with you last night and started that fire."

"You'd be surprised at how much help I had," Hrissif said.

"Shut your mouth," Valaric hissed. "This—all of this—it was you. You started it all. And now it falls to me—to the rest of us—to try to clean it up."

"I started nothing," Hrissif said, chancing a little smile. "We voted, remember? All but a minority favored a public demonstration, and you honored their wishes."

"A *demonstration*," Valaric said, "not a riot."

"I broke some baked clay," Hrissif said with a little shrug. "And what did they answer with? Cold-blooded murder! Grendan was just a boy, not seventeen—"

Valaric slammed Hrissif against the plaster wall again. "Those men trust us to lead them," he said through gritted teeth. "To guide them. We help them make good decisions— *honorable* decisions. What we touched off in the Warrens—that was not honorable!"

"Wasn't it?" Hrissif asked, one corner of his mouth curling now. "What else should we have done, eh? Those bloody pick-monkeys snatching our work—and our wages—right out from under us?"

"We all bid on that contract, and they won it, fair and square."

"Fair?" Hrissif sneered. "What's fair, Valaric? They're not human. They barely sleep. They work an eighteen-hour day without a pause. They keep no holy days and see no honor in leisure, and so they can work all six days of the week. They were built to dig and burrow and scrape in the earth beneath our feet—what patron among all the gods of the Panoply made them our equals? Entitled to our labor, our wages, in our own gods-damned city? I promise you, if that had been an Aemonist temple and not one of those bloody god-choked Panoplist dens, the winds would have blown in our favor."

"Stop it," Valaric said. "You're turning a labor dispute into a holy war, and I won't have it."

"Won't have it?" Hrissif asked. "Last time I checked, master steward, you were elected to your position, not appointed by the reconciled Aemon himself. If you're so squeamish about protecting the interests of these men, maybe I should move for a special election before the end of your appointed time?"

Valaric slammed Hrissif into the wall again. Hrissif's skull clopped hollowly off the plaster wall and he cursed in pain.

Out in the common room, the song had not ended. It was louder than ever. It sounded as if every man had joined in—not a tongue idle, not a voice silent.

As the men launched into a last, rousing rendition of the chorus, Hrissif smiled at Valaric. "Hear that?" he asked. "Sounds like holy war to me. And I didn't even get them singing."

Valaric stared at his second and listened to the song his men sang in the next room. It stole all the fire from him. Slowly Valaric set Hrissif loose and stepped away. Hrissif propped himself upright against the wall and shook his head, clearing his scrambled senses. Glaring at Valaric, the smaller man straightened his tunic and flattened his ruffled hair.

The song finally ended. The men cheered, whistled, and applauded, unified in both their grief and their fervor for justice.

"We go back a long way," Hrissif said to Valaric. "I've known you since you were an apprentice."

"And I you," Valaric said.

"For the life of me," Hrissif said, "I never would have expected the man I'd come to admire and follow as a leader to prove himself such a coward. Such a bloody *politician*." He sneered that last word as though it were a curse, the vilest of insults.

"Blind violence isn't the way," Valaric said. "You're smart

enough to know that. Anything we do that makes us look like mere brutes."

Brutes, like the sort that would corner a frightened young man fleeing a riot. Brutes that mangled the boy's face with their own stout fists. Brutes that crushed his hands with their stone-hammers. Brutes that answered violence against things with violence against flesh . . .

"Anything that we do," Hrissif countered, "to stake our claim and protect our laborers, we do as men, for men, and for all mankind. Those bloody tonkers in the Warrens have been living and breeding here long enough. Time they knew whose city this was and what comes of crossing true men, men of strength and honor."

Valaric was about to tell Hrissif that he was a fool—that there was no strength in wanton violence, no honor in letting his rage run wild—but Hrissif walked away before he could do so. Why did he feel so weak all of a sudden? So weary and aimless?

From the common room he heard his deputy address all gathered. "Let's drink to Grendan!" the deputy steward shouted. The men replied with, "Hear, hear!" When Valaric stepped back into the doorway and surveyed the room, their cups and mugs were still raised. All drank, their draughts long and deep.

Hrissif raised his cup again. "Now let's drink to the lot of us," he said, moving through the room. "Let's drink to our honor, that we might not soil it. To our courage, that we might not lose it. And to justice, that we might see it done, though all the world seems indifferent to our suffering."

Hear, hear, again. Everyone drank.

Valaric knew he should say something, but he could not bring himself to do so. Why was that? Was it fear? Indifference? Weariness?

There was something white hot and painful at the very

center of him. Something that left a bitter taste on his tongue and made his fists shake where they lay flat against the knotty tabletop.

What was its name?

Maybe we were wrong to go there, he thought. *Wrong to speak against them, wrong to break their bloody pots and their peddlers' stalls. Wrong to run riot through their streets.*

But they killed Grendan. They drew blood. We cannot abide that, can we?

"When do we hit them, then?"

A number of voices chimed in accord. *That's right*, they said. *When? How? We should! We must!*

"No, no, no," Hrissif said, but Valaric could hear the tone of disingenuous placation in his voice, the sense that his words were a game, meant to drive the men onward, not stop them in their tracks. "No, that won't do. We're stonemasons, lads—not assassins or mercenaries."

Groans and curses answered that statement. Hrissif threw a sideward glance at Valaric where he still sat. *See? They'll have none of your passivity. Your determination to forgive and forget.*

From across the room someone suddenly shouted, "I say we take to the streets right now—at this very moment—lay hands on the first dwarf we see, and make them pay!"

Cries of assent. Cheers. Cups clacked and goblets clinked.

"I say we go right to the dwarven temple," a young man said. "Leave some choice words on their walls, a pailful of shit on their altars, and anything that'll burn in flames!"

More cheers. More rage.

Valaric realized now why he could not name the feeling that stirred inside him. It was new to him, rarely encountered in everyday life, and even then usually chased away or suppressed as soon as he was aware of it. It coiled in his belly like a cold serpent, made his body tremble and shake, and turned his usually ordered thoughts into a cacophonic jumble within him. He could feel his own pulse in his temples. His hands shook as though he were caught in a blizzard.

Rage. The very same feeling that his men felt at the moment. It had infected him all the while he'd been trying to deny its presence. But now, hearing their words, imagining just what sort of damage they could do to the dwarves and their sacred spaces if they set their minds to it . . . it all made Valaric drunk. More drunk, more intoxicated, than all the beer he'd been drinking through the night. He did not care for the feeling—hated it, in fact—but there was a delicious sort of comfort in accepting its presence, of stewing in it, bathing in it, and letting its venomous poison soak him all the way to the bone.

We could simply scare the dwarves, he thought. *Humble them. Let them see what happens when they cross us. I swear, Holy Aemon, I swear upon poor dead Grendan, I'll not let my men hurt anyone, nor draw a drop of blood.*

But those dwarves should know fear. That Valaric could deliver, gladly.

"What say we line the city walls with dwarven heads on pikes?" someone suggested. The cheers were deafening for that one.

"What say we take their women?" another countered, the excitement clear in his voice. "Seed each and every one 'til they'll only spit out half-breeds! See how those tonker bastards like a new generation a head taller than they!"

"NO!"

Everyone fell silent.

For a moment Valaric wondered who had spoken—who had shut them up with a single short word. Then he realized it had been he. He stepped back into the room.

"No," he said again. "I'll hear no more of this."

The men murmured.

Hrissif watched, waited.

"If we're to strike terror into their hearts and yet protect our-selves," Valaric said, "we must be more cunning than this. More subtle. There can be no random beatings. No rape. No haphaz-ard desecration of their monuments. Whatever we do, hence-forth, must be done *deliberately*—with forethought, intent, and dedication. Nothing less will do."

Valaric looked to Hrissif. *Is this what you wanted?* he almost asked. *Is this the complicity you sought, you snake? Well, I see which way the wind blows. I hear their lamentations and their curses. These men are primed for action. I'll be damned if I let you be the one to lead them.*

If I can't stop them, I'll aim them.

And I always hit my target.

"We shall strike," Valaric said loudly. The men cheered. "We shall strike, and they shall bleed. We shall make our voices heard, and our words will move them to tears and shrivel their hearts with bitterness and loss. We'll show them—*we'll show them all*—that Yenara is a city of men! Built *by* men! *For* men!"

The roar in answer filled the great room. The men sounded as if they'd just seen the greatest joust of their lives, the most stunning reversal in a tournament melee. They shook their fists and cheered and drank and threw their arms round one another and made merry. To see them in such a state made Valaric's heart leap.

CHAPTER FOURTEEN

It was strange for Rem to be in the streets, working a shift, while the sun still hung in the sky. Strange, also, to be rooted to a particular spot, guarding a prescribed location, instead of patrolling the streets. Stranger still was the chance to take in a Yenaran sunset while on duty, even on what promised to be a cold, wintery night. Such were the myriad glories, Rem supposed, of what Ondego called a "swing shift"—midday to midnight.

Not so glorious were the circumstances. Rem and Torval had learned of their sudden shift change just as they'd finished their sundown-to-sunrise shift that very morning.

"Go home and sleep," Hirk had said when they returned to the watchkeep, the rising sun barely peeking over the eastern walls of the city outside. "We need you back by midday."

"You're joking," Rem said.

"Bollocks," Torval spat in disbelief.

Ondego appeared then, looking glum as always. "He's neither joking nor engaging in any commerce whatsoever with anyone's bollocks."

"So what, then?" Torval asked.

"I've decided we need a swing shift to bolster our presence on the streets during the high-traffic hours, and you two are on it."

"Cack," Rem muttered.

"I know it's a steaming heap of horseshit," the prefect said, sounding almost contrite, "but I need some of my best on this, and you two pillocky twats are that."

Only Ondego could compliment them and berate them in the same instant. The man was a masterly motivator.

"You can both still take the following day off," he continued, "but if I'm to grant you that, I need you two on this shift first. Understood?"

Rem and Torval had answered with nods and terse grunts.

"Sod off, then," the prefect said. "Get some sleep. Report at midday to the Panoply temple site. Queydon will be the warden in charge on the scene, and she'll give you your orders."

"The temple?" Torval asked. "What are we to do there?"

"Security for your kinfolk," Ondego said. "Including armed escort back to the Warrens when their shifts are done. Now get scarce, the both of you. Don't make me tell you again."

Rem had done as ordered and hurried home to sleep—or tried. In truth the combined excitement of hurrying home, cursing the day of Ondego's birth, and lamenting his poor luck in being one of the prefect's "favorites" had gotten his blood up and made real rest close to impossible. He dozed a bit but ended up reporting for his new midday shift almost as tired as if he hadn't slept at all.

He found many of his fellows of the Fifth on duty when he arrived, making up a loose, meandering cordon around the work site, separating the laboring dwarves from the milling public that streamed around the square. Rem found Queydon among his comrades, and the elf posted him at the far western end of the temple complex near one of the stairways that descended into the square from that plaza balcony he'd found Torval standing at a few days earlier. Before sending him off to his post, she bade him arm himself from a selection of staves, maces, and mauls piled nearby.

"I've got my sword," Rem said.

"Orders from Ondego," Queydon responded. "Blunt instruments only. If there's trouble, he wants arrests, not corpses."

Shrugging, Rem bent over the gathered weapons, chose a lightweight maul not unlike the one Torval always carried, then hurried off to his begin his shift.

It occurred to Rem that Tavarix might be about. As he skirted the edge of the construction site, he idly studied the dwarves he passed, all bent to their separate labors or bustling off on orders from their team leaders. There were bearded males, whiskered females, and an ample number of young apprentices and assistants—Tav's peers, Rem supposed—all focused, engaged and hardworking. Already a great deal of the wreckage from the fire had been cleared away, while still more was in the process of being gathered and discarded. Wherever walls still stood and the detritus had been hauled off, nests of new scaffolding rose and were being added to by the moment. Everywhere activity and industry. To be honest, Rem felt weary just watching them.

Or was that merely sleep deprivation?

Trudging on, Rem found Tav planted among a gaggle of young dwarven apprentices, all doing hammer-and-chisel work on great sanded blocks. As each boy and girl bent to their labor, tap-tap-tapping with mechanical regularity, their young, dust-covered faces masks of intense concentration, a pair of older master masons drifted among them. These two proctors hovered at the youngsters' elbows or loomed over their shoulders, offering casual praise when they were impressed, giving stern correction when disappointed. Rem stood for a time, watching Tavarix and hoping he might raise his eyes from his work so that Rem could wave to him. But it never happened; the boy was too deeply engaged in his work. Satisfied that he'd found him, Rem took up his post and began a slow, steady perambulation of the area, idly wondering when Torval would arrive to join him. Though tired and cold, he tried his best to enjoy the change of routine, to soak up the sunlight, and to appreciate the riotous colors of the sunset when it finally arrived.

As darkness fell, the workers lit torches and lamps around the work site and carried on with their labors. Teams stopped in orderly turns to quaff some ale and wolf down some coarse brown bread or nibble at a wedge of cheese before scurrying back to work again. They kept to their labors—slow, steady, uninterrupted—even as darkness engulfed the city around them and the air bit so sharply that Rem wished he could rush up to one of the torch stations that provided the workers with light and soak up the radiant heat.

It was shortly after sundown that he was finally approached by Torval. The dwarf carried with him two tin tankards with hinged lids, each trailing steam into the bitterly cold night air.

"And where in the sundry hells have you been?" Rem asked. "I've been out here alone, all afternoon long, thinking you were home in bed."

"Hardly," Torval said. He handed one of the tankards to Rem and bade him drink. "Queydon just posted me at the far end, that's all. I've been here just as long as you have."

Torval then explained that Osma had prepared the warmed spiced cider in the tankards and delivered them herself to the work site. Having something warm to drink as the night's chill dug its fingers into him made Rem feel like a king among paupers. He wrapped his benumbed hands around the piping hot tankard, thumbed back the little lid, and took tentative sips, desperate for the warmth, but in no hurry to burn his tongue.

The cider was the stuff of dreams—sweet and tart and spicy and hot enough to warm him through. It took all his self-control to keep from guzzling it all in one long draught.

"Gods, that's welcome," Rem said after a few sips. "You tell Osma she can send me an extra cup anytime."

Torval managed a crooked little smile. "She's a good lass, that sister of mine. Anything to report?"

Rem shook his head. He gestured with his tankard toward the dwarves at their labors. "Just what you see. They've been bent to it since I got here. I saw Tav, though."

Torval said nothing to that.

Rem carried on. "Frankly," he said, "I'm amazed they've accomplished so much in just a day or two. They really are hard workers, aren't they?"

Torval glanced at his kinfolk scurrying and swaggering among the half-built temple and its wreckage, hundreds of individuals, all engaged in distinct labors, but making progress collectively, as one. He gave a noncommittal grunt.

Rem knew what that grunt meant. Torval was still ambivalent about this assignment—protecting his people, being forced to work with them and treat with them and respect them, even though not a one of them would do the same for him in return. Even if the dwarf did think his laboring countrymen were hard workers and skilled laborers, he probably wouldn't deign to say so aloud. He'd spare not a word for them if that word was kind or gracious. Rem wished it could be some other way, but he knew it could not. Torval was many things—a great many of them surprising—but when he decided that he bore someone or something a grudge, that antipathy persisted...perhaps not white hot yet, but always there, pulsing in the darkness like a bed of embers just waiting to be stoked.

Are you so different, really? Rem thought. *You faked your own death and fled almost five hundred miles from the land of your birth! Could a person offer their kin any greater insult?*

Mine is a totally different circumstance! Rem reminded himself. *I didn't leave the whole human race behind.*

But Torval... These are his people. How must that feel, to hate them so? To feel so despised in return?

"You know," Rem said, "some people in this world are slow to change. Some institutions even slower. But that change always starts when one honorable individual stands before that group and says, 'We cannot go on the way we have. Times change, and so we must. Let's do it together.'"

"What are you gabbling about?" Torval asked.

"I'm gabbling about you, you bloody fool," Rem shot back. "You can't go through your whole life hating the very thing you're a part of, whether you like it or not."

"So," Torval said, "I should treat with them? And try to reason my way back into their good graces?"

Rem shrugged. "What'll it hurt?"

Torval snorted. "Cack," he said. "You're a dreamer, lad. It's your best quality and your worst."

Rem considered arguing his point further, but it seemed a useless distraction. Did he want to get into it all now? Out here? In the cold? On the job?

So instead of pressing the issue, he merely raised his tankard. "Fine, then. I'll say no more about it. To friends?"

Torval tapped his tankard against Rem's. "Friends," the dwarf said. "Now I'd better get back to my post. Keep warm, Bonny Prince."

The end of the dwarves' workday was announced a few hours later by a thunderous iron bell hung at the edge of the work site. The steady knells reverberated across the square and seemed to go quavering into the night, as deep and dirgelike as the hourly bells rung at the great temple of Aemon.

As the dwarven work teams reordered their workstations, secured their materials, and began amassing on the north side of the temple for their homeward march, Rem answered the call of his fellow watchwardens and happily rushed from his post to muster for the security escort. The lot of them—Rem, Torval, and all of those chosen by Ondego for the dubious honor of this special assignment—gathered along Shriver's Street in loose formation. Once they were there, Queydon undertook a silent head count to make sure all were present and accounted for. To Rem's great relief, Torval stood beside him in muster. It felt good to be reunited again after spending most of their shift apart. Rem hadn't anticipated how strange it would feel to be on duty and not have his partner beside him.

Pathetic, Rem thought. *A few hours separated during a shift and already I'm missing the little bastard.*

Queydon indicated a point in their line, midway through. "Separate here," she said. "Everyone to the right, take the south side of the street. To the left, the north. Demijon?"

The robust watchwarden stepped out of his place in line. "Sergeant?"

"You will accompany me, at the fore. Rhys and Sliviwit?"

The two watchwardens stepped forward.

"You shall bring up the rear," the elf said. "To the rest of you," Queydon said, speaking in her normal silky monotone, making no attempt to raise her voice but somehow, miraculously, being heard by all of them, "your columns will defend the dwarven ranks. Space yourselves appropriately and make sure none of our charges wander outside the cordon we make. Understood?"

The dwarven masons were gathered in a long, loose column

now. Rem did not take the time to count them, but he guessed there had to be almost a hundred, some hauling big leather bags or wooden crates full of tools, the senior members of the guild wearing leather aprons. Tav and the young apprentices— perhaps two dozen of them—were embedded behind the half-way mark of the column, with a large number of senior masons leading them and a smaller number trailing behind. Slowly but surely a balding, white-bearded dwarf steward moved down the line, checking the faces of his charges as he said their names, taking roll from memory. When he reached the front of the column and was satisfied, he turned to Queydon and hooked his thumbs in his apron belt.

"All accounted for," the old dwarf mason said. "Carry on, good watchwarden."

Queydon gave a curt nod and raised her fists to indicate that the watchwardens should form up. Rem, Torval, and the rest fell into their lines on either side of the dwarven column. To Rem's relief he and Torval were some distance forward from the group Tavarix was part of. Perhaps, Rem reasoned, Torval could better concentrate on their work if he knew his son was safe, yet was not marching right beside him. Their formation finally set, Queydon turned swiftly on her heels and set off at a steady march, Demijon trudging along at her side. The dwarven column trailed behind her, paced by its watchwarden escorts.

Torval strode about ten paces ahead of Rem, his eyes forward. As they left the open square, the streets and houses, taverns and tenements along Shriver's Street seemed to huddle in around them, leering and looming as the snaking column passed. From forward in the line, a dwarf began to sing. It was clearly a working song, given its steady rhythm and its call-and-response lyrical pattern, but Rem had no clue what it was all about, for it was all sung in the native language of the *Hallirwelk*. But no matter. The cadence was the thing, and after a block or so, it asserted itself over his step. Thereafter, almost unconsciously, Rem found himself stepping in time with the dwarven laborers, sometimes even humming the melody when the mood suited him.

As they traveled, passersby on the street were alternately charmed and perturbed by the sight and the sound of them. Some would stop and clap or stomp along, smiling broadly before carrying on about their business. Others hung out of their apartment windows or haunted low doorways, cursing the dwarves as they paraded by, urging them to shut their bloody mouths and take their short little legs back to the place that had borne them. More than once Rem heard a call of *pickmonkey* or *tonker*. It was a credit to the marching dwarves that, so far as Rem could see, they never once broke ranks or tried to engage with all those taunting strangers.

Rem noted that Torval kept his own pace ahead, occasionally glancing at his countrymen, scowling at them, even— usually at those moments when their song was most exuberant.

Rem turned to walk backward for a moment, curious and eager to check on Tav, farther back in the line. He could not see him—just the loose press of smaller dwarven bodies where all the apprentices were gathered. Only a little satisfied, Rem turned forward again and resumed his steady gait.

Ahead the column bent, heading eastward on a more direct path toward the Warrens. As their train snaked around that bend, Rem noted something out of the ordinary. All of a sudden there were no passersby. This section of the ward—made up of narrower lanes than that which came before, hemmed in closely on either side by taller, seedier buildings—seemed entirely deserted, quite unusual for this part of the ward. Rem picked out lamplight in every third or fourth window, espied moving shadows, even heard voices, some raised in argument, some laughing over a suppertime joke—but no one seemed to be out on the street, or even drawn by curiosity or the noise of their passage.

For some reason that made Rem uneasy. Could a usually busy boulevard such as this really be wholly empty, even after dark on a winter's night? Where were the drunks haunting tavern doorways? Where were the stoop-shouldered men and women shuffling home from a long day's work?

A dread rose in Rem. He turned to look behind them. Staring back, he noted that the end of the train and the two watchwardens bringing up the rear guard had just turned the shallow corner that marked their exit from Shriver's Street onto whatever narrow lane they now traversed. Looking forward and back, Rem could see the whole train stretched out along the length of the street in a long, straight line.

Off to Rem's right there came a great, thumping clamor. As he searched the gloomy little lane for some sign of the noise's source, he caught shadows moving on a rooftop off to his right. Then the missiles rained down: a storm of blunt, heavy objects falling upon the watchwardens and dwarves beneath those shadows on the far side of the street.

Someone cried out. A dwarf fell out of the line, groaning. Others shouted or screamed. The column halted, its aft end crashing into its fore and creating a swirling, unmoving mass of bodies in the middle of the crowded street. As the dwarves and watchwardens scurried for cover and tried to retreat, Rem realized what it was that rained down on them from that rooftop.

Stones. Bricks. Broken masonry. Anything heavy, jagged, and sharp. They seemed to come tumbling down by the bucketful, not thrown but simply dumped. With almost every round of attack, someone would grunt and topple into the cold mud. The dwarves who had no room to retreat simply fell to their knees and covered their hairy heads, cursing as the stones rained down and pummeled them.

"Ambush!" Demijon shouted from the front of the line.

Then Rem felt an intruder in his mind, a strange, alien presence—Queydon—eschewing subtlety entirely in favor of instant, unfettered communication. A single word—

Everywhere.

Then—

Coming.

Rem looked to Torval. His partner, ten paces away, was already yanking his maul from his belt and turning outward to face their oncoming foes. Torval threw a glance back at Rem.

"Stop gawping, boy!" he shouted. "They're coming!"

Rem got a good grip on his borrowed maul and scanned the darkness between buildings, every shadowed doorway and alley.

"Where are they?" he shouted.

Then more rumbling from above. Before Rem could react, he heard Torval's heavy boots pounding the mud. A second later the dwarf collided with him and they went sprawling in the cold, churned mud of the street. In the next instant, stones and bricks rained down from above, just a breath behind where they'd landed. Instinctively the two curled up and covered their heads, in no hurry to be brained by falling rock.

Their ambushers had both sides of the street. Basic combat strategy suggested that after you'd pummeled your opponent with long-range missile attacks and gotten them squatting in their trenches, you should follow up with—

Queydon's words bloomed in Rem's brain, a searing scream that made him wince.

Contact, vanguard.

Torval scurried to his feet, searching the gloomy world around them for some sign of where the attack would come from. Rem followed suit, eyes darting everywhere, breath starting to catch in his throat.

A chorus of war cries—high and savage—split the quiet night. From where he lay on the ground, Rem saw the whole line of dwarves and wardwatch escorts at the fore of the column buckle and slide backward. Steel rang off steel. Wood thumped flesh. Somewhere a bone cracked like a pine knot exploding in a fire.

Voices, shouting, and cursing. Iron and steel clanging like handbells. Many of the dwarves in the line were regrouping after their initial panic, snatching up whatever tool was at hand—a hammer, a chisel, a supping knife—and readying themselves to meet their attackers.

Rem, terrified that their edge of the column would have to withstand its own enemy onslaught at any moment, frantically turned and searched the dwarven line for some sign of Tavarix. He had to make sure the boy was safe in all this chaos—

"North side of the street!" Torval suddenly shouted. "Coming fast!"

Rem spun in answer. Out of a number of alleyways before and beside them, men charged to meet them. They all wore masks of roughly of the same design: simple, almost featureless, only the chin of the attacker left uncovered and exposed, all seemingly made of bleached leather. They wielded hammers, mauls, maces, bludgeons, truncheons, even twirling chains and wooden staves or clubs—but thankfully, not a blade or battle-ax among them. But those were all the impressions Rem could glean. In the next instant their attackers were upon them, barreling right into the flank of the column with ferocity and abandon.

Rem had to defend himself from a falling bludgeon that looked like a sawed-off broom handle. He traded several blows with the broom handle's wielder before managing to disarm the man and send him reeling, bent double, into the mud. A few feet away, Torval charged right into the oncoming horde, maul in one hand, lidded tin tankard in the other. To Rem's great astonishment, Torval was using the tankard as a weapon, blocking blows and swinging its broad side into would-be attackers. Gods, but that dwarf could defend himself with just about anything!

Rem found his own position more precarious. There were too many attackers, and the quarters too close, to truly go to work with his blade. Their enemies seemed to prefer speed and surprise over direct engagement. And so Rem found himself on guard against an onslaught of haphazard swipes and strikes from a dozen adversaries as they rushed by and plunged into the column itself, but no one bothered to stop and enter into a battle to the end with him. Every time he ducked or parried or narrowly avoided one attack, he'd be subject to another.

Hit and run, then, Rem thought amid the chaos, *like forest brigands. Not precisely sporting, but effective.*

Rem took more blows than a half-drunk boxer, got blood in his eyes from a glancing wound to his brow, then lost his breath to an unexpected gut blow that came in from his undefended right. As he tried to right himself, something hard and heavy slammed into his temple, filling his vision with a roiling darkness awash with exploding stars. As his vision swam and his ears rang, he was violently shoved into the mud, face-first.

Rem thrashed in the mud, eager to get his feet under him and avoid being bludgeoned while still sprawling. Somehow he scurried forward, made the brick wall of a nearby tenement, and turned there to survey the scene. He felt safer with his back to the wall, facing outward, but he desperately needed a moment to prepare himself before entering the fray again.

The whole street was choked with chaos and violence, the skirmish stretching from one end to the other. Despite their ill-fitting homespun tunics or cloaks, their cheap masks, and their battered and improvised weapons, the bandits seemed to be winning the battle, having managed to catch the watchwardens and their charges wholly off guard.

Torval went charging by, shouting something. He was backtracking toward the rear of the line. His maul was his only weapon now.

Aemon's tears—Tavarix!

Rem launched himself off the wall and went running after his charging partner. Torval was making straight for a knot of masked attackers that had surrounded a band of dwarven masters and apprentices. A stout dwarf maid with a wispy braided beard seemed to be the primary defender of that little group, hammers in both hands, sliding left and right to defend the youngsters anytime those brigands got too close. Some of the apprentices were cowering and crying, others stood their ground, wielding their mason's tools or any stout piece of wood at hand. Tav was one of the latter.

Torval plunged into the fray, knocking one attacker out cold with a swipe of his maul, then jabbing another in the gut with the maul's grip end. Four more of the masked villains turned their attention on Torval and swarmed him. Rem saw the dwarf's maul cast down quickly—knocked from his hand by an unlucky blow—but that didn't discourage Torval in the least. In the next instant the dwarf's fists were flying, and his hithertoeager attackers began to slowly retreat.

Rem charged a pair on the outskirts of the band, attacking with his own maul but finding his first few raging, sloppy blows parried and thrown aside by the men he'd engaged. Just as he fell back to prepare for another attack—this one more sensible, more focused—whistles began to shriek up and down the line.

For a moment Rem thought they were watchwarden whistles—the sort that they all carried to call for aid—but then he realized the pitch was too high, too shrill. As the whistles sounded up and down the street, their attackers disengaged and fled, all leaving one adversary or another flat in the mud or reeling from a last vicious blow before dashing for the safe shadows of the nearest alleyway. Rem's own adversaries slowly backed off, then ran for a nearby side street. When he turned to see how Torval fared, Rem saw the dwarf's own opponents all scurrying off as well. Two of them hauled an unconscious third between them.

Torval no longer cared about them, though. His only concern was Tavarix. Rem was warmed to see Torval with his son now, questioning him, searching him for signs of injury. Tavarix, clearly in shock, just kept nodding in answer to all of Torval's questions, withdrawing a little every time his father stepped closer.

Rem turned from the scene to survey the street. Tav and Torval were safe. No more worries there. Now, as for the rest of them...

Rem tried to catch his breath, to study the scene. All around him the sounds had changed. There were no more war cries or curses or shouts, no more ringing steel or thumping hickory. There was only the sound of wounded watchwardens and dwarves, groaning and bleeding in the street. Someone coughed. Someone else hawked and spat. A voice rose above the groaning and cried for a surgeon—someone was bleeding badly, unable to move.

Queydon's consciousness suddenly invaded Rem's fevered brain. *Remeck?*

Safe, he thought, and she receded, satisfied.

Torval appeared beside him. The dwarf's chest expanded and contracted like a bellows, gulping air desperately. He was splattered with a great deal of mud, a few stray splatters of blood, and a sheen of fresh sweat. Rem assumed he himself probably looked much the same. For a long time the two partners just stood there, side by side, surveying the damage.

"Who do you think they were?" Rem asked between breaths.

"Fools," Torval answered. "Trying to start a war."

CHAPTER FIFTEEN

Whistles blew. Runners ran. A nearby barber-surgeon and an innkeeping widow, both claiming experience with combat wounds, arrived on the scene to assist. In short order the critically wounded—those in need of immediate transport to the Houses of Healing—were separated from those in need of less acute care. Soon enough they had a tally of their casualties.

They'd begun the night with twenty watchwardens and sixty-eight dwarves. Four watchwardens and seven dwarves were critically injured, likely to survive, but only if they could be treated at once, possibly even if they were attended by true magic-wielding healers. Four dwarves and two watchwardens were unconscious, still breathing, but unresponsive to all attempts to rouse them. That group—all seventeen of them—were hurriedly gathered on improvised litters and hauled away for treatment by physicians and mages.

Of the seventy-one remaining, most walking wounded or wholly untouched, about half required some sort of stitching, bandaging, or binding. Rem had suffered a nasty blow to the head, but the widow innkeeper checked his eyes and his balance and pronounced him only superficially injured.

"Bell rung," she said, "but not cracked." She assured him that he'd likely sport a nasty bruise, maybe even suffer headaches for a day or two, but she thought it unlikely that his skull was fractured or his brain in danger of swelling. Assuming that the woman had, in her time, probably seen enough skull-cracked men and ejected enough of them from her public house to know what a potentially dangerous head wound looked like—and how the victim of one behaved—Rem took her at her word.

Rem found Torval sitting on a stone horse trough in front of a now-crowded tavern just a stone's throw from where the ambush had unfolded. Gawkers choked the tavern's doorway, appraising the damage, whispering among themselves. Torval, Rem noted, was doing a fine job of ignoring them. Even after Rem sat down beside him, the dwarf continued to stare into the middle distance, stoic and silent. Now that the mud and blood had been cleaned off him, it was apparent that Torval had numerous scrapes and bruises of his own, though most probably looked worse than they actually were. A short, deep cut along his temple had been stitched, while one elbow and both hands were bandaged entirely. Pink seepage through the bandages round Torval's hands indicated that his knuckles were bleeding.

Rem sat beside Torval on the horse trough. Most of the critically wounded had been helped away now. More watchwardens of the Fifth were on the scene, having answered the whistles and the runners sent to fetch help. Ondego picked a meandering path among the stunned and injured in the street, taking stock of how much damage had been done, while many of the lately arrived watchwardens interrogated the ambush victims—including their fellow watchwardens—and several others scoured the surrounding streets and alleyways for physical evidence.

"What do you think?" Rem asked Torval. "Was it them?"

"Them?" Torval asked, raising his head.

"The stonemasons," Rem said.

Torval grunted and shrugged. "Likely, I suppose."

Torval raised his eyes. He took in the surrounding roof-tops, the myriad dark alleyways radiating from the street they currently lingered in. "That attack was swift and sure. Hardly sophisticated, but that didn't matter. They hit fast, they hit hard, then they scurried away. I'm ashamed I couldn't bring one down."

Rem shook his head. "Don't beat yourself up, old stump. They knew we'd be a match for them if they really tried to stand and fight. Their only hope was to surprise us, make mince of us while we were still trying to get our heads straight, then flee the minute we did."

Ondego approached them. Just a moment ago, Rem had seen him having a discussion with two lower-ranking watchwardens, examining something they'd discovered. Now, approaching, Rem saw that the prefect carried something in his right hand. When he was just a stone's throw from them, he tossed it to Torval. The dwarf caught it.

It was one of the masks. Now that Rem could see one up close, free of the frantic demands of the moment of attack, he was satisfied that his first impression had been more or less complete. The mask was simple, largely smooth, made of boiled leather with inked tracing. It was a three-quarter sort, large enough to cover the forehead, the eyes, and the nose, but would leave the lower jaw exposed. Rem knew he'd seen something similar before, but he couldn't seem to recall just where.

"Recognize it?" Ondego asked.

"Well enough," Torval said, "since a whole slew of them just attacked us."

"I meant the style," Ondego said. "Do you know what sort of mask that is?"

"It looks familiar," Rem said. "But I can't place it..."

"Come now, Bonny Prince," Ondego chided, "certainly such a handsome historical artifact should jog your memory?"

Rem still winced every time he heard Ondego use that teasing nickname.

"If it were fancier or possessed of more flourish," Rem said after studying the mask, "I'd say it was from a mummer's wardrobe. Or maybe the sort of thing made for a rich house's masquerade ball."

"Not quite," Ondego said. "Two thousand years ago, during this land's darkest age, Lord Marshal Zabayus—"

"The statue on Zabayus's Square?" Torval interjected.

"The same," Ondego said, then resumed his tale. "Lord Marshal Zabayus, imperial governor of the province that Yenara stood as the capital city of, found his lands beset by reavers from Kosterland, horsemen from the steppe, orcs from the wilds, belligerent elves from the forests, and dwarves from the mountains—not to mention rival principalities from the four points. Everyone was at war with everyone in those days. The lord marshal's request for legionary support from the imperial seat was refused—they weren't having a much better time of it than he was."

"Where does the mask come in, then?" Torval asked impatiently.

"I'm getting to that," Ondego snapped. "Shut your sauce box. So... Zabayus realized that he was on his own, and that if he was going to mount a concerted defense against both human and inhuman enemies, he'd have to better organize his forces. He formed a militia, impressing every man between sixteen and sixty in the city and from the countryside surrounding, and he drilled them hard, day and night, until he could sift the martial chaff from the wheat.

"The story goes that the merely competent formed the core of the first homegrown Yenaran legion—a new beast, unaffiliated with the Horunic empire—while the best of the best, his strongest, smartest, fiercest warriors, were organized into an elite unit known as the Sons of Edath."

"Edath?" Rem asked. "The first man, from the *Scrolls of Derivation*?"

Ondego wobbled his head and offered mock applause. "At last the Bonny Prince recalls his ecclesiastical instruction! Took you bloody long enough, you plank."

"I don't get it," Torval said. "What has the first man from a bloody holy book got to do with Lord Marshal Zabayus or his elite soldiers, or that mask, even?"

"Visit the library," Ondego said, holding up the mask now. "Ask to see some of the old scrolls and their attendant illustrations. In every image of Zabayus and his elite troops, you'll see those soldiers wearing these masks, or something like them. Membership in that coterie and the sign of the mask bears such pride among old Yenaran families that most of them have these cheap replicas made for every newborn male in the family, if there's any reasonable way they can claim descent from one of those troopers."

"People and their bloody traditions," Torval muttered. "As if it matters twopence who your bloody grandmother or grandfather was…"

Rem broke in, finally dredging up a great block of text from the *Scrolls*. "'Then did the Maker traverse the garden of His Making,'" he recited. "'Thereupon he saw every beast and bird, every mite and every serpent of the sea.'"

"What a lovely singing voice he must have," Ondego quipped.

"Wait," Rem said. "I'm getting to the important bit. 'The

dragons were wanton and cruel, the elves indolent and deca-
dent. The dwarves grew trifling, consumed by greed, while the
orcs were as shallow as ponds, yet turbulent as seas. "Shall I rid
the earth of these, and let the beasts inherit all that I intended
for my awakened kith...or is there, I wonder, some way yet to
humble these knaves and arrest their excesses?"'"

"Get to the bloody point," Torval said.

Rem looked to Ondego, as if for approval to continue.

Ondego nodded. "Carry on. You're almost there."

"'And in that moment,'" Rem continued, "'the Maker conceived of humankind: as wise and wondering as elves, as tough
and industrious as dwarves, and strong, courageous rovers like
the orcs. Though their bodies were slight and trim, the Maker
ignited in their breasts the fire of dragons, and with it, mastery
over the world.

"'And the Maker said to the man and woman as he awakened them, "Though I made this world for those that came
before, now I say to you, this is your inheritance, your kingdom, your domain."'" Rem paused so that those words could
sink in. Torval's grim stare indicated that at last, he understood.
Rem carried on, slowly now to emphasize what followed for
all of them. "'"Where they bow to you, make friends of them;
where they ask of you, 'Whence came you?' point to my throne
and urge their swift return; but where they challenge you, my
children, my beloved, humble them with fire and sword."

"'And the man He named Edath, and the woman was
Yfrain.'"

"Wonderful," Ondego said drolly. "I've got chills."

"But I'm right, aren't I?" Rem asked. "These masks—
they're the mark of elite soldiers whose whole calling was to
protect mankind from all that was *not* mankind."

"Exactly right," Ondego said, nodding.

"'Where they challenge you,'" Torval quoted softly, "'humble them with fire and sword.' And the pillars shook..."

"Now do you see what we're dealing with?" Ondego asked.

"Dwarf killers," Torval said.

"Worse," Rem added. "Zealots."

Ondego stared at the mask in his hands. After a moment's contemplation he drew a deep breath and turned to leave them. "Watch your backs, boys..."

He left them in silence. Neither had words of comfort for the other.

The men celebrated, whooping and hollering, toasting with their frothy mugs while the fires of the hearth were stoked and their disguises were collected and hidden away. Valaric could not lie to himself; a deep and abiding part of his heart was moved by the sight. He loved the sounds of their laughter, their brotherhood, their exultation. He loved watching the men, all smiling and laughing from their full bellies, bending in close to tell tales of their violent confrontations with their enemies or hugging one another, slapping one another on the back. This sort of joy—this sense of absolute fraternity and oneness—had been unknown in the guildhall for some time, banished by worries about coin, negotiations with landlords for late rents and unpaid school tuitions, and normally robust wages undercut by unskilled—or nonhuman—workers. Seeing their joy return— a sense of carefree confidence and accomplishment—almost brought him to tears.

Never mind that it came from spilt blood and broken bones. Valaric didn't honestly think they'd killed anyone tonight— he'd certainly given orders to avoid any such blows, reminding the men, constantly, that their aim was simply to frighten the dwarves and humble them, not to murder them outright.

That was why all of their weapons had been the blunt sorts: bludgeons, mauls, maces, many wrapped in straw and burlap to soften their blows. All that their foray that evening needed to impart to their enemies was this: they were being watched, they were never safe, and if the fury of the men of Yenara was roused, they would be punished.

Valaric, having spent long enough watching the celebrations from a far corner of the room, finally decided to move among the men. He tapped the nearest keg and refilled his mug, then meandered off to hear their tales, to see the wonder and energy on their faces up close.

"Did you see that gaping little knuckle dragger I downed?" Keelix, one of the younger masons, said to a coterie of companions, all eager to hear the tale. "He came right at me— howling, like a goddamned ape!"

"Oh, he thought he had me," said one of the older men, Hobb, growling to his own private audience in a far corner. He was bald, clean shaven, his round ears standing out from his head. "But I made quick work of that waddling pickmonkey. Knock knock, right on his bloody skull!"

Valaric sipped his ale. A group of men just a few spans away raised their cups to salute him as he passed. He smiled to thank them. Another group leapt from their perches, chairs and stools overturning, and crowded around him, throwing their arms around his big shoulders, slopping their ale and mead all over him.

"There he is!" they cried. "There's our headman! Our fearless general!"

"The lord marshal of the Fifth Ward!" someone shouted.

"All hail the lord marshal!"

Valaric tried to silence them, but they could not hear his petitions to calm themselves, to stop singing his praises and raising him above the rest of them. He was no general...no lord marshal...no great man at all. He just wanted his brothers in trade to feel the old pride again, the old joy. Once being a stonemason in Yenara had meant something. They were celebrated and respected, both as craftsmen and as good members of the community. What had happened? Where had they lost that sense of service, that sense of purpose?

"The lord marshal!" someone else cried, far across the room. The whole great chamber of the guildhall exploded into cheers, and cups were held high. Before Valaric could say a word, the cheer became a chant.

"The Sons," they said, "the Sons! The Sons of Edath! The Sons! The Sons! The Sons of Edath!"

Then a new voice, splitting through the rest, loud and sure and crisp. Valaric turned and saw a lithe figure climbing onto one of the trestle tables, rising above the fray to address the men. It was Hrissif, smiling broadly as ever. Try as he might, Valaric was too moved and mirthful to let his mood darken at the sight of the man.

"That's what we can do, lads," Hrissif said as the men all quieted, little by little. "That's what stonemasons can do when they're mobilized! Barely fifty men, as mighty as an ancient legion!"

The men cheered and quaffed.

"And there's the man who's responsible!" Hrissif shouted, pointing at Valaric. "There's our good, strong leader! The leader we've always wanted and dreamt of! Smart! Savvy! Swift and secretive!"

The men cheered and quaffed again. By Aemon, weren't they out of ale yet? Valaric's warmth and good cheer were wearing off. All of this adulation was making him quite uncomfortable.

"And this is only the beginning!" Hrissif said, as though all that might follow was more barrels of ale, some mummers in motley, and a troupe of dancing girls. "We made those tonker bastards bleed tonight, and we were *barely* prepared. What will we do when we've taken greater pains to plan? To strike right at their coal-black little hearts?"

The men did not cheer that time—they did something worse. They nodded, quietly, approvingly. Solemn glances were exchanged. Cups were quietly clinked and dregs sipped off.

Step in, Valaric thought. *Step in and take charge of this before Hrissif steals it from you. If this is to work—if this is to strengthen you without corrupting you—it must be managed, controlled, every step of the way.*

But why should I? another part of him asked. *Why should I fight it any longer? We did the right thing. The joy of my men proves it. So long as our enemies bleed and we celebrate, all is right with the world, isn't it?*

Perhaps I've misjudged Hrissif. Perhaps he's been right all along . . .

Hrissif leapt down off the table he stood upon and started moving through the crowd. "We have the advantage, don't we? We know every alleyway, every shadow, every chimney and foundation. We have our shrouds, we have our fists and our weapons, and we have our mandate."

The men were all rumbling in agreement now, their passion gradually gathering force again. Hrissif had them in the palm of his hand.

"We struck at them right in the street, when they thought they were safe, and we made them bleed!" Hrissif roared. "What can we not do, having done *that*?"

"But the wardwatch!" someone shouted. "They were guarding them! They'll be ready for us next time! Armed to the teeth, most like!"

"Perish the thought," Hrissif said, turning and taking in

all the men with his challenging carnival barker's gaze. "We will not simply repeat ourselves, lads. We'll strike elsewhere next time... where they least expect it. No, our next sortie will be no hit-and-run on a bunch of tired day laborers marching home with a police escort. Next time we'll hit them where they live!"

More cheers. Fists clenched, raised, and shaking in fury. All eyes were turning to Valaric now, and Valaric did not like the feeling. As they all turned their gazes toward him, they seemed to be asking, *Where shall you next take us, good sir? Where shall the lord marshal next rally his troops? Where shall we next spill blood?*

It was that passion—that purpose—that he was desperate to harness. To control and direct. He could use those energies to good purpose, he knew, if he could but hold tight to the reins and get the horses galloping in the right direction.

Valaric tried to come up with some words to calm them, but all that leapt into his mind was an image. A single image. A target that he knew—that all of them would know—could make those dwarves tremble in their oversize boots if only they could leave their mark upon it.

And that's what came out of his mouth when he spoke. Not an admonition to calm themselves. Not soothing words to banish hatred and bitterness from their hearts. Not an alternative to Hrissif's belligerence. Only an object for their enmity.

CHAPTER SIXTEEN

"...And that's all I know," Rem said, completing his summary to Indilen of Torval's recent trials, with both the dwarven court and Tavarix. "It's my sincere hope that Tav's present tonight, and that things have been smoothed over a bit between them." The night air was cold and hard as glass. Every time Rem glanced over and saw Indilen's marten-lined cloak, he felt an urge to climb inside it. His watch-issued greatcoat seemed painfully inadequate tonight.

"It's awful," Indilen said, shaking her head slowly. "Such a proud, unbending folk. Still, parents and children do quarrel sometimes. I'm sure they'll come to some accord."

Rem nodded silently. He'd had more than enough years living under the yoke of his own hard-hearted, proud, and unbending father to know how such enmity between those who should love and support one another could poison one's outlook, not to mention one's sense of self. It was realizing that there could be no accord—no meaningful compromise—that had sent Rem into exile.

For a moment—the briefest of moments—that fleeting thought of his home and why he'd left it filled Rem with an overwhelming desire to finally reveal everything to her. To finally lay down the burden of the unknown, the unspoken, that he'd been carrying about with him. In the same instant, something equally strong held him back.

"So," Rem said, eager to change the subject. "This should be quite the experience. I've never been to a Fhryst feast before, but I take it as a great honor. And Torval specifically indicated that I should invite you—"

Indilen shot him a sideward glance that had become all too familiar. "Am I to assume," she said, "that bringing me along was not your first inclination?"

"You know full well that's not true," Rem countered. She was teasing him, and she wasn't. Rem had learned, the hard way, that Indilen was meticulous in matters of language and self-expression. Perhaps it was just a side effect of her chosen vocation—secretary, notary, copyist, and illuminator—but she seemed to delight in twisting his words against him and making him second-guess everything he said. She usually offered those sly, half-joking criticisms with that same sideward glance, suggesting to him that it was all in fun, but he sensed something deeper in it. It was as if she wanted him to gain greater control of his words, and by extension greater control of his thoughts—as though mastering each in relation to the other could somehow smooth his rough edges and shore up some of his insecurities.

He closed his mouth and hid his embarrassment behind a wry smile. As if to comfort him, to assure him that it was all in good fun, Indilen moved closer to him, locked her arm in his, and laid her head on his shoulder. They walked that way for a time, Rem loving the feel of her beside him. Her fur-lined cloak warmed her, and when she walked so closely beside him, she warmed him just as surely. That warmth seemed to radiate through him, and he thought he felt his heart beating just a little faster. All at once he wished he could ignore Torval's summons and take Indilen somewhere else—somewhere warm and clean, with a fire and some good honeyed wine. Maybe even a soft, fresh bed...

"Forgive me," she said. "Sometimes I like teasing you too much."

"Oh," Rem said dumbly. "Well, of course—"

"Don't," she said. "I hurt your feelings. A little, at least. I saw it in your eyes."

He cocked his head so that it touched hers. "No blood, no scars. I'll live."

They turned, moving from a narrow lane to a wider, better-lit boulevard that snaked in broad, easy curves toward the banks of the Embrys. Torval's home was just ahead, about four or five more blocks.

Indilen reached up, laid one hand on his cheek, and gently turned his face toward hers. "You're the best man I know, Remeck. Here or anywhere. If I tease you, it's only because I love you."

But you don't know me, Rem thought. *Not the real me, the me I ran from.*

Or is this *the real me? Here? Now? Perhaps that other man—the one I left behind—perhaps he* was *the pretender . . .*

Rem was suddenly overcome with an inexorable urge—an impulse both terrifying in its finality and gratifying in its spontaneity. He stopped, right there in the middle of the cold, darkening street. There were others out and about, but they passed at a distance, seeming to take no notice of him and Indilen. He drew away from her so that he could stand and meet her gaze, face-to-face. She looked worried. He couldn't stand to see that look on her face after she had just so generously opened her heart to him.

"Now," Rem said, but the words he intended to follow that pronouncement failed to tumble out of him.

"Now what?" Indilen asked.

"I think now's the time," Rem said. "For that talk. For... secrets."

"Rem, we're expected," Indilen said. "And it's cold as the grave out here."

"I've waited too long," Rem said, determined to see this through. Was he really doing this? What had gotten into him?

"Stop it," Indilen said.

"What?" Rem asked.

"I understand, I do," she said. "But this is neither the time nor the place, love. Let's save our confessions for later?"

"I just," Rem stammered, then swallowed his clumsy words and then tried to start again. "I thought this was what you wanted."

"Of course I do," Indilen said, smiling and cupping his face in her hands. They were warm, having been protected in her fur-lined cloak all this time. "Rem, my love, we've set forth on this journey together. It's already begun. You need not rush to prove anything now. Just enjoy this evening with me."

"I'm sorry," he said, lowering his eyes. "It's just...the things I've seen over the past few days. The rage, the violence simmering under the mundane stillness we take for granted every day. The other day, in the Warrens, when we were separated, I was terrified—"

"As was I," Indilen agreed.

"Terrified that something would happen to you!" Rem quickly added. "I couldn't stomach it, Indilen. It would break me—especially if something so horrible happened and we hadn't cleared the air between us. If I hadn't told you the truth."

"What is it?" she pressed, her normal poise now seeming to slip a little. She was studying him closely, as she often did, but he could see by the narrowing of her eyes and the slight down-turn at the corners of her mouth that she didn't quite know what he was thinking at the moment. His combined impulsivity and inscrutability seemed to disturb her deeply.

"You think you know who I am—who I really am," Rem said, lowering his eyes. "But I've never told you. Not the way I should have."

"Why is it troubling you so? Now, of all nights?"

He shrugged. "Because I'm afraid. I'm afraid that you can't truly love me if you don't know who I really am."

Indilen reached up and laid one soft hand on Rem's cheek. "I know who you really are, Remeck of the Vale. I've borne witness to your true self, in action, from the first moment we met in that market. A kind young man. A brave young man. A lonely young man."

"Not so lonely," Rem said, managing a cockeyed smile. "Not since I've had you."

"Partially true, perhaps," Indilen said, "but that loneliness... it's still there. I've seen you look lonely and lost in a crowded tavern surrounded by all your friends at their most boisterous, and with me right beside you. It's like your mind is a draughty old castle on a high, bald hill, and even when you could be outside, supping and drinking and laughing and exploring, you still get lost wandering its halls."

He could only nod. She knew him well in that regard. He knew he could sometimes grow melancholy or turn inward, whether the moment demanded it or not. In a way it was a relief to know that his unbidden moments of introspection had not escaped her notice.

"I'm sorry," he mumbled.

She put her hand under his chin and raised his eyes to meet hers. "Don't be sorry, you fool. I said what I said and I meant it. *I love you.* I love you reckless. I love you chattering. I love you silent. I love you pensive and paralyzed." She leaned a little closer. "I also love you atop me, and underneath me. But mostly I love you beside me. And, most importantly, I love you no matter who you were before you came here...no matter what you left behind. Tell me all of it when you feel you must—for the time being, *I know who you are*. I see it every single day. And I hope you can say the same for me."

Rem took her hand in his. Her fingers were cold now, and he rubbed them between his own roughened hands to try to warm them. Then, standing there in the cold street, staring at Indilen in the warm, dim light of nearby post lamps, with a frosting of silver moon- and starlight crowning her auburn hair, Rem thought he could not have asked for, or found, a better, more perfect partner, lover, and friend. And how strange that he'd had to leave everything he knew behind and come to this teeming, overwhelming place, and brave a million possible paths and forked roads that would have kept her away from him forever, just to end up, by blind luck—or by ordained fate— meeting her among the Saturday market stalls.

He drew Indilen close and kissed her. The kiss lingered. He was fairly sure it warmed the both of them, from the inside out.

When the kiss broke, he stroked her hair and stared into her large, lambent brown eyes. "I love you," he said. Simple, declarative, truer than any words he had ever spoken.

"And I you," Indilen replied. "Now can we carry on? It's bloody cold out here."

Rem pulled her close, threw his arm around her shoulders, and ushered her on. Down the street they went, onward toward Torval's family lair, Rem feeling that some boundary had been passed, some milestone marked, and that, whatever happened next between him and Indilen, it would be happening to a different pair of people: partners, inseparable and bound by silent oath.

He was a lucky man. If there was any part of the Fhrysting feast dedicated to giving the gods thanks, he would be sure to offer his sincere and undying gratitude.

For a time Torval and family had rented a pair of rooms at the King's Ass. But those rooms being unsuited to long-term family habitation, Torval had gone searching for a new place to ensconce his family: a suite of three small bedrooms and a great room built above a dressmaker's shop, on the western edge of the Third Ward. Though the rooms themselves were low-ceilinged and cramped by human standards—which had, apparently, resulted in the landlord's inability to keep tenants—they were a perfect size for Torval and his family.

One of the reasons Rem loved to visit was that the external staircase that led up to the rooms faced southwest, and the building was positioned on a slight rise before the land naturally sloped down toward the river. One could mount that staircase and, before knocking at the door, turn and study the larger part of Yenara, laid out before him, stretching away to the north, west, and south. On clear, moonless nights, when there was no fog and all the lamplights of the city winked under a black and star-strewn sky, Rem thought Torval the luckiest of men, for who could not appreciate such a stunning and lovely view as that which greeted Torval every morning and every evening when he came and went?

To Rem's great delight, Indilen enjoyed the view as well. They had often taken the time, during their handful of shared visits to Torval's home, to stand there at the head of the stairs and drink the view in. Tonight was just such a night as they both prized for appreciating that vista: the moon was a thin crescent, the stars were bright pinpricks of light in the broad, black firmament of the cloudless sky, and there was, thankfully, not so much as a ribbon of fog upon the great, sprawling city before them. They lingered before knocking on Torval's door, arms around one another, enjoying the view.

"Funny," Rem said, suddenly in a thoughtful mood. "I've been here such a short time. It's so far from everything I've ever known—five times larger than the largest city I ever visited in the north. For two thousand years this place has been here, growing and rotting and rebuilding itself and transforming, completely separate from my knowing or my existence. And yet, after such a short time, it already feels like home."

"Not the home you came from," Indilen said. "The home you were meant for."

Rem smiled. "Just so," he said. "Strange thought, I know."

Indilen shook her head, smiling brightly in the dark. "Not at all," she said. "We're not always from the place where we belong."

She rose on her toes and kissed him. Behind them the door to the apartment opened with the creak of old, unoiled hinges. Their kiss broke, and they both turned to find Torval standing in the doorway, occupying most of its width but only about two-thirds of its height.

"I thought I heard bandits out here on my threshold," Torval said. "Shall you vacate the premises with only a warning, or must I be rough with you?"

Rem stepped away from Indilen. "Don't make me let her off the leash, old stump. She's a pretty thing, but she's got teeth and claws."

Indilen slapped him playfully, then stepped toward Torval. "And more brains than either of you. Good evening, master dwarf." She bent and kissed Torval's bald pate, and Rem thought he saw his partner flash a self-satisfied smile.

"You're most welcome in my home on this auspicious night, lass. Come inside, it's freezing out here."

Torval stepped inside to free the doorway, and Indilen moved past him. As Rem stepped forward, Torval blocked the door again.

"Hold, you," he said in mock sternness. "The lady's welcome, but you're a stranger hereabouts, and little do I like the look of you."

"Out of my way, old stump, or I'll make you bleed."

Torval stepped aside to let Rem step in. "In your dreams, Bonny Prince. In your dreams..."

CHAPTER SEVENTEEN

The hour was late when the Fhryst service adjourned, the remembrances sung, the scriptures recited, the prayers of thanksgiving and petition all offered and done. In the wake of the last pious petitioner's exit and the dismissal of the temple acolytes, Bjalki and his fellow clerics undertook the slow, steady business of ordering the altars, securing the sacraments, and closing the temple for the night. Afterward they could return to their quarters and sit down with the temple priestesses and acolytes for their own Fhryst feast and a private service.

Bjalki was glad of it. It had been a long, tiring day, and he craved the good food and easy atmosphere that a holiday feast would provide for him. He thought the others might feel the same, for even craggy old Hrothwar and perpetually distracted Haefred seemed intent on expediting their separate postservice labors and clearing the way for the feast to come as quickly as possible. True to her position as leader of all holy services, Therba had assigned their tasks. Hrothwar had been charged with seeing the doors shut and the temple torches all dowsed, leaving only the undying flame burning in the brazier upon the forward dais. Meanwhile Haefred organized the scrolls used in the service and saw them restored to their home shelves in their proper order. Having received the two simplest tasks, the old priests were both finished before Therba had completed her reorganization of the holy sacraments in their consecrated arks, or Bjalki had finished dousing each of the hundreds of lit and flickering prayer lamps that bedecked the temple pillars and outer walls.

Bjalki's was an arduous task, but he took a special pleasure in it. During services, petitioners might light these lamps as they arrived, saying a special, direct prayer as the flame of the taper ignited the lamp oil. Now that the service was done and the petitioners all departed, someone had to extinguish the flames, one by one, offering a prayer for the petitioner who had lit each. With the torches that lined the temple's outer walls already doused, and the prayer lamps fast following, the darkness closed in by inches around Bjalki, and he found himself more than a little enamored of it. He half wished he could stay here alone when the others had gone, to soak up the solemn silence and shadows and contemplate eternity—and his place in it—while staring at the undying flame.

He had just doused the last lamp on a particular pillar, leaving only a few in a pair of side niches still burning, when Docent Therba interrupted him.

"Go below," she said. "See to the shrines and lower sanctuaries. I'll snuff the last lamps."

He nodded and began to walk up the aisle. "Are Hrothwar and Haefred already gone?"

Therba, bustling back down the aisle toward the still-flickering lamps, nodded. "I dismissed them. Hurry now. We've a feast awaiting us."

Bjalki nodded and mounted the forward dais, before the altar and the sacramental arks. "As you wish, *khoyra*," Bjalki said, using an old, affectionate term that the common tongue might render as *revered speaker*. It was an affectation, addressing her so, but Bjalki hoped she heard the warmth in his voice and took it as the genuine show of respect and affection that it was.

He moved past the altar and its attendant sacraments, then rounded behind the great stone edifice to start a circuit of the quartet of doorways that led from the main worship space into the outer chapels. As Bjalki saw to his tasks—starting with sealing up the four lesser chapels dedicated to specific gods and accessed by worshippers and the clergy only for specific purposes—Therba moved about in the gathering gloom of the great sanctuary, praying softly to herself as she doused the last of the lamps.

Bjalki's movements were rote, instinctive. The lesser chapels were open to any and all during the day, or during services, but once services were done and the late bells rung, those chambers had to be locked, the treasures within protected through the night. He closed them often, and thus had adopted a routine, involving a sort of drumbeat rhythm in his head that corresponded to his actions: close, lock, test the door, pocket the key. As he went about that business, the younger priest found his conscious mind drifting elsewhere—to his wife and children, hundreds of miles away and several more miles below-ground, in the Ironwall Mountains. He had not kept a Fhryst meal with them in—How long was it now? Ten years? A short time in dwarven terms, perhaps, but still, to his lonely and tiring heart, a seeming eternity. He missed the joy of reciting the creation story, of lighting and then dousing the ceremonial candles, of watching as his daughters hung on his every word and spoke the ritual responses when prompted. And Wettelin's bread. No one baked better onion-barley bread than his wife.

He knew that the feast to come in the temple refectory would be a good one—the wine spiced, the beer frothy, the meats steaming, and the bread fresh from the ovens—but there always seemed to be less to love in a meal taken with the familiar strangers who constituted his family away from home here in Yenara, while his own true family was so far away. Perhaps, once the meal was done and everyone retired, Bjalki would stay up late and write a letter to his wife, his daughters, his youngest son. Even if they would not receive his missive for weeks, it would still do his heart good to be alone in his chambers and to think of them, to record words of love and support for them that he knew they would read.

As though he'd been sleepwalking, Bjalki realized that he had just completed his final task: closing and locking the gates to the lower shrines and sanctuaries. Though there was nothing of material value to steal down there—lower sanctuaries were the dens of austere, chthonic powers, meant to be neither comfortable nor welcoming—the clergy were still in the habit of locking the wooden door and the iron gate that led below.

His work done, Bjalki turned and mounted the steps that would take him from the lower staircase back up to the sanctuary level. Reaching the surface, he could tell that the last of the lamps had been doused by Docent Therba. The sanctuary was now so dark as to almost be tomb-like, the only light yet burning the undying flame in its ceremonial stone brazier near the altar. As Bjalki rounded the altar from the rear, he saw Therba waiting there, her back to the altar, staring out into the dark vastness of the sanctuary, as though she could see something lurking out there that the absence of light rendered all but invisible.

"Why do you linger, *khoyra*?" Bjalki asked as he approached. "The feast is waiting. We should—"

Therba raised a single hand: *Silence.* She said nothing. She did not move. Her eyes stared fixedly into the tenebrous shadows that stretched away beyond the altar and the dais. Bjalki let his eyes follow the line of Therba's gaze. As the night vision that his people were renowned for took over and brought the sanctuary and its contents into sharper relief against the shadows, Bjalki suddenly saw what had drawn the docent's attention.

They were not alone.

Scattered throughout the sanctuary—in the aisles, among the benches, guarding the doors—were a number of strangers. They were not dwarves, but tall folk, somber and silent, all wrapped in the dark, ashy cloaks of mourners and wearing strange, pale masks that hid their faces. Many carried clubs and bludgeons. A few bore buckets and pails, though Bjalki could not see what they contained. Their silence persisted. Whether they were waiting for Therba to speak or daring her to, Bjalki could not say.

"Who are you?" the docent finally asked. Her voice was hoarse, dry, two stones slowly rubbed together.

One of the men stepped forward. Even masked, he was most impressive—wide of shoulder, strong armed. "We are the ghosts of Fhrystings past," the masked man said, "come to show you the error of your ways."

Bjalki took a step forward and opened his mouth to speak— but Therba stopped him. She took a long stride that placed her right at the head of the dais steps. She addressed the intruders sternly, but without malice.

"If you speak of the Fhrysting, you know this night is sacred," she said.

"Sacred to you lot, aye," one of the other masked men answered. He stood just a little forward of the leader, his frame smaller, his voice a little more reedy. "Pardon us if your feast days do little to instill reverence in our cold, dead hearts."

"You are no spirits," Therba snarled. "You're men of flesh and blood. Enough of this foolishness—"

"We *were* living, once," another man said from his place farther down the center aisle, "before your kind stole our honor and our livelihoods from us."

Bjalki heard himself speaking before he realized that he wanted to speak. "Our people take nothing that we do not earn! How dare you come into this holy place and—"

Before he had finished, the nearest intruder shot forward, grabbed Therba by her priestly robes, and yanked her down off the dais onto the stone floor of the central aisle. The old woman's ceremonial stave clattered on the flags. She grunted when she hit the ground, for she hit hard. As Bjalki watched, frozen by fear, the man who'd thrown her down snatched up handfuls of her robes again and dragged her farther up the aisle, toward his masked companions. Therba landed in a heap at the feet of their leader and the men closest to him.

Something in the leader's tentative step back told Bjalki that the man was shocked to find Therba cast down before him. A stunned silence settled on them all, the masked men looking back and forth to one another, as if wondering what came next.

Bjalki forced himself to step forward now. "Please," he said, "I beg you, don't hurt her—"

Then the wiry man with the reedy voice turned back to Bjalki. "You want the old woman back?" he said. "Earn her."

The leader said something, too softly for Bjalki to hear. The wiry man answered, but his response escaped Bjalki as well.

"I'm begging you," Bjalki said. "This is a holy night. There's no reason for violence—"

"There is every reason for violence," the wiry one said. "Two men, up here. Grab the other one."

Bjalki realized that "the other one" was he. He turned and tried to flee but crashed into the stone brazier where the undying flame flickered in the gloom. He moved to scurry around it, but it was too late. He felt strong hands grab his arms and yank him backward, whirling him around so that he was facing back up the aisle, into the sanctuary, where Therba stood surrounded by the masked intruders.

The wiry man with the reedy voice waved his hand—a summons. A larger man—one who had not spoken so far— answered the thin man's silent command and stepped forward, towering over Therba.

"Treat with us honestly," Bjalki said, struggling against his captors' iron grips and realizing it was pointless. "You need not even take off your masks—but tell us, what can we do for you? What restitution can we offer?"

The wiry man stepped forward, leaving the captive Therba in his wake. A few of those closest to the leader closed in, tightening their cordon around the dwarven priestess. A pair of masked men—including the leader—seemed to be engaged in a war of whispered words. But whatever they were saying, it did not change the fact that Therba was now surrounded. The docent, meanwhile, was feeling about, trying to reach her ceremonial stave, which lay about two arm's lengths off to her left.

"It would have been better for you if you hadn't been here," the broad-shouldered leader said, shoving his way forward, and Bjalki thought he heard real remorse in the man's voice. "Now you shall have to bear witness to our grim work."

"And what work is that?" Bjalki asked, helpless in the grip of the two men who held him.

"Justice will be done," the leader said.

There was a sudden commotion. Farther down the aisle, Therba had managed to snatch up her ceremonial stave again and now struggled to her feet. The men were trying to keep her down, but Therba managed to gain her feet and turn to face them. Then, to Bjalki's great astonishment, the docent thumped the man nearest her with her stave.

"Bjalki, run!" she cried. "Bring the Swords of Eld!"

Bjalki could not run, even if he'd been free to do so. He could only watch, horrified, as the masked men closed in around Therba as she swung her stave back and forth, threatening them.

"Stop her!" the leader of the masked men roared. "Get that stave away from her!"

"End her!" the wiry man barked. "Someone!"

"No!" the leader shouted in answer, and Bjalki realized that there really was a conflict among them. The wiry man was urging violence, while their brawny leader seemed to be trying to avoid it.

"I have no fear of you!" Therba shouted, strong and sure as Bjalki had ever seen her. "Invade our house of worship, will you? With masks, like bandits? What shameful creatures you are!"

"Therba," Bjalki shouted, struggling against his captors again, "stop it!"

The stave kept cutting the air. It came close to a couple of the masked men, but both dodged it. A third tried to step in from the side and got a faceful of the big gilded stick. As he went reeling, two more men, at Therba's back, dove in and tried to subdue the old dwarven priestess. One managed to almost get his arms locked around Therba's frame, but her dwarven shoulders were too broad. She shrugged off the man's bear hug easily and swung round, bringing her swishing stave with her. The other man who had been behind her tried to dive in under a strike from the stave, but collided with it instead. It came down hard on his skull and he hit the flagstones of the temple aisle, unmoving.

Therba suddenly stopped her thrashing and striking. She seemed to be in shock, as though her naturally compassionate instincts had taken over in answer to the harshness of her attack.

"Hold her!" someone shouted now amid the chaos.

Yet another intruder lunged in from Therba's left. The priestess dropped her stave and tried to rush to the side of the man she'd knocked cold, but the newcomer had her in a sloppy hold and wouldn't set her free.

"Let me go!" Therba shouted. "I want no more of this! Your companion, he's bleeding! Let me tend him!"

A number of the masked men had crowded round their fallen comrade now.

"He's bleeding!" someone cried.

Bjalki heard a rip and saw one of the masked men force his way forward. He held a scrap of his dark gray cloak in his hand. He drew back the cowl of the fallen man, found where he bled, on his scalp, and pressed the scrap of cloak there.

Therba was still struggling. "She's disarmed!" the leader shouted, now lost behind a line of his jostling men, all trying either to help subdue Therba or to attend to their fallen comrade. "Let her go!"

Bjalki heard the knife before he saw it. A slithering sound: steel rasping as it was drawn from a sheath. He lunged forward, desperate to break away from the men holding him, to stop what was about to happen. His mouth was open, he was about to cry out to warn the docent...and then it was too late.

The man holding Therba released her. She stumbled forward, clearly heading for the man she'd laid out on the flagstones with that head strike. As she moved, almost lost among a press of tall human bodies and whipping, slate gray cloaks, one of the men—the tall, wiry one, Bjalki thought—stepped into Therba's path. There was a blade in his hand, glinting in the near darkness. It flashed for the briefest instant, then disappeared up to the hilt in Therba's robes. The old priestess gasped. Wheezed. Choked.

Bjalki thought he heard one of the men say, "Aemon! What have you done?"

Then the press of bodies crowding around Therba dispersed. Everyone scurried backward, as though they wanted no part of what had just occurred. Only two men stayed close to Therba: the one whose knife now violated the docent's body, and another who seemed to be bracing her from behind. For a moment Therba stood frozen, the blade in her belly, knotty old hands grasping at her attacker's tunic and cloak. Then the knifeman twisted the blade—he must have, for Therba gasped and shuddered. A moment later, with a shudder and a thin exhalation, Therba fell against her attacker and slid to the floor.

"Aemon's bones," one of Bjalki's captors muttered, clearly shocked.

The other exhibited neither surprise nor remorse. "Dwarven bitch," he snarled. "Let her bleed."

The knifeman stood above his victim, blade in hand, its steel stained dark red, Therba's blood on his hands. One nearby masked man clapped the knifeman on the shoulder. Two others stepped away, as though they had no desire to be blamed for the sudden escalation in violence. A fourth bent over a nearby bench and vomited.

"What did you do?" the big leader whispered. His voice was low, strangled, but Bjalki heard him clearly nonetheless. He sounded just as shocked and frightened and enraged as Bjalki himself felt.

To Bjalki's surprise—and, no doubt, that of the intruders' leader—the knifeman said nothing. He only tilted his head slightly to the left, as though truly puzzled by his leader's reaction. Then, almost as a provocation, he turned to Therba's heaped, unmoving form, crouched beside her, and turned her over onto her back.

Bjalki made a weak, beastly sound when Therba groaned and stirred where she lay. She was dying, but she wasn't dead yet. "No," he said, truly ready to throw himself on his knees and beg for the docent's life.

He heard a single word from the leader as well. "Stop," the man said.

The knifeman did not listen. He stared into Therba's clouding old eyes, then slid his knife in one last time. This time he made sure the blade struck at a sharp angle, up beneath the ribs, seeking the old dwarf priestess's slowing heart. Therba gave a tiny gasp, then went still.

Bjalki threw himself forward, screaming—though the sounds he made seemed to have no words in them, only pain and fear and hatred and rage. This time his captors weren't ready for the force of his resistance. He burst away from them and shot forward, right toward the docent's still body. A massive form suddenly filled his world—the leader of the masked men, stepping right into his path. Bjalki plunged right into the man's open arms and found himself held fast in a strong, viselike bear hug, forced back toward the steps and the dais. Once they'd reached the low summit, the leader threw Bjalki down and towered over him. The two men who'd been holding Bjalki just moments ago had retreated to the wings of the dais now, not sure what their leader intended.

To Bjalki's astonishment, the leader only asked him a single question. "Is there a back way out?"

Bjalki could not answer. He could only stare at Therba—the

old, Rem loved it. He liked the familiarity, the fun, the
ulness. Gods knew he got little enough of that in his daily
avors.

There he is!" Lokki cried as he climbed Rem as though he
 an ambulatory tree. "The giant Mokhenrog, back for more
 at the hands of the dwarven hero Lokki, Son of Torval!"
Vithout warning the dwarf boy scurried higher, planting one
ver Rem's shoulder, then wrapping his arms round Rem's
. Suddenly Rem was blind.

For the sake of all the gods, Lokki!" Ammi said, exasper-
 "Let poor Rem go! He's barely through the door!"

Aye, that!" Torval barked. "He's dainty as a daffodil, that
 One wrong move from you, little hooligan, and you're
o crush him."

Your support is overwhelming," Rem said, still unable to
"But what if the giant had simply grown tired of always
g the battle, eh?"

Oh no," Lokki said, a delicious expectancy in his voice.
 can't do that. This is the way the story goes—the dwar-
ero fights Mokhenrog and cuts him down to size."

Vell," Rem countered, "what if I'm a *different* giant?"

say you're Mokhenrog!" Lokki insisted.

em gave a roar, tore Lokki from his shoulders, and brought
arefully down to the floor with mock fury. When he laid
 down, he started tickling the boy, who giggled uncon-
bly.

he giant's loose!" Lokki giggled. Rem pulled the young
—barely the size of a human toddler—up off the floor
ave him a few mock-savage shakes that stirred up Lok-
ughing fit, then brought him down again onto the floor.
then lifted his arms in triumph, his fists thumping rudely
t the low-hanging roof of the cozy rooms.

---

kind, the upright, the wise…now stone-cold dead, bleeding
all over the temple's flagstones.

The leader kicked Bjalki in the ribs. "Is there a back way
out?" he hissed, and Bjalki suddenly realized that the man was
trying to speak to him without being heard by the others.

"Hold that one," the knifeman said from farther up the aisle.
Three men rushed forward to mount the dais. One of the men
who'd been holding Bjalki closed in as well.

Bjalki was terrified. What was happening? He couldn't leave
her, could he? Why was this man asking about a back exit?

The masked leader now lifted Bjalki by his robes and set him
on his feet, then shoved him hard.

"Run," he said.

Bjalki could not think straight any longer. That simple
word—*run*—was all that he needed to hear. The animal part
of his brain took over and he turned to run. One of his former
captors lumbered closer, but he had the barest of head starts
on him. Stumbling, Bjalki scrambled toward the altar, caught
himself upon it, to steady himself, then broke into a run once
more. Glancing back, Bjalki could see his pursuing captor closing, right behind him, reaching out, ready to snatch his trailing
robe—

Then the leader intervened. He fell on Bjalki's pursuer,
yanked him backward, and threw him to the floor of the dais.
Then the masked stranger turned to Bjalki and roared his single order again.

"Run!"

Bjalki fled as fast as his feet would carry him, heading toward
the back corridors of the temple and the only other way out
that he could think of.

As he flew he heard the clamor of their voices behind him.

"Are you mad? You let him go?"

"What were you thinking?

"Aemon's tears, there's blood everywhere!"

"Do what we came to do!" the leader shouted above the rising din of his chaotic, excited companions. "Work fast, we've only minutes!"

As Bjalki ducked into the lower passages far behind the altar that would lead him to the rear door of the temple, he heard a great clatter and cacophony behind him. The men seemed to be upending everything, tearing it all down, tossing every ark and bench and scroll.

It sounded like his whole world coming to a brutal and sudden end.

CHAPTER EIGHTEEN

Torval's home smelled like a country kitchen, and
tering one at that. Clearly the family had been wo
to get the Fhryst meal prepared. The fruit of the
labor was laid out on the short trestle table that thei
for dining, and the moment Rem stepped through
eyes danced eagerly over the offerings. There wa
barley bread, salted fish, a pot of mutton stew, par
cheese, a pitcher of milk for the children, a large
beer or cider, Rem could not tell which—for th
hearth-roasted carrots, onions, and parsnips, a
soft butter, and a bowl of dried apple shavings
had learned, were a common dwarven table co
val's people often using those dried, wrinkled
to flavor everything from stews to porridge t
their bread. A warm fire licked at a new beech
hearth, and flickering candles lined the dinner

Lokki charged, and Rem bent down so L
onto him. In seconds the boy clung to his shou
dler's pack, nearly strangling Rem with his s
round Rem's throat. Rem knew the drill well
est loved his visits and took great delight i
him, bodily, until he could force Rem to the
him, and declare the challenged giant slain.
to scold and dissuade little Lokki, but it nev

kind, the upright, the wise...now stone-cold dead, bleeding all over the temple's flagstones.

The leader kicked Bjalki in the ribs. "Is there a back way out?" he hissed, and Bjalki suddenly realized that the man was trying to speak to him without being heard by the others.

"Hold that one," the knifeman said from farther up the aisle. Three men rushed forward to mount the dais. One of the men who'd been holding Bjalki closed in as well.

Bjalki was terrified. What was happening? He couldn't leave her, could he? Why was this man asking about a back exit?

The masked leader now lifted Bjalki by his robes and set him on his feet, then shoved him hard.

"Run," he said.

Bjalki could not think straight any longer. That simple word—*run*—was all that he needed to hear. The animal part of his brain took over and he turned to run. One of his former captors lumbered closer, but he had the barest of head starts on him. Stumbling, Bjalki scrambled toward the altar, caught himself upon it, to steady himself, then broke into a run once more. Glancing back, Bjalki could see his pursuing captor closing, right behind him, reaching out, ready to snatch his trailing robe—

Then the leader intervened. He fell on Bjalki's pursuer, yanked him backward, and threw him to the floor of the dais. Then the masked stranger turned to Bjalki and roared his single order again.

"Run!"

Bjalki fled as fast as his feet would carry him, heading toward the back corridors of the temple and the only other way out that he could think of.

As he flew he heard the clamor of their voices behind him.

"Are you mad? You let him go?"

"What were you thinking?

"Aemon's tears, there's blood everywhere!"

"Do what we came to do!" the leader shouted above the rising din of his chaotic, excited companions. "Work fast, we've only minutes!"

As Bjalki ducked into the lower passages far behind the altar that would lead him to the rear door of the temple, he heard a great clatter and cacophony behind him. The men seemed to be upending everything, tearing it all down, tossing every ark and bench and scroll.

It sounded like his whole world coming to a brutal and sudden end.

CHAPTER EIGHTEEN

Torval's home smelled like a country kitchen, and a mouthwa-tering one at that. Clearly the family had been working all day to get the Fhryst meal prepared. The fruit of their collective labor was laid out on the short trestle table that their family kept for dining, and the moment Rem stepped through the door, his eyes danced eagerly over the offerings. There was fresh-baked barley bread, salted fish, a pot of mutton stew, part of a wheel of cheese, a pitcher of milk for the children, a larger pitcher—of beer or cider, Rem could not tell which—for the grown-ups, hearth-roasted carrots, onions, and parsnips, a crock of fresh soft butter, and a bowl of dried apple shavings, which, Rem had learned, were a common dwarven table condiment, Tor-val's people often using those dried, wrinkled old apple pieces to flavor everything from stews to porridge to the butter on their bread. A warm fire licked at a new beech log beyond the hearth, and flickering candles lined the dinner table.

Lokki charged, and Rem bent down so Lokki could leap onto him. In seconds the boy clung to his shoulders like a ped-dler's pack, nearly strangling Rem with his strong little arms round Rem's throat. Rem knew the drill well; Torval's young-est loved his visits and took great delight in wrestling with him, bodily, until he could force Rem to the floor, climb atop him, and declare the challenged giant slain. Ammi would try to scold and dissuade little Lokki, but it never worked. Truth be told, Rem loved it. He liked the familiarity, the fun, the playfulness. Gods knew he got little enough of that in his daily endeavors.

"There he is!" Lokki cried as he climbed Rem as though he were an ambulatory tree. "The giant Mokhenrog, back for more abuse at the hands of the dwarven hero Lokki, Son of Torval!"

Without warning the dwarf boy scurried higher, planting one leg over Rem's shoulder, then wrapping his arms round Rem's head. Suddenly Rem was blind.

"For the sake of all the gods, Lokki!" Ammi said, exasperated. "Let poor Rem go! He's barely through the door!"

"Aye, that!" Torval barked. "He's dainty as a daffodil, that one. One wrong move from you, little hooligan, and you're like to crush him."

"Your support is overwhelming," Rem said, still unable to see. "But what if the giant had simply grown tired of always losing the battle, eh?"

"Oh no," Lokki said, a delicious expectancy in his voice. "You can't do that. This is the way the story goes—the dwarven hero fights Mokhenrog and cuts him down to size."

"Well," Rem countered, "what if I'm a *different* giant?"

"I say you're Mokhenrog!" Lokki insisted.

Rem gave a roar, tore Lokki from his shoulders, and brought him carefully down to the floor with mock fury. When he laid Lokki down, he started tickling the boy, who giggled uncontrollably.

"The giant's loose!" Lokki giggled. Rem pulled the young dwarf—barely the size of a human toddler—up off the floor and gave him a few mock-savage shakes that stirred up Lokki's laughing fit, then brought him down again onto the floor. Rem then lifted his arms in triumph, his fists thumping rudely against the low-hanging roof of the cozy rooms.

"The giant wins the day! The hero is slain!"

"I'm the hero!" Lokki said. "I can't be slain."

"Tell that to the giant crunching your bones about now," Torval said. The dwarf bent and hauled his little boy to his feet, then straightened his tunic and dusted it off. "Go help with the rest of dinner now. We're starting soon."

The boy did as he was told. Rem studied Torval, noticing the proud, almost melancholy look that he gave Lokki as the little one hurried to help Osma—a sort of bittersweet adoration, indicative of deep affection coupled with the sting of loss. No doubt that whenever Torval looked at the boy like that, he wasn't just thinking about how much he loved him, but also about how much he missed the lad's mother and two dead siblings. Staring at his friend and suddenly overcome with a great well of protective sentiment for him, Rem realized that he, too, was being watched. Indilen, three steps away, studied Rem in the candle- and hearth light, her eyes bright as two dark jewels holding stars in their depths, her smile broad and bright and perfect. Catching her like that—so beautiful, gilded by the light of the candles and the fire across the room, Rem felt his breath taken. Was she really his? Had he really gotten so lucky?

There was a long, loving silence between them. Finally Rem closed on her and swept her into his arms. "How was I? As a giant?"

"Terrifying," she said. "And thoroughly adorable."

"Shall the giant make you his prisoner, milady?"

She leaned in close. "He already has."

They kissed—only for a moment, because they didn't want to be rude. In that moment Rem made a decision. As soon as they were alone again, and the moment was right, he would tell her the whole, unadulterated truth about who he was and why he'd come here. If she did not storm out of his life or beg him to reclaim his birthright at that point, then he would keep her forever, and never want for anything more.

He became aware of a new presence at his elbow. When he turned he found Tavarix lingering nearby. The boy was cleaned up nicely, wearing a good, neat tunic and trousers, not the everyday work clothes Rem had seen him in just a few days ago, in the dwarven quarter. The young dwarf smiled expectantly, then offered his hands.

"It's good to see you, sir," Tav said. Rem offered his own hand and Tav shook it in both of his. "You're most welcome here, on this night. It's our great privilege to have you."

A pang of pride seized Rem. The boy was trying to offer heartfelt gratitude, a sense of welcome—all the things that a gracious man of the house might offer to an honored guest. Seeing Tav like that—still so young, yet so eager to be seen as gracious and mature—made Rem terribly proud of the boy.

"It's good to see you, Tav," Rem said. "The privilege is all mine." Conspiratorial, Rem cocked his head toward Torval—engaged with dinner preparations across the room—and spoke to Tav in a whisper.

"Any improvements?" Rem asked.

Tav's expression fell, his hospitable joy collapsing into sadness. "None. He'll barely speak to me."

Rem bent closer, to make sure Tav could see into his eyes and hear his still-whispered words. "He's proud," he said. "Keep at it."

Tav nodded, forced a smile, then hurried away to help his aunt and sister complete the preparations.

Rem turned back to Indilen. "I'm glad to see him here," he said quietly, "but sad to hear there's still bad blood between them."

"Don't overstep your bounds," Indilen said. "Torval knows

you love him, and you love his family, but if you push yourself into the middle of this—"

Rem held up his hands. "I offer encouragement, nothing more," he said.

He suddenly became aware of Torval at his elbow. "Encouragement for what?" his partner asked.

"I encourage you to not be such a belligerent little knob," Rem said with a smile. "Thanks to me, the whole world loves you."

Torval shook his head. "You think you're funny. Come on, it's time."

Rem and Indilen both nodded in unison and moved toward the table.

A still, solemn silence fell, subduing even eager little Lokki. Torval took the seat at the head of the table, while Osma, his sister, took another chair at the opposite end. The children filled the bench on one side of the trestle table—Tav taking the place closest to Osma, farthest from Torval. Rem and Indilen sat themselves on the bench opposite. As they all settled in, Rem noticed a line of candles running down the center of the table, all in unmatched holders. Osma held a burning reed in her hand, presumably to light the waiting candles. Currently the only light in the room came from the fire in the hearth and a pair of nearly burnt-down candles in glass holders on the far side of the room.

Osma looked to Torval—a silent inquiry regarding readiness. Torval situated himself in his seat, then nodded. All of a sudden, he looked profoundly uncomfortable to Rem—a dwarf about to bear witness to some ritual or ceremony that he would rather ignore or eschew altogether. His eyes dropped to the table and his mouth was set stonily.

Osma studied everyone round the table in turn, ending with the children.

"This is the story of how everything came to be," she said, her voice taking on the grave and evocative cadence of a born storyteller. "It's to be recalled upon the longest night of the year, in the midst of the world's cold and privation, to remember that from the emptiness we came, and to the emptiness we shall return."

Rem felt a pleasant shiver run the length of his spine. He loved storytelling, and Osma's invocation already seemed to be immersing him in another world—a world of primordial darkness and cold waste. Beside him he felt Indilen lean just a little bit closer.

Osma raised the burning reed in her plump fingers, its yellow light flashing in her large dark eyes. "When the world was young, and all was void and tempestuous, Stormblight, That of the Primordial Chaos, decreed that its servants should fill the world with teeming life, so that lonely, embittered Stormblight could savor their sufferings, their fears, their losses, and their pains.

"All manner of beasts, great and small, were formed from the stones and the sand and the waters and the winds by Stormblight's infernal brood, and all at once, the world was not barren, but fertile and fulsome." She reached forward and lit the candle nearest to her with the burning reed. The room became just a little brighter. As everyone stared at the newly lit candle, Osma rose from her seat. Slowly, deliberately, she moved along the trestle table behind the bench on which the children sat.

"Yet despite all the wonders now moving in the world, none of them pleased the rapacious Stormblight, for they were simple and unknowing, and their pain and fear were as fleeting as sparks, as shallow as ponds. Its efforts and impulses frustrated, Stormblight made demands once more, and the living spirits that it had planted in the very fundaments of the earth were stirred to make beings of their own—beings whose lives would be bound, but whose knowledge could be far-reaching, so that their awareness of their own mortality, their own helplessness, their lifelong suffering, and their eventual extinction, could enrich their pain and sate Stormblight's bottomless hunger."

Reaching between Tavarix and Lokki, Osma lit the next candle in the sequence with her still-burning reed.

"The Spirit of the Sky made dragons. They were proud and powerful, but in time Stormblight's own scouring winter winds tore them to pieces."

She lit the next candle, leaning between Tavarix and Ammi to do so.

"The Spirit of Wood made elves from the grass and the moss and the bark and the leaves. They were elegant, inquisitive, and supple, in love with their senses. Though they thrived for a time in ignorance, Stormblight finally beset the wending woodlings to test their mettle, and learned, in time, that it could torture them with longevity, and keen senses, and even keener knowing—for their depth and their wisdom were both their boon and their curse."

Rem suddenly felt Indilen's hand on his arm. He laid his own hand upon hers and took comfort in the warmth of it, but he never took his eyes from Osma. All this time he'd been supping at the woman's table, complimenting her cooking and her unwavering care for both her brother and his children, but he had never realized that she was also such a gifted storyteller—as charismatic and compelling as any bard from the north country that he'd ever seen.

"Then the Spirit of the River made humankind from its reeds and its clay."

And so, Rem thought. *We enter the tale . . .*

Osma lit the second-to-last candle on the table.

"Humankind, both weaker and less wise than the elves, were nonetheless more numerous and more fecund. In no time at all, Stormblight had learned the secret to humankind's pain: to shorten their years, to haunt them with promise, and to tempt them with power. Stormblight saw these flaws and exploited them, and took great delight in the cries and laments raised and the delicious suffering meted out upon these, the children of his children."

She rounded the end of the table, moving behind Torval and arriving at last just behind Rem and Indilen.

"Finally," she continued, "Stormblight said, 'I have conquered these pitiful souls and hold them in my power evermore. Give me another, my children! Give me yet more progeny to lord over and feast upon! For pain is my meat and mead, and I shan't be satisfied until I've gorged upon it!'"

Lokki was leaning close to Tavarix now, clutching at his big brother's arm. After a moment's pause, Osma carried on.

"And so the Spirit of the Earth, having long tired of Stormblight's rages and tyrannies, found the finest stones it could in the very bowels of the earth, and from these carved the first dwarves." She leaned forward, just past Indilen, and lit the final candle on the table, the one nearest Torval. "There was Leinar, the All-Father and first of our kind; Thendril the Womb of the World; Athura the Sower; Yangrol the Smith; Wengrol the Warrior; and Kondela the Speaker and, ever thereafter, the Judge of All. In its stony bosom did the Spirit of the Earth succor and wean these first of our kind, knowing that only patient formation and robust design could fortify them against Stormblight's depredations."

Rem stole a glance at Torval. His partner stood straight backed, utterly still, hands flat on the table before him. His eyes glinted in the near darkness. Clearly, for Torval, Osma's tale conjured bitter memories and unpleasant associations.

Osma continued. "When the dwarves were, at last, so plentiful that Stormblight's attentions could be avoided no longer, the Spirit of the Earth set them loose, and bade Stormblight do its worst to hinder and hamper them. And who knows what happened then?"

"They beat Stormblight bloody!" Lokki cried.

"They tore Stormblight limb from limb," Tavarix said solemnly.

"Stormblight found them strong and resilient," Ammi said, "and it punished them for their resilience."

Rem studied Torval again. He could see all the warring emotions at work in the dwarf's heart, subtly registering on his face, even as Torval tried to suppress them. Pride, loss, love, grief, warm memories, and bitter regrets—clearly Osma's tale, the special, ritual magic of such a gathering, stirred up a great deal in Torval's normally stout heart.

Rem wanted to reach out to him, to lay a hand on his friend's thick, square hand, to offer some comfort. Was that permitted? Was it even his place?

"Ammi knows well the end of it all," Osma was saying, her voice and tale now fading in Rem's consciousness, replaced by his concern for his haunted partner. "The dwarves were strong, and so they fought when Stormblight assailed them. They were also tough, so they endured, even when Stormblight punished them. And oh, how Stormblight cursed—"

Without warning, there came a pounding at the door. Rem nearly jumped out of his seat. Torval's inward reverie visibly collapsed. The dwarf turned toward the knocking at the door, blinking, like a man emerging from a dream.

Don't answer that, Rem thought. *No good can come of it. Who would come here so late, on such a night?*

But the spell was already broken. The tale of Stormblight,

the expectation of the feast, the sense of familial warmth and togetherness—that infernal knocking had scattered it all, like fallen autumn leaves blasted by a gust of wind.

Torval was up and across the room in four long strides. Rem, preparing himself for something terrible—he knew not what—lifted himself off his bench and stepped clear of the table.

Torval opened the door. A young boy in rough-spun woolen clothes stood outside.

"You're the dwarf called Torval?" the boy asked.

Torval nodded. "I am. What's the meaning of this?"

The boy handed Torval a folded note. "Just a runner, sir, begging your pardon. This is from the prefect. He needs you and your partner at the court of Eldgrim, in the Warrens."

Torval stared at the note, but did not open it.

"He said to hurry," the boy said.

Torval turned to Rem. Rem felt his stomach curl into a tight, sickening knot.

Gods, what now?

CHAPTER NINETEEN

The runner was tipped, apologies were issued to the family and Indilen, then Torval and Rem armed themselves and set out for the dwarven quarter. Thank Aemon Rem had worn his sword tonight—mostly just to assure his and Indilen's safety on their nighttime stroll. He hadn't truly intended to put it to use. Terrified of the prospect of Indilen heading home alone so late at night, Rem made her promise to stay with Osma and the children until morning.

"And don't give me that cack about how brave and capable you are," Rem said, smothering her sure-to-come resistance before it even appeared. "I know that well, but even I wouldn't walk these streets alone at night. That's why Torval follows me everywhere."

Indilen had accepted that, kissed him deeply, and wished him luck. Once they were out of the house and under way, Rem asked Torval what he thought awaited them.

"Whatever it is, can't be good," Torval muttered.

It was closing in on midnight, so the streets were largely deserted and an unnatural, almost funereal, silence seemed to press in around them. Every moan or sigh of the wind tumbling down a side alley was amplified, while every cat mewl and mongrel bark sounded as if it were just over their shoulder. Finally, after what seemed an eternity marching through the biting cold and oppressive stillness of Yenara's benighted streets, the pair arrived at the ethnarch's citadel. And there, to their mutual surprise and chagrin, they found ample activity and excitement.

The first sign that something was amiss was the crowd of curious onlookers—mostly dwarves, with a few curious humans among them—crowded before the citadel gates. They pressed forward, jostling as they went, shouting, inquiring, while a full platoon of house guards formed a broad picket line between the public and the compound gates. As Rem and Torval shoved their way through the milling, pressing throng, intent on the gate and the citadel beyond, they heard the guards admonishing the crowd, pleading that they fall back and make some space before the walls. When, after a laborious slog through the crowd, Rem and Torval finally made the gates, they flashed their lead badges and stated their business. The dwarven guards, too concerned with the crowd to care much about a pair of low-level watchwardens, all but yanked them forward, cracked the gate, and allowed the two of them to slip through.

Inside the compound there was no less activity. House servants and members of Eldgrim's court drifted and clustered about the dooryard and gardens, most wearing nightshirts or house robes, their talk all furtive whispers and hushed gossip. There were more citadel guards as well, their armored, liveried presence far more conspicuous and intimidating than it had been on Rem and Torval's previous visit. The guards were in loose formation, skulking on the periphery of the meandering knots of courtiers and house staff, but their primary duty seemed to be keeping everyone corralled near the ethnarch's manse and allowing only permitted personnel beyond the gardens, into the vicinity of the great temple. Rem and Torval's passage through the courtyard was aided by their badges, though none of the dwarven guardsmen seemed pleased by their presence. Whenever challenged, they'd flash their badges, then receive the same broad directions: carry on to the manse.

Hirk was waiting for them outside. The big, strapping second met them when they emerged from the milling crowd of dwarves, and hastily apprised them of the situation as the three of them mounted the manor house steps and approached the guarded front doors.

"It's bad," Hirk said. "Murder and desecration in the dwarven temple."

Torval stopped in his tracks. Rem and Hirk took a few more steps before realizing they'd lost him. When they turned back, they saw Torval standing by himself in the shadow of the ethnarch's manse, staring off over the heads of the courtyard crowd toward the temple itself five hundred yards away. Rem hurried back.

"Torval?" he asked. "Are you all right?"

His partner nodded absently. His eyes slid sideward, toward the looming temple, then back to Rem. Together, they once more approached the waiting Hirk.

"The victim?" Torval asked his superior.

"A priestess of the temple," Hirk said quietly. "One witness—a younger priest. A bunch of men in masks, he said."

"Masks?" Rem asked. "Again?"

Hirk shrugged. "That's what he said—the little bit I heard from him, anyway. Now come on, Ondego wants you two present."

He led the way. Rem and Torval fell in behind him. Present for what?

Eldgrim was speaking—shouting, actually, loud as a mad bull elephant—when two of the Swords of Eld escorted Hirk, Rem, and Torval into the great chamber. The audience for the ethnarch's outburst consisted of his wife, Leffi, two male priests whom Rem recognized from their previous visit, the ever-silent, ever-scribbling court secretary, and two armored, liveried dwarves whom Rem marked as high-ranking commanders of the Swords of Eld. Ondego and Queydon stood nearby—unlucky representatives of the wardwatch, stoically absorbing the brunt of Eldgrim's fury.

"It's clear to me," he was saying as Rem and company crossed the room to where Ondego and Queydon stood, "that your peace officers are woefully undertrained and undermanned to deal with this threat! If I'm not mistaken, Prefect, just say the word. I'll have the Swords of Eld on the streets bolstering your patrols by morning."

"If I'm not mistaken," Ondego said, droll as ever, "our jurisdiction ends at the gates to this compound. That means these vandals and murderers slipped by your Swords of Eld just as nimbly as they escaped the notice of my watchwardens. Your priestess died inside these walls, not outside them."

Eldgrim rose up off his throne and pointed a thick, accusatory finger at Ondego. "You dare make sport of this calamity?"

"Hardly," Ondego answered. "I'm trying to make sense of it. Now stop making threats and start working in concert with us, milord. You summoned us here, did you not? You ordered me, upon my arrival, to put my watchwardens to work studying the crime scene, did you not?"

Eldgrim saw Torval now at the prefect's elbow. His expression immediately darkened. "Why is this one here? What use has he?"

"He's one of my best," Ondego countered. "If you want answers, he's one of the bloodhounds most apt to track them down."

"He's an outcast," Eldgrim said. "A wretched vagrant. Given his hatred for his own kind, I would not doubt this foul deed was his own."

Torval took a single step forward. Ondego held out one arm, a silent command to stand fast and keep his gods-damned mouth shut. Rem entertained a moment's amazement: how many men or women, elves or dwarves, in all the world, had the power to both fetter Torval and keep him silent with a single movement?

The prefect's self-control was starting to slip. Rem could see it in the way his eyes narrowed, and in the ever-lowering sound of his voice as he answered the ethnarch's accusation.

"You see here," Ondego said slowly. "I don't give four turds and a bucket of piss for the mule-headed feud that exists between the two of you as dwarves. If there wasn't work to be done and my people waiting to do it, I'd say the two of you could each take up arms and have at it to settle your differences, right here, right now."

"The proud ram does not answer the challenge of a goat," Eldgrim said.

"And cocks shouldn't clash when there's a fox in the henhouse," Ondego answered, then barreled on before Eldgrim could interrupt him. "My point is, a member of this household lies dead, and we stand here—all of us, the goat included—ready to lend a hand and find those responsible. To see justice done. Don't waste another fucking moment of my time trying to settle old scores or tell me how to do my job."

"Were we both *Hallirwelk*," Eldgrim said slowly, "I would see you flayed for your insolence."

"But we're not," Ondego said. "And you won't. What say we end the pissing about and get to work, eh?"

Eldgrim, to his credit, seemed to be working—actively working—to calm himself. He paced before his throne. He breathed deep. He hung his head and thought before he spoke.

"Forgive me," the ethnarch finally said, "but I find it difficult to place my trust in you, Prefect. Your methods have, thus far, proved inadequate to protect us. How, then, can they be sufficient to find the criminals? To see them punished accordingly?"

Ondego sighed. Shrugged. "You'll never know 'til you try, mate. Will you or won't you?"

Eldgrim bristled at being addressed so informally. *Mate.* Rem had to fight an urge to burst out laughing.

"Go to it, then," Eldgrim said. "But I warn you, Prefect— and this is a promise—if your ragamuffin street brigands cannot keep my people safe, my personal guard will."

"They'll do no such thing," Ondego snapped, losing his almost-returned composure again. "Law enforcement within the city walls is the job of the wardwatch, period. Vigilante committees and mercenary security forces are strictly forbidden by the criminal code. You can deploy your Swords of Eld within these walls and as picket sentries all you like, but if I see a single pair of armed and liveried dwarves patrolling *my* streets, I'll clap them in irons and toss them into my deepest dungeons. And they won't see the light of day again until you, milord, come to pay their fines in person."

Eldgrim grimaced. Clearly he had not dealt with Ondego enough to know just what a belligerent, argumentative bastard the prefect could be—or how protective he was of his ward. After a moment of silent fuming, Eldgrim finally just reclined in his ceremonial seat and turned his face away from Ondego, like a petulant child giving his mother the silent treatment.

Ondego waited. Rem knew he would not set one foot inside

that temple—crime or no—until the ethnarch or someone in authority gave him explicit leave to do so.

Leffi saved the day. The ethnarch's wife stepped forward, folded her hands before her, and addressed the prefect with perfect courtesy. "My husband's heart is heavy, Prefect," she said to Ondego. "The events of the past days, and now this…"

"No explanation is necessary, milady," Ondego said, and he seemed to genuinely mean it. "Just give the word. We are here to help—to serve."

"Go, then," Leffi said. Rem saw Eldgrim turn toward her— ever so slightly, as though ready to scold her, then thinking better of it. "Go to the temple, glean all that you can, and find the men who took Docent Therba away from us. Her death is not just a tragedy… it is an abomination."

Rem heard her voice threatening to crack, but also noted how much control she still exercised over herself. Her eyes were dewy, on the verge of tears; her voice was wavering; but she maintained her composure. She remained strong, detached, and in the moment, no slave to her grief or her outrage.

Unlike her husband.

"An abomination indeed," Ondego said, almost sighing as he spoke. "You have my word, milady, justice will be done for her. For all of you."

Eldgrim snorted derisively from his throne. Leffi's eyes flicked toward him for the barest of instants before she turned her attentions back to Ondego.

"We ask no more," she said. "Go now. Our soldiers will assist you in any way necessary while you are on the grounds."

Ondego nodded, turned smartly on his heel, and marched straight for the door. Rem and the others fell in behind him, needing no explicit command to know that now was their best chance to be away before another argument started.

"My vow still stands!" Eldgrim shouted at their backs. "If one more drop of dwarven blood is spilt, it will be my Swords of Eld seeking justice for our kind! Do you hear me, Prefect?"

They passed through the door of the audience chamber into the grand foyer beyond, Eldgrim's voice still echoing behind them.

"I bloody well heard you, you prick," Ondego snarled under his breath.

Queydon was ordered back inside with Watchwarden Firimol to record testimony from the witness as an officer of the Swords of Eld led Ondego, Rem, Torval, and the others directly across the courtyard to the great temple. Armored house guards and watchwardens of the Fifth lingered outside the glowering edifice, both parties eager to get to work, but unable to do so until the prefect and the ethnarch had come to an agreement. The officer gave orders for the doors to be opened, the great iron hinges squealed, and in moments their grim little band advanced through a dark, broad foyer, emerging moments later into the temple sanctuary. It was dim within, the space vast and the available light unequal to the task of filling it, but the lamps, torches, and candles on hand would have to do. The gods knew the Fifth had accomplished more with less in the past. Rem said a silent prayer that they could work a miracle and resolve this mess before dwarf-human relations grew any rockier.

Once inside the sanctuary, Ondego turned to the lot of them, Rem, Torval, and Hirk having been joined by five more watchwardens to aid in their investigation: Djubal, Klutch, Hildebran, Horus, and Pettina. The watchwardens all clustered together now, shoulder to shoulder, as their prefect addressed them.

"Go over it—every inch," Ondego said. "Every crack, every

crevice. Do it fast. I don't know if our kind host will have a change of heart and shoo us off, so treat every moment like it's your last opportunity to see what there is to see."

"Sketches?" Torval asked.

"On it," Klutch said, brandishing a bag Rem had seen him with before, crammed with parchment, paper, and charcoal, so that hasty renderings of a crime scene could be rendered for later review. However Klutch vexed Rem with his teasing, the man was a true artist with his charcoal and worked at remarkable speed.

"Aye, then," Ondego said. "Get those back to the watchkeep the moment you're through, Klutch. Sketches or no, though, I want everyone here to give the place a once-over with their own eyes. Your intuition might pick something out that the sketches won't reveal. To work, you bastards."

He clapped his hands. The watchwardens present scattered into the sanctuary to start examining the crime scene.

Torval led Rem up the center aisle, past a great, black pool of congealing blood that stained the flagstones just a stone's toss from the altar. A rough outline of the slain priestess's prone body—already removed—was apparent both in the gelid mass of the blood pool itself and beyond, where seeping blood had stained the priestess's unfurled robes and haphazardly impressed her form on the flags. As Torval knelt and examined the pool, Rem moved around it, closer to the altar and the main stage of worship. He studied what he saw, trying to imagine what the temple might have looked like when orderly, for it was now in complete chaos.

The stone altar was too heavy to move, but a great pile of scrolls, brass lamps, censers, and bowls of unburned incense and old ash now lay scattered about its base. It also looked as if someone had taken a quarryman's hammer and chisel to the altar itself. Though the huge masonry could not be moved, it had been cracked and riven by several powerful blows. A heavy stone brazier lay toppled and broken to one side, the cinders and ash once contained within it now strewn everywhere, without a lick of heat or fire left in them.

Rem mounted the platform steps. Off to the right of the altar were a series of elaborate wooden arks—stoutly made chests of oak and hickory and ash in a number of sizes, all well lacquered and tightly fitted, chased with brass or bronze, hinges and lock assemblies rust-free and well oiled. Rem supposed these must have been reliquaries, to hold the holy sacraments and arti-facts employed in the course of dwarven worship. Every one of those chests had been demolished, overturned, their contents strewn all over the stone dais: a bottle of expensive, fragrant oil, smashed; more incense—the rare stuff, from the far east or the sunbaked south—scattered like kindling and crushed beneath heavy bootheels; bound codices and more artfully inscribed scrolls torn to shreds, their contents littering the worship area like oversize confetti.

A terrible smell suddenly tickled Rem's nostrils. He stepped nearer, trying to get a better look at the detritus and wreck-age. There were puddles, stains, and thick brown curds of some unknown substance stuck here and there. The smell and the color told Rem what he was looking at.

Feces. Probably human waste. Destroying the dwarves' tem-ple hadn't been enough for this lot. They'd been keen to violate it with a bath of piss and shit as well.

Monstrous. Simply monstrous.

Disgusted, Rem turned away from the altar and the reli-quaries. When his eyes fixed on the columns flanking the altar, he noted that the heinous desecration had not stopped on the dais behind him. On the pillar before him, it looked as if someone had dipped their hands in the priestess's spilt blood, then inscribed sloppy crimson words on the column itself.

Trifling, *Beset by greed*, and *Rid the earth of these* were scrawled hastily, one beneath the other. The other pillar, about ten or twelve feet away, on the far side of the altar, bore a message of its own, also written in blood.

Humble them with fire and sword.

Rem felt sick, and somehow knew that it was not just from the smell of shit emanating from the altar. The bitterness on display here—the naked hatred—made him honestly, physically ill. Rem knew what it meant to hate. He'd hated people in his lifetime, some of them total strangers, some of them his closest relations. But that was how he chose to hate: person by person, individually, for personal slights or observed miseries inflicted upon undeserving victims. He hated his father for being ambitious and cruel. He hated one of his cousins for being a boor, a fool, and a rapist, and for never being held accountable for his crimes. Once he'd even hated a perfectly kind and intelligent young man who had won the affections of a local girl they both pined for. But he could not, for the life of him, understand the sort of blind hatred that led a person to demonize an entire people, just for being who and what they were.

And yet here was that hatred, made manifest in all its ugly glory before him. *Trifling. Beset by greed. Rid the earth of these. Humble them with fire and sword*.

Those weren't just insults. They were declarations of war.

Torval hove up beside him and studied the haphazard inscriptions.

"Can you read them?" Rem asked quietly.

"Thanks to your Indilen I can," Torval said grimly. "By all the gods, I wish I couldn't."

Rem waited. For a long time Torval studied the words

directly ahead, on the pillar nearest them. After a time he turned and studied the other pillar. Finally he returned to the pillar before them. His expression had not changed. It was grim, thoughtful, and more than a little pitying.

"What do you think?" Rem asked.

"I think," Torval said slowly, easing nearer to his partner, "that things are about to get ugly." He searched the area, to make sure they were alone, then spoke to Rem in a hoarse, low voice, as though he feared being overheard. "This? This is bad. Terror. Cowardice. Hit-and-run. Masks. Spilling blood in holy houses. It's vile, plain and simple. But when those dwarves decide to strike back...? I promise you, it'll be just as bad... maybe worse."

"Well, then," Rem said, "we'll just have to make sure no more dwarven blood is spilt."

"Don't believe him," Torval said. "We can't trust a word from Eldgrim's mouth, not a one. It isn't that he's a liar by habit, mind. It's that he doesn't see the profit in keeping his promises to human authorities, or those who would claim to be his allies. In his mind, you tall folk are all the same—all envious, or hostile, or just eager to exploit him and his for your personal gain. I seriously doubt he'll wait to retaliate. He's probably got a plan brewing as we speak."

"Can we stop it?" Rem asked, meaning not just the two of them but the whole of the wardwatch.

Torval studied the pillar before him and the pillar adjacent, then turned his gaze toward the great pool of blood on the flagstones of the central aisle. He sighed.

"Not likely," he said.

CHAPTER TWENTY

Bjalki wandered the citadel like a ghost. He sat for a time in his seat beside the ethnarch's throne, hearing Eldgrim's wroth curses and furious threats to the wardwatch.

"I need to see meaningful effort from your wardwatch, or I shall send my swords into the streets of this quarter to protect my people. I'll fight the councils on it if they hinder me, and I'll see you stripped of your rank and badge if you challenge me!"

Eldgrim would do it, too. There was no reasoning with the ethnarch even at the best of times, let alone when his blood was up.

And he was not wrong, was he? Their people had been wronged. Justice had been denied them. If the locals could not protect them, why shouldn't they protect themselves?

Gods of old . . . we are on the brink of open war in the streets.

I should have saved her.

Why did I not fight harder to save her?

Eldgrim continued to froth and rage even after the questioning was complete and the watchwardens had departed. After a time Bjalki grew tired of the ethnarch's fury and excused himself. He meandered through the back corridors of the manse for a time, then out into the cold, clear night, haunting the shadows on the periphery of the courtyard. Outside the citadel gates curious onlookers clustered while citadel guards struggled to keep them back. In the shadow of the temple itself, across the courtyard, the watchwardens milled about, moving in and out of the temple, talking in furtive whispers among themselves about the senselessness and savagery of the crime, the great quantity of blood. Bjalki lingered within earshot of all these conversations, and unconsciously absorbed them, but in truth very little penetrated the frozen, sword-shocked stasis of his mind. He heard, but he did not comprehend; he saw, but he was not aware. At one point he found himself leaning against one of the outer walls of the great temple, palms high on the cold stone, head hung low, a steaming puddle of vomit at his feet. He did not remember vomiting, but whose else could it be?

After the excitement in the courtyard and the temple itself died down, Bjalki drifted inside the temple. A few watchwardens of the Fifth and a handful of citadel guards moved in the great, empty space, but for the most part the place was as dark and silent as a family tomb. A few lamps were lit, no doubt to support a closer examination of the premises. No one had attempted to clean up the wreckage surrounding the ceremonial altar. No one had washed the vile graffiti off the front pillars. No one seemed eager to bend to work with brush and bucket to scour away the great congealing pool of Therba's blood now staining the flagstones of the main aisle.

The docent's blood. Therba's blood. Dwarven blood. There it lay, a vulgar black puddle on the paving.

Something caught his eye, a dim glint in the shadow of one of the great pillars lining the main aisle. Bjalki moved nearer, crouching down to get a better look.

It was a rag... or rather a scrap of cloth. Though it was hard to tell in the dim light, Bjalki thought it was naturally dark gray. Presently, though, it was soaked with blood.

He remembered the masked man who'd been struck by

Therba, who'd fallen so hard and cracked his head on the flag-stones. He remembered the sound of the tearing cloak, and the man who had knelt at his wounded brother's side, pressing that scrap of cloth to his bleeding skull.

This is the blood of one of Therba's murderers, he suddenly realized.

In answer to a strange compulsion—a desire he could nei-ther articulate nor understand—Bjalki shoved the bloody rag in the pocket of his robes.

The grim trophy made him think of Therba again. Bjalki turned back to the great pool of her blood just a few strides away. He stared, unable to take his eyes off it. It seemed to admonish him. To taunt him. To shame him.

What could he have done? Those men had held him, hadn't they? And he was no warrior—he was a priest. He hadn't held a sword or an ax in his hands since he was a youth, and even then only for the few summary drills that all young dwarves were taught. He was neither especially strong, nor especially fast, nor especially brave. He was not, now that he thought about it, especially *anything*. And because he was not especially any-thing, the dwarf he'd called teacher—and friend—had died.

I could have fought them. Should have fought them.

I could have hurt them, if I'd only tried. I have hands. Fists. Teeth. Feet.

If I fought hard enough, I could have at least died fighting for her.

But instead I cowered and watched. I broke free of them eventually, didn't I? Perhaps if I'd fought harder, sooner. If I'd kept my wits. If I'd waited for the right moment.

But no. I cowered. I submitted. I only fled when their leader told me to run. I would praise his mercy if it had not come as too little, too late.

Like my own resistance.

What am I to do now, eh? What purpose can I possibly serve in a season like this? Therba was strong, learned, wise, courageous. She told Eldgrim the truth, even when he preferred not to hear it. She shamed her people to noble action when they would have fed their basest instincts. She moved our people—and our leaders—to deeper labors, more earnest penitence, more honest charity, and more true compassion. I cannot replace her. I'm not wise enough, or brave enough, or experienced enough.

And they will all know. Word will get round. Everyone will know that I could have fought, I could have tried to help her, so that we could either escape together or die together. But instead I saved myself, and I let her die. They will all know, and they will shame me. Even if they never say a single word, they'll shame me with their silence and their piteous glares and their whispers.

He had come to a door. He hadn't even realized he'd been wandering again—out of the temple, through the back corridors that led to the chapterhouse, down a series of dark, untrodden hallways. Somehow, through no conscious effort of his own, his feet had brought him to the place he always came to when seeking solace or insight: the library.

He pushed open the heavy oak door and slipped inside.

A single oil lamp burned under a clouded glass hood on a flat-topped stone column that stood just a few feet from the door. Bjalki was drawn, mothlike, to the flame and the way the translucent glass hood amplified and softened that light. He took up the lamp and carried the little brass bauble across the chamber to the reading table in the far corner—the very same table where Therba had found him poring over scrolls just days ago. There familiar candles waited. Carefully Bjalki lit each of them from the pilot flame of the lamp in his hand. When the candles were glowing and the light in the shadowy scriptorium had increased sufficiently, Bjalki withdrew and returned the parent lamp to its pillar. Then he crossed wearily back to the reading table and let himself sink into his favorite reading chair. For a long time he slumped there, trying to tease out just what it was he was thinking and feeling. He could determine neither.

The war is not coming, he thought. *It's upon us. The riot . . . the fire . . . Therba's murder and the temple desecration. They are no longer warnings of what might come—they are proof that the terror—the fury—has arrived.*

We cannot rely on the wardwatch. They owe us nothing and can promise us nothing.

We cannot deploy the Swords of Eld—no matter how justified we might be to do so. If the ethnarch's house guard metes out bloody justice to even one human in the dwarven quarter, the whole city will rise up against us. They will always protect their own, and see us as aliens and criminals.

What's left, then? How do we protect ourselves—avenge ourselves— if we cannot take up arms in our own defense?

Suddenly there was a sound in the chamber like a braying ass, and Bjalki realized he was crying. His whole body shook. Snot hung in long ropes from his nostrils. His vision was awash with tears. Stinging, bitter, copious tears. Try as he might, he could not stop. He wiped at his nose with his sleeve and kept trying to choke the sobs down, but there was nothing for it. All that he had failed to feel, to face, for the last few hours came rushing in upon him.

He relented. For a long, long time he sat there, slave to his sobs, hoping they would soon be exhausted. He never wanted to know this feeling again.

Bjalki blinked and wiped his eyes, trying to banish his tears. This was weak and foolish. If his heart was sick and his soul in mourning and his desire for justice stirred, he should do something. He should act—as Therba would have—not just moon about how helpless and confused he felt.

Our people need protection, he thought. *Retribution. How can I give that to them? What can one bookish priest do?*

He let his gaze wander to the table before him. A number of old codices and scrolls he'd been recently perusing lay nearby in reasonably neat piles. Idly, Bjalki studied them, letting his fingers trace their leather covers, their cracked and frayed old spines, their uneven leaves of parchment or vellum, their hasps of brass and silver.

Regarding the Gods. The *Book of Ormunda*. *Treatise upon Trials and Lamentations.*

His eyes returned to a single volume.

The *Book of Ormunda*.

Bjalki blinked. Ormunda, the most celebrated and accursed of dwarven mages. Had he and Therba not been discussing her only days ago?

In those days war was endless. Our people tried to live in peace, but Ormunda the Red saw how weak we'd become, how vulnerable. She showed our people the way . . .

She summoned demons from the Fires of the Forge Eternal.

And they fulfilled their purpose. They gave our people strength and resolve when they had none. They enacted the worst punishments—the most terrible depredations—upon our enemies, so that, in the end, we did not have to.

He heard Therba's voice then. *Do you think that absolved Ormunda? Savior or no, she blighted us. She damned herself. Do not lift her up as a hero, Bjalki. Even in her own tale, she is the villain.*

Bjalki's hand plunged into the pocket of his robe. He drew out the scrap of cloak that he'd picked up in the sanctuary . . . soaked in the blood of one of Therba's murderers.

This blood—blood tied to the perpetrators—it could be all that the right power needed to seek out their enemies, to deliver retribution.

Therba's voice echoed in his mind, wholly unbidden. *She damned herself. Do not lift her up as a hero, Bjalki.*

Bjalki shook his head and spoke aloud to himself. "Perhaps," he said in the gloomy, empty library. "But she made a choice, and that choice saved our people . . . even if it ultimately damned her."

He stared at the book before him and shuddered. Was he really considering this?

It only took him moments to decide. Bjalki sniffed. His tears were all gone now, as was his desire to weep. There was work to be done—hard work, bitter work, but necessary work. And this time, no matter what it cost him, he would be true. This was his only salvation . . . his only redemption.

Those who threatened his people would pay dearly, and Therba would be avenged.

CHAPTER TWENTY-ONE

The Fifth's answer to ambushes and temple desecrations by masked marauders? Armor. All those on the midday shift—Rem and Torval included—were set loose in the watchkeep armories and told to cobble themselves together a more or less full suit, complete with a shield and a few weapons of varying lethalities. Rem was a little excited about that prospect at first—he hadn't worn armor in years, since his last tournament melee, back home—but hunting through the forgotten, half-rusted hodgepodge of armor pieces littering the watchkeep armories proved far more challenging than just picking out a suit.

For one thing, no two pieces matched. No two greaves, no two gauntlets, no two pauldrons. Clearly everything available had been gathered by the wardwatch by slow accumulation. Second, even when matching was not a concern, there was the issue of sizing; a person could not simply snag a plate or banded cuirass and strap it on. One's armor needed to fit, at least somewhat, or it would prove uncomfortable, hindering, even potentially dangerous to the wearer in the heat of battle. And finally, of course, there was the issue of to what extent they should armor themselves. Ondego had given no require-ments. He had said only that he wanted his watchwardens to be protected and armed for pitched battle, and, likewise, capable of defending more than just themselves should things get dire. But protecting oneself for a street skirmish and protecting oneself for life-and-death fighting on a field of combat were two very different matters.

Left to his own devices, Rem tried to strike a balance between protection and mobility. And so, after searching the armories for almost an hour, he managed to gather a light chain mail shirt, a pair of mismatched greaves that fit the shape of his lower legs well, despite looking nothing like one another, a banded mail breastplate that afforded him excellent protection from direct attacks while also allowing some freedom of movement, and, miracle of miracles, what he assumed to be the only matching pair of vambraces—thin, light, steel sheathed in leather—hiding in the whole armory. To this cobbled-together outfit he added a stout wooden shield, then called it a day. Now he, like all his companions on the midday shift watching over those dwarves at the temple construction site, would be ready for almost anything their enemies could throw at them, even if they looked like a bunch of ragamuffin mercenaries in motley while they did it.

"Look at him!" a feminine voice said. "The Bonny Prince cuts a striking figure indeed!"

Rem turned, knowing the speaker instantly: Emacca, a tall, muscular Tregga horsewoman and one of his frequent sparring partners in the watchkeep courtyard. The nomad was striking in her own right, easily a fingerlength taller than Rem, wide at the shoulders and hard of limb, her soft, almost feminine face marked by a storm of ritual scars and tattoos from her days riding on the Great Steppe, off in the northeast beyond the Ironwalls. She'd chosen a fine complement of pieces from the armory, all providing a great deal of protection and movement without weighing her down.

Rem posed heroically, playing the fool and not caring. "What do you think, Emacca? Shall I strike fear into the hearts of my enemies?"

"Love and devotion, most like," said Sliviwit as he passed. He tickled Rem's chin as though he were a kitten as he hurried by. "Such a pretty, pretty lad."

"Too pretty for the likes of you," Rem shot back, knowing well that Sliviwit's jest was offered with affection. There was no subtlety in him, but he was always quick to laugh or offer a joke, and had a special knack for using that humor to mollify tense situations.

"Next time we spar," Emacca said, "we should wear these. It'll make us stronger, doing our blade work in all this junk."

"That's assuming we ever find time to spar again," Rem said. He turned to find Torval.

The dwarf was nearby, strapping himself into a fine, intricately banded leather cuirass—far superior to the blue-gray cast-offs they normally wore—made for, and probably by, a dwarf. The thick, hard, red-brown leather was supplemented by a mail shirt that fell all the way to Torval's knees, a mismatched pair of battered steel rerebraces sporting rust at their scalloped edges, and greaves—also mismatched and tarnished with long disuse—for Torval's shins. Torval's ever-present maul was joined by a hand ax he'd found among the stockpiled arms and a pair of broad-bladed dwarven daggers, one of them shoved in his left boot.

"Fearsome indeed, old stump," Rem said.

Torval grunted, still busily adjusting the straps of his various armor pieces and making sure everything was well situated and perfectly balanced. "I don't plan to be taken by surprise a second time," the dwarf said, then looked up at Rem. "Next time they come, I promise you, they won't all leave on their feet."

Rem nodded and surveyed the room again. Looking around the armory as his companions hunted among the castoffs, trying on and throwing down pieces that didn't fit or would not protect them, Rem idly wondered how many of those present had real combat experience. Several of them did for a fact, he knew—Sliviwit had told stories of his mercenary days, as had Blein and Blotstaff, Djubal and Klutch. Likewise, Rem supposed both Emacca and Brogila—both being from the steppe folk, whose lives were marked by intertribal wars and raids on undefended settlements—had probably seen their share of bloody battle in their time. But who among the rest? How many of these scrapping, hard-faced law dogs had even worn armor before, let alone donned it in preparation for true, potentially lethal combat?

Well, if one's talking about true, potentially lethal combat, Rem thought, *I suppose that leaves me out. Of course, I've owned armor and worn it—usually just for ceremony or tourneys—but I've never had to rely on it to save my life.*

And here they were, preparing themselves as though Yenara's streets were about to become a bloody war zone, desperate to prove that they could keep the peace, and that the city guard need not step in to do their work for them. How long could it all go on? How bad would it have to get before Eldgrim's dwarves and their mysterious masked adversaries finally decided that it just wasn't worth it? That whatever they were fighting over wasn't worth dying over?

If the whole of history was any indicator, only when it was too late, and the terrors had progressed so far that they could never be atoned for.

Three days passed. Each day Rem and Torval arrived for their midday shift at the work site, accepted their assigned guard post, and spent the day milling about on the same little plot of ground, as the dwarves continued their labors on the Panoply temple and passersby stared at the now-armored watchwardens as if they were some alien occupying force. Every night the watchwardens escorted the dwarves back to their homes and guildhalls in the Warrens, then spent the remainder of their shifts on patrol in and around the dwarven quarter itself.

Two or three times they broke up potential brawls between humans and dwarves, none of which had progressed beyond the lobbing of insults when interrupted. A half dozen times they dispersed suspicious gatherings of tall folk on the edge of the quarter, those parties all lingering street side or in the courtyard of some tavern facing the Warrens just across the street, seemingly whispering among themselves and clearly up to no good. What they talked about or planned or discussed, neither Rem nor Torval could ever tease out. But they knew troublemakers when they saw them, and when they saw them, they broke up their little conclaves and chased them all away.

The worst, though, was the graffiti. Four times in three days, they came across words scrawled on walls in chalk or charcoal, or, once, painted in bright, dripping green—words that boded ill for human-dwarf relations in Yenara.

Fire and sword, one of them said.

Another, probably written by a dwarf, based on its low placement on the wall: *We weren't here first, but we'll be here last*.

Another dwarven retort to human enmity: *Outlive them, outlast them*.

And, perhaps the worst, clearly written by human hands: *Tonkers die*, scrawled coal black on a wall in the Warrens for all to see. Those two words were so blunt, so ugly, that, if Rem had caught the man or woman who'd written them, he probably would have beat them bloody.

Torval took it all in stride, though—not so much optimistic as grimly resigned.

"No shortage of cunts in the world, eh?" he'd mutter. "Come on, let's wash it off."

Every night they checked in with Hirk or Ondego to both report on and learn about the progress of the temple fire investigation. Rem had enlisted Indilen for an early-morning visit to the city archives, to peruse the temple construction contracts as Ondego had ordered. Rem wanted not only to take advantage of Indilen's helpful associates at the archives, but also to glean her impressions of the contracts as written. She was a scribe and notary, after all, and had a better grasp of legal rhetoric and written contracts than Rem himself, so while he was capable of doing his own review and drawing his own conclusions, he thought her more experienced eye would be invaluable. Unfortunately, their reviews offered no insights.

"Clean as could be," Rem told Ondego. "No hidden details, nothing to contradict or reframe what we know of the situation."

Regarding the Stonemasons' Guildhall: watchers had been posted in rotating shifts, day and night. In the three days that they had been watching, while Rem and Torval cooled their heels on temple guard duty, nothing out of the ordinary had been reported.

"They know they're being watched," Torval surmised. "If they're up to something, they're up to it secretly."

"Shouldn't we question them again?" Rem asked in frustration.

Ondego shook his head sadly. "Orders from on high," he'd said with a sigh. "We made our first foray—asked routine questions and the like. Now the council and the tribunal don't want us to go back in there and stir the pot or bust heads unless we've got clear cause."

"So it's a stalemate, then," Rem muttered to himself. "Everyone just staring down everyone else over the hedges."

"Not a stalemate," Torval said. "The calm before the storm. Mark my words, something will touch it all off again."

As it happened, the old stump was right.

CHAPTER TWENTY-TWO

Hrissif sped his pace, then realized Foelker was falling behind. The night was bitterly cold, and his younger brother seemed to lag with startling regularity, as if keeping warm and keeping up could not be accomplished at once. For the third time that evening, Hrissif stopped and waited for the younger man to catch up.

"You sure you're all right?" he asked as Foelker approached.

Foelker nodded. "Fine," he said, a little impatiently. "It's just bloody cold out here."

Hrissif stepped nearer and peered at the bandage wrapped around Foelker's crown. The wound on his right temple wasn't seeping, nor did Foelker seem unusually dazed or confused. Hrissif had been worried about his brother ever since he'd taken those double thumps to the head a few nights earlier, first brained by that dwarven priestess's blasted stave, then hitting the ground so hard that everyone nearby heard the crack of his skull on the flagstones. Truth be told, in those first moments, Hrissif had been terrified Foelker wouldn't last the night. There'd been so much blood, after all.

Though not as much blood as that priestess lost when I stabbed her, eh? Foolish bitch. If she hadn't fought so hard—hadn't hurt Foelker—she'd probably still be alive.

And I'd probably still be in Valaric's good graces.

To Hrissif's great relief, after returning to the guildhall that night, they'd called in Frendel's wife, Molla—a barber-surgeon by trade—and she'd taken care of the poor bastard. She stitched Foelker up nicely, then pronounced that he'd likely suffer head-aches for a few days, perhaps a little wooziness, but that none of it would persist. Soon enough he'd be right as rain.

So, Hrissif told himself, *maybe there's nothing wrong. Maybe I just walk faster than he does. Just like when we were young—always yanking him along.*

"Keep walking," Foelker said, sounding a little annoyed. "I know where I'm going. I'm not a babe in these woods."

"Well," Hrissif said, "keep up. We need to get home."

Foelker gave an impatient nod and Hrissif turned and led the way, doing his best not to look back over his shoulder every few breaths to make sure his little brother kept up.

They'd just come from the Hammer and the Square, a work-ingman's tavern on the edge of the Fifth, where they'd met with some allies from the distant Fourth Ward, Thorven and Irenus. A Fourth Ward watchman and carpenter, respectively, the two men had expressed an interest in opening brother chapters of the Sons of Edath after Hrissif had told them of their opera-tions. In retrospect, Hrissif supposed it had been a dicey move, letting anyone outside the masons' guild in on their secret activ-ities. But Thorven and Irenus were very old mates, with hearts and minds equal to Hrissif's own. If the Sons were to grow—to become a force of power and purpose in the city and not just a momentary stir of ancient pride and primacy—it would need to grow beyond its founding circle.

Especially after Valaric's pronouncement when last he and Hrissif spoke, three days ago, in the aftermath of the temple desecration.

It's over, Valaric had said. *The Sons of Edath retire, here and now.*

Hrissif hadn't bothered to argue at the time...but he'd already known his plans for the Sons involved the very opposite of retirement. No, from where he sat, it was time to expand.

That's what their clandestine meeting at the Hammer and the Square had addressed: how Thorven and Irenus and their eager cohorts could further the mission and swell the ranks. They'd been so awed by Hrissif's account of the temple operation, so eager to undertake missions of their own in the name of the Sons, they'd treated Hrissif like a bloody general—a hero out of some old bedtime story who rode a big white charger at the head of a shining army.

Hrissif smiled to himself in spite of the bitter cold. He liked that feeling: being powerful, being renowned and respected. He'd spent most of his life in the shadow of bigger men like Valaric or men who were better at giving stirring speeches or men who had basically inherited their influence and positions from more famous parents. But now *he* had something to offer. He was at the tip of a spear, on the boss of a shield, and men such as Thorven and Irenus—friends to their cause, patriots— were eager to cultivate the seed that he had planted. If only his dead, drunken, belligerent father could see him now.

You'll never amount to a speck of shite on a cow's rump, the old man had said when he was young. *Too scrawny, too sneaky, too cowardly. You'll be arse-raped by a drunken Kosterman and left for dead before you've even got curlies on your sack.*

But, of course, that hadn't happened. Hrissif's and Foelker's lives had changed immensely—and for the better—when their father was found dead in a dung pile on a side street near the wharves. Terrible accident, that...fell on someone's knife a dozen times. Even managed to cut his own throat. They never did catch the bloke who did it...

If he'd just lifted us up, once in a while, instead of beating us down, Hrissif thought, completely free of remorse, *it wouldn't have come to that. Didn't I deserve better? Didn't Foelker?*

"Aemon Almighty," Foelker swore, shrinking from a freezing gust.

"Hang this," Hrissif said. "It's no good for either of us to be out in this. Let's take a shortcut, shall we?"

Foelker shrugged in his cloak. "Lead the way, Brother."

Hrissif changed course and Foelker followed. The wind blew hard around them—savage, probing, greedy. It seemed to swirl through every tiny little gap in Hrissif's clothing, over every inch of uncovered skin, searing his lungs and make his extremities ache toward numbness. Such a bitter night! He hated the winter. Summers in Yenara could be chilly enough, what with all the winds and fog from the bay. Going about in winter and braving the wind-racked streets was positively torturous. He'd have to build them a good fire in the little iron stove that graced his chamber when he got home. He had no wood to burn, but if memory served, there were a few dark kernels lying at the bottom of their coal bucket. Those should help them through the night. Too bad he couldn't afford a pair of buxom ladies to do the warming, so he could save the coal, but there was nothing for it. It was too late to go buy companionship, anyway. No telling how long he'd have to search around in this infernal rime for a molly to rent. And hadn't he already indulged himself a little too often this month? Wasn't that the whole reason they had no wood to burn and only a handful of coal remaining? These were lean times, after all—their combined severance from the Panoply job had been spent almost to the last copper. No, Hrissif and Foelker would just have to make do with the dregs of their coal tonight, then go buy some more—along with a cord of wood or two—in the morning.

There was the wind again—biting, clawing, snarling. Caught off guard by its lurching attack, Hrissif stopped right in the middle of the street, shrank against the gale that scoured him, and cursed all the saints and angels. Foelker stamped his feet and muttered something that Hrissif couldn't hear above the wind. The gust subsided. Hrissif carried on.

"We're going through here," Hrissif said, indicating the dark alley looming before them, black and hungry. "Keep your eyes peeled for some scraps of wood. Anything that'll burn."

"I'm cold, Brother," Foelker said, and though he was well past thirty years old, something in his voice still sounded like the little boy who'd always followed Hrissif around, or fled to him for comfort when dear old da was on the rampage.

"Almost home," Hrissif said, and then the darkness closed in around them.

It was dark—painfully so—but there was just enough starlight that the alley wasn't completely black. As his eyes adjusted to the gloom, Hrissif noted that they could still navigate safely, avoiding most of the larger obstacles—refuse piles and the like—during their passage. With any luck the closeness of the tenements and row houses back this way would give them some shelter, so they wouldn't be so vulnerable to the damnable freezing winds that kept attacking them. More rubbish in alleyways, too, of course. That improved their chances of finding some fuel.

The wind had, mercifully, subsided now that they were threading the alley.

"A vast improvement," Hrissif muttered aloud, and marched on.

"It stinks," Foelker said.

Hrissif only grunted in response. He couldn't argue.

One of those nights, I suppose, he thought. *Cold, lonely, nothing to look forward to and nothing of import to bask in the glow of. Good news about Thorven's and Irenus's people, though. Once I tell the boys in the guild—the dedicated sorts who've gathered around me— they'll be pleased to know the Sons of Edath need not retire just because old Valaric's lost his kingly jewels. We're onto something with this— discovered a need in this city, a hunger that's long been ignored. I'd wager if we can swell our ranks and do our work in the coming months, we might soon rival the wardwatch as the most fearsome keepers of law and order in this stinking, infested old city.*

Hrissif felt a pang of warmth at that—satisfaction, perhaps. Or smug assurance. He'd always known he was destined for better things than his father allowed, better things than his street-urchin childhood and almost-career as a sneak thief and accidental apprenticeship with the stonemasons would have allowed. He knew he was a man of humble origins and limited means, and even that he sometimes rubbed people the wrong way with his arrogance or eccentricities. But he was cunning, ambitious, adaptable, and, in the right setting, with the right audience, charismatic and capable of leading. No one would have guessed so based on his younger years, but he'd always known, even if no one else did. Hells, Foelker could have told them. Hadn't his big brother always done his best to keep them both safe, housed, and gainfully employed? Had Hrissif ever once tried to cut his simple brother loose or run out on him? No. Hrissif was loyal, to the bloody end. Where he went, Foelker went. What bounty he reaped, Foelker shared in.

The problem was men like Valaric. Habit and tradition led everyone to look to the big men, the strong men, the *impressive* men, to be leaders. That's why men like Hrissif had to work so hard to ingratiate themselves with their potential allies, to prove their worth, to earn their trust and deliver on their promises. Some people just had to work harder to be respected and elevated, that was all. It was a bitter truth, but one Hrissif had never ducked once he'd learned and accepted it.

They were almost to the end of the alleyway now, after interminable twists and turns. Once they were back on an open street, they'd have only a block left before they arrived at the little boardinghouse they called home. The men of the guild often asked him about that—why he and his brother still lived like students or errant troubadours when he was an officer of the guild and gainfully employed (usually, anyway). Hrissif's answer was simple: he had no wife, no children, and no responsibilities or ties other than Foelker, his brothers in the guild, and his work. Why build a house or waste coin on lavish accommodations? All he needed was a bed, a piss pot, and a little warmth, after all. That left more coin for the finer things: food, drink, whores, a roll of the dice, weekly wagers at the pit fights, maybe even a few hours in a witchweed parlor if it'd been a hard month.

They were almost home. Hrissif did not relish stepping out into the windy street again, but it would be easy now that—

Something scraped behind them. It was a loud, sudden sound. Metal on stone. A flat clank. Then a crunching sound of some sort—stone on stone this time. Hrissif stopped and turned. Foelker had stopped, but he wasn't looking behind him. He was staring at Hrissif.

Hrissif peered back into the darkness beyond his brother's broad shoulders. That sound had come from somewhere behind them, deeper in the alley, or off on one of its tributaries, but he couldn't place exactly where.

"What is it?" Foelker asked.

"You didn't hear that?" Hrissif asked. Why didn't he just turn and go? Who cared what was moving in the alley? Probably just a dog or some cats looking for a place to screw.

But then he heard it again. A scrape and a clank. What could make a sound like that? A heavy iron box picked up off the pavement, dragged a little, then dropped? Some old, discarded stew pot in a rubbish pile knocked over and dragged by a stray sniffing for victuals?

Or maybe one of those metal shields that covered the access shafts to the sewers? He'd seen city engineers working with those blasted things before. They were iron, and heavy (to discourage idle or clandestine explorations). One of those could make a sound like that as it was lifted from its lodgings and slid aside to allow someone into the stinking tunnels beneath the streets.

Or out of them.

Hrissif snorted. Preposterous. What would venture out of the underground? True, he'd heard the stories—the city was rife with them. Whole legions of mutated vermin; diseased, devolved men; ancient, shit-stinking demons—according to legend, they all lived down there, a virtual shadow kingdom, vital day and night, unseen beneath Yenara's streets. And it was true, people *did* disappear more often around the open portals where the sewers flushed into the river or canals. But surely if something lived down there, it would hunt where the pickings were easiest, would it not? It wouldn't possibly be equal to the task of lifting and moving one of those iron lids...

Hrissif took a step toward his brother, still trying to scan the darkness and see what might be making those noises behind him.

"Hrissif," Foelker said, shifting back and forth on his feet now, impatient, "let's go. It's cold."

"Just wait," Hrissif said.

Footsteps now, heavy and ponderous. They didn't sound like regular bootheels, though. It was a short, thumping sort of gait, like someone trying to walk with large stones tied to their feet. He could just make out the rocky scrape of each step, and something that sounded like earth moving or bones being ground in a low, rhythmic sawing.

Hrissif was curious—but he shouldn't be foolish. They were steps away from the street. Time to carry on and leave whatever was moving through the alley—toward them—to its business, whatever that might be.

"Come on," he said to his brother. "It's nothing."

Hrissif started to turn.

Foelker suddenly cried out—a yelping, surprised sound, as though he'd been seized or yanked by something or someone.

Hrissif spun round. It was too dark to see clearly, but he could still see the impressions of things, and the impression that he saw filled him with instant, disbelieving horror. He saw Foelker squirming and jostling in the air. His booted feet were off the ground. His surprised yelp now became a frightened, beseeching scream, a torrent of almost-words that conveyed no information, only emotion.

Fright. Need. Desperation. Disbelief.

Something tall and wide held Foelker in its hands. Though Hrissif could not see what the thing was, exactly, he could see its starlit outline, and what he saw made no sense. He saw a low head, but no neck. Broad shoulders. Strange, skeletal projections and protrusions that looked like bones. And its eyes—two bright red-gold eyes, like lamplights in the dark, burning from the bottom of deep wells.

"Hrissif!" Foelker screamed. "Brother, help me!"

His cry was swallowed when the thing opened its mouth—what passed for a mouth, anyway—and roared. As it roared, it made a sound like boulders rolling down a mountainside and blew hot, ashen breath before it, like the scorching air wafting from a smith's forge.

What is it? Hrissif wondered, his mind working hard to understand what he was seeing. *Not a man . . . made of stone . . . or is it bone . . . and that smell . . . like old, damp earth . . . the earth of a rotten cellar . . . the earth of a graveyard . . .*

Then the thing jerked Foelker sideways with terrible force. Hrissif heard his brother's head connect with the immovable stone wall beside him just before the force and weight of the thing's enormous hands crushed Foelker's skull against that wall like an eggshell. Hrissif heard the snap of bone, smelled salt and copper, then felt hot curds of brain and ropes of blood splatter his face.

Then the hulking beast turned its firelit gaze toward Hrissif. It took a single step toward him. In that instant Hrissif knew that he would be its next target, that if he did not move, and fast, his brains would be on the wall as well. That terrible realization set Hrissif's feet pounding the half-frozen mud beneath him, and he fled into the night, screaming.

CHAPTER TWENTY-THREE

Bjalki woke with a start when he realized a shadow had fallen upon him. For an instant—just an instant—he forgot all that had preceded that moment, and there was only terror; he was alone in the dark with only a single oil lamp to provide any light, while a monster stared down at him with pitiless, firelit eyes.

Bjalki screamed, leapt up from where he lay, and pressed himself against the cold, damp stone wall. The echoes of his cry ricocheted through the catacombs beneath the temple.

His shock fled an instant later. Sense returned. The watcher—the monster—was no stranger, but his servant and charge. He had formed it, empowered it, summoned the spirit to inhabit it, and given it its mission.

This monster was wholly of his own making.

I am Bjalki, he'd said when he first faced the risen beast, *the one who called you and commands you. And this*—he'd drawn out the scrap of cloak from the sanctuary, the one stiff with the blood of the man Therba had struck down—*this will lead you to those who've wronged us.*

That was hours ago. He'd waited so long in the darkened catacombs that he'd started to wonder if the creature would return before morning at all. Yet here it was, having caught its master napping on his vigil, staring with its dumb, lamp-like eyes as if awaiting a new command. Bjalki slowly edged around it. The Kothrum rotated its body, keeping its eyes always trained upon him as he crossed the empty chamber to where his oil lamp stood burning atop the lip of a long-dry stone cistern.

As though it were tracking prey, Bjalki thought. *Gods, make it stop staring at me like that...*

Bjalki took up the lamp and studied his creation in the flickering golden gloom. There had been a number of theoretical models in the texts, from primitive, doll-like effigies of clay or mud to intricate, elaborate automatons rife with gears, clockwork, and forged, oiled joints. Bjalki, though, had decided to use materials close at hand that were both easily manipulated and carried with them a useful symbolism: the frightful majesty of incarnate death. That rough beast now stood before him, molded by his own hands of damp grave earth mixed with ashes from Therba's funeral pyre and encrusted all over with dwarven bones pilfered from the builders' tombs beneath the temple: animate, obedient, lethal. Though the Kothrum's eyes were nothing more than a pair of deep wells in its oddly small head, a mysterious, witchy light pulsing in their depths, there was yet a strange, childlike avidity in them, as if the thing awaited something, *craved* something, from the one who had created it.

Craving... that's ridiculous, Bjalki told himself. *It's an automaton, pure and simple. It has no feelings—only a purpose.*

Bjalki raised the lamp as high as he could, closely examining its malformed symmetries and primitive, charnel plumage of chalky old bone. The creature looked much as it had when he'd given it orders and it had left him. All except its hands.

Those hands, large and splayed and ugly and bestial, were covered in sticky, clotted, slowly coagulating blood.

"Oh, merciful Thendril...," Bjalki breathed, and lowered the lamp so that its weak light better illuminated the beast's bloodied talons. As if in answer to his close scrutiny, the Kothrum lifted its hands. It displayed them like a child proud of a fresh finger painting. Most of the blood had congealed, turned black and sticky, but there were still thick red rivulets here and there, rolling sluggishly along its upraised fingers or trembling whenever the beast made even the most minute movement. Bjalki also thought he saw something caught in the joints of its bony fingers: milky curds of some bodily tissue, along with a few sharp bits of bone that attested to something's having been broken—nay, crushed—in the creature's bare hands.

The Kothrum had killed this night.

I've done it, then, Bjalki realized. *I've raised an avenger. I've delivered death.*

Based upon what Bjalki had gleaned from the texts, the thing should have sought the man whose blood stained that scrap of cloth first. Once he'd been located and dispatched, the creature would now seek any accomplices magically associated with the murder of Docent Therba. To the Kothrum, Therba's death tied together every human present at her death, and the blood left behind by that single wounded man created a path that the Kothrum could follow to find them.

Bjalki forced himself to meet the Kothrum's implacable glowing gaze. The creature stared down at him, unmoving, unmoved.

"I will ask you a question. You will answer in the affirmative by nodding your head, in the negative by shaking your head from side to side. Do you understand these instructions?"

To his great surprise, the Kothrum slowly nodded the comically small head on its broad shoulders.

Bjalki started to speak again, but his voice caught in his throat, which was suddenly dry as baked clay under a summer sun. He wet his tongue, then pressed on.

"Did you kill one of the marked men?" Bjalki asked.

The Kothrum nodded.

"More than one?" Bjalki added.

The creature's head slid from side to side: no.

"Good," Bjalki said, feeling a strange sort of relief. "You've done well, then. Was it the man whose blood stained the rag I showed you?"

The Kothrum nodded.

Bjalki had thought that knowledge would satisfy him . . . but, shockingly, it did the opposite. In that instant, what had hitherto been an abstract concept—an exercise of sorts—struck him as damningly irrevocable.

The man whom Therba had thumped headwise with her stave, a man who had been unconscious and uninvolved when Therba was ultimately murdered, had just been executed—ended utterly—by this thing that Bjalki had brought to life.

Who was he? Did he have a name? A family? A wife or children? A father and mother?

Stop it, a voice inside Bjalki hissed. *Waste no sympathy for that man, for he wasted none for Therba, or for yourself. Just because she knocked him out cold before he had a chance to take part in her murder doesn't mean he would not have.*

And yet, Bjalki thought, *he could have meant her no harm. He could have been angry and misguided, like the others . . . but perhaps, when Therba was truly in danger, he would have tried to help her, to stop the man who wielded the knife? Just as their leader helped me escape?*

Bjalki felt a strange sickness in the pit of his stomach and realized that it was self loathing. He'd taken definitive action, committed a grievously mortal sin, and had done so without knowing, beyond any doubt, that the man—or men—he sought to murder were, in fact, those most directly responsible.

One man held her, he reminded himself. *One more plunged*

the knife in. Two guilty parties, without a doubt. The others were
accomplices—but they did not truly kill her, did they? Can I pass fatal
judgment on them when they were not, in fact, directly responsible for
her death?

And yet, they were all there. All in masks. All intent on desecrating
our temple and terrorizing us and humiliating us. Even if Therba's
murder was the result of a single man's overzealousness, they were still
there to spread fear and do harm, were they not?

Should that absolve them? Does that mean they deserve to live when
their brother took Therba from us?

Bjalki stared at the Kothrum. The Kothrum stared back.
What had he done, summoning this thing he did not understand, to punish guilty men he could not, realistically, name
or pass judgment upon? What had ever given him the notion
that he, a fortune-telling, omen-reading auspice, was worthy
or powerful enough to traffic with these dark powers and try
to see justice done?

Because you were there! that angry voice within him countered. *You saw her die! You feared for your own imminent death! And*
now that your people need you and the men who wronged you might
escape mortal justice, you would see vengeance—directed vengeance—
visited upon them just as they think they've escaped it! That is why!

"No," Bjalki said aloud, the sound of his own voice sounding feeble even to him. "This can't be allowed to go on."

The Kothrum stared down at him as if awaiting orders, but
made no move to respond to his words.

Of course he hadn't given a command. But what could he
do? What options did he have?

The stone—that was it!

Every Hallirwelk temple in the world held, among its holy
relics, a collection of magical stones recovered, in the most
ancient of epochs, from the underground mines that were the

homelands of Hallir's Folk. These stones were discovered at intervals through the ages, always by accident, and usually set apart from the other produce of dwarven mining by a latent glow evident within them. From the dawn of time, his people had cherished these stones whenever and wherever they were discovered, and gathered them together in a single holy coffer at the Mother Temple, to be venerated, prayed over, and sometimes employed in the working of communal wonders or the invocation of miracles from the gods. When Hallir's Folk began to scatter into the world of men and elves, to build temples to their gods away from their subterranean birthplace, the founding clergy of those far-flung temples would be granted a trio of those stones of power for their own reliquaries, as miraculous seeds of a sort—some small measure of the ancient power the gods afforded all their kind, to be kept and venerated in a consecrated house of worship.

To enact his plan, Bjalki had stolen one of those sacred gems from the temple reliquary, an emerald so dark it was almost black, inscribed with dwarven runes and pulsing with a sickly green inner light. He had been keenly aware, when he'd purloined the gem and brought it down into the catacombs for his ritual, that to use such a holy gift for such an unholy purpose was most unseemly, if not blasphemous. But all the texts had been in agreement about one thing: the constructed body that the Kothrum-spirit would inhabit needed an energy source, and those runestones were the most frequently invoked example of such a source.

Thus, in accordance with the rites he'd compiled, Bjalki had dug a hole in what passed for his dirt-beast's small round head, then forced the glowing gem deep into the hole he'd made and packed in dirt on top of it. As an afterthought he'd placed a half-broken skull over the place where he'd planted the stone, as a grim helmet of sorts.

And so, if he wanted to deactivate his creature, perhaps that was all that was required: lift off that broken skull cap, dig his fingers into the soft soil of the Kothrum's skull, and yank that gem out.

It couldn't hurt to try, anyway.

"Kneel down," Bjalki said, trying to sound as commanding and forceful as he could.

The Kothrum did as commanded, finally lowering its hands and falling to its knees with a crunching of soil and bone. Its head was now more or less at Bjalki's eye level.

"Lower your head," Bjalki said.

The Kothrum obeyed, as if awaiting a blessing.

Bjalki reached up and tried to lift off the skull cap. It stuck fast, as though it had somehow been glued to its perch.

Strange, he thought. *I didn't affix it. I simply placed it there.*

He pulled with both hands. Yanked. Tried to get his finger-nails beneath the broken edges of the shattered hemisphere of bone.

Suddenly the Kothrum shoved him. The beast seemed to expend no force on the gesture, but Bjalki was nonetheless thrown back violently and rolled across the earthen floor of the chamber. His lamp had fallen from his hands, just a few feet from the where the Kothrum still knelt.

Bjalki stared for a moment, then scurried to his feet again. He studied the beast in the dim lamplight. Its faceless coun-tenance remained blank and impassive even as its eyes still burned, two miniature forge fires in the murky darkness.

And yet it *had* shoved him away—defended itself from what was, essentially, an attack.

Bjalki stepped forward. He pointed to the skull cap. "Remove that," he commanded. "Take it off. Let me see the bare earth beneath it."

The Kothrum did nothing.

"I said remove it!" Bjalki shouted, then lunged forward again, reaching out for the skull cap. Perhaps, if he could just get a purchase on it again—

This time the Kothrum did not shove—it grabbed. Both bloodied hands shot up, took hold of his robes, and tossed him aside. Bjalki hit the damp stone wall of the underground chamber and tumbled to the earthen floor, breath knocked out of him. He lay for a time in the dirt, sputtering and coughing, trying to understand what had gone wrong. When he'd finally regained himself, he tottered upright and sat where he'd fallen.

The Kothrum stood above him, looming, its lamplike eyes burning down upon him.

"I am your master," Bjalki said, and struggled to his feet again. "How dare you lay hands on me!"

He reached out for it again, not even sure what he intended to do. He struck it in the torso, like a petulant child, just to see how it might respond. To his great surprise, it responded with violence. Once more he was struck and sent sprawling, head over heels. Once more, when he regained his senses and sat upright, the Kothrum stood above him, staring at him, its silence and implacable face a strange sort of taunt.

Bjalki stood again, toe to toe with the beast.

"I command you to stand down!" he shouted. "There will be no more murders! No more justice! I revoke my summons!"

The Kothrum stared, doing nothing.

"Will you obey me in this?" Bjalki asked.

The Kothrum shook its head slowly.

"But I command you!" Bjalki said. "I summoned you!"

The Kothrum nodded.

"But you will not obey when I try to revoke that summons?"

The Kothrum shook its head.

"What will you do, then?" he asked, starting to realize how foolish he sounded. "Now that you've begun, you'll not stop until the warrant I gave you is satisfied? Until all those marked men are dead?"

As he'd dreaded, the Kothrum gave a single curt nod.

"No," Bjalki said, shaking his head. His knees buckled beneath him. "No, this isn't what I wanted...It can't be..."

The Kothrum offered no more responses. No nods, no shakings of its tiny head. It simply stared, even as tears filled Bjalki's eyes and he became aware of the blood from the creature's hands now staining his robes, now smeared on his face, imparted in their momentary contact when the thing had tossed him about the room.

The blood of the slain. Marking him. Condemning him.

CHAPTER TWENTY-FOUR

Rem and Torval were just about done with their shift, trudging back to the watchkeep and dragging under the weight of their recently mandated armor, when they heard the scream of a watchwarden's whistle just to the west of them. The partners exchanged mordant looks, sighed, then broke into a jog, heading off in the direction of the call. It took some searching—they pounded down the wrong street or alleyway at least twice in an effort to home in on the whistle calls—but finally they arrived at a short, bent lane between two larger thoroughfares, a depressingly ordinary street of shabby old boardinghouses and dingy little shop fronts. A crowd clotted the center of the street, right near the mouth of an alley. Flickering torchlight was visible deeper in the alleyway, throwing warm light and dancing shadows on the wide-eyed, staring faces of the gathered onlookers.

Torval led the way through the crowd, holding up his badge and barking that all the gawpers needed to make way for the wardwatch. Rem followed suit and noted uncomfortably that more than a few of the people present eyed Torval warily, as though he were vermin carrying some disease. That observation made Rem more than a little uneasy. He knew well that all over Yenara—especially in the Fifth Ward—there were neighborhoods where anyone with a badge was unwelcome and regarded with suspicion. But what he saw now—narrowed eyes, disgusted frowns, even a few whispers—seemed to have nothing to do with the two of them, or their office, but only with Torval specifically.

It's spreading into the streets, he thought as they forced their way through the crowd. *This business that began with a single group of humans and the dwarves. Soon enough it'll turn into one of those bitter, bloody feuds that spiral into madness and stir hatred on both sides, with the original slight or insult long forgotten . . .*

Gods of the Panoply, he prayed it never came to that.

At last they made it through the crowd and broke into the mouth of the alleyway. Four other watchwardens—Djubal and Klutch, Pettina and Firimol—were already present. Djubal and Klutch stood by with blazing torches, trying to light the grim tableau as Pettina—a compact, tattooed Kostermaid from the north whose well-honed tracking skills were often employed in just such a fashion, to parse murder sites for faint but usable clues—studied the mess before them. A few feet away, deeper in the alley, Watchwarden Firimol took testimony from a man whose choked, lowered voice Rem could barely hear and whose face he could not see.

Rem lowered his eyes to the body crumpled on the floor of the alley. He didn't fancy himself of a sensitive bent, but the sight made his stomach churn a bit. Just beneath the smell of the resin torches he caught the charnel, coppery tang of blood and the musty barnyard scent of exposed organs—in this case the dead man's dashed brains.

Torval groaned. "Sundry hells," he said. "What befell that poor bastard?"

Djubal, skin dark and eyes bright, shrugged. "Your guess is as good as ours, old stump. This is how we found him."

Rem studied the wall of the alley about six feet above the man's lifeless body. There was a horrible garish splash of gore

there, thickened by a few curds of brain matter, slowly coagulating as it dripped down the uneven surface of the wall.

"Head crushed against the stone?" Rem asked, by way of an
affirmation.

"My guess," Klutch said, moving the torch in his hand a little closer. "And look there—outside the main bloom. These two
marks, and this third over here. What does that look like to you?"

"Fingers?" Torval asked.

"But what's only got three fingers?" Klutch added.

"An orc that lost two?" Pettina offered from her crouch.

"Maybe a Kosterman wearing split mittens?" Djubal countered.

"It doesn't have to be fingers," Torval said impatiently. "Those
could just be smears."

"Or the smears of three fingers," Rem offered, "when the
murderer actually had five."

"I'm a little more concerned about the force involved," Djubal
broke in. "Look at this poor sod's head, will you?"

Rem and Torval crouched to get a better look. It was true—
the victim's skull had been smashed utterly, brains everywhere,
face squished into a vile, narrow parody of a human visage, like
a doll missing half its stuffing. Worse, the collapse of the victim's
skull and jawbone stretched his open mouth into an elongated
oval that made it look as if he were yawning or screaming—a
hideous detail that Rem half wished he could instantly forget.

"Who is he?" Torval asked.

"He's my brother," a hoarse voice answered. It was the man
Firimol was questioning, just a few feet from them.

Rem recognized him instantly: Hrissif, that smirking stonemason who'd tried so mightily to blow them off the other
night when they'd come to ask their questions.

"Well," Torval said beside Rem. "Here's a familiar face."

Hrissif pushed past Firimol, leveling a finger at Torval. "I don't want him here!" he said, and Rem saw something strange in the man's manner—a true, bone-deep fear, an unspoken hysteria. Rem had pegged this fellow for the sort who was never rattled by anything—the sort more likely to do the rattling, and stay calm as a coiled adder all the while. But here, now, he could see clearly that the man seemed to literally hate and fear Torval, all at once. That he wasn't simply grieving the loss of his brother—he was truly, deeply shaken by something.

Firimol edged up behind the stonemason. He was a strange, slender man—always seeming to Rem more like the fussy butler for some proud old patrician family or a canny artist of some sort than like a keeper of the peace. Nonetheless, everyone swore the man was most dependable on the streets, eager to keep the peace most of the time, quick to enforce it when things got out of hand, refined manners notwithstanding.

"Here now," Firimol said to the agitated Hrissif. "Watchwarden Torval's one of our best."

"He's one of *them*," Hrissif said. "And if I were a betting man, I'd put this"—he pointed at the corpse—"at *their* doorstep."

"Them," Rem repeated. "You mean dwarves?"

"Of course," Hrissif said. "The little pickmonkeys think we're threatening them now, so they're sending messages."

"Mind your tongue," Torval said, taking a single step toward the man.

Rem threw his arm in front of his partner, hoping that his attempt to quietly hold him back wouldn't make the old stump more angry. "So," Rem said slowly, "you're saying dwarves did this? To your brother?"

Hrissif shook his head. "It wasn't a dwarf," he said. "It wasn't anything I've seen before. But I'm betting they're responsible, somehow."

"He's not making any sense," Torval growled.

"I know what I saw!" Hrissif shouted. "At least—I don't *know* what it was, but I know it was nothing natural."

"Smelled like damp earth," Firimol recited, clearly parroting some of what he'd gleaned in his conversation with Hrissif before their arrival. "A little taller than Hrissif. Wide shoulders. Big hands. Bones."

"Bones?" Rem asked.

"Aye," Hrissif said, nodding. "Studded with them, like. I couldn't see clearly, it was dark, but the outline was somewhat clear, picked out by the starlight."

"Smelled like earth," Torval muttered, almost to himself, "and covered in bones...?"

Hrissif lunged at Torval. Firimol and Klutch caught him. "Don't mock me!" the stonemason spat. "That's my brother lying there! Look at his goddamned skull! Look at how he died! I've still got his blood on my face!"

Rem studied his long, angular face. He was right. For just a moment Rem entertained the possibility that Hrissif's brother had died by Hrissif's own hand. But no, that made no sense... His face was bloody but the rest of him was clean—especially his hands. And besides, he could not have done such a thing— crushed his brother's skull so utterly—without a weapon of some sort. A sledgehammer or a giant stone block. And even then, the force required would certainly be greater than Hrissif's ropy frame could produce, wouldn't it?

As Rem shook his head, chasing away that momentary consideration, he caught sight of Torval, lingering just beside him. The dwarf had a puzzling look on his face—blank and pensive, as if something Hrissif had said had jogged a memory within him.

"Torval?" Rem asked, trying to get his stunned partner's attention.

"Its eyes," Hrissif said, now appealing to anyone who would listen, turning his desperate, hounded gaze on each of the watchwardens present in turn. "Its eyes burned, like two infernal fires in deep stone pits. I've heard stories, had nightmares, but I've never seen anything like it. Not in the flesh. Not ever. It's some kind of foul dwarven magic, I tell you—"

"You need to stop," Rem said, stepping close to the man and speaking as quietly as he could. "If you say another word about dwarves or what blame should be laid upon them—"

Hrissif sneered, but there was a terrible sadness behind the expression now, as though he pitied Rem. Pitied his naivety. "You won't even stick up for your own kind?"

Rem jerked his head toward Torval. "See that badge he wears? That makes him *my kind*. But you, sir...you're a stranger."

Hrissif stared at Rem for a moment, studying him, appraising him. Rem never let his gaze waver. *Look here*, he thought, *right into my eyes. Measure me and tell me what you find. I won't back down on this.*

Then, as if he realized that there was no intimidating Rem—no shaming him—Hrissif swung his gaze aside and focused on something else. A moment too late, Rem realized what it was.

The crowd, just beyond the mouth of the alley.

"Do you see this?" Hrissif shouted. "Here lies a man—*my own brother*—dead! Murdered! And when I offer my suspicions, these fools with their badges try to tell me I'm wrong—because it's inconvenient! Because the enemy"—he leveled a finger at Torval—"is one of them!"

The crowd beyond the alley's mouth began to rumble and murmur.

Rem looked to Torval, half expecting his partner to unleash himself on Hrissif, to defend his own honor if not the honor of his people. But to Rem's great astonishment, Torval offered no such rebuttal. Instead he just stood staring at the ruined corpse of Hrissif's poor dead brother, that dazed, puzzled look still on his broad face.

What's gotten into him? Rem wondered. *Since when does Torval let insults pass so easily?*

"What do you wager," Hrissif began, voice rising, still addressing the crowd, "that it's dwarven gold paying the wages of these sorry, whoring head-breakers?"

Rem lost control. Almost without realizing what he was doing, his fists balled around Hrissif's cloak and he threw the man right into the wall of the alley. He heard the stonemason's head thump against the brick and saw the dazed look in his eyes—shock at Rem's sudden rage, a wincing against the pain of his ringing skull.

"Shut your mouth!" Rem hissed, shaking the stonemason. "Don't say another gods-damned word—"

Rem felt hands clutching at him, arms folding round him, trying to yank him away from their witness.

"Not helping," Djubal said.

"That'll get us nowhere," Firimol whispered.

"You see that?" Hrissif was shouting now, still addressing his audience in his daze. "My arrow hit too close to the mark, I'd say. What does that tell you?"

Firimol yanked Hrissif aside, then shoved him along, deeper into the alley. "We're finished here," he said. "You can go, sir."

Hrissif took a step back toward them. "I want my brother's body," he began.

"When we've finished," Firimol said. "I'll deliver it myself. Go, now, before you make this any worse."

Rem glanced at the crowd, just a stone's throw from them. Judging by the looks on some of their faces, the way they whispered and shook their heads, Hrissif already had. And Rem had played right into his hands.

Hrissif snorted and tugged his cloak closer around him. "I'll expect him at the guildhall by sunrise," he said. "Fail to deliver him and I'll see that each and every one of you pays for what you've done tonight."

And with that he was off.

Rem looked to Djubal, who still held him. "I'm sorry," he said.

"No apologies," Djubal said quietly, and let go of him. "I was on the verge myself."

"That wasn't our first run-in with him," Rem said. "And I'm guessing it won't be our last."

"Gentlemen!" Pettina chimed in. She'd moved away from the argument and taken a torch deeper into the alley. Clearly, by the way she stood, staring at the muddy floor of the byway with her torch lowered for better light, she'd found something.

They all hurried to her side. To Rem's great relief, Torval finally seemed to snap out of his daze, and he joined them. Rem heard the crowd at the mouth of the alley surge forward to see what the watchwardens had found. Djubal and Firimol doubled back to block their way and urge them to keep their distance.

Pettina pointed at a section of the alley floor that was more mud than detritus or rubbish: a two-yard span that allowed for clearer footprints to be made by anyone passing through. She gestured to one track of human feet moving along the length of the alley toward where Hrissif's brother lay, stiffening.

"Those are the brothers' prints," she said. Then she pointed to something else: a strange agglomeration of footprints that didn't look like feet at all. They were instead strange round depressions in the mud, easily a foot in diameter, but sporting nothing like the contours or textures left by the bare or booted feet of anything in the known world. And yet those strange, circular depressions were arranged and spaced in such a way as to clearly suggest footsteps.

"What in the sundry hells?" Rem muttered.

"Footprints," Torval said, that single word carrying a terrible, ominous weight.

"There is our murderer," Pettina said grimly. "And Hrissif was right: it wasn't human."

CHAPTER TWENTY-FIVE

The day was waning, dusk just an hour or two away, when Bjalki arrived at the conclave of elders. Those present included the ethnarch, his good wife, Trade Minister Broon, Elder Hrothwar, Arbiter Haefred, and Bjalki himself. Eldgrim's ever-present, ever-silent secretary—recording their minutes—haunted the proceedings like a shadowy spirit, and Godrumm, the captain of the Swords of Eld, stood by in silence, usually content to listen without chiming in. Bjalki knew not who had called the meeting, nor why, precisely. He knew only that it was of some import, because the audience chamber had been cleared and the mood upon those gathered was grim and silent. Bjalki wondered if it had something to do with him, for he was the last to arrive, and all their eyes swung toward him when he did, weighing him down with silent recriminations the moment he slipped into the room.

"Am I late?" he asked.

"Not late," Eldgrim said, "but last. Come, sit." They were all gathered at the great conference table, beer, bread, cheese, and a half-carved ham laid out untouched before them.

Bjalki took an empty seat between Hrothwar and Godrumm. The captain of the house guard's chest and shoulders rose and fell like a bellows as if he was trying to calm himself, regain himself, after some outburst.

After a long, awkward silence, Lady Leffi leaned forward.

"It appears that someone murdered a stonemason in the Fifth Ward last night," she said slowly. "A member of the very same chapter that lost their contract to our laborers. The man's death is seen as both malicious and suspicious."

Bjalki kept his eyes down. He remembered greeting the Kothrum when it returned to him, underground, in the wee hours of the morning. Its dreadful, bony hands stained dark with blood and clotted with something Bjalki opted not to analyze too closely. It had displayed those stained hands proudly for its master, as though it were a child, its fingers splashed with finger paint.

Bjalki's memory of the predawn hours was interrupted as Eldgrim muttered something and shifted in his seat. Leffi waited for a moment, expecting him to say something. He did not. She carried on. "Naturally, given the hostilities of late between these craftsmen and our own, suspicions fall upon us, or someone in this community."

"Did they report the manner of this man's death?" Haefred asked.

"Apparently," Leffi said, "his skull was crushed. Upon a wall."

"I swear," Godrumm broke in, "that neither I nor any of the men in the Swords of Eld had anything to do with this man's murder...though I wish we had."

That got Eldgrim to snap himself out of his dyspeptic silence. "You and I both, Captain," the ethnarch rumbled. "There's little honor in someone else slaying your enemies for you."

"You should not say such things, Husband," Leffi said. Bjalki noted the tone of her voice—not soft or disturbed at all, but hard, scolding, reproachful.

"And why can't we?" the ethnarch countered. "We are alone here—Hallir's Folk, all of us. There are no outsiders here to hold our words against us, or to suggest that our inward enmities are proof of actual criminality."

"This is most grave," old Hrothwar said, and leaned forward. "They will come for us now!"

"Who?" Eldgrim asked. "That rabble that pass for a ward guard? They're thieves and drunkards, the lot of them . . ."

"All of them!" Haefred hissed. "Every man, woman, and child! If word gets around that a workingman of that sort was murdered, and that it was dwarven hands that spilt his blood—"

"But they don't know that dwarven hands spilt his blood!" the ethnarch snapped. "Let them prove it."

"This is a season in which proof is of little consequence," Leffi said solemnly. "The sage and the arbiter speak aright. If the people of this city—even of this ward—get stirred up like a nest of hornets and grow eager to avenge that man's murder, they shall look for the closest and most convenient scapegoat . . . which could be us."

And then, Bjalki thought solemnly, *I shall have to turn the Kothrum on them as well. Gods, it really never stops, does it? First the murderers. Then any who come to fetter or accuse or punish us. What have I done?*

"We *are* outnumbered," Trade Minister Broon said quietly. When they all turned to him, amazed that he'd deigned to speak, he could only shrug. "Aren't we? If they decide to come for us—"

"No one shall come for us," Eldgrim said, hand pounding the table. "We'll double the house guard. Arm everyone, from the chambermaids to the brewer!"

I must stop this, Bjalki thought. *Now, before it's too late. Reassure them—do what a priest is supposed to do—then I shall see to the Kothrum. There must be a way to stop it . . . something I've missed . . . something in the texts—*

"There is no doubling, milord," Godrumm said. "Every sword is now deployed."

"Then build a militia," Eldgrim snapped. "Go to the streets, drag in every able-bodied dwarf who loves their country and their countrymen, and explain to them what's going on—what's at stake! They cannot refuse us—and if they do, it's the dungeons for them! Our law—our traditions—give me the right to demand such fealty, to mobilize such a force—"

"What's going on, precisely?" Bjalki suddenly asked. They all stared at him as though his words were the strangest they'd ever heard. He drew a breath and carried on a little more forcefully. "We have suspicions, fears, anxieties," he continued, trying to talk himself as much as the rest of them into a place of calmness. "But what proof do we have that the people of this city will blame us, or come for us? Perhaps this man's death will end it all. We've lost one of ours, they've lost one of theirs. Surely that should signal that things have gotten far enough out of hand—"

For they have. And I am to blame. The sin is mine, and mine alone.

"Blood cries out for blood," Eldgrim said, eyeing Bjalki like the lowest form of life he'd ever encountered. "If someone—friend or kinsman—does not seek justice for this man's murder, then he was a poor man in life indeed. And since we've become the embodiment of all these stone breakers hate—"

"That is not true," Bjalki said. "They were angry over their dismissal from the temple project. They made that anger known in the streets. They threatened our people and caused trouble in the marketplace. In answer, some of our own folk caught a hapless boy who may or may not have had a thing to do with the trouble they caused and beat him senseless. Do we even know if he lived or died? If he had a name?"

"If they did not want reprisal against the innocent," Eldgrim said archly, "they should not have threatened the innocent with that riot in the market."

"I lost someone I cared for as well," Bjalki countered. "I was there when Therba was murdered! I saw her bleed her last! I saw the life leave her!"

"And yet," Eldgrim countered, "you did *nothing* to stop it. Little wonder you come to us now talking of a subservient, wheedling peace. You are a bloody coward, Auspice Bjalki. I knew it from the moment you were forced upon this court."

"Eldgrim!" Leffi snapped.

"This needs to stop," Hrothwar said.

"When one's people are threatened," Eldgrim said, slowly and deliberately, "one defends them. That is both natural law and holy law. There are no questions to be asked, no soul-searching to be done. If one chooses not to act—decisively—in that moment of trial, then one is a dishonorable cur."

Someone started pounding on the outer door of the chamber. Amid the pounding, Leffi broke in upon Eldgrim's pronouncement.

"There's no need for all this," she said, clearly at her wit's end with her husband's belligerence. "Apologize to the auspice, milord."

Eldgrim looked at his wife as though she'd just struck him in front of the court. "What did you say?"

"I said," she responded, slowly and patiently, "apologize. We accomplish nothing by fighting among ourselves."

Eldgrim stared at her for a long moment. The pounding at the door continued. Clearly someone wanted into the room, and urgently.

"I was not fighting," Eldgrim told his wife. "I was commanding. That is, after all, my anointed and sacred duty. As it is yours to serve and obey me."

Leffi wanted to fight with him—Bjalki saw it in the squaring of her shoulders and the set of her mouth. And yet...she also knew the wisdom of retreat. Eldgrim could not be overcome head-on. He had to be finessed, manipulated. At the very least convinced behind closed doors. She knew—they all knew—that if she challenged him here and now, he would only redouble his resistance to her.

The pounding came. Again. Again. Again.

Leffi sat, not saying another word.

At the other end of the table, nearest the door, Godrumm shot to his feet and spun out of his chair.

"Come in, damn you!" he shouted.

The door to the audience chamber opened a little, and the house herald slunk in. "Pardon the interruption, milord," he said, addressing the ethnarch, "but there is a visitor. He demands an audience with the court."

"A visitor?" Eldgrim asked. "Official?"

The herald shrugged. "I am unsure, my lord. It's that watchwarden—the dwarf. He's all alone."

Bjalki watched as everyone at the table exchanged puzzled glances, as though no one knew what to say or do. Finally Leffi looked to the herald and nodded.

"See him in," she said.

Eldgrim shot his wife a baleful glare, as though issuing even that simple order, to a house servant, should not have fallen to anyone but himself.

Bjalki hung his head. *Gods, deliver us from this petty tyrant... from the spirit of hate that moves him and stains us all...*

The herald slipped out. A moment later he returned with the watchwarden in tow. Bjalki recognized the dwarf immediately, that same fellow having petitioned the court and the temple just weeks earlier in order to see his eldest son educated and apprenticed among his people now that he was of age. If he remembered correctly, this dwarf—Torval—had been guilty of some long-ago slight against their people. Was it challenging members of the martial class to a duel? Insult to priests? Bjalki could not remember the details.

But he remembered well how Eldgrim had made the dwarf pay for his sins. The ethnarch's apparent relish when it came to a final pronouncement on the issue of reparations and reconciliation with Hallir's Folk.

Kneel, he had said.

In truth, Bjalki had thought that a harsh punishment— evidence that Eldgrim bore the dwarf some grudge and was eager to break his spirit. In practice, forcing a repentant enemy to kneel after reparations had already been petitioned for and agreed to was reserved for the most intractable of foes, those whose transgressions were of greater moral import—rebels, usurpers, and the like. Though it was well within Eldgrim's power to demand such a show of humility, the demand had nonetheless struck Bjalki— and the others present, given their grumblings afterward—as excessive and spiteful. And yet, to everyone's great surprise, Torval had done what the ethnarch asked. He had knelt and begged forgiveness for his son's sake, though his gnashing teeth and burning gaze made it clear he did so under the greatest of duress.

Clearly this Torval was determined, and strong, and loved his son deeply; otherwise how could he have endured such humiliation? That sort of power—even in apparent defeat— would forever elude a proud, contentious dwarf like Eldgrim.

The herald let himself out. The dwarven watchwarden strode forward, stopped about five paces from the conference table, and stood. For a long time he said nothing. No one at the table said anything, either, though most of them adjusted their seats so that they would face him and see him more easily.

"Good watchwarden," Leffi finally said, "how can we help you today?"

The dwarf drew a deep breath. "Milady, I come to you—to all of you—as a private petitioner, not a member of the watch."

Eldgrim frowned. "A private petitioner..."

"You know my son is in your care at present," Torval said. "I humbled myself before you to secure his fostering and apprenticeship."

"Humbled," Eldgrim said, then sniffed. "Tetherix, was it?"

"Tavarix," Leffi corrected him. "His name is Tavarix."

"Just so," the watchwarden said. Bjalki could see the rage in him, simmering just behind his blue eyes, clear in the balled-up, white-knuckled hardness of his fists at his sides. The dwarf continued. "Coming to you now, in this fashion, is not easy for me...just as asking for you to accept him was not easy, given my...history."

"'A father's sins scar a son's back,'" Eldgrim said, quoting from the *Pillars of Kondela*.

Torval looked right at the ethnarch, eyes narrow, gaze steely and unwavering. "I should think the homage I've already paid has squared my debt to our people. Now, as for my son...speak of him again as bearing any scars not earned by his own endeavors, and you shall have some of your own, good ethnarch."

Bjalki literally heard everyone's breath catch. He could not believe the dwarven watchwarden's audacity. Neither could anyone else, apparently.

Truth be told, he admired it.

"You dare," Eldgrim snarled.

"I dare," Torval answered. "I gave you what you asked for, Eldgrim, and you gave me what I requested in turn. I'll not give you a copper more, nor another *milord*, nor a single knee dropped in obeisance. Our deal was struck when I knelt to satisfy your pride; now I expect you to hold up your end of it."

Eldgrim shot to his feet. "Remove this impertinent worm," he said.

Godrumm moved to do so. Torval offered the captain of the Swords of Eld a burning glare and a spoken challenge.

"Try it," Torval said.

Godrumm froze. Torval swung his gaze back toward Eldgrim.

"Let's cut to the chase here," he said. "I came and begged your forgiveness so that my son could regain a place among his people. When you accepted him, you made a pledge of your own: to protect him and keep him safe and see him through the end of his boyhood. But the violence in this city—the violence perpetrated *against* you and *by* you—"

"Violence!" Eldgrim shouted. "We are guilty of nothing, you—"

"I don't believe you," Torval said, looking right at him. "But I also can't prove it. I have only my instincts, but I trust those. And I know my own people. I know that at least some of you—if not in this room, then out there, in those streets—would take the wrong done to you and seek to revisit it on your enemies tenfold. That is the dwarven way, is it not? Unbending pride? Unending vengeance?"

Leffi stood now. She stepped away from the table and toward Torval. Bjalki could see on the courtly lady's face that she wanted an end to this little meeting, not only to protect them, but to protect this watchman as well. The rage, the naked hatred, was clear as a cloudless dawn on Eldgrim's face. Bjalki almost fancied he could see gears and clock springs turning and tumbling in the ethnarch's mind, working out any and all methods of attack to humble the proud little watchman before him, or to end him entirely.

"Why have you come to us?" Leffi asked Torval. "Surely not only to cast aspersions and insult us?"

Torval looked contrite—a little, anyway. It was as though she were the only member of the court whom he could take seriously, whom he could truly respect. "Milady," he said slowly, "I mean no insult. I just need my son back, at least until this mess is over and done with. At that time he can continue his education and apprenticeship. But for the time being, he should be home, with his family, where he can be safe. Not right in the line of fire. Not where *your* sins"—he indicated all of them seated at the table—"can scar him."

"Once again," Eldgrim said, "the father's cowardice stains the son."

Torval stepped forward then. Every muscle in his body went taut, every vein standing out like creepers on the bark of a tree.

"Try me, if you think I'm a coward," he growled. "When my people took my locks and beard and exiled me, it took nine of them to get me on my back! How many men have *you* got, Ethnarch? Or do you think you can take me alone?"

The ethnarch was on his feet, striding forward now. He held out a hand to Godrumm.

"Your sword, Captain!"

"Sir?"

The ethnarch roared, "Your sword, so that I may cut this fool down where he stands!"

"Please," Leffi shouted. "Control yourselves! I shall have no bloodshed in here! Not a drop!"

"There is no cowardice in wanting to keep one's kinfolk safe," Bjalki offered, entering the fray in an effort to allay the mounting tension. "Lord Eldgrim, this dwarf's intentions are honorable, and his request simple and clear. I beg you, stand down and let him be."

"Quiet, you," Eldgrim said. "You hedge priest. You sniveling wretch."

Bjalki felt his heart start to hammer in his chest.

"Ethnarch!" Hrothwar shouted. "Control yourself!"

Eldgrim now seemed to forget Torval was even there. He turned on Hrothwar. "This priest, as you call him, let good priestess Therba die at the hands of sneak thieves! He ran when he could have fought! Why, in all the sundry hells, should I show him any respect or deference when there is no honor in him?"

"There we are," the watchman broke in, "back to honor. You're so very concerned with everyone else's honor, Lord Eldgrim. I wonder that you don't pay more attention to your own."

Eldgrim's head swung toward the watchwarden. "Say one more word, *sweppsa*, and it won't be the humans that your boy will need to fear."

Bjalki watched, horrified, as the watchwarden Torval lunged right at the ethnarch, seized his ermine-lined robe, then lifted him and hove him a good ten feet from where he stood. In an instant Captain Godrumm was on his feet, sword ringing as it leapt from its sheath. Eldgrim hit the wall with terrific force, then slid to the floor. Though stunned, he regained himself almost immediately.

"Please," Bjalki said, his voice sounding weak even in his own ears. "Please, all of you, stop this."

The dwarven watchwarden was armed now, a sturdy maul in his hand. He stood on guard, eyes darting back and forth between Captain Godrumm on his right and the ethnarch directly in front of him. Captain Godrumm, for his part, seemed too shocked to move. His sword hovered in the air, bent toward the watchwarden, trembling.

"Guards!" Eldgrim shouted.

The doors to the audience chamber thundered open, and a bevy of house guardsmen poured in, scale mail rattling as they ran, swords and pikes at the ready. It didn't take the newcomers long to realize what was happening; there stood their captain, sword drawn, facing off against an armed stranger, while their ethnarch stood, back to a wall, face a mask of red rage. As Bjalki watched, the guards encircled the dwarven watchwarden, lowered their weapons, and raised their shields.

Torval made no move for a moment. Finally he lowered his maul and raised one hand in deference.

"My weapon's lowered," Torval said calmly.

"You dare," Eldgrim said, teeth gnashing so hard Bjalki thought they might all crumble.

"You threatened my boy," Torval answered. "Gods-damned right I dared."

"Seize him," Eldgrim said.

"Stop this!" someone roared. Bjalki turned toward the raised voice, the sound of thunder and rage and despair. It was the Lady Leffi.

The ethnarch's wife stood there, body shaking, face betraying sorrow and pity. Everyone stared at her, amazed and awaiting the next word.

"You do not rule here," Eldgrim said, leveling a finger at her.

"For this moment—this *one* moment—I do." She stared him down, unwavering, unbending, unafraid. A long, pregnant silence fell upon them.

Finally the Lady Leffi spoke again, more calmly this time. "Captain Godrumm, lower your sword and disengage."

"With respect, milady," the captain began, making no move to obey her.

"Now!" she shouted. *"There will be no bloodshed here today!"*

Godrumm finally took two long steps away from Torval,

then lowered and resheathed his sword. He hung his head, afraid to look the seething ethnarch in the eye.

"Break that circle and let the watchman go free," Leffi commanded. The guards looked puzzled for a moment, not sure whether to obey or not. Finally one of them took two steps back, swung aside, and opened a space for Torval to retreat through. The others remained as they were. Torval stepped through the breach in the cordon and marched toward the door. When he had reached it, he turned back to face Eldgrim, who still stood with his back to the chamber's outer wall.

"This is why they hate us," the watchwarden said, seeming to address only Eldgrim, and no one else. "We break before we bend. We'd rather die fighting than change and live in peace."

Eldgrim stepped forward, closing the distance between him and Torval. He held out his hand and let his oppressive gaze sweep over the captain and his gathered guardsmen.

"Someone give me their sword," the ethnarch commanded. "Let me see this forsaken outcast silenced."

"Husband," Leffi said, and there was real love in her voice, sincere worry. "Kill him and we'll have the whole city in arms against us."

"Probably not, milady," Torval said, still staring at Eldgrim. "You overestimate my importance."

"Give him what he wants," Leffi continued, still addressing the ethnarch. "End this."

Bjalki waited, reminding himself to inhale and exhale with each passing silent moment. Gods, how had it all spiraled so far out of control?

Eldgrim licked his lips. "Your son will be delivered to you, once he's returned from his day's work," he said to Torval. "But let this be the end of his place among us, as well as yours. If you take him, under these terms, he will never again be welcome among us, nor shall you, nor shall any who share your blood. Dwarven tradition has been challenged once too often by you, Son of Jarvi. Henceforth there shall be no room for you or for your whole blighted line within it."

Torval raised his head, studied the lot of them for a moment, as if he hoped—or expected—someone to counter Eldgrim's pronouncement. No one did. Bjalki was especially ashamed of himself. He knew that all of this—the conflict, the bitterness, the inability to forgive or forget—was wrong. Why could they not simply give him what he asked? Why could they not understand that the watchwarden only feared for the safety of his son? And that he was right to do so?

Because this is not our way, he realized. *Negotiations, capitulations, compromises . . . none of these are the dwarven way. Our codes and mandates stand, unchallenged, from the holy scrolls, and unbending dwarves wielding power like a hammer on an anvil—dwarves like Eldgrim—make sure that all challenges to that way are shattered, utterly, before they can change us.*

And why could Bjalki himself not find the strength to speak his mind, and shame them all into the right course of action?

"Your decision will cause my boy much grief," Torval said finally. "Myself? Not so much. Piss on the lot of you."

He spat on the floor then, turned, and left the audience chamber. A long silence fell upon them in his absence.

"My lord," Godrumm finally said. Bjalki could not tell if he was concerned about the ethnarch or asking permission for some unspoken action.

"Leave him be," Eldgrim said. "What concern is it of ours what one exile does with his whelp? In any case, Captain, you have more important things to do."

Godrumm looked as confused as Bjalki felt. "More important . . . ?"

"The Swords of Eld shall take to the streets," Eldgrim said. "Liveried, armed, expressly under my orders."

"Husband," Leffi said.

"Silence!" the ethnarch snapped. "You are fortunate, good wife—*so fortunate*—that I can forgive weakness and folly in you, no matter how great."

The veiled threat in his voice—the clear disdain—kept the Lady Leffi silent.

"Now," Eldgrim continued, "I don't give a fig for what that bastard does with his own brood, or on his watch for this city, but the dwarves in this domain are *my* responsibility! Curse the wardwatch, curse the city guard, curse the whole bloody Council of Patriarchs and Circle of Alders—*I will not let my people be threatened!* If those longshanked bastards out there want a war, we'll give them one."

Bjalki felt sick. He looked to Godrumm. The eyes of the captain of the guard betrayed his hesitation, even if his words did not.

"Your orders, then?" the captain asked.

"Take to the streets," Eldgrim said. "Day and night. The only business humans have among us is to trade coin for goods—that's all. Any one of them so much as spits in the mud or utters a harsh word during a haggle, I want them broken and ejected from the quarter, so that their fellows can see what happens when our people are not respected! Am I understood?"

"As you command, lord," Godrumm said with a nod.

"As you command, lord," the guards parroted.

Bjalki turned back to the table and hung his head. They were going to start a war in the streets. What should he do? What *could* he do?

The Kothrum, he thought. *It still has men to hunt, retribution to deliver. Perhaps—just perhaps—I can finish this. If I can send it after the rest of them—all of them—tonight and provide Eldgrim with proof that the perpetrators have been punished . . .*

What then? Eldgrim would relent? The ramping tension in the city could be dispersed?

No. This can't be the way. More death—more blood—cannot be the way, even if it's the blood of the guilty.

But standing there, listening as Eldgrim barked commands at the Swords of Eld, then turned on his wife and his councilors and gave them each a tongue-lashing in turn, all his fury and ire directed at them and what he took to be their disloyal hearts, Bjalki started to realize that more death, more blood, was, in fact, the only way.

Let the Kothrum lay their heads at his feet, he thought sickly. *Let him see the beast, and its filthy work, in all its hideous and awesome glory.*

Perhaps that is all that will settle him . . . all that will silence him . . .

CHAPTER TWENTY-SIX

Einar Egulsson, sergeant in the Swords of Eld, was one hundred and twenty one years old. By dwarven reckoning that meant he was well out of adolescence, but still young and untried. He boasted neither wife nor children, for he had spent the last several years as a member of the ethnarch's elite house guard, hoping that such a posting could, in the fullness of time, win him trust and respect sufficient to return to the Ironwalls and his renowned warrior clan. Serving an ethnarch, wearing the livery, proving one's mettle and loyalty, were all honorable undertakings, after all, even if they were not terribly exciting.

Presently, for instance, he stood stock-still on a street corner in the Warrens, on the lookout for malfeasance. The dwarves of his squad were spread out around him, having adopted a similar stance and mien: shoulders squared, weapons at their sides, raptors' gazes scanning the knotted streets for any threat of violence. Such work—police work—was, in Einar's estimation, far beneath a warrior of his quality, or the combined quality of his squad. But this was their duty, as ordered by the ethnarch and their captain. Patrol the streets, keep the peace, meet all hostility or wrongdoing with force and fury.

A war hammer to squash a gnat, Einar thought. But his was not to question. His was to obey. And he would obey, for there was no other path to honor, glory, and a journey home.

It was after dark, and the streets of the dwarven quarter were subsiding toward emptiness and silence. Einar was certain that the night would prove so banal and unexciting that he might not make it 'til sunrise with his sanity intact.

That's when he saw the man.

There was nothing special about him, no singular quality of appearance or movement that would mark him as special (and all the tall folk looked alike to Einar, anyway—gangly things, with their long, sticklike legs and almost dainty feet). This man walked alone, singing low to himself some old drinking song from the bygone days of his father or grandfathers. All around the strolling man, activity unfolded in the little beer halls and taverns that lined the avenue, interspersed with a number of shops that had been closed and barred for the night, their windows gaping into the cold, wintery streets like staring, somnambulant eyes. The man moved in a more or less straight line, right down the center of the deserted street, heading, apparently, toward a fountain that stood alone in the little square at its far end.

He's drunk, Einar thought. *That bloody longshanks is going to fall headlong into that icy water, I'll bet, and we'll have to fish him out.*

The man reached the fountain. He stood for a time, seeming to study it. Finally, after a good, long survey of the fountain— one of hundreds in the city, neither its most memorable nor its largest, nor even its most frequented, Einar wagered—the man stepped up onto the stone lip of that fountain, quickly unlaced his trousers, pulled out his tackle, and loosed a strong, yellow, steaming stream of piss into the water of the fountain.

Einar was frozen by shock for a moment—just a moment— before he finally found his voice.

"You there!" Einar shouted, breaking into a run toward the fountain. Without orders his squad followed behind him, murmuring and snickering among themselves about the man pissing in their fountain, the man they were about to beat bloody and make an example of, the man who had chosen to muck about with the *wrong dwarves* on this particular night.

Einar reached the man first. He drew his blade and leveled it.

"Get down from there!" he commanded. "Just what in the sundry hells do you think you're doing?"

The pissing man raised one hand, one finger: *Wait, please.*

The others arrived, fanning out around Einar. Einar stepped forward and reached out for the man with one mailed fist.

"I said, get down from there!" he barked, grabbed a handful of the man's tunic tail, and yanked. The human toppled from his perch with a yelp and hit the mud a moment later, coughing as the wind was knocked from his body.

Einar stood over the man and leveled his sword. *I cannot believe this*, the dwarf thought. *I am a warrior—I aim to be a slayer of orcs and the scourge of mountain bandits. I should not be here, arguing with these fool tall folk, especially one with his* sluuk *dangling about.*

"What did you think you were doing?" Einar demanded of the downed man.

The man, still on his back, blinked and shrugged a little. "Pissing," he said, then went about stowing his tackle back in his trousers.

"That's a public fountain," Einar said. "People drink from that."

The man struggled to his feet, looking a little perturbed but hardly threatened by the armed dwarven soldiers who now surrounded him.

"People don't," the man said to Einar. "Your kind do ... *tonker.*"

Einar blinked. Had he really just called him that? To his face? When Einar held a sword and this fool held nothing but his gods-damned trouser snake? Einar stepped forward, feeling a strange mix of furious impatience and honest puzzlement.

"Go," Einar finally said. "I'll forget what I've seen, and I'll forget what you said."

The man looked around as though searching for someone to back him up. There were none of his kind apparent. He crossed his arms.

"I won't," he said. "I've just had a good piss, and now I'm eager for a little tot and tipple. Where are the brothels, pray tell?"

Einar shook his head. His anger was rising now. Once more he leveled his sword and shook it as he spoke, to punctuate his orders. "There are no brothels here. Now, you need to—"

"Not a one?" the man asked incredulously. "Are you all eunuchs? I know you've got womenfolk! Where are you hiding them?"

"Now see here," Einar began.

The man lunged and spat in Einar's face. Einar had barely registered the insult before the pissing man turned and broke into a desperate sprint.

I'll kill him, Einar thought, wiping the gob of phlegm and saliva from his face. Then, without even giving orders to his men to fall in behind him or follow their prey, he pursued. A moment later he heard his three squad mates pounding the mud in his wake.

The pissing man hurtled, fast and loose, toward the far end of the street. Once Einar caught their quarry glancing back over his shoulder, a peculiar look on his flushed face.

He's not frightened, Einar thought, *but smiling. There's something wrong here—*

Then the fugitive cut right, disappearing from the main street into a long, dark alleyway between two tenements. Einar and his dwarves altered course, their chase never flagging, and

Einar's momentary foreboding was lost in the headlong rush of their pursuit.

Barreling down the length of that long, narrow alley, the man called back over his shoulder.

"I'm sure they're down here!" he shouted to his pursuers. "Those womenfolk of yours! I can smell their mushroom-scented cunnies from a mile off!"

Einar increased his pace. Behind him the rattle of his fellows' scale mail told him they matched his speed. Up ahead the alleyway split, like a tree limb with two forks. At the intersection, their quarry rushed into the smaller passage that veered right.

Einar led his dwarves on, leaning into the turn as he rounded the corner...then skittered to a halt. Frozen and dumbfounded, he struggled mightily to arrest his forward momentum and nearly landed on his face. His three squad mates all slammed into him from behind, bunching them up as a group in the narrow, darkened alleyway, mouths agape, eyes wide.

There were men in the right-hand fork, waiting for them. Thanks to their dwarven night vision, the lot of them saw their statuesque human frames, their broad shoulders, their dusk-colored cloaks, and their bland, pale masks easily. The pissing man had run right through the cordon of masked marauders and waited on the other side, gasping for breath.

As Einar stood there, trying to decide how best to extricate himself and his men from this situation while not trading the greater measure of his honor and good name, there came a strange sound just behind them—the scraping of flint on steel. Before Einar could even turn to see what was happening, he heard a breathless whoosh, then saw the alleyway filled with light, heat, and the stink of sulfur and hot pitch. Already suspecting what had transpired, Einar turned to take it in.

A raging fire now burned just before the intersection of the two forking paths, its high, hungry flames blocking their exit via the main alleyway. A human stood beside those flames, face covered in the same strange mask as their ambushers'. The man stared at Einar and his dwarves, daring them to retrace their steps through the inferno.

From the left-hand fork, another threat appeared, drawn out of the dark by the firelight: more men, six of them, all masked and cloaked like their silent companions. Einar turned back to face the ambushers before them. He counted six more.

Three exits, two blocked by the masked men, one by a raging wall of flame. Twelve masked men in all, against him and his three guardsmen. Worse, every one of their adversaries was armed. Most bore blunt melee weapons—hammers, mauls, maces, even stout wooden staves—but a few carried humble swords, long knives, even a woodsman's ax, every honed edge gleaming horribly in the undulating firelight.

This is how you die, Einar thought calmly. *Tonight you may breathe your last, but make them pay for your murder.*

"Sergeant?" one of his dwarves whispered. "Orders?"

Einar fell into a half-crouching battle stance and faced the adversaries directly ahead of him.

"Let us pass," he said. "We have no quarrel with you."

"But we've got a quarrel with *you*," a masked man at the front of the band said. "With every stinking stump among you."

Einar swallowed. One of his soldiers shouted from over his shoulder.

"Sergeant, they're coming up behind!"

"Make them pay dearly to put us on our backs," Einar said, then charged the knot of men before him. They were ready for his attack and guarded themselves well against it. One or two revealed that they carried shields, and they rushed forward now, lifting those shields to block Einar's blows and arrest his advance while their companions closed on his undefended flanks.

A stone's throw away, Einar's fellow dwarves had fallen into savage combat with the men from the adjacent alleyway. In moments the muddy floor of the alley, gilded by the lurid fire lit to prevent their retreat, was awash with churned mud and hot blood, clanging and clamoring with the sounds of their voices, their curses, their calls for aid, the rattle of their scale mail and leather harnesses. Einar's ears rang with the sound of steel on steel, wood on flesh, bone breaking under heavy blows.

Einar fought, his compact frame working to his advantage in the cramped space. But the men who beset them knew they had the edge—overwhelming force, along with superior reach. Time and again their ambushers worked in concert, several occupying Einar or one of his men, keeping him pinned while their masked companions sneaked in for furtive blows when the dwarf's back was turned, his attention drawn elsewhere.

Einar felt something sweep against his right leg. It knocked something loose, painfully, and down he went, hitting the mud hard on the ruined joint before pitching over and roaring in pain. He tried to hold on to his sword, but someone snatched it from his hands. As the humans closed in around him, their bludgeons rising and falling, their blades poking at him, drawing blood but never daring to give him the blessing of death, of release, Einar rolled and searched and managed to see what had become of his men. He saw broken spears, his dwarves on their knees or on their backs, fighting with ruined weapons or bare hands. In moments the masked marauders would have them subdued, and the killing blows would finally come.

Curse me, Einar thought. *That's why I caught him smiling! It was a gambit—a trap—all along! I should have anticipated it, suspected it, but instead I led us right—*

Someone screamed. Searching the chaos that hemmed him in, above and beyond the tumult and turmoil, Einar watched as a man's body arced right through air—through the very flames blocking their retreat—then heard bones crunch as the masked man slammed into an alley wall and slid to the cold, muddy ground, lifeless.

Everyone froze, man and dwarf, searching every approach to their narrow, muddy little battleground, wondering just what could have yanked that man off his feet and thrown him so forcefully. Einar struggled where he lay, trying to see what, precisely, had happened—who, precisely, was responsible.

Then the mystery stepped through the flames, fury incarnate, so terrible and strange that Einar could barely believe his own eyes. If every man and dwarf around him had not gasped or cried out almost at once in shared disbelief, he might have thought the thing was just some phantom summoned by his fevered, frightened mind in the moments before he took his last breath.

But no—to Einar's great wonder and dread, that thing that strode through the flames was real—as real as the blood he tasted in his mouth, as real as the smell of human sweat and burning pitch that now surrounded him. It was roughly the height of a man, but broader, as if someone had stretched a stocky dwarven body to a height of six heads or more. It was neither human nor dwarf, but something altogether alien, molded of an agglomeration of materials—mud, soil, bones, broken stone, all stacked and pressed and bound together by some unknown, otherworldly force. Though it was roughly anthropoid in shape—two arms, two legs, a torso, a head—it was lopsided, uneven, its unpleasant shape an indicator of its probable origin as a thing not born, but *made*.

It was the stuff of nightmares, brute force and remorseless vengeance personified.

For a moment Einar wondered if it was a demon, come to punish them all for their foolish hatred, their embattled wickedness. Then the beast turned its dire and fiery gaze on the nearest masked men and, with a roar that sounded like a mountain avalanche, lumbered into their midst.

From the alley floor Einar watched as it tore into the parcel of men surrounding his dwarven comrades, snatching them up and casting them every which way as though they were mown-down chaff. He felt a strange thrill when he saw the beast move to grab one of his companions, hesitate for the barest instant, then simply shove the dwarf aside and reach for the next human scrambling to escape it.

It snatched men by their cloaks and flung them against the alley walls. It took up one man by his head, then closed its huge, blunt fingers around his skull, crushing it like a grape. As that man's now-headless body crumpled to the mud, the creature felt another man laying into its hunched, bone-encrusted shoulder with what looked like a stonemason's hammer. The creature reached over its shoulder, grabbed the attacker by his night cloak, then hove him forward, slamming him bodily to the mud. As it stepped forward to continue its onslaught, it crushed the man's rib cage beneath its blunt, rounded feet.

Einar saw the knot of masked men around him quickly dispersing. Some fled outright. Others tried to do battle with the beast, but it maimed or killed all who opposed it, every injury and killing undertaken with no hint of either malice or struggle. It simply struck and killed as though it were swatting flies. It lumbered, it swung, it grabbed, it threw, it struck. There was only blind, blunt force—nothing else.

Einar watched from the muddy ground, terrified, as the beast painted the alleyway with the blood of their enemies. When at last there were no more to kill, or cripple, or send fleeing into the night, the thing simply turned and lurched away from them, offering no acknowledgment to those whose lives it had just saved. It trudged back through the dying flames in the main alleyway, then off into the deep shadows and cold night beyond.

Einar, astonished and silent, looked to his men. They were broken and bleeding but, miraculously, still alive. It occurred to him then that he should see how many of their enemies had fallen to their mysterious avenger, but when Einar rolled about and surveyed the damage in the alleyway, he was sorely disappointed. So far as he could see, almost every human body that had littered the mud and refuse choking the alley just moments ago had been removed. Clearly their attackers did not want anyone or anything left behind that could identify or incriminate them. Not only the wounded but even the dead had been shuttled away.

Somewhere whistles shrieked. Bootheels pounded near. By the sound of their steps—light compared to a dwarven tread—those approaching were humans.

Someone had called out the watchwardens.

Nearby a groan. Einar tried to rise, keen to investigate, but his ruined right knee made standing impossible. Nonetheless he pressed on, sliding along as best he could, using his good left leg to propel him. Crammed into an alcove just off the intersection of alleyways, about a stone's throw from where the fire had been ignited to arrest their retreat, two human bodies lay, twisted around one another, a tangle of limbs awash with blood and mud and soot. Einar wriggled past his men, each tending his own wounds, struggling to regain his own feet, and made straight for the groaning and vaguely stirring pile of human flesh that lay there.

The watchwardens were arriving now. Einar could hear

them approaching from two directions—the mouth of the main alley, where they'd chased their quarry into this death trap, and at the far end of the tributary that bent off to the left. He would have to move quickly. He intended to have some answers of his own, if he could. He prayed that the groaning man he heard was not only alive, but coherent.

Einar disentangled the limbs and yanked. On top was a corpse—one of the masked men, blood leaking from his nose, his open mouth, and his ears, the mask itself askew on his ruined face. His body seemed to have collapsed, most of his bones shattered when he hit the wall.

But beneath him someone stirred.

Einar's squad mates were gathering round now, all pressing in for a good look. He reached down, laid hands on the curled-up figure pressed against the clammy brick wall, and hauled him to his feet. The cowering figure beneath the corpse was a young man. The leather strap holding his mask in place had broken, and the mask had fallen away. The boy's smooth, youthful face was streaked with mud and blood, and he shook uncontrollably, seemingly in shock.

But he was alive.

Einar held the young human upright and studied him, noting that, despite his bloodied and begrimed appearance, he didn't seem injured—at least not in any significant way. A few scrapes and bruises, perhaps. A couple of fingers stood out from his left hand at a strange angle. Overall, though, he seemed undamaged.

And that meant that, finally, Einar's people might have an advantage. Here was a prisoner, and prisoners could be interrogated.

Strong hands suddenly fell on Einar and yanked him away

from the boy. The wardwatch had arrived, having converged from all directions. Einar counted five: four humans, one dwarf. As the watchwardens handled them, jostling them roughly and snatching the young prisoner right out of their dwarven hands, Einar tried to explain.

The dwarven soldier started shouting at Rem and Torval the moment they dragged him off the half-conscious young man on the alley floor.

"We were the victims in this!" the banged-up dwarf stammered, as though trying to explain his ragged state. "We gave chase to a miscreant and he led us right into this alley, into an ambush."

Torval tried to help the armored dwarf stand, but the younger dwarf immediately fell, his right leg clearly refusing to support him. Before Rem could even ask what had happened, how he'd become so bloody and battered, Torval broke in, already in a froth.

"Victims—is that right?" Torval snarled. "And just what gave you lot the right to go chasing miscreants? Last time I checked, you were Eldgrim's house guard, not a police force."

The dwarf offered Torval some sort of answer—defiant, dismissive. Rem didn't pay much attention. He was more interested in the body that lay beside them. Rem gave the dead human a quick study, including a few experimental pokes and prods.

"Torval," Rem said, trying to interrupt the heated flurry that was under way between Torval and the wounded dwarven guard, "this one's cracked as milled corn. His bones are broken like a bag of glass."

Torval, taking a moment to consider Rem's report, turned

and shoved the dwarven soldier up against the wall. "Is that how you treat miscreants?" he asked. "Chase them into an alley and beat them 'til they're nothing but a bag of gravel?"

"See here," one of the dwarf's squad mates shouted, "let the sergeant go!"

The dwarven sergeant held up one hand to his soldiers: *Quiet, I'll handle this.* He looked to Torval now, then to Rem, then back to Torval. He seemed to be struggling to calm himself, to start talking sense. "It didn't happen that way," he said to the two of them, "and I'll explain it if you'll let me."

Torval shook a thick finger in the sergeant's face. "I warned your master what would happen if he set you lot loose in the streets! I *warned* him!"

"Torval," Rem said softly, "Look what I've found."

Torval turned away from the sergeant in answer to Rem's call. Rem crouched near the wall of the alley now, his own coat thrown around the shoulders of the only still-breathing human in the alley who wasn't a watchwarden. Rem hoped that Torval could see his face clearly in the light from their fellow watchwardens' torches now. The young man, though conscious and alert, was clearly in shock, eyes downcast, mouth hanging open, breathing quick and shallow.

"Is that...?" Torval began.

"Jordi," Rem said, nodding. "From the masons' guildhall."

"He's one of them!" the dwarven sergeant blurted. "He's the last of them! The rest fled! They took most of the injured and the dead with them, but that one was among them!"

Torval stepped forward, studying Jordi's pale, begrimed face.

"We should have a right to question him!" the dwarven sergeant said, lunging, as if to grab the boy and yank him right out of Rem's arms. "His friends attacked us! They nearly killed us!"

"Oh, is that right?" Torval asked. "Then why are the four of you still standing, and the only dead body I see is that of a man? And this boy, who you clearly failed to kill?"

"We held our own!" one of the other dwarven guardsmen said. "We were outnumbered, but we beat them back. It was that *thing* that saved us!"

"What thing?" Rem asked.

"It walked right through the flames!" another of the sergeant's dwarves said. "Waded right into them. Broke them and crushed them, tore them to pieces!"

Torval looked puzzled by all that. He looked to the sergeant, as if for corroboration. The sergeant nodded soberly.

"They're telling the truth," their leader said. "I don't know what it was, but it came out of nowhere, and it saved us before lumbering off again."

"Bones," Jordi suddenly muttered. "Eyes on fire. And earth... earth that smelled like death."

"What's he on about?" Torval asked, looking annoyed.

"I'm taking him back to the watchkeep," Rem said. Truth be told, he understood that dwarven sergeant's desperate need to lay hands on the boy, to beat his own answers out of him. Understanding that need was what convinced Rem that, one way or another, he had to get Jordi away from here. The boy wouldn't survive the night—and wouldn't yield any of the answers the wardwatch needed—unless he could be secured and protected in a watchkeep cell. To make his intent clear, he looked to the dwarven sergeant. "We'll lock him up," he assured him. "He's not going anywhere."

"By rights he should be ours," the sergeant said. "His men tried to murder us."

"But this thing," Torval interjected. "What are you on about, *this thing*? This thing that intervened on your behalf?"

"It was like that beast from the old stories," another of the dwarves stammered. "Don't you remember? The demon that Ormunda the Red made, during the great orcish tyranny."

"Those are bedtime stories," another dwarven guard scoffed.

"Maybe," the first barreled on, "but that's what it reminded me of! The Koff...the Kroft—"

"The Kothrum?" Torval offered.

The dwarven guard snapped his thick fingers. "That's it! The Kothrum! You know the stories, don't you? You're one of us!"

Torval studied the dwarven guard, then looked to the sergeant for affirmation. The sergeant could only nod and shrug. "I don't know if I'd call it that," he said, "but he's right—that's certainly what it brought to mind."

Rem studied Torval's face in light of that strange news. His partner looked as if he'd been punched in the gut. For a moment Torval stood staring at them, incredulous, shocked, dumbfounded. Finally he turned to their fellow watchwardens.

"Get their statements and see their wounds tended," Torval said. He turned and faced the sergeant as he offered his last order. "See that they make it back to the ethnarch's manse safely."

Rem looked to the dwarven sergeant. It was on the tip of his tongue to say something—anything—that might assure the battered dwarf that, whatever had happened, the watchwardens now on hand would keep them safe. To Rem's great relief, the dwarven sergeant gave him a silent nod before Rem had offered even a single word. Clearly he was satisfied that they'd now been treated with some fairness—some dignity. As Rem nodded in answer and got to his feet, ready to help Jordi to his own, he looked for his partner.

Torval had wandered away from them, off into the dark

tributaries of the alleyway, moving like someone adrift in a dream…or a nightmare. Once more Rem wanted to offer words of assurance, this time to Torval, but he could summon none. So, satisfied that the scene was secure and there was nothing more for him to do, he yanked the still-shocked Jordi to his feet and urged the boy to take his first steps on their long walk back to the watchkeep.

CHAPTER TWENTY-SEVEN

Rem delivered the young stonemason, Jordi, to the lockup. Soon after his arrival back at the watchkeep, Torval joined him, looking preoccupied by something—haunted by it, even—but remaining tight-lipped as to what that something might be. For a time Rem was content to keep his head down, slowly writing out a report to justify the young stonemason's arrest, while Torval sat nearby and brooded. Finally, after a little less than an hour, Djubal and Klutch arrived from the crime scene with the body of the dead stonemason in a wheelbarrow. The corpse was removed to the dank lower chamber that served as their informal mortuary, Djubal and Klutch wrote their report, and the night's strained silence persisted.

It was in the midst of that silence that Rem found himself lost in thought, trying to tease out just what it was that had Torval so bound up. It wasn't the worries of the previous weeks—all that mess with Tavarix and the ethnarch—but some new concern. Rem was fairly certain it had been brought on by the testimony of the dwarves at the crime scene, but he was loath to simply come out and ask.

In the midst of all that watching and wondering and Rem's silent attempts to dare himself to ask Torval to open up about whatever now troubled him, Hirk arrived and ordered both of them to the dungeons.

Hirk led them into the bowels of the watchkeep. Surprisingly, though, it was to the mortuary and not to the dungeons themselves. There Rem and Torval were urged into the damp, cold little chamber where the dead stonemason from the crime scene was stretched out on a sweating stone slab. Eriadus, the quartermaster and the watchkeep's default surgeon, circled the stone table and the corpse, examining every inch of the dead man in his own inimitably haphazard fashion, with a method that Rem had learned only resembled disorganization and madness and belied an astonishing thoroughness.

Just as Rem was about to ask why they were here and not in the dungeon proper, interrogating their prisoner, Ondego arrived with the boy, Jordi. Queydon trailed in after them, her presence clearly announcing that they were about to begin an interrogation.

Ondego gave young Jordi a shove, heaving him right up to the stone slab where his dead companion lay. As the young stonemason's apprentice stared at the dead man on the table, Ondego threw one of the confiscated leather masks from the scene on top of the corpse's chest.

"Playing goblin in dark alleys at midnight?" the prefect asked.

The boy shook his head. Rem studied him. He looked genuinely sickened, genuinely scared. Breaking him couldn't possibly take them long. Rem almost felt sorry for the lad...

Ondego slapped the boy headwise. It was a hard strike. He delivered the blow without even changing his bored, hangdog expression.

"Talk," Ondego said. "We'll get it out of you one way or another. Don't make us pry it from you."

Someone moved at the corner of Rem's vision. He turned and found Torval slowly examining the dead man's body. As

Rem watched, the dwarf gently felt the broken bones beneath the corpse's pallid skin, fingered shattered ends where they had broken through, and seemed to make a long, deep, silent appraisal of the corpse, never uttering a word as he did so. What was the dwarf thinking? Rem could not remember the last time he'd seen him so troubled...

"It shouldn't have come to this," the boy finally said. "We didn't want it to come to this."

"False," Queydon said simply. Hirk stepped in, snagged the boy's left arm, and folded it behind him. The boy shouted and beat the stone slab with his free hand.

"Hurts, doesn't it?" Hirk asked. "Now try again—and no cack this time. The straight truth. Nothing more, nothing less."

"That *was* the truth," the boy squealed. "I didn't want it to come to this!"

"Better," Queydon said.

Hirk released him. "*You* didn't want it to come to this," the lieutenant said, "but *your friends* did, didn't they? This—an eye for an eye, blood for blood—was *exactly* what they were after, wasn't it?"

The boy stared at the dead man. Tears cut tracks down his cheeks, and he shook his head as though struggling to will away the terrible sight before him. He bent over the stone table and wept. Hirk looked to Ondego, silently asking if he should urge the boy along. Ondego shook his head.

Rem caught the prefect's eye and gave a little sideward nod. Could he try? Ondego, having often deferred to Rem's softer touch in interrogations as a means of keeping the prisoners on continually shifting ground, shrugged and nodded, indicating that Rem was more than welcome to do so. Rem approached the table then, directly opposite the weeping young man. He settled himself down on his elbows and lowered his head, so that he could try to catch the young man's gaze on the same plane. When the boy raised his tear-reddened eyes for a moment, Rem gestured to the mask discarded on the dead man's chest.

"Start with the masks," Rem said quietly—his words a friendly invitation. "Tell us what they mean." He'd spent enough months questioning suspects in tandem with Torval—the dwarf threatening them, beating them, while Rem tried to win them with empathy and compassion—that he finally felt worthy to try his method while Ondego watched.

The boy sniffed, wiped his tears, shrugged. "They hid our faces," he said. "Made us mysteries—something unknown, to be feared."

"Is it a cult of some sort?" Rem asked.

The boy shook his head. "Oh no, sir, no! We would never! We're all Aemonists, true of heart and dedicated!"

Rem tried to keep from losing his patience. He hated being called sir.

"We were the Sons of Edath, that's all," the boy said. "Like in the old stories. Defenders of the faith, of the city...We just...we just wanted to do what was right."

Rem looked to Ondego, recalling the prefect's earlier summary of the old Sons of Edath legends. The prefect smirked with relish: *See? Sometimes the old man knows what he's talking about...*

Jordi carried on. "We thought, perhaps, if we could frighten them—the dwarves—then we could win justice—"

"Justice for whom, exactly?" Ondego asked. "What justice is there in terrorizing peaceful folk who just want to work? Getting your way through fear and intimidation instead of fair competition? I don't see much justice in that, lad—"

"It wasn't meant to become *this*!" the boy howled, suggesting his dead companion on the table. "But what else could it be...after Grendan?"

"Who's Grendan?" Rem asked.

That opened the floodgates. The boy told them the whole story: the riot in the dwarven market, Grendan being waylaid and beaten to death, the cries of the stonemasons for blood and justice, the power struggle between Hrissif and Valaric. The tale he told made perfect sense, and filled Rem with a deep sense of shame that they had not managed to challenge the stonemasons more directly, to haul a few of them in when they only suspected their involvement. Perhaps if they'd taken the right steps, asked the right questions—

"But what about all this?" Torval asked, suggesting the dead man on the slab. "Almost every bone in this man's body is broken, boy! What did this?"

The young apprentice shook his head. "Master dwarf, I assure you, I don't know. I mean, I saw it—saw the beast with my own two eyes—but it was like nothing I'd ever seen. Maybe something out of a nightmare..."

"Don't name it, then," Rem said. "Just describe it."

The boy nodded. "It was big—as tall as a man, but broad in the shoulders and through the chest. It had enormous hands—only two fingers and thumbs, I think—and its feet just looked like round, flat columns. It had the strangest shape—all out of proportion and lopsided, as though molded right from the earth by a child or something. And it seemed to be made of the earth itself. Damp mud. And bones—lots of bones."

"Bones?" Ondego asked.

The boy nodded again in assurance. "Bones, sir, just pressed right into the mud and dirt that it was molded of. Its eyes were the worst, though; they were just a pair of deep wells dug into its head, but there was a light burning at the bottom of those wells—a terrible, infernal light..."

They all looked to one another, searching for some name to lay to the thing described.

"Necromancy?" Eriadus suggested.

"Of the foulest sort, by the sound," Hirk agreed.

"But it wasn't an animated corpse?" Rem asked. "Neither a revenant nor a lich?"

The boy shook his head. "I don't think so, no. I'm not sure how to say it. It looked like something animated, but not *re*animated."

"And it just came upon you?" Torval asked. Rem studied his partner. The dwarf's face was drawn, his eyes wide. Clearly there was something in the boy's description that had upset him.

The boy nodded slowly, gravely. Tears began to glint in his eyes again. "We set those dwarves up for an ambush, and they fell right into it. We'd set a pitch fire in the main alley so they couldn't retreat—but then that thing lumbered in. It came right through the flames and laid into us. Cribben here wasn't the only one it killed—his was just the only body left behind."

"Your companions took the others?" Ondego asked.

"Aye, sir. We'd all been given a partner before the mission. If that man fell, his partner was to make sure his body wasn't left behind when we fled. Cribben and I were sworn to carry each other out, if need be...but of course he couldn't, and I was in no shape to..."

He fell to weeping again.

Rem turned to find Torval, but his partner had suddenly disappeared from their little circle. Searching the chamber, he saw the dwarf lingering across the room, by the door. When

Torval saw Rem staring at him, he waved him nearer. Without a word Rem joined him.

"Got something to share, old stump?" Rem asked quietly. He stole a furtive glance to make sure that the others were still busy with Jordi.

"It may be nothing," Torval said, also keeping his voice low. "Or it may be the worst thing imaginable."

Rem felt his stomach churn. He did not care to learn Torval's version of "the worst thing imaginable."

"Tell me," Rem said, hoping that just this once, Torval wouldn't waste time trying to protect him or keep his fears to himself.

Torval made sure that Ondego and the others were still on the far side of the room, then plunged in. "There are old legends among my people," Torval began, "of a time, millennia ago, when we tried to put violence and bloodshed behind us. But after renouncing the old ways, we were immediately beset by the wicked and the bloodthirsty. Orcish warbands, Tregga horse nomads, human conquerors—they all fell upon our people in turn, slaughtering us, enslaving us, terrorizing us. Hallir's Folk were so desperate to be a people of peace—a people of honor and righteousness—that they would not even take up arms to defend themselves. They only resigned themselves to their new place in the world, slaves and prisoners, at the mercy of the gods and the creatures that oppressed and exploited them."

Torval drew a deep, shuddering breath then. Rem sensed the story was about to take a dark turn.

"There was a witch, a sorceress, who sought a means of freeing and vindicating our people. She decided that if we would not fight for ourselves, then we should have a merciless champion to fight for us. She appealed to the eldritch powers that haunted the earth itself—its depths, its bowels, its unending memory—and she summoned just such a beast. It was called a Kothrum, and it was made of earth and ash and bone."

Rem studied his partner's face. The worry in the dwarf's eyes and the pained, preoccupied look on his ruddy face told Rem all he needed to know. Torval was dead serious—terrified, even—and he offered this theory, as bizarre and unreasonable as it sounded, with utter sincerity.

"So," Rem said, still keeping his voice low, "you think the dwarves in the quarter summoned one of these things? Set it loose on the stonemasons?"

Torval shrugged. "It's all that makes sense. The strength displayed, those strange footprints, the descriptions..."

Rem nodded. Admittedly, it did fit. And Torval would know better than he what the marks of a Kothrum were, or how it should look. And while magic was a capricious practice, even its simplest operations often subject to the most arbitrary and unpredictable of laws, it wasn't exactly outside the realm of possibility, was it?

"What do we do, then?" Rem asked. "How do we stop it?"

Torval shook his head. "That's what troubles me: I don't know. I don't even know if it's true, to be honest. I don't want to believe it. But I do know this: if it *is* true, and the people of this city see that thing, or figure out what it is and who unleashed it—"

"Garn's forge," Rem cursed. "They'll burn the whole dwarven quarter to the ground!"

The partners stole glances toward their fellows across the room. Ondego was ignoring them no longer. Now he and Hirk were moving nearer.

"I've got to go," Torval said. "Tell Ondego I've gone after Tav, and to make sure my family's safe. That's half-true, anyway. But as to that thing—"

"Do what you must," Rem said, clapping Torval on the shoulder, "then send for me—send for all of us—when you need us. Just don't try to take it on alone, do you hear me?"

Torval offered a crooked smile. "I'm hardheaded," he said, "but I'm no fool."

Rem studied his partner's face. He knew, deep down, that Torval was lying. It was true, the dwarf was no fool...but if he thought he could settle this business, be the one to subdue the criminals among his people and end the Kothrum's reign of terror, Rem did not doubt Torval would try to do it. He would see it as his duty not only as a watchwarden, but also as a dwarf.

And worse, Rem knew there was nothing he could say to convince Torval otherwise.

"Go," Rem finally said.

Torval stared at Rem for just a moment, as though searching for the right words. Finally he offered them. "You've made me proud," he said.

Rem wanted to offer something in return, but it was too late. Torval turned and departed. Ondego arrived just as Torval disappeared through the door.

"Where's he off to?" the prefect asked.

"Family business," Rem said, feeling a great pang of fear and sadness in the center of him. He shouldn't let him go, should he? He should join him, protect him—

"We need to snatch them, now," Ondego said, "before they've too much time to regroup or scatter."

"Snatch who?" Rem asked, his determination to run after Torval now blown to dust.

"The stonemasons," Ondego said. "Since you've talked to them, and you know their faces, I need you on point in the raid."

Rem considered for a moment—the barest instant—telling

Ondego about Torval's fears regarding the Kothrum...but thought better of it. He feared for Torval, true, but he also needed to trust him. Let the dwarf do what he had to do, learn what he had to learn. In the meantime Rem should see to his duties here.

"Ready, sir," Rem said with a nod. "Lead on."

Ondego looked back to where Jordi stood, still weeping, over the body of his dead companion. The sad-eyed prefect sighed and shook his head.

"Cocks and cunts, this is going to be a mess," Ondego said.

CHAPTER TWENTY-EIGHT

Queydon was put in charge of the raid, but she made it clear that once the stonemasons were apprehended, she would count on Rem to do the dragon's share of the talking and finger-pointing, since he'd already treated with the men they were about to arrest. Their first stop would be the guildhall itself, where they would gather any and all present, as well as any printed rolls they could find of the membership. From there the team of watchwardens they'd assembled would spread out through the ward in search of the men on those rolls. Rem thought that as fine a plan as any, despite all the ways it could backfire on them. The simple fact was, there was no easy, stealthy way to snatch these men without a lot of research and preparation. If Ondego wanted them now, his men would have to move fast and bring in as many as they could—secrecy and finesse be damned.

At the end of the block nearest the guildhall, Queydon divided the party. Four of them would slip in ahead and take up stations on the northern and southern sides of the guildhall, in adjacent alleys, to make sure no one managed to slither out through a window or some such. A squad of six would be ready at the mouth of the courtyard at the guildhall's back door to snatch any who tried to flee that way. The rest of them—close to twenty—would guard the front entrance or go in to arrest any and all they found on-site.

As they prepared to take up their positions, Queydon pulled

Rem aside. "Not first," she said. "Second. Let Hildebran lead the way. You follow, keep your eyes open, make sure the key figures don't slip away."

Rem nodded. "Aye, Sergeant. As commanded."

Queydon nodded, satisfied. Hildebran, the big northerner, took his point position on the opposite side of the door from Rem. He carried with him an iron battering ram—the perfect size to be wielded by a single man, albeit one of considerable strength. Inhaling, he drew the big, blunt instrument back for a strike. Just as he prepared to ram down the guildhall door, Queydon gave a standard watchwarden's greeting. Her voice was louder, harder, than Rem had ever heard it.

"Wardwatch!" she shouted. "We're coming in!"

Hildebran slammed the battering ram into the door, and the slab of banded oak all but leapt off its hinges. Before they were even through the door, the house dog barked and snarled and charged the barbarian. Rem watched as Hildebran smoothly stepped aside, allowing one of the other men to slide in with a looped catchpole—the sort used by beast handlers in blood sport rings to hold their angry contestants at bay. As the snarling guard dog charged, the dog handler slipped the noose at the end of the catchpole around the beast's throat and pulled tight. The dog snarled, snapped, bit, scratched, but it was no use. It was held fast, unable to approach its captor or anyone else. As the dog man wrestled the fighting mongrel into the street and away from the entrance, Rem and the rest of the watchwardens poured into the guildhall.

What they found inside surprised Rem, who had half expected an empty hall at such a late hour. Before them, however, were nearly fifty men, all crammed into the great room around a roaring fire. True, they were now running to and fro, colliding with one another, seeking exits or preparing to stand and fight as the watchwardens poured in, but from the large number of dropped ale horns and beer steins evident, the brightness and warmth of the fire, and the great number of men on hand, it looked as if the watchwardens had interrupted an official gathering.

As they sped into the room, Rem scanned his surroundings. Immediately he picked out the steward, Valaric, along with the bearded fellow Valaric had named as their treasurer. He saw no sign of Hrissif, the sneering man whose brother had been killed. Rem waved his arms and cried out, "There! Those two! Officers of the guild!"

Several watchwardens streamed around Rem, charging right toward Valaric and the old treasurer. Before Rem could see if they nabbed their quarry or not, someone came speeding in from his left and tackled him. Down he went in a frenzy of flailing arms, hitting the floor with terrific force, the breath knocked out of him almost immediately. He tried to regain himself, but already his adversary was beating him mercilessly. If Rem was not mistaken, his attacker's weapon was a pewter serving tray.

Rem kicked, rolled, struggled. He kept his arms over his face and head, trying his best to deflect the worst and most direct blows. The man was straddling him, cursing him, and the force of his blows, coupled with the fierceness of his attack, suggested that he was ready to kill Rem—or, for that matter, anyone who dared violate the sanctity of his fraternal guildhall.

Just as Rem was about to raise his voice and call out for help, the man was suddenly snatched right off him. He seemed to rise up into the air with a surprised croak, then went flying, slamming into a trestle table six feet away, smashing it with his muscled bulk. Rem uncovered his face and blinked. Hildebran stood over him, hand out to help him back to his feet.

"Trouble, valley boy?"

Rem took the barbarian's hand and was yanked upright. "Nothing a savage from the fjords of Kosterland can't fix, eh?"

Hildebran smiled crookedly. "You're welcome. Don't let it happen again."

Rem nodded and they rejoined the fray. Across the room Valaric didn't seem to be putting up a fight at all. He stood calmly as watchwardens clapped him into manacles, and seemed to be working hard to be heard above the din of all the fighting and chaos around him. Rem stepped nearer to hear what he was saying, and realized that he was, in fact, urging any men in his vicinity to surrender without resistance—to stand where they were and offer their hands for shackling.

Not the actions of a guilty man at all.

Or perhaps the actions of a *very* guilty man, totally untroubled by the blood on his hands, eager to be a martyr for his cause. Gods, weren't those sorts always the worst?

But Rem could not tell, for the moment, just which of those sorts this Valaric was. He knew only that the steward was now in custody, and that a number of his companions were already in chains. A few brawls unfolded around the room. Shouting down a back hallway suggested that some men had escaped entirely, or were still fighting in the rear courtyard. But here and now, so far as Rem was concerned, their primary mission was complete.

The sense of satisfaction that Rem briefly entertained within the guildhall fled entirely when he emerged again into the cold night air. A crowd had gathered in the street outside the hall, held at bay by the watchwardens who'd been left to guard the entrance. A few stonemasons snatched in their attempted flight were gathered nearby, on their knees in the gelid mud, hands manacled behind their backs. While two watchwardens over-saw the gathered prisoners, another four walked the perimeter, forcing back the locals as they pressed in to get a good look at the unfolding chaos, to make their doubts known and their dissatisfaction plain.

"Is this how the wardwatch treats honest, law-abiding trades-men?" someone shouted from the crowd.

"Just what are these men guilty of, pray tell?" someone else yelled.

"It's those bloody dwarves in the Warrens," a third voice cried out. "They've bought half this city with their smithies and gems, and now they own the wardwatch, too!"

Rem was tempted to engage the crowd, to respond directly to all those aspersions and more. But he knew it was a fool's errand. There would be no point in engaging these folk; they were frightened by what they saw, and they did not fully under-stand it. It was right that they should be a little upset by it all, even if some context might have changed their minds. But most important was the abiding wisdom that one should never, ever try to engage in a logical argument with a person in emotional distress. You would not be heard, and you could not win. And so, much as it pained him, Rem resolved to go on about his business and do his duty, whether it made him look like the enemy to these folk or not.

He checked with Emacca and Blotstaff, the two watchwar-dens guarding the prisoners. They seemed to have things under control. He joined the line holding back the locals then, and promised himself that he would not engage with anyone per-sonally, nor speak a single word to explain or defend the ward-watch's actions. To be honest, he was surprised by the size and relative ferocity of the crowd. It was well past midnight, and most of these folk probably had a hard day's labor ahead from sunrise to sunset. Didn't any of them need sleep? Did no one have more pressing personal business to attend to? He saw a number of ale tankards and cups in the hands of those gathered, so he guessed a great many must have drifted out of the nearby grogshops in answer to the noise. Big operations of this sort always drew a few drunkards and troublemakers, bored with their own lives and eager to see a fight unfold, some blood spilt. But to Rem's chagrin, the drunken gawkers did not constitute the majority of the crowd—only one small part of it. No, the bulk of those gathered seemed to be truly sober workaday folk—men and women all shouting and shaking their fists and cursing horribly at the watchwardens who kept urging them back, back, to give them room lest they, too, end up in irons.

Injustice! they cried.

"Tyranny!" someone brayed.

Some bastard deep in the crowd started a chant.

"Let them go! Let them go! Let them go!"

Gods and monsters, devils and angels, Rem thought. *That's all we need now: a bloody mob!*

The crowd's fury subsided, for only a moment, falling into sudden, stunned silence. Rem turned to see what had their attention and saw the steward, Valaric, and another dozen of his men led out of the guildhall in chains and gathered together with the other prisoners. That's what did it, apparently: the sight of that one man—tall, proud, strong, a pillar of this community and a paragon of its best intentions—shamed in front of his peers. A moment after the crowd had fallen silent, it began to murmur. Soon the murmurs rose once again toward a horrified, furious roar.

"Set him free!" a woman screamed. "Not Valaric!"

"Let's rush 'em!" someone else barked, and Rem felt his whole body tense. *Rush them?* Was the speaker mad? If this crowd surged on their little band, there was no telling what sort of violence might erupt. The watchwardens were trained to defend themselves, after all, and every one, to the last, was armed.

"Right! They can't arrest us all!" someone else shouted.

A strange, shrill whistle split the night. It was high, strident, almost painful. Only a moment after it began did Rem suddenly realize it was not an actual sound in his ears at all, but a strange psychic tone, shrieking right through his consciousness.

And, apparently, the consciousness of everyone else present. He and his fellow watchwardens felt it, but the civilians seemed to be getting the worst of it. A great many of them were on their knees now, shouting, begging for it to stop, teeth gnashing and eyes squeezed shut against the strange sound that was not in their ears, but in their heads.

Mind still aching, Rem searched the street and finally realized where the bizarre mental whistle was coming from.

It was Queydon. The elf stood calm, severe, staring at the crowd now reeling under the weight of her psychic attack.

Then, without warning, it stopped. The watchwardens blinked and stood tall again at their posts. The onlookers slowly regained their feet and studied the world around them, not sure what had just befallen them or where it had come from.

"Listen to me!" Queydon shouted now, her voice carrying far into the night. To Rem's astonishment, the crowd fell silent. They listened.

"These men," Queydon continued, "are lawfully charged with the crimes of murder, conspiracy to murder, and conspiracy to foment civil unrest."

The crowd booed. Queydon wisely waited to continue, letting them boo themselves back into silence again.

"They will be held, questioned, and tried. Some may be

innocent, others guilty, but none will suffer if they have nothing to hide, and nothing to atone for."

Liar, a few in the crowd shouted.

"Elven bitch," Rem heard.

"Believe what you wish," Queydon answered. "But these men are headed for the watchkeep. Who would like to join them?"

A frustrated murmur ran through the crowd. A few men and women cried out in defiance, but, Rem noted, none of those crying out ever stepped forward or showed themselves. After a good long while, it was clear that Queydon's gambit had worked: no one seemed eager to charge the watchwardens or cause trouble any longer.

"Go home," she said finally. "Go back to your ales, your dice, and your beds. Let us deal with these men now, and trust that they'll be judged fairly."

"Fairly, my arse!" someone screamed, then an object came arcing out of the crowd toward Queydon. Rem took a step toward the sergeant, not sure what that missile might be, but expecting it was nothing good.

It hit Queydon's cuirass and winter coat. Just a ball of mud. It left a smudge and little more. To the elf's credit, she did not move. She did not even blink. But, a moment later, it was followed by more handfuls of mud and excrement from the streets. Queydon barely made an effort to duck or avoid the sudden barrage, she only raised a single arm to protect her face, then signaled to the other watchwardens present. Time to go. Rem himself threw up his arms and retreated a few steps, caught in the crossfire.

"Get them up and marching," Queydon commanded.

She was obeyed. The prisoners were brought to their feet and pressed into a tight column. As mud and refuse continued to be lobbed by the crowd, Queydon hurried to the front of the impromptu marching line and led the way. Rem fell in at the rear.

The crowd jostled, yelled, screamed. Mud still flew, some of it quite solid, half-frozen by the winter cold. Rem felt a great relief when they'd finally made it around a corner and out of sight of the angry mob by the guildhall.

The men they'd arrested were guilty of myriad sins—among them conspiracy and murder—but the hysteria they'd sown struck Rem as perhaps the most poisonous of them, the most potentially long lasting and destructive. They had provoked the world to madness, stirred its latent enmities and paranoid suspicions, and those maladies now threatened to spread like a wildfire through the city streets.

Rem only hoped that if those fires caught, there was some tide, some waiting storm, capable of putting them out...

CHAPTER TWENTY-NINE

Torval had known that Ondego would not want him taking part in the arrests. Such a thing had never happened before, but Torval—despite his reputation as a brawler and his noted lack of social graces—was not stupid. He knew how it would look if even a single dwarf were in a party that raided the guild-hall, rounded up the stonemasons of the Sixth, then dragged them into the watchkeep. And so he had removed himself. He wagered that would free Ondego of the need to be delicate or to spare his feelings. More importantly, he realized that the Fifth Ward was about to explode. When that happened he wanted his family all together, in one place, possibly even hidden away in another ward, with friendly souls and stout walls between them and the coming chaos. Since Torval could not take part in the arrests or interrogations, assuring his own family's safety became his most pressing priority.

So Torval had slipped out of the watchkeep and rushed into the night. He took the straightest path possible from the watchkeep down to the riverfront, then pounded up the outer stairs to their rooms and burst in without knocking. Osma and Ammi sat by the fire mending torn shirts. The two of them leapt to their bare feet the moment Torval slammed through the door, Ammi uttering a little scream before clapping her hand over her mouth.

"Torval, have you gone softheaded?" Osma scolded as she threw down her sewing. "You scared us half to death—"

"Where are the boys?" Torval demanded.

"Lokki's asleep," Ammi said, still shaking a little.

"And Tavarix?"

"He's not here," Osma said, looking at him as if he'd suddenly gone senile. "You know he's at the citadel, with his fosterers—"

"No," Torval huffed and pounded through the apartment to the closed doorway that marked the boys' bedroom. Therein Lokki lay asleep, completely oblivious to what was happening in the world around him. Tav was nowhere to be found, his bed unslept in. "No no no!" Torval cursed, closing the door with all the delicacy he could muster.

"Father, what's happening?" Ammi asked, the first glint of tears in her lovely blue eyes. "You're frightening me."

"Exactly," said Osma, exasperated. "What's all this stomping about and—"

"There's trouble coming," Torval said to his sister. "A terrible one. We're likely to be caught in the middle of it."

"A storm?" Ammi asked.

It took considerable effort, but Torval struggled toward it. He had to calm down, to explain to Ammi and Osma so that they'd understand. If he had to go after Tavarix, they'd be left alone here with Lokki. He normally hated to tell them about his nightly business—the filth, the hard and hollowed souls, the blood and bruises, the close calls with death and dismemberment, the casual cruelty of strangers, the idle tragedy of everyday life as seen by those who cleaned up the messes and saw the malefactors punished. Those were fell things, *evil* things, that he wanted to keep away from his family, to protect them from. But here, now, he realized there could be no secrets kept. He had to tell them the truth—some version of it, anyway.

And so Torval told them—though he kept busy as he did so, gathering up the personal arsenal he'd amassed over his years as a watchwarden: not only his favorite maul, but also a pair of broad-bladed dwarven daggers confiscated off a dwarven assassin for hire some years earlier, as well as a short sword bought during a watchkeep auction that had struck him as remarkably comfortable in his thick hands, heavy but well balanced. These he added to the red-brown banded leather cuirass and mail shirt that he already wore, supplemented by a pair of battered, mildly rusted rerebraces and tarnished greaves. He discarded the hand ax that he'd claimed from the watchkeep armory— too clumsy—but held on to the two supplemental daggers that he'd taken to wearing in his boots.

A blunt instrument, one long blade, four short ones. If that didn't keep him alive, nothing would.

As Torval gathered his implements he told Osma and Ammi everything, in the shortest, simplest fashion possible. The contracts, the feuds, the violence…and now the possible escalation of it from a private vendetta to a citywide persecution.

"What can you do, then?" Osma asked. "Your place is here, with us—"

"No," Torval said. "Not yet. I've got to go get Tav and drag him back here."

"Drag him…?"

Torval lost his patience. Their questions were too many. "I went to the ethnarch and his court! I told them to hand him over! They said they'd do so after his shift, but his shift should be long done by now! That means they've broken their word, and if I'm to protect him, I now have to go fetch him! Don't you understand?"

His sister and his daughter stared at him. Clearly Ammi was disturbed by everything he'd explained to them; he could see the struggle on her face, in her trembling hands, in her quivering shoulders. She was scared because she did not entirely understand. But Osma... Torval saw in her eyes that she understood all too well.

He saw, too, that his sister understood what he had not said: that he went now to fetch his son from those dwarves he'd entrusted the boy to; that he anticipated they'd try to hold Tavarix, perhaps as a bargaining chip, perhaps just out of spite; and that if they defied him in any way, he'd be willing and ready to kill them all to tear the boy from their grasp.

Or he would die trying.

He was right back to where he'd started, fighting with his own folk, daring their acrimony and reprisal for the sake of those he loved.

Torval knew he'd lingered too long. He had to go. He looked to Ammi and forced himself to put on the bravest, kindest face he could. As he did so, he opened his arms and she fell into them.

"Don't fret, lass," he said softly. "Just be good and stay inside. Go into the bedroom and watch over Lokki. Don't leave him alone or let him fear. That's your job—that's what I need from you while I'm gone. Can you do that?"

Ammi nodded, tears streaming down her cheeks. She was a good girl—strong and determined, just like her mother. If Torval gave her instructions and made it clear he was counting on her, she'd likely die before disappointing him or dishonoring herself. Torval kissed his daughter on the forehead and urged her off. Ammi responded with a gentle kiss on his rough cheeks, then hurried into the bedroom where Lokki was sleeping.

Torval offered his sister a last sorrowful look. It was on the tip of his tongue to ask her about the signs he'd read at the crime sites—that stonemason's talk of walking mounds of earth and bones, the flat, unrecognizable footprints, the statement from those dwarven house guards that a Kothrum was loose in the streets. But what good would that do? He'd only frighten her more. Instead Torval simply made for the door, offering not a word. He heard Osma following close behind.

"What aren't you telling me?"

"There's nothing," he said, opening the door and letting in the cold night air.

Osma laid hands on him, yanked him back in through the door, and slammed it shut. She was strong when she wanted to be—stronger than even Torval had realized. Her rough handling left him more than a little stunned.

"You spared the children," she said quietly. "There's no need to spare me, Brother. We've both got the same scars on us. If I'm to protect these wee ones, I need to know what I'm protecting them from."

Torval swallowed. His throat felt lined with scree from a mountain rock slide. Still, if his sister begged a direct answer, he could not keep anything from her, could he?

"My main fear is the chaos to come—what the tall folk of this city will do when they see those stonemasons in chains. The anger bred in such moments is vile enough... but if they find dwarves in the streets, outside the enclave..."

He let that thought linger, and he saw clearly, by Osma's falling face and glinting eyes, that she understood.

"But there's more," he said, this time barely above a hoarse whisper. "Some of these men—these stonemasons—have died by unknown hands. I saw strange tracks around a murder site just last night. Saw a man's skull crushed like an egg. Tonight there were more, right inside the borders of the dwarven quarter—a brawl between these angry men and a squad of the ethnarch's house guard. Something plowed into the middle of that fray, killed a handful of those men without hesitation, then left again. The house guards, they said...they said..."

"Spit it out," Osma urged.

"One of them said it was a Kothrum," Torval finally said, not believing the word was actually passing his lips. He looked to his sister, hoping she believed him. "Just like in the old stories."

Osma clearly did believe him. She looked as frightened and sickened as he felt. "That can't be. That magic's ancient, forbidden. Who would...Who could...?"

"Maybe they're wrong," Torval said. "Maybe it's just a single dwarf—or a knot of them—out for blood. But if those witnesses weren't lying...if our folk truly unleashed one of those things in this city..."

"Oh, Torval," Osma muttered. "Pillars of the Blessed...it won't stop. Not until everyone its master marked is dead and buried."

"And worse," Torval said, "if the people of this city see what terrible, bloody magic our folk are capable of...what one of them unleashed..."

Osma clapped a hand over her mouth, as though trying to trap the despairing words now in danger of flying out. Her brown eyes shifted to her brother. She removed her hovering hand.

"Go get Tavarix, Brother," she said. "Bring him home safely. That's all you should do. That's all you can do."

"That's what I will do," Torval said, opening the door to finally take his leave. He didn't add the thought that followed close on that statement's heels, for he knew it would give Osma no comfort.

That and more. Tav comes first . . . but if our people have unleashed a demon from the Forge Eternal to wreak vengeance upon their enemies, then only a dwarf can cut that beast down and send it back to the fires it was born from . . .

Torval kissed his sister's hand.

"Keep them safe," he said, then fled into the cold night.

CHAPTER THIRTY

"That's it," Valaric said, eyes still downcast, hands fidgeting on the worn wooden table before him. "That's the whole story."

Rem looked to the others in the interrogation room: Ondego, Hirk, Queydon. Clearly, Valaric's account of his guild's villainous activities had rocked them all. They'd had their suspicions before now, but hearing it all laid out...that was a different matter altogether.

"Where's your deputy now?" Rem asked. "I noticed he wasn't among those we hauled in here."

"Your guess is as good as mine," Valaric said. "I've no love left for the man, so if I knew where to find him, I'd happily tell you. He wasn't in the party that ambushed those dwarves in the quarter tonight, so I can't even say when he left the guildhall, or where he might have gone."

"There's one bit we're still fuzzy on," Ondego said, crossing his arms over his chest. He stood on the opposite side of the table from Valaric. Rem had never seen the prefect bother to take a seat during an interrogation—he much preferred to stand, to look down at his prisoner and intimidate him. "Just who is it that killed your deputy's brother? Or the men who died in that alleyway ambush tonight, for that matter? The reports we're getting are bizarre, to say the least."

Valaric shook his head. "That I don't know, Prefect, I swear. The men say—"

"The men spoke of a monster," Rem broke in. "Even the dwarves attested to it."

"I wasn't there," Valaric said. "Not when Foelker died, not tonight. I told you, though we all decided on the sortie into the Warrens, it was also decided that some of us should sit it out, establish alibis. But if I knew who was responsible for this—"

"He'd already be dead?" Hirk finished.

Valaric shook his head. "No. If I knew who was responsible for killing my men, I'd have already gone to them—face-to-face—and begged for an end to this. I would've offered my own throat if it might've kept my brothers safe."

Rem studied their prisoner. The stonemason was a big man—strong, roughly handsome, imposing in stature, regal in bearing, despite his rough hands and his working-class Yenaran accent. He seemed to speak truly, without any guile or duplicitous charm. It was sad in a way—a man like that could've made a good watchwarden in another life. He had the charisma, the presence, that special uncanny quality that made others instinctively respect and follow him. But here he was, a stonemason who had lost work to fierce competitors, fallen victim to his own desperation and bitterness, now having led himself and his followers down a path they could not retreat from. And what still puzzled Rem was this: how little Valaric seemed the sort to do what he'd done—to even countenance such actions in others. Time and again during his confession, the mason had made it clear that he blamed himself, and no one else, for the choices made, the lives lost, the damage done. Even in admitting his guilt, he was a man to respect, a man of quality.

But none of that had been enough to stop him from going down that path to begin with, had it?

Where there's need, there's no decency, Torval had said when they'd chased after the thief who'd taken Dorma's house idol.

No, Rem supposed there was not. Nor, it seemed, could under-standing or compassion grow in a garden whose soil was poisoned with wounded pride and the sense that someone *other*—someone *less than*—had taken something inherently deserved by oneself.

And now Valaric would probably die for his pride, for his sense of entitlement. Ondego had already made that clear to Rem in the moments before they'd entered the interrogation room. A confession, the prefect assured him, would mean the man's death, because that was the prescribed punishment for conspiracy, incitement to violence, desecration of holy ground, and participation in murder. The question, now that Valaric's confession was complete, was only this: How many of his men would join him?

"Take him out," Ondego said then.

Rem looked to the prefect. "Pardon, sir?"

Ondego nodded at Valaric. "Take him out—back to his cell. Bring us another."

Valaric raised his eyes. "My brothers aren't to blame in this. I'm their leader—punish me. But let the rest of them go."

"As much as I respect that offer," Ondego said, "I'm afraid that's not to be. You're not a watch captain or an officer in a mil-itary company—you're a bloody stonemason. I don't care how much your men respect you or honor your leadership; they're still free men who made their own choices. You're guilty, it's true—but so are they. No one gets to wriggle out of this by say-ing they were just following orders."

That seemed to pain the stonemason deeply. "But I confessed—"

"And it's most appreciated," Ondego said, sounding, to Rem anyway, truly appreciative. "You've saved us a great deal of trouble. But now we need to figure out who else in your merry little band has blood on their hands. In simple factual terms, it can't be all of them. I'd prefer to isolate the truly guilty and see only them pay the highest penalties, while the rest get off with lesser sentences. But if all of you keep falling on your swords and claiming sole responsibility...well, we'll just end up with a nice bloody execution rally in Zabayus's Square, won't we? Could take all day to see the lot of you hanged or top-chopped."

Ondego's tone was entirely too casual, considering what portentous words he was offering. Rem knew instantly that this was a gambit. He wanted Valaric to start naming names, to point out which of the men had been at the fore of the violence and which had been just followers and hangers-on, to incriminate a few in an effort to spare the rest from the noose or the blade.

Valaric, however, didn't seem willing to play that game. "You want me to offer up my men—my friends—for torture and death now? By name? *I* was their leader, *I* am the one that should be punished!"

Ondego looked to everyone else in the room—Rem last. He seemed truly taken aback. Rem recognized this act as well. It was one of the prefect's favorites. "Am I talking to myself? Am I speaking Quaimish?"

Valaric's gaze grew dark, his anger rising. "Don't insult me, Prefect. It's beneath you."

Ondego scowled at him now. "Then don't aggrandize yourself," he spat, sounding suddenly furious. He bent down over the table, face inches from Valaric's. "I know in your own mind you're an old imperial general, leading his men on all sorts of bloody adventures through the wilds of the west, telling yourself that you command and they jump, that you're special somehow, while they are, by and large, unique only in the severity of their love and loyalty for *you*. But I'm here to tell you, boy:

it just ain't so. You're a bunch of stonecutters in a trade guild. What power you have over those men was given to you by them, in a fair and open vote. You're not an emperor or a general or a real leader of anything; you're just the biggest man in the gang, and they only follow you because doing so lined their pockets and made them feel good."

Valaric shot to his feet, knocking over the chair he'd been sitting in. At his full height he was at least a handbreadth taller than Ondego. He glared at the prefect across the table. Ondego glared back—completely unintimidated by Valaric's height or muscular frame. Rem wagered Ondego had probably killed larger and meaner men with table cutlery.

"This all started," Valaric said slowly, "because one of our own died. Grendan, just a boy, beaten within an inch of his life and left in a gutter in the Warrens to choke on his own blood until that life finally left him. When some of his friends found him, he was still there—barely—but it was too late. I sponsored that boy's guild membership, Prefect. He was *my* apprentice, *my* charge."

Ondego was unimpressed. "I assume he was in the Warrens because he was part of your little demonstration?"

"Aye," Valaric shot back. "Loyal. Obedient. He trusted us and maybe we failed him—but did Grendan deserve *that* end? I say no, and there was no way, after I'd presented his body to his mother and heard her cries, that I could ever let those who'd murdered him escape justice."

"Because honor demanded it?" Ondego asked, sounding so dismissive that even Rem felt the sting of the words.

"You're a petty little dictator," Valaric said, seeing that his appeal had fallen on deaf ears. "What do you know of honor?"

"I know you might have had it once," Ondego said, "but your desire to take all the guilt for this upon yourself isn't honorable;

it's the mark of an arrogant, overproud fool. If you can't finger the bloodied ones among you, then you can all hang. Every gods-damned man in your company, from the pensioners to the fresh-faced apprentices. And with none of you left behind to pay your guild dues or distribute the surplus, what happens to your widowed wives, your orphaned children? They suffer, they starve, they turn to crime and prostitution—all because you lot were too proud to mark the truly guilty among you and try to save the rest."

Valaric's internal struggle was apparent to Rem, and it hurt some deep, hidden part of him. Watching this proud man forced to make such a choice, to betray a few of his guild brothers or condemn them all, truly made Rem's heart ache. But even amid his sympathy, Rem knew that Ondego was right: it was foolish to assume that those men bore no guilt in what they'd undertaken, and more foolish still to condemn them all when only a few were truly guilty of the worst crimes they'd perpetrated. The choice before Valaric was an impossible one—justice or honor—but because he struck Rem as a good man, an honest man, a man unwilling to sow suffering where he could assuage it, Rem hoped that he would, in the end, make the right choice.

It was just a question of how long it would take him to come around to it.

The silence in the room persisted. It was long, awkward, sharp edged. Finally, Ondego waved one hand toward the door. "Get him out of here," he said.

Rem laid a hand on Valaric's shoulder. "Come on, then," he said, jerking his head toward the door of the interrogation room. "Back to the dungeons."

Valaric looked at Rem, seeming to truly notice and study him for the first time. "What's your part in all this, boy? I can hear in your speech you're not even from here."

Rem made sure that he met Valaric's gaze, that his own never wavered. "You're right," he said. "I'm not from here. But now that I've made this my home, I'll be damned if I let a bunch of hateful tradesmen tear it down around me."

Valaric fell silent and let Rem lead him from the room. After Rem and Valaric stepped into the hall and set off down the right-hand passage, toward the dungeons, Rem noted that Ondego and Hirk set off in the opposite direction, back toward the administrative chambers upstairs. Queydon followed Rem and his prisoner at a distance—a little backup, just in case.

The dungeons were quite full. Though they hadn't managed to nab all the stonemasons, they'd still arrested a great many of them—thirty or forty in all. Rem made straight for the cell that Valaric had come from—a cramped cell, set apart from the main cages, with no one else waiting inside. He assumed this was Ondego's doing—to keep the leader isolated and alone, to keep his men at a distance, wondering just what Valaric had told the authorities, or what deals he might have struck. Likewise, that solitude would give Valaric time to sit and think, deeply, about how his choices might affect his men.

"There they are," one of the locked-up masons said from the far side of the room. "Bloody coin-gobblers! Hired hands of the *welk*!"

A chorus of jeers and curses followed. Rem tried to keep his eyes down as he unlocked Valaric's cell and shoved him back into it. As he shut the door again and locked it, he threw a glance back toward Queydon. The elf shook her head: *Don't listen to them. Just lock that door and let's get out of here.*

"Yenara's not a city for mankind any longer!" another of the stonemasons shouted. "It's a city for the hired help and the rich who buy them! Workingmen? Free men? Bah! Who cares for them?"

The bars of the cages rattled. The men shouted, spat, cursed. A chant rose among them, gradual, but soon adopted all round.

Turncoats. Turncoats. Turncoats.

Rem kept his eyes down. Had it really come to this? Did these men, guilty of murder and terror and conspiracy, really think they were innocent, while the watchwardens who tried to maintain order and keep the whole city from being burnt down were guilty? Hate and fear could do terrible things to a human heart, Rem thought as he moved to rejoin Queydon. Worst of all: those twin demons—hate and fear—tended to blind human eyes and cloud the human mind. There was no truth in the world that could survive the frenzy of perceived threats or obligatory vengeance. What a sad, sorry lot they were as a species...

Though were the others—the elves, the dwarves, the orcs— really any better?

Queydon led the way out of the dungeons, shutting the door behind them with a metallic squeal, drowning out, at last, the screaming and rebukes from the locked-up stonemasons. As the sound of their threats and hatred subsided to a dull roar, Rem and Queydon began a slow trudge down the long, dark corridor that would lead them to the stairway.

"Are we wrong?" Rem asked. Queydon—elvish aloofness and propensity for surprise appearances aside—was a good person, a thoughtful person. Rem admired her. Her opinion mattered to him.

"We do our jobs, we fulfill our roles," Queydon said. "What more is there?"

"And what of the dwarves?" Rem asked. "They share blame in this, as well, don't they? Whatever it is they've set loose on these men, whatever murdered those few—"

"They shall be dealt with," Queydon said, and for the first time Rem thought he heard real emotion in her voice, though he couldn't be sure.

"But how?" Rem countered. "The old treaties protect them, don't they?"

"Treaties protect those who honor them," Queydon said calmly. "If we can prove they've broken their word—that they sought personal justice instead of deferring to city authorities, that they disturbed civil order by deploying their own private police force—then we can make them subject to our justice. Or, at the very least, expel the guilty parties and restore order."

"But how often does that happen?" Rem asked, still remembering the outcome of the last major crime they'd solved: a human-trafficking ring run by a vile elf with a deep black hole where his heart should have been. The elven authorities had taken him away, never to be seen again. Somehow Rem doubted he'd met with any true justice at their hands.

Queydon stopped. The force of her ageless gaze made Rem stop as well. She looked at him like an older sister or a kindly aunt—a little pitying, a little patronizing, doing her best to help a witless youngster navigate the bitter forest that was life. All at once Rem felt ashamed. He shouldn't have carried on like that—it was beneath him. He was no bairn in the woods. He should know that this was the way of the world, bitter though it might be.

"It happens when it must," Queydon said quietly, "and seldom ever else. I do not know what will come of all this, Remeck—but if you think about it, you will realize that it's not even our concern. Our job is to find the wrongdoers and arrest them. It is someone else's job to judge and punish them."

"It's just so bloody vile," Rem spat. "All this hate."

"We hate what we fear," Queydon said, "and we fear that which challenges our supremacy, our privilege. Neither humans nor dwarves hold a monopoly on that iniquity."

"How do you carry it all?" Rem asked. "The weight of it? With such...calmness?"

Queydon shrugged a little, then looked—to Rem at least—deeply saddened. "Practice," she said, then carried on down the hall.

Just as Rem took his first steps to catch up with the elf, he heard bootheels pounding down the stairs at the far end of the corridor. Rem quickened his pace to draw up beside Queydon and reached her just as Hirk appeared from the stairway and strode toward them. The big man's face was a mask of panic. Rem, far more used to seeing the deputy prefect implacable and nonplussed, found that look on his normally stony, stubbly face more than a little unnerving.

"Both of you," Hirk said, "upstairs, now. We need all hands."

"What is it?" Queydon asked.

Hirk shook his head. "Just hurry." He turned and pounded back down the hall. Queydon looked to Rem and gave a curt little nod, and the two broke into a run.

Upstairs, the administrative chamber was in chaos. Watchwardens ran to and fro, many amassing at the front, near the short passage that led to the main foyer and the front entrance. A few more hustled in and out of the armory off the back corridor, shuttling with them armloads of armor, weaponry, and shields. Already a great number of their fellows were slipping into steel plate cuirasses, gauntlets, greaves, and helmets, donning mail shirts when no plate presented itself, choosing from the coterie of weapons hastily assembled: swords at their sides, shields on their arms, polearms or spears in their grips.

Rem stared. What in the sundry hells was happening?

"Hirk?" Ondego roared from the entryway. Seeing his second and Queydon approaching, he waved them forward hurriedly. When Rem moved to follow, Ondego raised a hand to stop him and gestured toward the contents of the armory, now strewn around the administrative chamber.

"Suit up!" he said. "That's an order!"

Rem needed little suiting up, in truth. He'd been wearing a mishmash of armor gleaned from the watchkeep armories to work ever since that ambush on the dwarven laborers. He already wore a breastplate of banded mail, a chain mail shirt beneath, and his sword ready at his side. Confused and frightened, Rem hurried toward Hildebran. The brawny man was trying on a series of helms in search of one big enough for his large skull.

"What's happening?" Rem asked. "What are we suiting up for?"

Hildebran gestured toward the outer wall of the chamber. "Friends of the stonemasons, massing outside."

"Friends of...? That's preposterous! Do they think they can besiege the watchkeep? How many of them are there?"

Hildebran studied Rem for a moment, half-bemused. "Don't believe me, copper-top? Go, see for yourself."

Rem turned from the Kosterman and hurried to the outer wall. There were three windows there—high, narrow, with lead mullions and thick glass. Normally they were opened to allow night breezes to sweep through the administrative room and keep it from growing stuffy. Presently they were all closed tight. Rem chose the center window and pressed his face against it.

The glass warped the scene outside, but his field of vision was clear enough. The square before the watchkeep was crowded with jostling bodies—men, women, even a few children and youths. The crowd was enormous and filling every available space on the watchkeep side of Sygar's Square. Some of those outside carried torches that lit the gathered throng with a malevolent golden light that made all their faces look nightmarish and twisted through the warping effect of the glass itself. They shouted, chanted, shook their fists, and exhorted the watchkeep and its occupants to some end that Rem could not understand or discern—though he guessed what it might be.

How many of them are there? Rem had asked Hildebran, doubting and incredulous. How many allies could the stonemasons of the Sixth Chapter truly have in the Fifth Ward?

Based on what Rem now saw through that little window, he guessed it might be everyone...

CHAPTER THIRTY-ONE

Torval first stopped in at the dormitories where Tav and his fellow apprentices were housed, a collection of broad slate-roofed buildings huddled just outside the citadel's walls. The proctor informed Torval that Tavarix had been summoned to the ethnarch's house some time ago, just after the apprentices' return. If the boy had not been sent home, then it was possible he was being guarded there. Torval thanked the proctor and stalked off toward the citadel gates. Somehow he doubted that Tav was being kept in the ethnarch's manse to assure his safety . . .

The gate guards readily admitted him. Within the compound things were silent and still, as though everyone was already in bed or engaged in other pursuits. Only a few lamps burned in the windows of the ethnarch's palace, while the great temple across the courtyard was so dark and quiet that it seemed deserted. Torval carried only his maul, leaving his sword and quartet of daggers in their sheaths. With luck he could convince them that he only wanted Tav and that he didn't give a miner's flaming fart for any other concern. If they thought it in their best interest to release the boy without a bloody contest, they just might do so, no matter how much they hated him or what he represented.

Or maybe, he thought grimly, *Eldgrim will try to teach me a lesson . . . put me in my place . . . humble me before my boy.*

And that was what the blades were for, wasn't it?

Two more guards urged Torval through the doors of the manse without challenge. The great banded doors groaned on their iron hinges, and a little warmth from within wafted out into the night, strangely comforting against the biting winter air. Without bothering to peer in to see what he was walking into, Torval stepped through the open portal and heard the door shut with a tomb-like finality behind him.

Torval stopped just inside the doorway and studied the broad, high-ceilinged foyer before him. A house porter—bald on top, hair long and plaited in the back, smooth, silky beard falling in a gray cascade against his barrel chest—busily rearranged logs in the massive fireplace that dominated the wall to Torval's left. Hearing the groan of the door, the porter turned to look. He gave the logs on the fire a last annoyed shove with the iron poker in his hand, then rose and crossed the marble floor toward Torval.

"You are expected," the porter said, head high and shoulders square, like any good butler.

"Then take me to the ethnarch," Torval said slowly. "Sooner begun is sooner done."

The porter had opened his mouth, no doubt about to respond in the affirmative, when another set of heavy hinges gave a metallic creak. Beside the enormous fireplace, the oaken doors that led from the grand foyer into the audience chamber swung open. Eldgrim stood there, a pair of armored members of the Swords of Eld just a few paces behind him.

"There he is," the ethnarch said, with a strange sort of relish. "Our wayward son, returned."

Torval felt his muscles tense, a wholly unconscious, anticipatory response. Eldgrim was planning something. This parley would not go as he'd hoped.

"Where is Tavarix?" Torval demanded.

Eldgrim strode into the foyer, his guards following. He wore his familiar long, ermine-lined cloak of command—a regal symbol, sumptuous and indicative of his importance—but Torval noticed something else about him that once more put him on guard. Beneath his cloak the ethnarch wore a breastplate. It was the ceremonial sort—lightweight steel, busy with decorative chasing and inlays—but no less effective for all that embellishment.

"Your boy is here, Son of Jarvi. Safe. Safer than he would ever be in those streets, or under your protection."

Torval sighed. "I don't want to hurt you, Eldgrim, just give me my boy and let us be on our way. You gain nothing by refusing me."

"Guards!" Eldgrim roared. He had crossed the room now and arrived at its center. The Swords of Eld must have been nearby, because Torval heard their heavy, tramping footsteps almost instantly in answer to Eldgrim's summons, along with the rattle of their armor and the creak of leather harnesses. In moments a sextet of guardsmen in their familiar blue-gray surcoats and square-scaled mail pounded into the room from a side corridor. They formed a straight, well-spaced line across the width of the room, from the door beneath the great staircase that they'd emerged from to the fireplace on the far wall. They all bore shields. Two had swords, one carried a great battle-ax, and the other three had matching spears.

Torval felt a sinking feeling in the pit of his stomach. He still hadn't seen Tav, and Eldgrim was offering a rather vulgar display of force. None of it boded well.

I knelt before this pig once, Torval thought. *I'll not give him the satisfaction a second time. And by all the gods and forebears, if he's harmed a single hair on Tav's precious head . . .*

"I am Eldgrim Sastrummsson," the ethnarch now said, voice

ringing with pride and pretension. "For twenty generations my forebears have been arbiters, magistrates, and custodians of the laws of our people. I came here—was sent here—to be the pillar of strength, justice, and righteousness for Hallir's Folk in this foreign territory. By virtue of those laws and my birth, I am the sole and sovereign authority over our people in this house and throughout the city beyond. I am not bound to grant you anything, Torval, Son of Jarvi, until you acknowledge my authority."

Torval considered his words carefully. Before saying what he wanted to say—what every drop of blood in his body and every bone beneath his flesh exhorted him to say—he drew a deep breath and made one last petition.

"Show me my son," Torval said to Eldgrim. "Let me see that he's safe before we take this any further."

Eldgrim seemed to weigh those words for a long time, then gave a curt nod. "Captain!"

On the balcony above them, at the head of the great curving staircase that dominated the right side of the grand foyer, Captain Godrumm, commander of the Swords of Eld, appeared from a side hall. Tavarix walked before him, the captain's heavy hand on the boy's shoulder. When Tav emerged and saw his father below, he lunged for the stone railing of the balcony.

"Papa!" he shouted.

Torval's heart almost stopped beating. The boy looked untouched, perfectly healthy, but there was terror in his voice. Godrumm grabbed Tav's collar and yanked him back from the railing before he had a chance to say anything else. It took every ounce of self-control that Torval had to keep from roaring like a rabid bear and charging up that staircase.

"Don't touch him!" Torval shouted, leveling his maul at the

captain across the great span that separated them. "Lay hands on my son again, and I'll—"

"You'll what?" Eldgrim interrupted. Torval looked once more to the ethnarch. Above, at the periphery of his vision, he saw the captain of the house guard urging Tavarix onward, down the stairs.

"This is beneath you," Torval said, trying to appeal to the ethnarch's self-importance. "Threatening a boy who never hurt you, provoking violence from a dwarf who would just as soon leave this place and never darken your doorstep again."

"I disagree," Eldgrim said. "This is *precisely* why I was made ethnarch in Yenara—why our elders in Bolmakünde sent me here. This world that we move in and ply our trades in, it does not want us. It hates us, in fact, for it knows that we are outside it and beyond its petty concerns. My whole purpose—my reason for being—is to protect our people here and remind them who they are, and where they came from."

"As you never fail to remind me," Torval countered. "Not only where I came from, but how right it was that I should have been exiled from there."

"You *are* an exile, true," Eldgrim said, and Torval thought he sensed some sadness in the ethnarch's voice. "But that boy, as you are so fond of pointing out, is innocent. He should not have to pay for your mistakes, nor should he have to live beneath the yoke of your shame, your unworthiness."

Torval took a step forward. "I'm warning you, Eldgrim."

"No," the ethnarch said, "I am warning *you*, Torval, Son of Jarvi. If you persist, you will bleed and you will die. That boy is under *my* protection now, has become *my* responsibility. While the tall folk hunt us and smite us, I can protect him, whereas you cannot. You have neither the mettle nor the authority."

"I am his father," Torval answered. "That is all the authority I need. As to my mettle—"

"Take him!" the ethnarch suddenly shouted.

Three of the guards—two spears and the battle-ax—broke from the line behind Eldgrim and charged across the marble floor. Torval stepped forward, drew his sword to join his maul, then roared an order of his own.

"Stop!" he barked.

The soldiers stopped. They did not look intimidated, precisely, just curious.

Torval eyed each of them in turn, then pressed on. "My name is Torval, Son of Jarvi. I am a watchwarden in this city, and I have come here on business of my own, as one of your kin—"

"I said," Eldgrim roared, "take him!"

To Torval's great amazement—and great relief—the guards still stood, listening.

"You've all heard me make demands of this ethnarch," he pressed on, "fair demands, and honest. If you cross steel with me now, shed blood now, it is because that dwarf, in his ermine cloak, refuses to treat honorably with me."

"Now!" Eldgrim pressed.

The guards started forward again. Torval took one long stride forward to meet them. His movement stopped them in their tracks. The four of them stood frozen—Torval and his three opponents separated by just a cart length, weapons ready, each on guard.

"Withdraw now and there shall be no quarrel between us!" Torval said hurriedly. "Advance and you bleed!"

The captain spoke from the staircase. "The ethnarch gave you orders."

Two guards charged. The third, the one with the battle-ax, hung back. Torval bent to his bloody work.

They were good, he gave them that. The two spearmen coordinated their attacks, one engaging directly while the other circled to try to draw blood from Torval's exposed flank. Torval had mauled his way out of enough bar brawls to know how that sort of coordination went, though, and what was required to counter it. He traded fierce blows with each of his opponents, parrying spearheads with sword or maul, using his blade to thrust his adversaries' shafts aside and open their defenses. He aimed for their soft bits, their joints, anything that would give him an advantage. The spears were formidable, but they were also clumsy for close combat. He only hoped he could use that to his advantage.

Steel rang, squealed, rasped. Torval and his enemies grunted and barked. In the midst of his onslaught and defense, Torval managed to connect his maul to one dwarf's ribs. He heard a sickening crack below the dwarf's scaled mail, then his adversary doubled over, falling to the floor.

Torval did not wait to see him fall. He whirled on the other to deflect his thrusting spear attacks. Sword and maul were employed in equal measure to fend off his blows before Torval finally managed to land a stunning strike that broke his opponent's shaft hand and sent his spear clattering to the floor. As the dwarven guard raised his shield and charged—a last-ditch attempt to put Torval on his back—Torval brought his maul around in a flat arc above the lip of the shield. The war hammer's blunt head rang on the guard's helmet and he toppled like a sack of turnips. The other guard, still rolling on the floor with the pain of his broken ribs, quickly scurried aside when Torval turned to check on him.

On came the next, howling mad, battle-ax raised high for a skull-splitting strike. In the bare seconds Torval had remaining before the guardsman was upon him, he dropped both sword and maul, snatched up one of the fallen spears, then lifted the shaft two-handed to meet the falling blade. The blade's keen edge dug deep into the ash shaft but did not break it. The guard tried to pull the battle-ax loose, but it held. Torval tried to use his grip on the spear shaft to yank the weapon from the guard's hands, but the dwarf's grasp never slipped.

"What is the meaning of this?"

It was the Lady Leffi, frozen in the doorway to the audience chamber beside Trade Minister Broon and the young priest Bjalki. Torval guessed they had heard the ringing and grunting. A moment after the lady spoke, Torval's opponent turned his head, just the slightest bit, toward the sound of her voice.

Torval seized the moment. With both hands he wrenched the spear shaft sideways. The battle-ax left the guard's sweating hands, dislodged from the shaft, and hit the marble floor with a terrible clatter. Before the guard could right himself or dive for his weapon, Torval swung the blunt end of the spear upward, right under the guard's mail shirt, toward his testicles. The guard bent forward to try to save himself the pain that was about to come—and that's when Torval had him. Abandoning his nut strike, Torval shifted his weight and reversed his swing, connecting the shaft's other end—just below the sharpened point—with the guard's helmeted head. The dwarf hit the floor, dazed and groaning.

Torval looked to the newcomers—the ethnarch's wife, the trade minister, the priest—and made sure he held them with a damning gaze as he struggled to catch his breath. His fallen adversaries moaned around him, slowly crawling out of reach.

Torval heard more bootheels. Moments later a new contingent of house guards arrived, some from the corridor beneath the staircase, others at the top of the stairs and fanning out across the balcony. Godrumm had stopped halfway down those stairs, with Tavarix still held tight by the collar of his tunic. The boy stood, scared to move, beseeching his father with his eyes, though Torval could not tell if it was rescuing he wanted or simply his father's withdrawal, to spare any more bloodshed.

It would have to be rescuing. Torval wasn't leaving without him.

"Let all bear witness," Torval said, addressing the wide-eyed Lady Leffi and her companions. "I've come for my son, and the ethnarch refuses to hand him over."

"Eldgrim," Leffi said, "this is foolish, wasteful—"

"Quiet!" the ethnarch roared. "I am sovereign here, and I will decide what is foolish and wasteful."

"Do not test me!" Torval answered, now facing the ethnarch. As he spoke, he snatched up his fallen sword and maul again. They felt good in his hands. "I told you I wanted Tavarix returned to me. Honor your word, you son of a whore, or I'll leave every guard in this house broken, bloodied, and worthless for further service."

"He boasts," Eldgrim said, addressing all present—including his guards.

Torval spat on the floor. "Ask these who lie at my feet if I boast."

"You are strong," the ethnarch said. "You are fierce. In your own mind you might think you're brave, but I think you're stupid, like an angry ox that won't be broken to the yoke."

"Husband, please," Leffi began.

"Silence, woman," Eldgrim snapped.

"There's no need for this," the priest, Bjalki, said from the Lady Leffi's elbow. "Can we not settle this—"

"There is nothing to settle," Eldgrim said slowly. "This dwarf is a disgrace. He was cast out for defying the laws of our people, and now he would come here—into this house—and make demands that further undermine the gods-ordained order that we hold dear. Why we ever agreed to school his spawn after he'd so stained the boy with his own failings remains a mystery to me..."

"Call my boy stained again," Torval said, "and I will kill you."

"And why should you care what I say?" Eldgrim countered. "You criminal. You broken, isolated little castaway. Clearly you left your home and your kind because you knew better. You were stronger than us, braver than us, above our traditions, our justice. Why should you bristle now if I call that little whelp of yours stained, or an outcast, or a shameful mistake, wrought upon the world by you? Unless there is truth in it... unless, deep down, you believe it."

Torval knew the ethnarch was trying to bait him—to get him to fly into a rage and make a mistake. He wasn't entirely sure he could resist taking that bait.

Rem would be proud, he thought absently. *The very fact that I haven't slain this fool yet shows I'm not the dwarf I once was...*

Eldgrim advanced now, all but swaggering as he crossed the marble floor. "We should do that boy a favor and make sure you take your last breath tonight, so that he can find a new family—*a new father*—worthy of his birthright as one of Hallir's Folk."

"Stop it!" Bjalki shouted, stumbling forward as he did. "Stop it, milord, I beg you! We cannot have this!"

"We most certainly cannot," said Trade Minister Broon.

"Save your breath," Lady Leffi said, and Torval heard both exasperation and resignation in her voice. "He's not listening any longer."

Eldgrim's head snapped toward his wife. He speared her with a burning, hateful glare, but Torval saw clearly that the lady would not back down.

"Milord," the young priest now said, standing in Eldgrim's path, "has enough dwarven blood not been shed already?"

"Get back in your corner, cur," Eldgrim snarled, then struck the priest backhanded. The priest hit the floor in a heap. Torval took a step forward, something about Eldgrim's violent rebuff of the young cleric giving his already-heated blood a sudden stir. The young priest raised his sad eyes to Torval. He waved him off.

That's when Eldgrim threw off his cloak, revealing the fine ceremonial armor that he wore beneath . . . and the heavy sword sheathed at his hip.

"I'll do it myself, then," Eldgrim said, then loosed his blade and charged across the floor toward Torval.

CHAPTER THIRTY-TWO

Once, when he was a youth in Lycos Vale, Rem had seen a crowd of angry yeoman farmers gather in force outside a local baron's castle. It had been a bad summer, at first too dry to get the crops seeded, then too rainy for the late-planted crops to take hold and flourish. By harvest time most of the farms in the area, serfs' and yeomen's, had struggled to produce a yield of any sort. Of course, since the local lords took their share first, they left most of those farmers with nothing to stock their own stores for the winter, let alone surplus to sell at market. When the farmers banded together to beg a reprieve from their annual duties, the baron and his peers refused, and fined the farmers by taking a deeper cut of their produce. In a single case, when the house guards of the local lord came to collect their due, the farmer they'd come to visit put up a bloody fight, and ended up dead and bleeding in a puddle of mud. It was soon after that bit of bloody business that the yeomen of the region banded together, marched to the baron's castle, and camped before his gates, demanding to be negotiated with and dealt with reasonably and compassionately.

The baron in question had been a longtime friend of Rem's father, and had turned to his old friend in that time of turmoil for support. Rem's father, regarding the baron as a good earner, a stout defender of the march's borders, and a reliable retainer, was more than happy to march a company of his own men to the castle and meet the farmers on the field.

Rem watched from the battlements as those men—honest, hardworking plowmen who owned their farms and little plots of land outright, asking nothing more than a postponement of their annual tax payments so that their families could survive the winter after a bad harvest—were surrounded, threatened, and finally openly attacked. Four died that day, twenty more were injured badly or crippled for life, and the remainder fled the field, delivering their surplus to the baron before the week was out.

Let this be a lesson to you, Remeck, his father had said in the aftermath. *The low-born will take all they can from you if you let them. Sometimes they need to be reminded just how lucky they are to own anything at all, and that what they do own is by your largesse and good graces alone. Fail to keep them in their place and they'll walk all over you.*

Rem supposed that might be true. But now he stood in a shield line, shoulder to shoulder with his fellow watchwardens, wearing mismatched bits of armor that were probably rusted before he was born, facing down an angry mob of Yenaran citizens whose demands for the release of their stonemason neighbors were both terrifying in their intensity and not wholly unreasonable. He understood their anger, as well as their determination to make the wardwatch the villains in all of this. Perhaps the watch could have handled things differently. Perhaps mediation of some sort, a dialogue, might have averted the bitterness and bloodshed that followed in the wake of the riot and the Panoply temple fire. At the very least, perhaps the remaining space in their dungeons needed to be filled with dwarven miscreants, and not just the men of the city who'd lashed out in anger at their smaller cousins.

But Rem supposed all of that was an academic question now. Here, in the present, there was only anger and unrest, shouts and demands. The crowd filled a good portion of Sygar's Square before the watchkeep, and when they raised their voices as one, it made a deafening roar that drowned out all the sounds of the world and seemed to make the stone walls of the watchkeep itself shake on their foundations. Rem wasn't sure if there was a plan in place, but there certainly didn't seem to be.

This will end badly, Rem thought. *These people—they just want to be heard. And us? We just want to survive the night. If they charge, we'll fight to survive. If we advance, they'll do the same. How in the world can we keep this situation from escalating? The casks are burning and the oil inside is already boiling. The only options are to flee, or stand fast when it all explodes.*

To Rem's right, something clonked against Emacca's shield. Rem was fairly sure that it was just a clod of mud or horseshit, but the collision put him on edge. Emacca, to her credit, hadn't even blinked. The former Tregga horsewoman, face grim beneath the long-healed ritual scars that decorated her cheeks, kept scanning the great mass of angry citizens before them as if the mob were a quiet tree line at the edge of a forest clearing.

Then there were more. *Clonk*, farther off to his left. *Clonk*, right beside him. *Whiz*, right over his helmeted head. *Thump*, right into his shield. The whole crowd was lobbing half-frozen loam and horse apples now. What had started as a sprinkling turned into a deluge.

"Shields up!" someone cried, and Rem obeyed. He raised his shield until its upper lip almost covered his field of vision. No mean feat, the damned thing was so heavy. A chorus of thumps, clonks, and clangs followed as stones, old fruit, mud, and excrement continued to arc out of the crowd. Rem stood fast, held his shield high, and kept his head down. There was no telling when it would end.

He heard bootheels behind him. When Rem craned his

head sideways for a better look, he realized it was Hirk, in old, creaking armor of his own, running along with his head down, barking as he went.

"Ondego's about to address them," he said as he passed. After another minute or two of thumping and thwacking against their raised shields, the volley subsided. From the back of the line, Hirk shouted for the watchwardens to stand at attention. Rem lowered his shield again and drew his boots in beside one another, straightening his back. Though most of his body was still covered by the shield, its base now resting on the muddy ground, he still felt horribly exposed, standing right in front of an angry crowd. When he looked out across them, he saw that many had paused in midwindup, lumps of mud and steaming dung still in their hands. Rem stole a quick glance toward the front stairs of the watchkeep and saw Ondego descending. He wore a fine, well-cared-for old breastplate that looked to be of Loffmari make—one could always tell by the molded muscles and the angular geometric chasing. Decked out as he was in more or less a full suit of armor consisting of both mail and plates, the prefect of the watch had never looked more like a general. Rem supposed this must have been what Ondego looked like long before he came to Yenara, when he was still a campaigning mercenary, renowned across the known world as a fierce warrior and a hard leader of harder soldiers.

Ondego descended the watchkeep stairs. The line of watchwardens standing at attention split and allowed him to pass through. Fearless, he stepped out in front of his men, occupying the churned-up no-man's-land between their shield wall and the front ranks of the protesters.

A few more clods of earth and shit arced toward Ondego, but he avoided them with ease. The man betrayed neither panic nor fear. He eyed the unruly throng as if they were a gaggle of teenage boy-soldiers in a barracks about to be given latrine duty. While the crowd continued to seethe and surge, Rem could clearly see that some of the folk at the fore had appraised Ondego and knew that this was an adversary not to be trifled with. Gradually their shouting and cursing subsided to a dull, indecorous murmur. Ondego waited. His stare—impossibly patient—suggested that he wouldn't say a word until they closed their mouths, and that they would, most like, want to hear what he had to say.

Silence reigned at last—or the closest thing to it. Ondego drew a breath and spoke, projecting his voice like an actor holding forth from an amphitheater stage.

"I am the prefect!" he shouted. "This is my ward, and you're all gathered in violation of its laws! Let it be known, here and now, that if anyone else casts a single stone our way, we'll tread down the lot of you and drag those we can lay hands on back into our dungeons!"

Boos and hisses rose from the crowd. Someone tried to start a chant, but it didn't catch on. Once more, Ondego waited until they grew silent.

"If you have demands," he said, "I'll hear them! If you're just a mob out to entertain yourselves, I urge you to take your asses homeward forthwith, before you end up a guest in my watchkeep or a bloody salt mine! Now who's willing to treat with me?"

The crowd began to titter. Small groups within the larger seemed to turn inward on themselves, as if trying to work out if there was a leader, and who that might be. While many of them argued or tried to press a single member of their little band forward, one man stepped out of the crowd, seemingly without any encouragement. He headed straight for Ondego.

Rem knew the man instantly: Hrissif, deputy steward of the Sixth Chapter of the Yenaran Stonemasons' Guild.

Cack, Rem thought.

"You're the leader?" Ondego asked.

Hrissif shook his head. "Just one of many. No one else was stepping forward, so I thought I might."

Though Rem was still some distance away from where Hrissif and Ondego stood, he managed to hear most of what passed between them.

"Good man," Ondego said, with real admiration. "Say what there is to say."

"My name's Hrissif," the stonemason said. "I'm deputy steward of the Sixth."

"Deputy steward, you say?" Ondego asked, then raised an eyebrow. "You're lucky I don't clap you in irons here and now and throw you in with the rest of your brothers below."

"Why don't you, then?" Hrissif countered.

"Because I'm still listening," Ondego said with a sigh. "Say your piece."

Hrissif nodded. "Very well. I lost my own brother to dwarven violence, just last night. Now, the men of my guild are locked in your dungeons, even though we are the ones wronged—"

"Dwarven violence," Ondego said, as though chewing on the words. "Has that been proven?"

Hrissif offered that familiar sneer of his. "Are you going to try to convince me they're not responsible?"

"I read the reports," Ondego said. "I don't remember you describing a dwarven assailant."

"Maybe not a dwarf," Hrissif said, "but sent by them, I'm certain."

"Until you can prove that," Ondego said, "I'd appreciate it if you'd keep your suspicions to yourself."

Hrissif's sneer broadened into a mordant, bemused grin. "You wardwatch cunts," he said, shaking his head. "So sure you know it all."

"Call us cunts again," Ondego said, "and you can join your brother masons in the dungeons."

Hrissif raised his voice now, still staring at Ondego but clearly addressing the crowd. "Did you hear that? The prefect doesn't like to be called names! To have the honor of his precious ward-watch besmirched!"

The crowd booed and jeered. Rem knew exactly what Hrissif was angling for now, and wished he had the authority to step out of line and knock the man cold.

"Don't talk to them," Ondego said. "Talk to me. What is it you want?"

"These people," Hrissif said, indicating the enormous crowd, "they're only here because they think you've made a mistake."

"Enlighten me," Ondego said impatiently.

"You think we're criminals, fine," Hrissif said. "What I'd like to know—what everyone here would like to know—is why only those of *our* kind are in that dungeon. Where are the tonkers, eh? Surely, if two sides are trading bloody blows here, both should be questioned, shouldn't they?"

"How do you know they're not down there already?" Ondego asked. "Have you seen the inside of our dungeons?"

Hrissif opened his arms. "Take me down to look them over," he said. "I'll be happy to come back up here and tell everyone what I see."

"No doubt you would," Ondego said sourly. "What say you let me worry about who's in the clink? You and yours worry about making sure the wives and children of the men we've arrested have food, rent, and warm beds for the days to come. Isn't that what your guilds are supposed to do in times of trouble?"

"Show me the dungeons," Hrissif said. "Let me ease the minds of these agitated people."

"I'm inclined to show you the dungeons," Ondego said slowly, "though I'm not sure I'd let you out again."

"Hear that?" Hrissif asked, addressing the crowd again. "The prefect's threatening me! *Me!* An innocent man! A man who just lost his brother to dwarven violence!" He turned away from Ondego, no longer even pretending that the prefect was his preferred audience. "Suddenly, when I come and beg justice of the authorities, *I* am the criminal!" he shouted to the crowd. "But what about the criminals in the Warrens, eh? Those bloody pickmonkeys? How many cells do they occupy? How many of them are crowding the Fifth's dungeons as we speak?"

"If you've got stumps in your dungeons, Prefect," someone shouted from the crowd, "we'd like to see them! And not just one or two! Parade the lot out here!"

A cheer answered that suggestion.

"Show us you're holding both sides accountable, Prefect," someone else cried from the back. "Then we'll leave you to sort it all out!"

More cheers. Hrissif turned and stared at Ondego, holding out his arms in a gesture of smug exaltation.

Ondego looked as if he was about to answer.

Then, from the rear of the mob, someone screamed.

Rem raised his eyes and tried to get a better view. At the back the throng pressed and seethed, then seemed to tear right down the middle as a great many people in that part of the gathered mass became eager to flee. But those in flight were blocked by the sheer numbers on hand. As the crowd tried to split and scatter, Rem saw bodies churned underneath, heard people crying for aid, buried as the lurching mass tore itself to pieces.

A roar sounded out of the horde—hoarse, elemental, bestial. From his vantage point in the shield line, Rem saw people in the center of the crowd thrown left and right, as though something large and hulking were driving a wedge right through them. Ondego saw it, too, as did Hrissif. As the crowd dispersed, the prefect and the deputy steward slowly backed away from the turbulence toward the line of watchwardens behind them.

In the next instant the square fell into total pandemonium. Ondego grabbed Hrissif's arm and tried to yank him toward the safety of the shield wall. Hrissif pulled away and retreated.

"The hell with you," he spat. "You'll not get me in your dungeons that way!"

"Don't be a fool!" Ondego barked. "Get behind the line, man! Now!"

"Shields up!" Hirk shouted.

Rem and his companions fell into formation again, shields rising and jostling against one another as they prepared to meet whatever now drove a path through the center of the roiling mob.

"What is it?" one of the watchwardens on the line called.

"Gods defend us," someone muttered nearby.

People from the crowd crashed into the shield wall, trying to press through, to flee the scene and leave the watchwardens to defend their retreat.

"Steady!" Rem heard Ondego shouting above the din. "Let the runners through but keep your shoulders close! We might have to tighten that wall with little notice!"

"Against what?" someone yelled.

Finally the crowd thinned enough for Rem to see clearly. All of Rem's hopes that Torval's strange theory about a dwarven vengeance demon and black magic had been unreasoned fears and idle fantasies evaporated. There, wading through the crowd, moving straight toward the shield line, was the Kothrum. Rem had never seen one, never heard the word spoken before that very night, but now, recalling Torval's description of it, he knew there was nothing else it could be.

For a single moment, Rem's mind unearthed childhood stories of grave dirt–smeared boggarts roaming the countryside in search of naughty children to flay and dismember for their supper. He recalled his old nurse's bedtime tales about child-devouring trolls in the deepest woods and flesh-eating goblins haunting shady bridgeworks and dark, root-encrusted over-hangs in twisty rivers. He remembered the stories told by him and his young friends when they were barely into adolescence about ghouls and wights lurking in local graveyards, visible only when the moon shone on the fog that choked the gravestones. This thing—this infernal, avenging angel of ash and bone and grave soil—was all of those childhood phantoms rolled into one.

And now the beast came right toward Rem and his com-panions. Nothing stood between the bone beast and the line of watchwardens behind their rusted old shields.

Someone suddenly stumbled into Rem's field of vision—a lone member of the roiling crowd, seeking a path of escape.

It was Hrissif. He was confused by all the chaos and jostling bodies around him, tossed about by the human tide, thrown back time and again like a man on a reef pummeled by incom-ing waves. Too late he saw the Kothrum, almost upon him.

"Get out of there!" Rem shouted, in spite of himself.

Hrissif tried to do just that, lunging toward the shield wall. Before he'd gone even two strides, the Kothrum was upon him, moving right toward him, intent, purposeful, when all its previous movement had seemed mindless and haphazard. The creature yanked Hrissif backward in one huge hand, tossed him onto the ground, then lifted one heavy, flat foot and brought it crashing down upon him. Rem heard Hrissif's ribs shatter, saw cloth and skin tear, smelt blood and shit on the cold, churned mud. A gout of blood gushed from Hrissif's open, screaming mouth, and then he was silent. With its next step, the Kothrum crushed Hrissif's skull.

Someone appeared at Rem's left and shoved their own shield into the line. It was Ondego, now wearing a helmet. The prefect bent into the same stance he'd demonstrated for his watchwardens at the start of this mess and shouted so that everyone could hear.

"Shields up! Close ranks! Dig in your heels, the lot of you!"

Rem did as his prefect commanded. All around him he felt the line of his compatriots doing the same. Their shields were interleaved, each broad curve protecting the wielder's front and the right side of the man or woman to their left.

Standing there on Hrissif's smashed, pulverized corpse, the Kothrum seemed to take a moment. It was like watching a hunting hound that had run down its prey work out what came next.

The Kothrum turned its fiery gaze on the shield wall. For a moment Rem thought it was looking at him, but that wasn't it. No, the beast was looking *through* him—through their shields, through the barrier they offered—its burning glare fixed right on the watchkeep behind them.

Then the beast plowed forward and hit the line, slamming into Ondego's shield, sweeping its enormous arms left and right. For just a moment Rem could smell it—damp earth, funereal ash, the coppery reek of fresh blood, and the sulfuric stench of hellfire.

Then he was flying, not sure when or where he would land.

CHAPTER THIRTY-THREE

"Papa!" Tavarix screamed from the stairs.

"Milord, no!" Godrumm shouted, sounding terrified and panicked.

Torval dropped his maul and raised his sword just in time to catch Eldgrim's first strike and parry it. He countered with a great sideward chop of his own. The ethnarch managed to avoid the tip of Torval's blade with a clumsy backward lurch, but recovered quickly and lunged for another round of slashes and thrusts.

"Stop this!" the trade minister cried.

"Guards!" the Lady Leffi pleaded, "draw my husband off!"

"Stand where you are!" Godrumm commanded from his perch on the stairs. "Neither help nor hinder him!"

Peripherally, amid the lust and terror of their fight, Torval saw the guards all shuffling and looking to one another. Attack? Don't attack? Help Torval? Help the ethnarch? Torval could not blame them. They'd been trained and conditioned all their lives to serve powerful dwarves, to protect them and deliver justice by their orders and lay down their lives when their superiors were threatened. But Eldgrim had stolen something from them when he'd drawn a sword of his own and engaged Torval in a duel. He was the sole, gods-ordained authority over all the dwarves in Yenara, that was true... but by taking up arms, he had also stepped outside of his appointed purpose and powers.

His duty was to lead, *theirs* was to fight. Now that he had taken that from them, it was little wonder they opted to do nothing at all.

Torval was alone in this, then. Perhaps he'd escape their wrath, but he certainly wouldn't get any help, either.

They circled and danced and stomped around the grand foyer's marble floor, toward the fireplace, across the great handwoven carpet in the center of the room, over to the staircase, back toward the front door. Eldgrim, though not of a warrior clan, was nonetheless a fierce opponent, pressing, always pressing, furious and enraged but never, ever sloppy. Torval had only the sword in his hand to keep himself safe from the thrusting point and honed slashing edge of Eldgrim's own broadsword. He felt a sting on his cheek suddenly and realized Eldgrim had drawn blood. Enraged at that, Torval pressed his attack, driving the ethnarch back with a series of savage blows until he almost had him pinned against the base of the grand staircase. At the last moment, as Torval drew back for a powerful swing, the ethnarch dove aside and scrambled across the floor, out of reach. Torval's sword blade nicked the stone wall with a spark and he turned, eager to avoid Eldgrim attacking from behind.

Torval and Eldgrim faced each other across the floor, each dwarf drinking in great draughts of air, harried, sweating, streaked with fine streamers of blood from his superficial wounds.

"Husband," Leffi said, and this time Torval thought he heard true concern, a deep beseeching, in her tone. "Drop your sword. If you persist in this, it will mean infamy for you…for your family."

"Infamy?" Eldgrim answered. He held Torval in his burning gaze. "My only crime would be to give this outcast what he asks without putting my people and their collective honor first."

Torval met Eldgrim's fell gaze. "This is your last chance," he said slowly. "I will leave you and never return again if you just give me my boy and let us walk away."

"He deserves better than you," Eldgrim said, his earnestness truly unsettling. "Every son with a failure of a father does. I will not let him lose a precious connection with his people—*his legacy*—because of his father's foolish pride."

Then, with a fearsome battle cry, the ethnarch charged.

Torval parried, struck, feinted, thrust—then stepped aside. Eldgrim overextended and struck empty air. As he bent, threatening to topple over, Torval raised his sword and brought it down in a steep, powerful arc. The pommel of his sword connected with the back of the ethnarch's skull and Eldgrim Sastrummsson sprawled, face-first, to the floor. The ethnarch's sword fell from his hand, ringing loudly on the marble. Torval kicked it aside.

Silence reigned. Torval could hear only the pounding of his own heart in his ears and the ragged rhythm of his breathing. He waited, his blade hovering expectantly, as the ethnarch groaned where he lay.

"Mercy," someone said. Torval glanced sideward. It was the young dwarven priest, Bjalki.

"He shall have mercy," Torval said, eyes back on the ethnarch, "if he will but offer it in return."

The young priest knelt, still some distance from Eldgrim. He seemed to be trying to meet the ethnarch's downturned eyes, to implore him directly.

"Milord," the priest said. "This has gone far enough—"

"Not so," said Eldgrim, and he lunged, arm extended, toward Torval.

Torval searched for the ethnarch's kicked-aside sword, thinking for a moment that the blade was what he reached for. Then he realized too late how wrong he was.

Eldgrim's fist closed around one of the dagger hilts protruding from Torval's own boots. The ethnarch, newly armed, drew back the blade and struck, plunging it deep into Torval's left thigh. Torval grunted, raised his sword, and struck without thought.

His blade bit halfway through Eldgrim's skull, entering just above his right ear, splitting his right eye, and stopping at the bridge of Eldgrim's large hawkish nose. For just a moment, Torval stared into the hateful old ethnarch's remaining eye, noting something like surprise or self-reproach there. Then, as though someone had blown out a candle, the lights went out. Eldgrim went limp and fell to the floor, dragging Torval's lodged sword with him.

Torval stumbled back, the pain of the knife wound in his leg suddenly announcing itself. He tried to stay upright but unceremoniously fell on his ass.

"Husband," he heard the Lady Leffi say from across the room. He could not tell if she was saddened or simply relieved.

"Captain?" one of the guards near Torval called, begging some direction from his commander. "The ethnarch...He's..."

"I see," Godrumm said from the stairs.

Torval heard them, but he did not bother looking at them. He could not take his eyes off Tav, still held back by the captain of the house guard. Tears streamed down the boy's reddened face, but he was smiling. If Torval wasn't mistaken, that smile was full of pride.

"My boy," Torval said, knowing that his voice would break, that tears would come, that he would howl like an animal if he spoke even one more word.

"Go to your father, lad," Godrumm said, and took his hand off Tav's shoulder. Tavarix took the stairs two by two and pounded across the floor. Still sitting, still bleeding, Torval opened his arms and welcomed his son into them. The boy held him up. He had a strong embrace, despite his youth.

"Forgive me," Torval said, and though he would have liked to ask for absolution for so many sins—so many ways, large and small, in which he'd failed his son—he could not, at that moment, decide which he should name first. And so those two simple words came again. "Forgive me, boy. Please forgive me."

"Shut your mouth, Papa," Tav said against him. "It's I who should ask . . . who should beg . . ."

Someone slid into Torval's peripheral vision. Without hesitation Torval shoved Tav away from him, reached down, and snatched up his other boot knife, ready to gut whoever now threatened them. But it was no threat at all, just the young priest, hands up in surrender, trying to edge closer.

Torval lowered his knife. He slumped. Tav was there to catch him.

"You're hurt," the priest said. "Let me bind your wound."

"Fuck binding," Torval said, then jerked his head toward the fireplace. "Lay that iron poker in the fire. When it's red, we'll put it to work."

"This night," Bjalki said, lowering his eyes, "it's not over for you yet."

"What does that mean?" Torval asked, honestly confused by the priest's words.

The younger dwarf raised his eyes to Torval's now. They were red rimmed, brimming with tears, and they bespoke a terrible shame, a terrible sadness, that Torval knew all too well.

Those were the eyes of someone who'd done a horrible, irrevocable thing and knew not how to atone for it.

"You have to help me," the priest said. "What I've done . . . it's unforgiveable."

Torval thought he understood. "You summoned it, didn't you? The Kothrum?"

The priest's voice caught in his throat. He only nodded.

"Do you know where it is?"

The priest nodded again. "It will be wherever the masons are, assuming it hasn't murdered them already..."

Wherever the masons are. Cold panic swept through Torval as realization dawned. When he'd left the watchkeep, Ondego was preparing to raid the guildhall. If the masons were already in custody, they'd be packed into the watchkeep's dungeons.

The watchkeep.

His friends.

Rem.

"See to that poker," Torval snapped. "There's no time to lose."

Chapter Thirty-Four

For just a moment, Rem was convinced that Hirk would close the door and lock him out. From his vantage in the square, amid the fighting and the fleeing, it was a wonder Rem heard the burly second call out to him at all. But somewhere on the wind, he'd heard his name, turned toward the sound, and seen Hirk behind the half-open front door of the watchkeep, waving him up frantically. Rem took a last look around the square, to see what else he could do to help. The Kothrum kept advancing toward the watchkeep, waylaid for moments at a time by eager watchwardens or brave bystanders who dared engage the thing. In all cases the Kothrum simply shoved or swatted aside its opposition, then carried on.

Some of those brave, unlucky souls might be dead, Rem supposed—more than a few still lay where they'd fallen, unmoving—but most of them simply got tossed aside and scrambled away with only some bruises or, at worst, a broken bone or two. Based on observation alone, Rem wagered the beast wasn't out to kill them. Hrissif had been the only one murdered outright as it plowed through the crowd. Now something within it, something magnetic and undeniable, drew it toward that watchkeep. If the Kothrum wasn't kept from its appointed task, it posed no threat to anyone it encountered...but they couldn't just let it waltz inside and kill those men, could they?

Off to Rem's right, the Kothrum lumbered toward him.

Brogila, the Tregga horseman, rushed into its path, sword in one hand, a castoff ax in the other.

"Brogila, come on!" Rem shouted. "You can't stop it! Fall back!"

"*You* fall back!" Brogila shouted over his shoulder. "And take Donal with you! I don't think he can walk!"

Donal—a brown-haired, pale-faced Warengaither, younger than Rem himself but a wardwatch veteran because he'd been on the force since his sixteenth birthday—was sliding through the mud, trying to drag himself into the waiting shelter of some winter-bare shrubs growing around the watchkeep's base. He didn't seem entirely present in the moment—eyes foggy, mouth hanging slack—but he was determined to reach those bushes, even if he couldn't use his legs.

Rem hurried to the boy, scooped him up, and threw him over his shoulders. Straining under the weight of him, he tottered toward the front stairs, climbed each painfully slowly, then slipped in through the half-open doors. Hirk waited just inside. When Rem was through, the second slammed the door shut and threw a heavy oaken bar across it.

Rem swung Donal off his shoulder and handed him off to Eriadus and Minniver. The old man and young woman accepted the half-delirious boy and shuttled him away.

"I want eyes on those front windows!" Ondego shouted from the administrative chamber beyond the cramped front vestibule. "Get polearms and spears up there to repel the thing if it tries to climb in!"

"Polearms and spears?" someone shouted back incredulously. "Against *that* thing?"

"Did I stutter?" Ondego asked. "Do it!"

Rem turned to Hirk. "Unbar the door! Brogila's still out there!"

"I know," Hirk said. He had his eye pressed to the little peep-hole drilled into one of the two entry doors. "He's engaged it."

"He'll be killed if it gets his hands on him," Rem said.

Hirk smiled a little, still staring out the peephole. "Brogila's unstoppable, it won't get its hands on him," he said. A moment later his expression fell. "Cack and piss...it got its hands on him."

Rem ran to the nearest window, a tall, narrow loophole designed more for defense than for visibility. When he peered out into the night, he saw Brogila rolling in the mud, face bloodied, trying to regain his senses after a mind-scrambling fall. From his vantage through the loophole, Rem could no longer see the Kothrum.

"Where is it?" he asked himself.

The front doors suddenly buckled and shook. A moment later they thundered again. Rem saw dust sifting from the bolts that held the door's great hinges to the stone arch containing them, saw the boards of the door bending weakly, splintering after each heavy collision.

Hirk and his door guards had leapt back at the first strike. "There it is," the second said. "It wants in."

Ondego appeared in the doorway to the administrative chamber. Their compatriots were gathering as well, bringing the spears and polearms they'd been ordered to arm themselves with.

Crash! Another collision as the thing threw its considerable bulk against the doors. The great oak plank that barred those doors was stout, surely, but Rem guessed it wouldn't hold out forever against that thing.

"What is it?" Hirk asked, looking to his prefect for some guidance.

"It's called a Kothrum," Rem said. He turned to Ondego then. "Torval told me about it, feared that might be what the dwarves had unleashed."

"Nice of him to tell his commander," Ondego offered as the doors continued to shudder as the beast battered its way in.

"He was scared," Rem said quietly. "Afraid what people might think—"

"Enough," Ondego said. "How do we stop it?"

"We cannot," Queydon said, now joining them in the vestibule. "This is old magic, magic born of pain and loss. If it was animated to hunt the dwarves' enemies and punish them, it won't stop until those enemies are all dead."

Crash! One of the doors splintered, breaking at its center, just above where the bar held it. Everyone shrank from the flying splinters. A moment later another fierce strike punched a hole clean through the other door. More splinters flew. The thing would be inside in moments.

"What if we set them free?" Rem asked.

"Those men need to pay for what they've done," Ondego said.

"I'm not saying they shouldn't," Rem said. "But we can't let that thing just march into the dungeons and murder them in their cells. It's only a threat to us if we try to stop it, and it will follow the men it's hunting wherever they go. What if we try to buy ourselves some time by drawing it off?"

Ondego nodded, finally understanding. "That's good," he said. "What did you have in mind?"

In truth, Rem hadn't formulated much of a plan—he just knew that trying to stop the thing or keep it from its quarry was pointless. But the prefect wanted a strategy . . .

"We need to gather them and move them, fast," Rem said, the door still thundering and splintering behind them. "Get everyone out of here—out of the beast's path. Queydon and I can go to the dungeons, free the masons, and get them out the back. If you could have horse carts or some other conveyance ready—"

"Say no more," Ondego cut him off. "Hirk, go to it."

The second nodded and rushed into the administrative chamber. Rem heard him shouting, gathering all available hands and directing them toward one of the back exits. Ondego looked to the rest of those gathered in the vestibule, ready to meet the beast when it burst through the almost-ruined doors.

"Get back!" the prefect said. "Stay out of its path! Don't engage and it won't lay a hand on you!"

They obeyed. Ondego urged Rem and Queydon along, back toward the common room.

"Queydon," the prefect commanded, "snatch the keys to the clink and take the Bonny Prince here with you."

Queydon hurried off to fetch the keys. Rem fell back into the center of the room, ready to see the Kothrum come marching through at any moment.

Crack! One of the doors had lost its top half. The beast's great fists and long, strangely proportioned arms swung in now, trying to tear the rest of the barricade apart.

Queydon fell in by Rem's side. The elf threw him a daring sidelong look—a strange mixture of deadly irony and thrilled anticipation.

"You're enjoying this," Rem asked, "aren't you?"

Queydon shrugged. "Such respites from the mundane should be appreciated."

Rem had no answer for that.

"Go," Ondego said. "If it takes another path or breaks from the program, we'll let you know. Just get those men out. Use the back stairs. We'll have transportation waiting."

Queydon clapped Rem's shoulder—one comrade urging another to action—then took off at a run. Rem fell in behind her. As they rushed to the stairs that led down to the lower levels and the dungeons, he heard Ondego behind him.

"I want everyone back! Retreat to the outer chambers or hug the gods-damned walls, but don't take a single step in this thing's direction. Stay out of its way!"

"Retreat?" someone shouted. "How are we supposed to stop it if we fall back?"

"Did I say we were going to stop it?" Ondego barked back.

Rem took the stairs two at a time. When he made the bottom and took off at a dead run down the long central corridor that led to the dungeons, he saw Queydon already far ahead of him, practically to the dungeon doorway. Get the prisoners out... load them into horse carts... draw the beast off... and then what?

Aemon's tears, what kind of a plan was that?

And why had Ondego listened to him?

Queydon reached the dungeon door. She plunged in the iron key, turned, and threw back the several locks barring the dungeon from the outside, then took the door handle in both hands and yanked. The door swung wide with a groan and a squeal of hinges thirsty for oil. As he arrived at the door, Queydon tossed Rem the keys that would open the inner cells. While he went to work, she waited outside.

Rem began with Valaric's solitary cell. When he undid the lock and swung the gate open, the stonemason only stared at him quizzically.

"What is this?" Valaric asked.

"There's a dwarven vengeance demon here to kill you," Rem said. "We need to go, now."

"Kill me?" Valaric asked.

Rem rushed to the next cell. "Yes, you. *All* of you."

He tripped the next lock and threw open the gates. "Out! Now! Follow the warden in the corridor! We're leaving by the back door and we'll have transports waiting outside!"

The men in the cell seemed just as puzzled as Valaric had been. They stared at Rem for a time, then at one another. Valaric was out of his cell now, but he still hadn't taken a single step toward the door.

Rem threw open one more cell. Seeing that those freed thus far hadn't moved, he stopped before going on.

"Did you not hear me?" he asked.

"I just don't understand," Valaric said.

Rem lost his patience. He barked like Ondego as he stomped to the next cell and went about unlocking it. "There's a beast made of grave dirt and bones forcing its way into the watchkeep as we speak! I saw it kill Hrissif myself—crushed him, right under its heel! It's the thing that killed Hrissif's brother Foelker and ruined your ambush in the Warrens! We think it's coming down here to slaughter the lot of you! Our plan is to get you all out of here, split you up, and try to lead it somewhere where it can be trapped or waylaid! So if you want to survive the night, follow me out of here!"

That seemed to do the trick. The men all surged forward, rushing toward the door. Outside, Queydon led them back down the corridor that she and Rem had just run the length of. About halfway down, on the left, Rem knew that another passage diverged from the main toward a series of shadowy, little-used storage cells and a final chamber with winding stairs that led up to the surface. That was their destination, their only means of escape. Rem just hoped there were more watchwardens waiting topside, to keep the stonemasons from fleeing into the night.

He had the final cell opened now. As the last man came running out, Rem followed him and brought up the rear. He trailed the long, crowded line of them—thirty or forty in all— as they jostled down the corridor toward the side passage that would lead them to the back stairs.

Just as the vanguard of their little column rounded the corner into that side passage, Rem saw something moving at the far end of the main corridor: dark, hulking, formidable, descending the stairs with deliberate patience.

The Kothrum had arrived. In the flickering light of the passage torches and the dungeon level's deep, oppressive shadows, it looked even more nightmarish than it had above.

The Kothrum stood for a moment, as though orienting itself. The men in the middle of the column had seen it. Panic rising, they all began to shout and shove one another aside, eager to escape the thing now striding toward them.

Rem started pressing the men ahead of him. He really didn't want to be here, right in its path, when it finally met them at the passage intersection.

"Move!" he shouted. "Move, gods damn you!"

Someone up ahead stumbled. As he fell, he drew several men with him into a chaotic pile. Those who avoided the fall parted and surged around their prone comrades, while only two or three stopped to help their fallen brothers.

Rem saw that the Kothrum's pace quickened as it got closer. It seemed to have acquired a target—one of the men in that dog pile on the flagstones. Rem sped up, pressing through the bodies just before him in an effort to get to the fallen men. One of them, a young man, still assisted his fallen friends, back to the creature, completely oblivious to its advance.

Rem skated around the dog pile, reached for the young mason who was completely unaware of what was about to happen, and yanked him into the divergent passage. Just as the young man shouted and stumbled toward Rem, the beast reached the spot where he'd been standing and brought one of its great, bony fists down upon a man struggling to rise. That man had a single moment to cry out, then the beast's fist crushed his skull and he was silent.

Rem tugged at the boy he'd saved, urging him on. "Go, don't look back," he said. The boy took off at a run. Rem retreated after him, but kept his eyes on the advancing Kothrum.

A few men tried to flank it, to flee back up the main corridor toward the stairs. After crushing one man's skull, however, the Kothrum turned its attentions on a certain man in the group of three angling to edge around it. It reached out, seized the stonemason in its dreadful hands, and swung him against the opposite wall of the passage. The force of that impact probably crushed every bone in the man's body instantly. The other two fled up the hall, ignored by the creature. Another mason threw himself at the beast to try to save the one it had just crushed. The Kothrum cast him off with a shrug that sent him flying and returned to beating the life out of the limp man in its grip, apparently unsatisfied that its first strike had killed him. As Rem watched, horrified, the beast finally dropped the corpse at its feet and turned toward its next target.

For a moment Rem thought it was looking at him. A second later he realized it was tracking one of the men from the dog pile who'd scrambled to his feet and now pounded along the corridor right toward Rem.

As Rem watched, the Kothrum took three long strides, snagged the fleeing man in its grip, and yanked him backward. Rem saw the look in the man's eyes as he was torn away from freedom, away from life itself. He struggled in the creature's grip for a moment, but it was no use. In a deft, smooth movement, the beast spun and drove the man's body—headfirst—into the opposite wall of the passage. Rem saw a terrible bloom of blood and brain matter paint the sweating stones, and the man's ruined corpse went rag-doll limp.

That was enough. Rem turned and ran, falling in behind the other fugitives and trying to put as much distance between himself and the Kothrum as possible. Only when he'd reached the far end of the hall did he dare to look back.

The Kothrum strode on, unhurried, intent on its prey. Rem knew that it wanted nothing to do with him—that it was not looking at him and probably could not even *see* him. And yet the sight of those deep, burning, malevolent fire pits that seemed to be its eyes, and the way it came on, steady and sure, in no hurry because it knew there was no escape...

Rem suddenly collided with a wall of jostling bodies. All the men freed from the cells were now crammed into the little chamber that held the spiral staircase leading to the surface. He saw them crowding the stairs, all the way up and out of sight.

"What's going on?" he demanded. "It's coming!"

"Hinges rusted!" someone shouted back. "The door's stuck!"

"Bloody well push on it!" Rem shouted. "It'll be here in moments!"

Maybe it didn't want him, but he really didn't want to be standing here, between it and its quarry, when it arrived.

Rem peered back around the corner. The Kothrum was less than a hundred yards away and closing. It passed through a deep well of shadow where no torches burned, and in that instant all Rem could see was those terrible eyes burning in the dark, its considerable bulk a black mass on the deeper blackness of the shadow enfolding it. There was nowhere to run down here. The passage dead-ended into this chamber. If they couldn't get that door open—

Above there was a sudden cheer and a mad surge. Rem looked over his shoulder and saw the men streaming up the stairs as fast as they could go. Those at the back shoved their mates forward, urging them on, pleading for them to hurry. Up above, the already-freed masons called out to their brothers, telling them to get out of the way and clear a path for those coming behind.

Rem fell in behind them, backing toward the stairs so he could watch for the Kothrum's imminent arrival. Just as he placed his boot on the lowest step of the staircase, he saw the beast round the corner. It came toward him.

Rem turned to the men choking the narrow passage above him. Though they were moving as fast as the space allowed, they seemed impossibly slow. Rem couldn't believe what a panic he felt—how his heart hammered in his chest, how it seemed to beat like a boatman's drum in his ears, how his vision seemed energized and enlivened. His whole body knew only one desperate need: to be out of here, away, to clear the Kothrum's path and escape sure death by its cold, bony hands.

There it was, below him. Without hesitation it mounted the stairs. Rem expected it to be on him in moments, but something miraculous saved him. As the beast tried to climb, its round, flat feet failed to find purchase on the narrow stairs. The beast slid and tripped, almost sprawling on its face. With a strange, guttural huff, it started digging its bone claws into the stairs themselves and the stones of the stairwell walls, drawing its body up laboriously, inch by inch, using the strength of its forelimbs to give its clumsy legs and feet a better hold.

Rem pressed on, still blocked by the men crammed into the passage ahead of him. Below him the Kothrum came to the place where the passage of the stairway narrowed around the spiraling stairs. The creature hesitated again, unable to move. It was too broad to fit, its stout, barrel-shaped body hindering its advance. As the beast pressed forward, determined and implacable, its soil-and-bone bulk became more aggressively wedged into the narrow passage. Rem heard the rattle and rasp of its bony ornaments against the stone of the stairwell, saw clods of earth littering the stairs, heard a few of the more obtrusive bones protruding from its torso breaking as the beast shoved itself forward a foot at a time.

That's where Rem left it. The men ahead of him had finally cleared the way. He felt the cold wind of the night kiss his face, felt hands grasping his arms and yanking him through the narrow little doorway at the summit of the stairwell. Suddenly, blessedly, he was outside. He was out of the beast's path, safe and free. He'd done his duty, fulfilled his mission; what happened now wasn't his problem.

He looked around, blinking. At each end of the street and off two side lanes, the fleeing stonemasons were urged into waiting carts by eager watchwardens, while more of Rem's comrades stood sentinel, creating a broad perimeter around the scene to await the Kothrum's emergence. Standing just beside Rem were Queydon and Valaric. It had been the two of them who'd yanked him out of that cramped stairwell into the blessed, wide-open, freezing air of the Yenaran night.

"You need to go," Rem said to the steward. "It's stuck in the passage, but that won't stop it. It'll be up here in moments."

"I was the leader," Valaric said. "I should be the one to bear its wrath. If that'll stop it—"

"Not alone, you're not," a familiar, stone-roughened voice broke in. Rem, Queydon, and Valaric turned toward the sound of that voice.

It was Torval. That youngish dwarven priest—Bjalki, was it?—stood beside him.

"About bloody time," Rem said, relieved.

"Sorry I'm late," Torval said. "The ethnarch proved... difficult."

Below the Kothrum roared, angry and frustrated by its slow progress.

"All of you go," Valaric said. "Get my men out of here. I'll meet it."

Torval marched up to the steward, shaking his head. "The Kothrum has a number of targets among your men," he said. "You could all flee to the ends of the earth. Sooner or later the Kothrum will catch up with you—all of you."

"And how do you know that?" Valaric asked.

"Because that's what I summoned it to do," Bjalki said.

Rem saw Valaric's dumbfounded expression and assumed he wore something similar on his own face. *This* was the Kothrum's summoner? This bland, soft-spoken, young-faced dwarven priest?

Down in the passage, Rem heard bone scraping stone. The Kothrum would soon make the surface.

"We need to go," Rem said, "It'll be up here any second—"

"Stand fast," Torval said, laying a hand on Rem's chest. "Forget about drawing it off or getting these men to safety. We can make our stand here."

"Here?" Rem asked.

"Here?" Queydon parroted.

"Right here," Torval said to them all—Valaric included. "This is where you'll help me kill it."

Suddenly Rem no longer wanted to cheer for his partner's return.

CHAPTER THIRTY-FIVE

Below, the Kothrum gave an impatient roar. Though they had withdrawn some distance from the doorway, that roar yet made Rem feel too near, too vulnerable. He looked to the priest.

"You're the one who summoned it?" Rem asked.

"I am," he said.

"Then why can't you just unsummon it?" Rem asked.

The priest shook his head. "I had to dig deep to find the spell to raise it," he said. "So far as I know, there are none that banish it. The only way to stop it is for its mission to be completed, or for its source of power to be destroyed."

"Fine," Rem said. "What's the source of its power?"

"It's a runestone," Torval broke in. "Bjalki here told me all about it."

"They're sacred artifacts," the priest explained, "discovered as our people mine and dig. We recognize them because they glow from within, containing fantastic energies from elder ages. When we come across them, we polish them and carve holy runes into them and add them to our temple reliquaries, evidence of the gods' power manifest in physical form. Every dwarven temple from Kosterland to Quaim has them."

"And you employed one of these holy stones in the raising of that demon?" Queydon asked.

Bjalki nodded. "I did. It's buried in the middle of the thing's head. I tried to remove it myself but the Kothrum wouldn't let me."

"So," Torval said, "if we can get it out—"

The Kothrum bellowed from the stairwell, closer now, sounding far more angry and impatient. Across the street, Ondego broke from a line of watchwardens encircling one of the wagons and marched toward them, calling as he came.

"What the fuck are you lot doing over there?" the prefect called.

"Stay back!" Torval shouted at him. "Keep everybody back! We've got this in hand!"

Ondego stopped. "Have you?"

"Just hold the perimeter!" Torval barked back. "Be ready to get the prisoners out of here if the Kothrum gets past us!"

The prefect raised his hand and trotted back to the cordon. Torval turned to Rem and the others. Only then did Rem see that Torval carried a weapon Rem had never seen before: a big dwarven war hammer, balanced on his shoulder, far larger and heavier than Torval's usual maul. The dwarf brandished it.

"This is for the smashing," Torval said, then dropped it at his feet with a heavy thud and pulled two more implements from a scabbard on his back. Rem recognized them immediately: a pair of rock hammers—stunted picks of a sort—commonly employed by miners in confined spaces, or by those climbing mountains, to keep them from sliding down sheer slopes. "These are for digging."

"This is mad, Torval," Rem said. "How are you supposed to dig into that thing? If you try to approach it or fetter it, it'll kill you!"

Valaric chimed in then. "I can distract it," he said. "I'm one of its targets, aren't I? Shouldn't it give me its attentions, so long as the dwarf doesn't stand right in its way?"

They all looked to him. He was dead earnest, without fear. Rem admired the mason's determination even as he damned him for letting this whole mess escalate to these mad ends.

"It wants me," Valaric said. "Myself, or one of my blood-stained brothers. If it's truly drawn to me, then I can keep it busy, stay right out of its reach. While I do that, the dwarf here can—"

"If Torval threatens it or interferes with it while it's trying to get to you," Bjalki said, "it'll tear him to pieces. It doesn't care that he isn't the target—he's an obstacle."

"Then give it better obstacles," Torval said. "Rem, Quey-don, hit it hard. Threaten it and strike it and get the beast's blood up. If it's chasing Valaric, and it's troubled by you two, I should be able to do my work."

"This is insane," Rem said, wishing they had more time to build a better plan. He looked to Bjalki. "Can't you call it off? Even give it pause? Won't it listen to you?"

Bjalki shook his head. "I've already tried," he said. "As I said, I created it for a purpose. Its only reason for being right now is to fulfill that purpose. I am its summoner, but I am not its master."

Behind them there was a loud, shattering crack. They all turned and saw the Kothrum shouldering through the too-small doorway, splintering the wooden frame and cracking the stone that surrounded it. Free and clear, standing tall at last, it once more did that strange little trick that Rem had seen it pull in the dungeons—stopping, waiting, as though searching for the scent of the nearest prey. After a moment it slowly turned its head, its blank and burning gaze, toward their little band.

Toward Valaric.

It advanced.

"If anyone wants to argue," Torval began.

"Fine," Rem said. "We'll go with your plan."

Torval nodded and resheathed one of his rock hammers. He suggested the big war hammer on the ground. "When I toss you the stone, lad, you bring it here and smash it—clear?"

Rem nodded. There was nothing else to say. Ready to start, he drew his sword. It looked frail and pitiful compared to the hulking juggernaut of bone and grave earth now stomping toward them. Rem broke left. Queydon drew her own curved sword and slid right. Torval followed Rem, intent on looping all the way around the beast and getting at it from behind. Valaric stood his ground.

"No heroics!" Torval called to Valaric as he trotted off. "You're only useful while you're still alive. Keep it occupied, but don't get too close!"

"This is my redemption, brother dwarf," the stonemason said. "I'll not let you down."

As Rem got into position on the Kothrum's right, he saw Bjalki edging closer to Valaric, as if to stand beside him.

"What are you doing?" the stonemason asked the dwarven priest.

"Let me try," Bjalki said, pointing to the advancing Kothrum. "I have to try."

The Kothrum closed.

Torval had withdrawn to about thirty feet directly behind the beast.

Opposite Rem, on the Kothrum's left, Queydon paced the beast, stalking sideways, waiting for her turn to distract it.

Rem lingered on its right, waiting for some sign that he should intervene.

The Kothrum lumbered forward, slow and patient. Directly before it, Valaric and Bjalki stood their ground. As the distance between them closed, Bjalki suddenly rushed forward, right into the Kothrum's path. The dwarven priest held up his arms and addressed the thing directly.

"Stop," he said. "As your summoner, I command you! Stop!"

The Kothrum swept Bjalki aside, a dismissive gesture that—despite its apparent carelessness—still sent Bjalki rolling with terrific force. Then, to Rem's great surprise, the ever-patient Kothrum charged.

For something so bulky and unwieldy, it moved fast. One moment it stalked—the next it leapt forward, taking three long, bounding strides in succession toward the startled Valaric. For a moment—a terrifying instant—Rem thought that the stone-mason had frozen, his shock at Bjalki's fall and the Kothrum's charge too sudden to overcome. Then the stonemason dove aside, scrambling for safety on all fours as the Kothrum tried to arrest its headlong rush and redirect.

Across the street the watchwardens and stonemason prisoners directly in the Kothrum's hurtling path scattered. The thing barreled forward and smashed into the horse cart that had—only moments before—held almost a dozen of the prisoners. The cart crumpled under the weight of the impact, and the horse tied to it bucked in its traces. Half-buried in the broken running board of the cart and yanked sideways by the bolting horse that could go nowhere with such a heavy burden now holding it in place, the Kothrum struggled to disentangle itself.

Torval saw his chance and took off at a sprint, strong, short legs pumping hard. He launched himself into the air just shy of the creature. Rem watched, awestruck and terrified, as his partner rose on the air and slammed hard into the Kothrum's hunched and bone-studded back. Because the thing was so knotty—so covered in arching ribs and protuberant shinbones and fanning pelvises—Torval found purchase quickly and easily. As the Kothrum tore itself out of the cart, Torval held fast.

Free of the cart, the Kothrum was suddenly aware that something was atop it, overbalancing it. It began a strange, whirling dance, arms bent awkwardly, trying to reach the hanger-on now riding its hunched shoulders. As one arm curled round, bony fingers sweeping dangerously close to Torval's huddled form, Rem realized it was his turn. He ran right up to the beast, shouting and calling, then swung his sword into its exposed flanks. A few chips of bone sprang forth, and some clods of earth fell away. The Kothrum turned on him, towering and grim, burning eyes livid in the wintry night.

Rem beat a hasty retreat, reeling backward as quickly as his feet would take him. Something snagged his heel and down he went. He hit the mud hard, on his back, and the Kothrum loomed above him. For a moment he thought he was done for, and he cursed his stupidity and uselessness.

Then Valaric sped into Rem's vision from behind the Kothrum. "Here!" the stonemason cried. "Here! I'm the one you want!"

The Kothrum's head jerked upright. Mechanically it strode toward Valaric.

Rem trailed after it, watching Torval as he went. His partner had climbed up onto the beast's shoulders now and was crouching there, in danger of toppling off at any moment. Fierce and sure, Torval raised the rock hammer in his hand and brought the sharp little pick down, its point cracking right through a scalloped formation of shoulder blades near his feet. Torval gave the couched pickax a yank to make sure it had gone deep and held fast. Satisfied, he rose up a little on his perch, using the embedded rock hammer as a sort of handgrip to keep him steady.

Valaric gave the Kothrum a wide berth now, leading it in a broad circle, back toward the center of the street, away from the cordon of watchwardens and stonemasons. Queydon slipped in from behind him, preparing to offer distraction if the beast charged or made a sudden play for its quarry again. Bjalki lingered on the periphery of the strange, clumsy dance, as though eager to join but not sure how.

Rem, still trailing the beast, turned his attentions back to Torval. His partner had drawn his other rock hammer out now and brought it smashing down on the half-shattered skull topping the creature's crown. With the pick buried in the skull cap, Torval began to tug, trying desperately to lever the bony carapace off the creature's too-small head. Once more the Kothrum seemed to become aware of something troubling it, despite the fact that a potential target lay dead ahead. Its forward motion slowed. Confused, the beast turned a little, pivoting back and forth. Its arms rose to reach for the unwanted passenger on its shoulders.

Rem was about to close when Queydon charged. In a series of deft movements that made her little more than a blur, the elf struck at the Kothrum with her elegant curving scimitar—first a strike on its right; a spin, then a thrust at its chest; ducking, finally, then whirling once more, capping off her attack with a trio of hard, fast blows to the Kothrum's left hip.

The Kothrum edged toward her, more aware of her attack now than of Torval's labors atop it.

Rem stared, amazed. It was working!

Queydon kept at it, dancing in a circle around the thing, striking, drawing sparks when her steel nicked stone embedded in the grave earth that the thing was molded from, easily evading its clumsy grasping and ham-fisted retaliations. Valaric, meanwhile, stayed right in the thing's line of sight, drawing it slowly, surely, toward him.

Rem slid left, intending to come around from behind the thing, opposite Queydon and Valaric, ready to attack if a distraction was needed. Valaric, meanwhile, moved in the opposite direction. Up on the Kothrum's shoulders, Torval brought the pick down again and again, still trying to break through the bone and tightly packed stone that made up its head.

"Careful," Bjalki said, lingering nearby. "It's not smart, but it's cunning. It—"

Without warning the Kothrum summoned one of its shocking surges of speed. With uncanny swiftness the thing stretched out one hand and swatted the dancing Queydon like a fly, almost as if it had anticipated where she would be in the next instant. The elf collided with its swiping hand, arced through the air, then hit the dirt with a grunt.

Rem charged toward her. "Queydon!" he shouted, hoping, praying that he would see her stir and rise in the next instant.

The thing's sudden movement almost threw Torval off its shoulder. At the last instant, the dwarf managed to arrest his near fall by planting the point of the pick he'd been using in the Kothrum's left shoulder. For a moment Rem watched as his partner literally hung off the beast, a climber clinging to a moving mountain, only his rock hammer's sharp point standing between him and the Kothrum's heavy, stomping feet. Satisfied that Torval was safe, at least for the next few breaths, Rem hurried to Queydon's side and dragged the still-dazed elf away from the chaotic action. Just as she waved him off, assuring him that she was sound and ready to rejoin the fight, sudden movement drew Rem's gaze.

The Kothrum was aware of Torval. It reached for him, ready to tear him free.

"Here!" Valaric cried, waving his arms. "Forget him! I'm your prey! Have at me!"

The Kothrum froze, as if the twin targets—the dwarf that hung from it and the man it had been summoned to kill—scrambled its primitive instincts. After only a moment's hesitation, it lurched toward Valaric.

Rem studied Queydon. She had suffered a few superficial cuts in the fall, but otherwise seemed unruffled. Her large honey-colored eyes displayed no hint of worry or need. She blinked at him.

"What are you waiting for?" she said calmly. "Help him."

"Right," Rem said, and rushed off to distract the monster.

Torval had regained his perch on the Kothrum's shoulder. He kept one hand on the planted pick, eager not to fall again. With his free hand Torval reached out for the first rock hammer, still stuck in the Kothrum's right shoulder, its handle pointing skyward. With a yank he dislodged the little pickax, then brought it crashing down onto the beast's crown, trying to break through its stone pate and expose the magic gem at its center.

"Come on!" Valaric cried, taunting it. "I'm right here! Catch me!"

The Kothrum lumbered toward him.

Rem paced the beast again. As he watched, Torval brought his pick down, hammering again and again through the Kothrum's smooth, boulder-like skull. Suddenly, a giant shard of the stone sheared away and went flying. Rem almost cheered—until he saw what happened next.

That shard whirled through the air and hit Valaric right in the forehead. With a startled groan the stonemason reeled backward, blood sheeting down his face. He was stunned, blind, reeling...

Rem was about to rush in, to yank the stonemason out of harm's way, when Bjalki broke into Rem's field of vision in a mad sprint toward Valaric. He reached the stonemason just a moment before the Kothrum did, tackling him hard, and the two went rolling. Rem closed on them, ready to attack the thing and draw it off—

But it was too late. The Kothrum bent, reaching out with its enormous, inhuman hands, ready to close them around Valaric's now-bleeding skull and crush it.

"Stop!" Bjalki shouted into the Kothrum's featureless face, rising on swaying legs to place himself between the beast and its prey.

The creature swept Bjalki aside carelessly and reached again for Valaric. Bjalki, undeterred, leapt onto the beast's reaching arm and held fast, like a man lost at sea clinging to a broken, wave-tossed mast.

"Stop," he pleaded, trying to pull the creature's arm aside. Rem saw that the priest really was begging now, tears streaming down his face. "Stop this! I don't want this...I never wanted this."

Atop the Kothrum, Torval had uncovered something. A sickly-green glow emanated from the Kothrum's cracked-open skull. Unfortunately, whatever glowed did not want to dislodge. Torval hacked at it with his pick, sending stone chips flying every which way.

Rem reached the fallen Valaric, snatched handfuls of his tunic, and yanked him clear. For the moment, at least, the stonemason was out of the Kothrum's reach...but poor Bjalki still held to its arm, pulling, sobbing, begging it to stop and leave the fallen mason be.

Perhaps the beast was incapable of emotion, but suddenly it seemed to lose its patience. With a strange, stony snarl, the Kothrum scooped up Bjalki and shifted his wriggling body into its grip. Both of its large, bony hands held the struggling dwarven priest. It studied him for a moment, Bjalki's legs pinwheeling above the ground, his fists still beating at the creature that he himself had given life to.

"Torval, hurry!" Rem shouted.

Valaric struggled to his feet again, wiping blood from his eyes. When he saw Bjalki in the Kothrum's iron grip, he lunged. Rem had to grab him to hold him back.

"No!" the stonemason shouted.

The Kothrum held Bjalki in both hands, like a strong man studying a baby for the first time—puzzled, cautious.

"Take me if you must," Bjalki said, breathless. "Just, please, stop—"

The Kothrum squeezed. Bjalki made a strange rasping sound and spat up a terrible gout of blood as his internal organs collapsed. With a convulsive jerk, the last life left the dwarven priest's body and he fell limp, a doll in the arms of his killer, every bone from his lower ribs to his pelvis shattered.

Rem felt as though something in him had been crushed, as though he could not breathe. The Kothrum dropped Bjalki and turned its burning eyes toward Valaric. On it came.

"Move," Rem said to the stonemason. As Valaric stumbled away, Rem broke right, trying to hook around behind the Kothrum. Before he'd traveled far to its periphery, he lunged and laid into the vile thing with his sword. His blade sent bone chips and clods of earth flying. The Kothrum turned toward Rem, his presence a distraction, an afterthought. It seemed to pause for an instant, hesitant, as if it couldn't decide which it should pursue—its true target, ahead, or this attacker, close on its flank. Finally it decided to swat at Rem.

He ducked the backhanded swipe—lucky, really, as it came so quickly—then scurried away, putting a safe distance between himself and the creature. He looked for Valaric.

The stonemason circled toward the beast on its opposite

side. He moved slowly, regaining his senses, blood still flowing from the cut in his forehead—but he was also actively trying to engage the beast.

"You missed me again!" he cried. "You'd kill your own master and still leave your target upright? Come on, you bloody bastard! Come and get me!"

The Kothrum made straight for him.

Torval brought his pick down. Rem saw something fly free from where Torval struck. For a moment he thought it was another shard of stone, but almost instantly he realized it was no such thing at all. Against the black night sky, the tumbling, arcing object glowed with a noxious, otherworldly light, a black gem with green fire burning within.

The runestone!

It rose, rose, then started its descent, describing a steep arc. Rem sped toward where it was about to come down, just a few feet behind the Kothrum itself.

The Kothrum reached for Valaric, who slid sideways, trying to turn the thing around in a broad circle. Just as the gem hit the mud, Rem did as well, sliding forward with his arm outstretched. He'd thrown his sword aside. All that mattered was the gem now.

Valaric's gambit worked. The Kothrum turned. Unfortunately, it was turning right toward Rem.

Rem slid to a stop, his hand just inches from the gem. He drew himself up and leapt forward, pouncing on the glowing stone and pulling it toward himself. The Kothrum was directly in front of him now, lumbering forward, looming tall in his vision.

Gods, this is it! Rem thought. *It's over now!*

Then something leapt through the air, right over Rem's prone form. It was Valaric. He was literally bounding into the

Kothrum's embrace. He hit the beast with stunning force, like a child leaping into the arms of a father he hadn't seen in ages. For its part, the Kothrum accepted Valaric's strange embrace, though it seemed to hesitate for a moment—as though it knew only how to chase things that ran away, not sure of what to do if they came willingly into its arms.

Rem stared, amazed.

"The hammer, lad!" Torval shouted from atop the Kothrum. "Smash it!"

Rem searched his surroundings for the great dwarven hammer. There it lay, a few yards from him. He scrambled toward it and almost landed on his face, but somehow managed to right himself. Arriving at the spot where the weapon lay, he tossed down the gem and snatched up the hammer. It was heavy, even for a human wielder.

Rem brought the hammer down on the gem. It cracked, but did not shatter. The unearthly glow still pulsed inside it.

"Rem, hurry!" Torval shouted again.

Rem chanced a look back at Valaric, still held aloft by the Kothrum. Torval beat at it with his rock hammers, trying to get it to release the stonemason. Valaric was still alive, eyes glinting between the Kothrum's bony fingers. He didn't struggle at all.

Queydon's voice split Rem's thoughts. *Now!* she commanded.

Rem raised the hammer again and brought it crashing down. This time he heard the gem shatter, saw tiny black-green shards go flying out from under the hammer along with a strange, sudden waft of green smoke.

He turned to the Kothrum just in time to see its last act: crushing Valaric's skull between its huge, shovel-like hands. An instant later the earth and bones collapsed, as though whatever held them together had evaporated in a single breath. Torval fell upon the heap. Valaric's corpse crumpled to the mud.

Rem studied the tableau before him: Torval, sitting upright and regaining his senses; Valaric's corpse, skull crushed and mangled; Bjalki, tossed aside, a twisted rag doll with no stuffing at its center, a widening pool of blood steaming on the cold mud around him; Queydon, approaching slowly, studying the horrible scene with her sad, ageless gaze. Rem knew it should feel like victory, but, gods help him, he couldn't summon anything like exultation. Instead he found himself suddenly weeping, totally unable to stop.

CHAPTER THIRTY-SIX

In the end the only way to settle it all—restitution for damages, inquiries into the large numbers of dead, an after-the-fact investigation that attempted to piece together what was known and what could be settled regarding the Sons of Edath and their short, bloody feud with the Swords of Eld—was that time-honored default of solicitors and litigants everywhere: mediation. All parties gathered in one of the many great tribunal chambers high on Founder's Hill, above the First Ward, and spent interminable days in uncomfortable chairs around overly large tables, under the watchful eyes of city judges, an army of notaries, and Black Mal, the ardent chief magistrate.

Torval was subjected to the circus for far longer than Rem, for he had spilt blood in the execution of his fatherly duties. Throughout, Rem remained in the chamber, having convinced the administrators that he was his partner's special counsel. When he heard the story of what Torval had endured at the dwarven citadel, delivered with clinical bluntness in excruciating, cross-examined detail, Rem nearly broke the solemnity of the proceedings by crossing the chamber to give his partner a great hug. He resisted the urge, though, knowing that it would be frowned upon by all present—Torval most of all. After tense days of deliberation, during which Torval was barred from active duty, the grand jury finally determined that Torval would not be held liable for the slaying of Eldgrim Sastrummsson, the late ethnarch, since ample evidence—a great deal of it from the Swords of Eld themselves—proved that the ethnarch's death was wholly a matter of self-defense. Torval was summarily dismissed to resume his duties, and the two partners left the Halls of Justice to carry on with their lives.

A verdict arrived weeks after their personal testimony had been given. The surviving members of the Stonemason's Guild, Sixth Chapter, would be impressed to repair the damage done to the Fifth Ward watchkeep. Their chapterhouse would be torn down to its foundations, the debris burned to ash, and some new structure raised in its place. There would no longer be a Sixth Chapter of the Yenaran Stonemasons' Guild, that number henceforth being banned. The survivors were welcome to seek membership in other chapters, subject to the acceptance of the sitting members of those chapters, but any of them caught within the city limits working stone without a license after two turnings of the moon would be subject to prosecution. In short: get someone to vouch for you henceforth, or get out of the city and never come back. When Rem heard of that resolution, he supposed he could not think of a better one. Apparently there had been discussions regarding harsher punishments, especially for the half dozen remaining stonemasons who had either been named by their fellows as, or outright confessed to, being present at the murder of Docent Therba. But, in a rare instance of Yenaran justice opting for mercy instead of castigation, the courts decided that enough blood had already been spilt, enough lives ruined.

How to deal with the violence and unlawful magic attributable to the dwarves was a more sensitive matter. The greater share of blame clearly lay with the priest, Bjalki, who had summoned the Kothrum, and with the belligerent ethnarch, Eldgrim, but as those two poor sods were stone-cold dead, no punishment could be meted out. Any members of the Swords of Eld with permanent injuries or handicaps resulting from the violence were deemed to have suffered enough and released. Any who would heal normally were told to leave the city forthwith and never return. When the issue of who should stand for the dwarven people in the ethnarch's stead was raised before the court, the Lady Leffi was readily enlisted. So far as every dwarf who testified was concerned, she was the only choice to lead them now that the ethnarch's seat was empty.

The judges thus decided: the Lady Leffi would be nominated as the new dwarven ethnarch in Yenara, as there was ample evidence now in the record that she had tried, at several junctures, to keep the situation in the dwarven quarter from spiraling out of control while her husband had exacerbated it. Her position would be secured pending the approval of the Brood of Elders back in Bolmakünde—but no one expected them to overturn the appointment. Leffi's sense of quiet command and humble satisfaction left everyone sure that she expected to be confirmed without opposition.

And just like that, after weeks of cleanup, deliberation, and whispers of promised punishments, it was all over. They had passed the five cursed days that ended the old year and ushered in the new by then. Most of the way through the month of Kythras, the air was far colder, but a warmer world was visible just over the horizon. However terrible the winter had been, spring would arrive, and not a moment too soon. The city— and the wardwatch, and Rem and Torval—had weathered the storm and come through it bloodied but still, wondrously, alive.

With all said and done and their routines more or less reestablished, Rem and Torval found themselves finally enjoying a free evening at the King's Ass. The fires were stoked, the great room was lively but not overcrowded, and Torval was recounting their harrowing adventures to a genuinely enthralled Aarna. The special that night was a slow-roasted boar provided by a local hunter, and the spiced ale was wonderful.

Indilen, warming the seat beside Rem at the corner table they all occupied, bumped Rem to get his attention. Rem hadn't even realized that he'd withdrawn into himself, Torval's tale and the rumbling conversation in the room around them all having receded to a dull murmuring at the edge of his awareness. But the moment Indilen nudged him and he raised his eyes to see her smiling back at him, he knew that he'd drifted and she was doing her lover's duty by drawing him back to the here and now.

He offered a smile. "Sorry."

"And where were you off to?" she asked. "Torval's just getting to the best part, I think—where he saves the day single-handed, and you once more owe your life to his quick thinking and unrivaled ferocity."

"No need to hear it," Rem said, and lifted his ale mug for a long sip. "I lived it."

He drank. When he lowered his mug, he glanced sideward and saw that Indilen still stared at him expectantly.

"I'm still waiting," she said, leaning closer. Her hand fell on his arm. He laid his own free hand atop it and smiled again.

"I was just thinking," Rem said quietly, "that when we've had our fill and left this place tonight, I might have a story of my own to tell you."

Indilen's eyes widened. "Do tell."

"It's all about a boy who ran away from his home and family," he said, "off into the wide world, to find a new home, and make a new family, all on his own."

Indilen's eyes, always warm and crystalline, now flashed, offering the first hint of joyful tears. Her smile widened.

"That," she said, "is the sort of story I never tire of. I can't wait to hear it."

"Can't wait to hear it, eh?" Torval asked.

Rem and Indilen, the spell broken, both looked to the dwarf. He was on his feet now, half-bent over the table before them. Aarna had bustled away to fetch their boar.

"Sorry?" the two lovers said simultaneously.

"The story is yet unfinished," Torval said. "Didn't you hear me?"

Rem and Indilen exchanged puzzled glances. They shook their heads in unison.

Torval's eyes rolled. "We should like you back at our table," the dwarf said. "The both of you. Our Fhryst feast was interrupted—the tale remains unfinished!"

"Another dwarven holiday?" Rem asked. "Less exciting than the last, I hope."

Torval only nodded. He wore something of a strange, bemused expression—wistful and a little melancholy. "We should hope so," he said. "Just say you will."

"We'd be delighted," Indilen said. "Perhaps you should invite Aarna as well?"

Torval started to answer—mouth open, breath drawn—but then, as Rem watched, the dwarf stole a furtive glance over his shoulder, saw Aarna approaching bearing a huge platter of roasted boar meat and vegetables, and shook his head.

"Not this time," Torval said, then sat down again. His final words were spoken quietly, almost to himself. "Someday, perhaps…"

Rem felt Indilen's grip on his arm tighten. "It's your table, Torval. Just tell us when…"

And so, a week later, Rem and Indilen once more took a long walk on a bitterly cold night through the Third Ward down to the riverfront, and there climbed the stairs to Torval's door and knocked. It was a moonless night, the sky black as a vein of coal, the city twinkling beneath that ebon dome like a great convocation of banked coals, smoldering, waiting to be stoked. Rem almost imagined he could warm his hands by that malevolent light. Torval greeted them as always, with compliments for Indilen and insults for Rem, then ushered them inside. All was as it ever was: Lokki attacked Rem as though he were an ogre from an old bedtime story, Tavarix told tales of his ongoing education and training—for he had been readily accepted back into the dwarven stonemasons' fold as an apprentice—and Indilen lent a hand to Osma and Ammi as they prepared the meal and laid the table. In short order, everyone took their seats. For a moment, before Osma started speaking, Rem studied all now jostling for a place at the table—their familiar faces, their smiles, the love and concern for one another that all but wafted off them, like smoke from a bevy of bright candle flames. In that instant Rem had a strange and comforting thought.

Yenara was no longer his adopted home. It was simply home, and that was that.

Moreover, these people—Torval; his sister, Osma; Torval's children, Ammi, Tavarix, and Lokki; and most of all Indilen, the lovely girl beside him—they were no longer merely his friends. They were his family. At that moment, basking in the warmth they created from their own hearts, about to share their lore and their bread and their celebration of another day of remembrance and a new turning of the seasons, Rem thought that they were the only family he would ever need.

The reason for their gathering: the completion of their interrupted Fhryst feast. The rituals were repeated, including the lighting of the candles and Osma's harrowing account of the dwarven creation story. Rem loved it even more this time, and found himself strangely primed—strangely eager—when they finally came back to where they'd been so rudely interrupted on that night so many weeks ago.

"And so," Osma said, "the Spirit of the Earth, long tiring of Stormblight's rages and tyrannies, found the finest stones it could in the very bowels of the earth, and from these carved the first dwarves." She lit the final candle on the table, the one nearest Torval. "There was Leinar, the All-Father and first of our kind; Thendril, the Womb of the World; Athura, the Sower; Yangrol, the Smith; Wengrol, the Warrior; and Kondela, the Speaker, and ever thereafter the Judge of All. In its stony bosom did the Spirit of the Earth succor and wean these first of our kind, knowing that only patient formation and robust design could fortify them against Stormblight's depredations. When they were, at last, so plentiful that Stormblight's attentions could be avoided no longer, the Spirit of the Earth set them loose, and bade Stormblight do its worst to hinder and hamper them. And who knows what happened then?"

"They tore Stormblight to pieces!" Lokki cried.

"Stormblight found them strong and resilient," Tavarix said, his eyes settling on his father, glimmering with the possibility of tears yet beaming with pride, "and Stormblight punished them for their resilience."

Rem and Indilen stole looks at one another; seeing the rupture between father and son now healed warmed them immensely.

Osma nodded proudly at her nephew. "You are correct, and we know well the end of it all. The dwarves were strong, and so they fought when Stormblight assailed them. They were also tough, so they endured, even when Stormblight punished them. And oh, how Stormblight cursed! Those dwarves—*our* people, *our* forebears—were too stout and too grounded to be tempted by sensual wonders, by earthly riches, or by any of the offerings that had so punished the dragons and ensnared the elves and made sporting fools of humankind. Though beasts were sent against them, the dwarves hewed them down. Though storms and floods and fires and rains were brought down upon them, they stood, and smiled, and took all that Stormblight offered, and asked for more. Being made of stone, and bound to the earth, the dwarves were *as* the earth—abiding, eternal, slow to move, slower to change...but also resilient. Stormblight sought their tears and their lamentations, and all it received for its pains were defiant laughter and bitter scorn.

"In its rage, great Stormblight made the earth a wasteland. It slaughtered its own eternal progeny, the Great Spirits of Wood, the River, and the Earth, and their progeny in turn—elves, men, dwarves, and the last of the dwindling dragons—made their homes among the bones and the unquiet spirits of those that had first made them. Yet still our people would not yield."

Osma had reached the first candle again now. "When Stormblight burned down their houses, the dwarves settled on the riverbanks." She blew out the candle and retreated along the table again, to the next in line.

"When Stormblight flooded the riverbanks, the dwarves took to the woods." She blew again. Another candle went out. The room grew darker.

"When Stormblight tore down the woods with frost and wind," Osma continued, then blew out yet another candle, "our people stole fire from Stormblight's own gaping maw, then retreated into the deepest caves and the darkest caverns, and there they made their home. And that home, despite all of Stormblight's best efforts, could not be taken from them."

She had arrived at the head of the table again, and stood just behind Torval. The dwarf's blue eyes—glinting in the candlelight in a way that Rem had never before known—focused deeply on that last, lonely candle burning before him. They all did. That candle was the last hope for their people—for the world. That candle was the survival of the dwarven race—of all races—the lone light of hope, sanity, and goodness in a dark world built to satisfy one mad god's bottomless hunger for pain and suffering. Rem thought it one of the most beautiful stories he'd ever heard, and the light of that candle the brightest he'd ever seen.

"When others cried or begged or lamented, or simply lay down and died before Stormblight's fury, our people stood, brave and proud and unafraid. We opposed. We endured. And down to this very day, to the light shining in the center of each and every one of you at this table"—she seemed to make a point of including Rem and Indilen in this pronouncement, and Rem felt himself profoundly moved by the gesture—"we stand as a testament to their courage and their defiance of a mad god's tyranny. We have *all* struggled. We have *all* lost. We have *all* cried in despair, or wept for that which the mad god's wrath has taken from us—but as of this moment, around this table, before this single, enduring flame, we *live*. We *remain*. We *are*...until we are no more."

She leaned forward and blew the candle out. Once more the room was dark, the only light the glow of the hearth and the dim illumination from those burned-down candles against the far wall.

"And that," Osma said in the darkness, "is why we give thanks, and remember."

Without another word she moved back down the length of the table to her seat and took it once more. There was a long, solemn silence. Rem looked to Torval and his children, to Osma herself, and realized that it was not simply a pause, but a prayer of sorts. Each seemed to be peering into a dim, half-remembered past that could never be recovered. No doubt they were all remembering Olian, Torval's slain wife, along with Gedel and Rinnit, the children's lost siblings, who had died when their mother did, under the same terrible circumstances. Rem saw the warring emotions in all their eyes—the warmth, the grief, the gratitude for the time they had known with their mother and siblings, the bitterness at having only that brief season to hold on to now that they were gone. The feeling of bearing witness to something personal and profound—something that by rights Rem should not be bearing witness to, something that should have remained private among this scarred and loving family—filled Rem with a deep and abiding sense of appreciation.

"We give thanks," Osma said, and the spell was broken in an instant. "And so we feast."

The children all smiled and repeated, in unison, "We feast."

Their hands went for the food before them.

Rem felt Indilen squeeze his arm lightly. "Hello?" she said. "Are you still in there?"

He leaned close and gave Indilen a long, sweet kiss. Clearly she hadn't been expecting that. She stared at him when he withdrew, pleased and puzzled. Rem vaguely realized that the children were watching, too, with wide eyes and open mouths.

"Here now!" Torval said from his seat at the end of the table. "What's all this kissing about? There are wee ones present here!"

"Sorry, old stump," Rem said, and squeezed Indilen's hand. He looked into her eyes when he offered his next words. "Just happy to be home."

He turned to see what Torval thought of that. The dwarf was beaming, his smile so true and bright Rem could scarcely believe it was on that dwarf's broad, rough-hewn little face. Torval took up a pitcher from the table, bent forward, and proceeded to slosh beer into all their cups. When he'd finished, he raised his cup to Rem. Rem raised his in answer.

"Welcome home," Torval said.

"Home," Rem added. "Among friends."

"No," Torval corrected him. "Among family."

They all drank to that.

Look out for

THE FIFTH WARD:
GOOD COMPANY

by

Dale Lucas

Humans, orcs, mages, elves, and dwarves all jostle for
success and survival in the cramped quarters of the city of
Yenara, while understaffed watch wardens struggle to
keep its citizens in line.

Rem and Torval are tasked with escorting a notorious thief
through a dangerous forest to nearby city. But the criminal's
companions are waiting, and the soldiers Rem and Torval
travel with may not less honourable than they seem.

www.orbitbooks.net

ACKNOWLEDGMENTS

Friendly Fire is a book about building a home in a place you didn't come from, building community with strangers whom you don't always understand or even like, and growing families from bonds other than flesh and blood. It was born of my desire to show my heroes as members of families and communities, and to test the limits of the bonds and loyalties that define (and confine) them. Little did I know when I conceived of that story and began it that the year ahead of me would basically dramatize all of those thoughts and fears, and force me to confront both the best and the worst that I, my family, my country, and the world at large are capable of.

In 2017 I got to make my major imprint debut; I got to watch my country wrestle with its better angels and its most pernicious devils; I got to shepherd my five-year-old through a scary—but ultimately successful—surgery; I got to enter bitter, heated arguments with members of my own family about what is right and wrong, and soon after thanked those same family members, with tears in my eyes, for their generosity and compassion; and amid all of that, I got to revisit Yenara and follow Rem and Torval as they wrested order from chaos, struggling to see justice done in an often unjust world. Hopefully, we've all come out the other side as they have: beaten, battered, but somehow smarter, stronger, more humble, and more aware, knowing a little more now than we knew before.

Whatever else I've learned, I know this: when someone helps you, you say thank you, and you mean it.

So special thanks go to Lindsey Hall, my now-former editor at Orbit, who decided the world needed to meet Rem and Torval, and who guided me through the hard work of shaping *Friendly Fire*. Lindsey's blazing new trails on other frontiers now, but her faith, support, and rigorous editorial instincts were instrumental in bringing Yenara to life, and I can't thank her enough for the opportunity she gave me to share this world and its denizens with all of you.

That said, I couldn't have followed through and crossed the finish line without the inimitable Emily Byron from Orbit UK and my new stateside editor, Bradley Englert, both of whom helped me maintain my focus and find the heart of a big, unwieldy book just as I was despairing of ever doing so. Like everyone I've worked with at Orbit, Emily and Bradley are awesome collaborators, true professionals, and fabulous human beings. Where the book shines, give them credit; where its rough edges show, blame yours truly.

Behind it all there is my ever-loyal and inhumanly patient agent, Emily Keyes, whose faith in my work and willingness to answer any ridiculous question about this business that I pose to her (not to mention hearing a constant stream of new project pitches, 99 percent of which will never be written) probably qualify her for sainthood.

Closer to home, this year's special blessings and trials showed me the true mettle of the engaged and compassionate circle of souls that surrounds me. Chief among those whose faith and love humble and empower me are my sweet Liliana, the love of my life; my superhuman cyborg son, Gabriel; and my parents, Jim and Carol. Come what may, these four people collectively hold my heart, keep it safe when it's endangered, and squeeze it hard when it freezes over and needs a kick-start. What's best in me is because of them; what's worst in me persists in spite of their example.

Finally, to all of you who ventured with me to Yenara: thank you. A writer is nothing if they are not read, and hearing from so many of you over the past year who enjoy what I've done and want more of it has meant more to me than words can express. With bold hearts and a little luck, I'm sure we'll all reunite in Yenara, preferably in a quiet nook at the King's Ass over a couple of frothy pints.

Until the next time: be brave, be kind, and keep your eyes open, your fists clenched, and your backs to the wall.

Dale Lucas
January 2018

extras

www.orbitbooks.net

about the author

Dale Lucas is a novelist, screenwriter, civil servant, and armchair historian from St. Petersburg, Florida. Once described by a colleague as "a compulsive researcher who writes fiction to store his research in," he's the author of numerous works of fantasy, neo-pulp, and horror. When not writing at home or trapped in a cubicle at his day job, he loves travel, great food, and buying more books than he'll ever be able to read.

Find out more about Dale Lucas and other Orbit authors by registering for the free monthly newsletter at www.orbitbooks.net

if you enjoyed
THE FIFTH WARD:
FRIENDLY FIRE

look out for

THE THOUSAND DEATHS OF ARDOR BENN

by

TYLER WHITESIDES

AN EXPLOSIVE TALE OF DARING DEEDS, DECEIT AND DRAGONS

Ardor Benn is no ordinary thief — a master of wildly complex heists, he styles himself a Ruse Artist Extraordinaire.

When a mysterious priest hires him for the most daring ruse yet, Ardor knows he'll need more than quick wit and sleight of hand. Assembling a dream team of forgers, disguisers, schemers and thieves, he sets out to steal from the most powerful king the realm has ever known.

But it soon becomes clear there's more at stake than fame and glory — Ard and his team might just be the last hope for human civilisation.

CHAPTER

1

Ardor Benn was running late. Or was he? Ard preferred to think that everyone else in the Greater Chain was consistently early—with unreasonable expectations for him to be the same.

Regardless, this time it was all right to keep his appointment waiting. It was a stew tactic. And stew tasted better the longer it cooked.

Ard skipped up the final stairs and onto the third floor. Remaught Azel clearly wasn't the big fish he purported. Rickety wooden tri-story in the slums of Marow? Ard found the whole thing rather distasteful. Especially after Lord Yunis. Now, that was something! Proper stone mansion with a Heat Grit hearth in every room. Servants. Cooks. Light Grit lanterns that ignited with the pull of a chain. Ard half suspected that Lord Yunis wiped his backside with lace.

Different island. Different ruse. Today was about Remaught Azel, no matter how unaccommodating his hideout appeared.

Ard shifted the Grit keg from one arm to the other as he reached the closed door at the end of the hallway. The creaking floorboards would have already notified Remaught that someone was coming. *Interesting*, Ard thought. *Maybe there is something useful about holing up in a joint like this. Floorboard sentries.*

The door swung open, but before Ard could step through, a hairy, blue-skinned arm pressed into his chest, barring entrance.

"Take it easy," Ard said to the Trothian man. This would be

Remaught's bodyguard. His dark, vibrating eyes glared at Ard. Classic. This guy seemed like a tough son of a gun, although he was obviously past due for one of those Agrodite saltwater soaks. The skin on his arm looked like it might start flaking off.

"I'm a legitimate businessman," Ard continued, "here to do... legitimate businessy things."

He glanced past the large bodyguard to the table where Remaught sat, bathed in sunlight from the western window. The mobster wore a maroon velvet vest, a tricornered hat, and a shoulder cape, currently fashionable among the rich folk. Remaught seemed tense, watching his bodyguard detain Ard at the doorway.

"Search him."

"Really?" Ard protested, holding the Grit keg above his head so the bodyguard could pat his sides. "I left my belt and guns at home," he said. "And if I hadn't, I could easily shoot you from where I'm standing, so I find this whole pat down a little unnecessary, and frankly uncomfortable."

The bodyguard paused, one hand on Ard's hip pocket. "What's this?" he asked, his voice marked by a thick Trothian accent.

"Rocks," Ard answered.

"Rocks?" Like the bodyguard had never heard of such things. "Take them out—slow."

Ard reached casually into his pocket and scooped out a handful of small stones that he'd collected on the roadside before entering the building. "I'll need these for the transaction."

In response, the Trothian bodyguard swatted Ard's hand, sending the dusty pebbles scattering across the room.

"Now, that was quite uncalled-for," Ard said to the mobster at the table. "I find your man to be unnecessarily rough."

"Suno?" replied Remaught. "Three cycles ago, he would have fed you those rocks—through your nose. Going soft, I fear. Fatherhood has a tendency to do that."

Ard wondered what kind of father a mobster's bodyguard would be. Some fathers made a living at the market or the factories. This guy made a living by stringing people up by their toes at the whim of his boss.

The Trothian moved down, feeling around Ard's thighs with both hands.

"At the very least, you should consider hiring a good-looking woman for this step," Ard continued. "Wouldn't hurt business, you know."

The bodyguard stepped back and nodded to Remaught, who gestured for Ard to enter the room.

"Were you followed?" Remaught asked.

Ard laughed as he set the Grit keg gently on the table, stirring a bit of dust that danced in the sun rays. "I am never followed." He adjusted the gaudy ring on his index finger and sat down across from the mobster. "Except occasionally by a bevy of beautiful maidens."

Ard smiled, but Remaught Azel did not return the gesture. Instead, the mobster reached out for the Grit keg. Ard was faster, whisking the keg away before Remaught could touch it.

Ard clicked his tongue. "How about we see some payment before I go handing over the Grit in a room where I'm unarmed and outnumbered?"

Remaught pushed backward in his chair, the wooden legs buzzing against the floor. The mobster crossed the room and retrieved a locked safe box from the window seat. It was no longer than his forearm, with convenient metal handles fastened on both sides. The Regulation seal was clearly displayed on the front beside the keyhole.

"That looks mighty official," Ard said as Remaught placed it on the table. "Regulation issue, isn't it?"

"I recently came by the box," replied Remaught, dusting his hands. "I like to keep my transactions secure. There are crooked folk in these parts."

"So I hear," answered Ard. "And how do I know the safe box isn't full of sand?"

"How do I know that Grit keg isn't empty?"

Ard shrugged, a smirk on his face. They had reached the part of the exchange that Ard called the Final Distrust. One last chance to back out. For both of them.

Remaught broke the tension by reaching into his velvet vest and producing a key. He slipped it into the lock, turned it sharply, and lifted the lid.

Ard squinted at the coinlike items. They looked real enough in this lighting. Most were stamped with seven small indentations, identifying them as seven-mark Ashings, the highest denomination of currency.

"May I?" Ard plucked out a coin before Remaught granted permission. Ard lifted the Ashing to his mouth and bit down on the edge of it.

"Taste real enough for you?" Remaught asked. Ard's relaxed nature seemed to be driving the man continuously more tense.

Ard studied the spot where his teeth had pressed against the coin, angling it in the sunlight to check for any kind of indentation. He preferred to gouge suspicious coins with a knifepoint, but, well, Remaught had made it pretty clear that weapons were not allowed at this meeting.

The Ashing seemed genuine. And if Remaught wasn't planning to slight him, there would be 493 more in that safe box.

"You ever been to the Coinery on Talumon?" Ard flicked the coin back into the open box. "I was there a few years back. On legitimate business, of course."

Remaught closed the lid and turned the key.

"Coining," Ard went on. "Sparks, that's an elaborate process. Just the effort it takes to grind those raw scales into perfect circles…And you know they follow up with a series of chemical washes. They say it's for curing and hardening. I hardly think a dragon scale needs hardening…"

Across the table, Remaught was fidgeting. Ard suppressed a grin.

"Is something wrong, Rem? Can I call you Rem?" Ard pressed. "I thought this information would be of particular interest to a man in your line of work."

"Perhaps you can save the details for some other time," Remaught said. "You're not my only appointment today."

Ard leaned back in his chair, pretending that the mobster's words had really put him out.

"I'd prefer if we just get along with the transaction." Remaught gestured to the Grit keg. "What do you have for me there?"

"One full panweight of Void Grit," said Ard. "My source says the batch is top quality. Came from a good-sized block of indigestible granite. Passed through the dragon in less than five days. Properly fired, and processed to the finest of powder." He unlatched the cap on the Grit keg and tilted it toward Remaught. "The amount we agreed upon. And at an unbeatable price. I'm a man of my word."

"It would seem that you are," answered the mobster. "But of course you understand that I'll need a demonstration of the product."

Ard nodded slowly. Not all Grit could be demonstrated, especially indoors. But he had been expecting such a demand for this transaction.

Ard turned to the Trothian bodyguard, who leaned in the doorway like he was holding up the frame. "I'll be needing those rocks now."

Remaught grunted, then snapped at his bodyguard. "Suno! Pick up the blazing stones."

Wordlessly, the man hunted across the floor for the stones he had slapped away. As he searched, Ard quickly picked up the safe box, causing Remaught to jump.

"Relax," Ard said, crossing the room and carefully setting the valuable box on the wooden window seat. "I'll need the table cleared for the demonstration."

A moment later, Suno handed the rocks to Ard and lumbered back to the doorway, folding his dry, cracking arms.

There were nine little rocks, and Ard spread them into a loose ring on the tabletop. He unclasped the Grit keg and was about to reach inside, when Remaught grabbed his arm.

"I pick the Grit," the mobster demanded. "No tricks."

Ard shrugged, offering the container to Remaught. The man slipped his hand inside and withdrew a pinch of grayish powder. Ard pointed to the center of the stone ring and Remaught deposited the Grit in a tiny mound.

"That enough?" Remaught asked, as Ard brushed the pinch of powder into a tidier pile.

"More than enough," Ard said. "You trying to clear the whole room?" He clasped the lid on the Grit keg and set it on the floor behind him. "I assume you have a Slagstone ignitor?"

From his vest, Remaught produced the device Ard had asked for. It was a small steel rod, slightly flattened at one end. Affixed at the center point along the rod was a spring, and attached to the end of the spring was a small piece of Slagstone.

Remaught handed the ignitor to Ard, the tiny fragment of Slagstone wobbling on its spring. "With the amount of Void Grit you've laid down, I'd expect the blast radius to be about two feet." Ard said it as a warning. Remaught caught the hint and took a large step backward.

Ard also positioned himself as far from the table as he could, while still able to reach the tiny pile of gray Grit. He took aim and knocked the flat end of the steel rod against the table. The impact brought the spring down and the small piece of attached Slagstone struck the metal rod.

A respectable spark leapt off the Slagstone. It flashed across the wooden table and vanished instantly, with no effect.

"Ha!" Remaught shouted, as though he'd been waiting to make an accusation. "I should have known no one would sell a panweight of Void Grit at that price."

Ard looked up. "The Grit is legitimate, I assure you. This Slagstone ignitor, on the other hand…" He held up the device, gently shaking the spring as though it were a child's toy. "Honestly, I didn't even know they sold something this cheap. I couldn't ignite a *mountain* of Grit with this thing, let alone convince the spark to fall on that pinhead target. Allow me to throw a few more sparks before you let Suno rip my ears off."

The truth was, the tiny pile of powdered granite hadn't lit for two reasons. First, Remaught's Slagstone ignitor really was terribly inaccurate. And second, the Void Grit was definitely fake.

Ard leaned closer to the table, pretending to give the ignitor a close inspection. With his right hand hovering just above the pile of gray powder, he wriggled his fingers, spinning his heavy ring around so he could slip his thumbnail into a small groove and slide the face of the ring aside.

The gesture was subtle, and Ard was drawing Remaught's attention to the ignitor. He was sure the mobster hadn't noticed the fresh deposit of genuine Void Grit from the ring's secret cavity.

"Let's see if this does the trick." Ard repositioned himself, bringing the ignitor down, Slagstone sparking on impact.

The genuine Void Grit detonated instantly, the powder from Ard's ring creating a blast radius just over a foot. It wasn't at all like a deadly Blast Grit explosion of fire and sparks. This was Specialty Grit, and the particular demonstrated effect was far less dangerous.

A rush of energy emanated from the pinch of Void Grit, like a tremendous wind blasting outward in every direction from the center.

It happened much faster than Ard could withdraw his hand. Caught in the detonation, his arm was shoved backward, the Slagstone ignitor flying from his grasp. The stones on the table flew in every direction, the Grit pushing them to the perimeter of the blast, their momentum sending them bouncing across the floor.

The Void Grit was spent, but hovering around the table where the detonation occurred was a dome of discolored air. It would have been a spherical cloud if it had detonated midair, but the tabletop had been strong enough to contain the underside of the blast.

Remaught stumbled a step closer. "How did you do that?"

Ard wrinkled his forehead. "What do you mean? It's Void Grit. Digested granite. That's what it does." He bent down and retrieved a fallen pebble. "It voids a space within the blast radius. Clears everything out to the perimeter. The effect should last about ten minutes before the blast cloud burns out."

To prove his point, Ard tossed the pebble into the dome of discolored air. The little stone barely touched the perimeter before the effect of the Grit pushed it forcefully away.

Remaught nodded absently, his hand drifting to his vest pocket. For a brief moment, Ard thought the mobster might pull a Singler, but he relaxed when Remaught withdrew the key to the safe box. Remaught stepped forward and set the key on the edge of the table, just outside the hazy Void cloud.

"I'm ready to close the deal," he said, producing a few papers for Ard's inspection. Detonation licenses—or at least forgeries—which would allow him to purchase Grit.

But Ard wasn't interested in the legalities of the transaction. He dismissed the paperwork, picking up the keg of false Void Grit and holding it out to Remaught.

"Of course, I'll need a receipt," said the mobster, tucking his licenses back into his vest.

"A receipt?" That sounded frightfully legitimate to Ardor Benn.

"For my records," said Remaught. In a moment, the man had

produced a small square of paper, and a charcoal scribing stick. "Go ahead and notate the details of the transaction. And sign your name at the bottom."

Ard handed the Grit keg to Remaught and accepted the paper and charcoal. Remaught stepped away, and it took only moments for Ard to write what was needed, autographing the bottom as requested.

"I hope we can do business again in the future," Ard said, looking up from his scrawling. But Remaught Azel didn't seem to share his sentiment.

"I'm afraid that will not be the case." The mobster was standing near the open doorway, his Trothian bodyguard off to one side. Remaught had removed the cap from the Grit keg and was holding the cheap Slagstone ignitor.

"Whoa!" Ard shouted. "What are you—"

Remaught brought the ignitor down. A cluster of sparks danced from the impact, showering onto the gray powder housed in the open keg.

"Did you really think I wouldn't recognize an entire keg of counterfeit Grit?" Remaught asked.

Ard crumpled the receipt and dropped it to the floor, lunging for the key on the edge of the table. He scooped it up, but before Ard could reach the safe box, the Trothian bodyguard was upon him. In the blink of an eye, Ard found himself in a headlock, forced to his knees before a smug Remaught.

"I believe I mentioned that I had another appointment today?" Remaught said. "What I didn't tell you was that the appointment is happening now. With an officer of the Regulation."

A man appeared in the doorway behind Remaught. Not just a man—a veritable mountain. He had dark skin, and his nose was somewhat flat, the side of his face marked with a thin scar. The Regulator ducked his shiny, bald head under the door frame as he entered the room.

He wore the standard long wool coat of the Regulation, a crossbow slung over one shoulder and a sash of bolts across his broad chest. Beneath the coat, Ard thought he could see the bulge of a holstered gun.

"Delivered as promised," Remaught said, his tension at an all-new high. The Regulator seized Ard's upper arm with an iron grip, prompting Remaught's bodyguard to release the headlock.

"What is this, Remaught?" Ard asked between gasps for air. "You're selling me out? Don't you know who I am?"

"That's just it," said Remaught. "I know exactly who you are. Ardor Benn, ruse artist."

"Extraordinaire," said Ard.

"Excuse me?" Remaught asked.

"Ardor Benn, ruse artist extraordinaire," Ard corrected.

The giant Regulator yanked Ard to his feet. Prying Ard's fingers open, the man easily removed the key to the safe box before slapping a pair of shackles around Ard's wrists.

"Now wait a minute, big fella," Ard stalled. "You can arrest *me*, an amicable ruse artist trying to eke out a humble living. Or you can take in Remaught Azel. Think it through. Remaught Azel. *He's* the mobster."

The bald Regulator didn't even falter. He stepped forward and handed the key to Remaught with a curt nod.

"The Regulator and I have an understanding," answered Remaught. "He came to me three weeks ago. Said there was a ruse artist in town selling counterfeit Grit. Said that if I came across anyone trying to hock large quantities of Specialty Grit, that I should set up a meet and reach out to him."

"Flames, Remaught! You've gone clean?" Ard asked. "A mobster of your standing, working with a Reggie like him? You disgust me."

"Clean? No," Remaught replied. "And neither is my Regulator friend."

Ard craned his neck to shoot an incredulous stare at the Regulator holding him. "Unbelievable! A dirty Reggie and a petty mobster make a deal—and I'm the victim!"

Remaught addressed the big official. "We're good, then?"

The large man nodded. "We're good. I was never here."

The Regulator pushed Ard past Remaught, through the doorway, and into the creaky hallway, pausing to say one last thing to the mobster. "You got him to sign a receipt like I told you?"

Remaught scanned the room and gestured to the crumpled piece of paper on the floor. "You need it for evidence?"

"Nah," said the Regulator. "This lowlife's wanted on every island in the Greater Chain. The receipt was for your own protection. Proves you had every intention of making a legal transaction. Buying Grit isn't a crime, providing you have the proper licensure." He gave Ard a shove in the back, causing him to stumble across the rickety floorboards. "Give me plenty of time to distance myself before you leave this building," the Regulator instructed. "Understood?"

Ard glanced back in time to see Remaught nodding as the door swung shut. Ard and the Regulator descended the stairs in silence, the huge man never removing his iron grip from Ard's shoulder. It wasn't until they stepped outside into the warm afternoon that Ard spoke.

"Lowlife?" he said. "Really, Raek? That seemed a bit much. Like you were enjoying it."

"Don't lecture me on 'a bit much,'" answered the Regulator. "What was that whole 'ruse artist extraordinaire' slag?"

"You know I like that line. I saw an opportunity and I took it," Ard answered.

Raek grunted, tugging at the collar of his uniform. "This coat itches. No wonder we can always outrun the blazing Reggies. They're practically choking themselves on the job."

"You almost look convincing," Ard said. "But where's the Reggie helmet?"

"I couldn't find one that fit," answered Raek. "And besides, I figure I'm tall enough no one can see the top of my head. Maybe I'm wearing a tiny Reggie helmet. No one would know."

"Sound logic," Ard said as they turned the corner to the west side of Remaught's building. "You swapped the key?"

"Child's play," Raek answered. "You leave the note?"

"I even drew a little smiling face after my name."

Raek led them to a sturdy hay wagon hitched to a waiting horse.

"Straw this time?" Ard asked, finding it difficult to climb onto the bench with his hands still shackled.

"Should pad the landing," Raek replied.

"Look at you! Good idea."

"You're not the only person who can have one, you know." Raek pulled himself onto the bench beside Ard and stooped to grab the reins. "You're getting bored, Ard."

"Hmm?" He glanced at his friend.

"This little stunt." Raek gestured up to the third-story window directly above them. "It's showy, even for you."

Ard dismissed the comment. Was there a simpler way to steal the safe box? Probably. But surely there wasn't a more clever way.

Remaught had to be feeling pretty smug. In his mind, the exchange had gone off without a hitch. The mobster had been gifted a Regulation-issue safe box, partnered with a crooked Reggie, and taken some competition off the streets by having the ruse artist arrested.

By now, Remaught was probably reading Ard's note on the receipt—a simple message thanking the mobster for the Ashings and informing him that the Reggie was as fake as the Grit. This would undoubtedly send Remaught scurrying to the safe box to check its valuable contents. All he needed to do was thrust Raek's replacement key into the lock, and... *boom.*

Any moment now.

The idle horse stamped its hooves, awaiting Raek's directions.

"We're sparked if he moves the safe box," Raek muttered after a moment's silence.

"He won't," Ard reassured. "Remaught's lazy."

"He could have the bodyguard do it."

"Suno was going soft," Ard repeated what he'd heard from Remaught. "Something about fatherhood. I'm more worried that the window won't break…"

Three stories above, the glass window shattered. The safe box came hurtling out on a perfect trajectory, landing in the back of the hay-stuffed wagon with a thud.

Remaught Azel was blazing predictable. Classic mobster. Maybe Ard *was* getting bored.

"I'm actually surprised that worked," Ard admitted, as Raek snapped the reins and sent the horse galloping down the street.

"That doesn't give me much confidence. Tampering with the safe box was *your* idea."

"I knew *that* would work," Ard said. They'd tipped the replacement key with a tiny fragment of Slagstone and filled the inside of the lock with Void Grit. The detonation would have cleared everything within the blast radius, undoubtedly throwing Remaught backward. The box of Ashings, still latched shut, was hurtled outward by the force of the Grit, smashing through the glass panes and falling three stories to the hay wagon waiting on the street below.

"I had full trust in the Grit." Ard gestured behind him. "I'm just surprised the box actually landed where it was supposed to!"

"Physics," Raek said. "You trust the Grit, but you don't trust physics?"

"Not if I'm doing the math."

"Oh, come on," said the large man. "Two and a half granules of Void Grit detonated against a safe box weighing twenty-eight panweights falling from a third-story window…"

Ard held up his still-shackled hands. "It physically hurts me to hear you talk like that. Actual pain in my actual brain."

Behind them, from the shattered window of Remaught's hideout, three gunshots pealed out, breaking the lazy silence of the afternoon.

"Remaught? He's shooting at us?" Raek asked.

"He can't hope to hit us at this distance," answered Ard. "Even with a Fielder, that shot is hopeless."

Another gunshot resounded, and this time a lead ball struck the side of the wagon with a violent crack. Ard flinched and Raek cursed. The shot had not come from Remaught's distant window. This gunman was closer, but Ard couldn't tell from what direction he was firing.

"Remaught's shots were a signal," Ard assumed. "He must have had his goons in position in case things went wrong with his new Reggie soulmate."

"We're not soulmates," Raek muttered.

A man on horseback emerged from an alleyway behind them, his dark cloak flapping, hood up. The mob goon stretched out one hand and Ard saw the glint of a gun. He barely had time to shout a warning to Raek, both men ducking before the goon fired.

The ball went high. Ard heard it whizzing overhead. It was a Singler. Ard recognized the timbre of the shot. As its name implied, the small gun could shoot only one ball before needing to be reloaded. The six-shot Rollers used by the Regulators were far more deadly. Not to mention ridiculously expensive and illegal for use by the common citizen.

The goon had wasted his single ball, too eager to fire on the escaping ruse artists. He could reload, of course, but the process was nearly impossible on the back of a galloping horse. Instead, the goon holstered his Singler and drew a thin-bladed rapier.

"Give me the key," Ard said as another horseman appeared behind the first.

"What key?" replied Raek. "The one I swapped from Remaught?"

"Not that one." Ard held up his chained wrists and jangled them next to Raek's ear. "The key to the shackles."

"Oh." Raek spit off the side of the wagon. "I don't have it."

"You lost the key?" Ard shouted.

"I didn't lose it," answered Raek. "Never had it. I stole the shackles from a Reggie outpost. I didn't really have time to hunt around for keys."

Ard threw his chained hands in the air. "You locked me up without a way to get me out?"

Raek shrugged. "Figured we'd deal with that problem later."

A cloaked figure on foot suddenly ducked out of a shanty, the butt of a long-barreled Fielder tucked against his shoulder.

Raek transferred the reins to his left hand, reached into his Regulator coat, and drew a Roller. He pointed the gun at the goon with the Fielder, used his thumb to pull back the Slagstone hammer, and pulled the trigger.

The Slagstone snapped down, throwing a spark into the first chamber to ignite a pinch of powdered Blast Grit in a paper cartridge. It detonated with a deafening crack, the metal gun chamber containing the explosion and throwing a lead ball out the barrel.

The ball splintered through the wall of the shanty behind the goon. Before he could take proper aim at the passing wagon, Raek pulled back the Slagstone hammer and fired again.

Another miss, but it was enough to put the goon behind them. Raek handed the smoking Roller to Ard. "Here," the big man said. "I stole this for you."

"Wow." Ard awkwardly accepted the gun with both wrists chained. "It looks just like the one I left holstered in *my* gun belt at the boat."

"Oh, this gun belt?" Raek brushed aside the wool Reggie coat to reveal a second holstered gun. "You shouldn't leave valuable things lying around."

"It was in a locked compartment," Ard said, sighting down his Roller. "I gave you the key."

"That was your mistake."

Behind them, the Fielder goon finally got his shot off. The resounding pop of the big gun was deep and powerful. Straw exploded in the back of the wagon, and one of the side boards snapped clean off as the Fielder ball clawed its way through.

"Why don't you try to make something of that Reggie crossbow?" Ard said. "I'll handle the respectable firearms."

"There's nothing disrespectful about a crossbow," Raek answered. "It's a gentleman's weapon."

Ard glanced over his shoulder to find the swordsman riding dangerously close. He used his thumb to set the Slagstone hammer, the action spinning the chambers and moving a fresh cartridge and ball into position. But with both hands shackled together, he found it incredibly awkward to aim over his shoulder.

"Flames," Ard muttered. He'd have to reposition himself if he had any hope of making a decent shot. Pushing off the footboard, Ard cleared the low backboard and tumbled headfirst into the hay.

"I hope you did that on purpose!" Raek shouted, giving the reins another flick.

Ard rolled onto his knees as the mounted goon brought his sword down in a deadly arc. Ard reacted instinctively, catching the thin blade against the chains of his shackles.

For a brief moment, Ard knelt, keeping the sword above his head. Then he twisted his right hand around, aimed the barrel of his Roller, and pulled the trigger. In a puff of Blast smoke, the lead ball tore through the goon, instantly throwing him from the saddle.

Ard shook his head, pieces of loosely clinging straw falling from his short dark hair. He turned his attention to the street behind, where more than half a dozen of Remaught's men were riding to catch up. The nearest one fired, a Singler whose ball might have taken him if Raek hadn't turned a corner so sharply.

The wagon wheels drifted across the compact dirt, and Ard heard a few of the wooden spokes snapping under the strain. They were almost out of the slums, but still a fair distance from the docks. Raek's stolen hay wagon was not going to see them to their journey's end. Unless the journey ended with a gut full of lead.

Ard gripped the Roller in both hands. Not his preferred way of aiming, but his best alternative since his wrists were hooked together. Squinting one eye, he tried to steady his aim, waiting for the first goon to round the corner.

The rider appeared, hunched low on his horse. Ard fired once. The man dropped from the saddle, but six more appeared right behind him. And Ard's Roller only packed two more shots.

"We need something heavier to stop these goons!" Ard shouted. "You got any Grit bolts on that sash?"

Raek glanced down at the ammunition sash across his chest. "Looks like an assortment. Anything specific you're after?"

"I don't know...I was hoping for some Visitant Grit," Ard joked as he reached over and pulled the crossbow off Raek's shoulder.

Raek chuckled. "Like you'd be worthy to summon a Paladin Visitant."

"Hey, I can be downright righteous if I need to be," he answered.

Ard didn't favor the crossbow. He preferred the jarring recoil of a Roller, the heat from the flames that licked out the end of the barrel. The lingering smell of smoke.

"Barrier Grit." Raek carefully reached back to hand Ard a bolt from his sash. The projectile was like a stout arrow, black fletchings fixed to the shaft. The Grit bolt had a clay ball serving as an arrowhead, the tip dyed bright blue.

The bolt was an expensive shot, even though Barrier Grit was one of the five common Grit types. Inside the clay arrowhead, a chip of Slagstone was nestled into a measurement of glittering dust: digested shards of metal that had been dragon-fired and processed to powder.

Ard slipped the bolt into the groove on the crossbow, fitting the nock against the string he had already pulled into place—a difficult task with chained wrists. The goons were gaining fast now. Definitely within range.

"What's the blast radius on this bolt?" Ard pulled the crossbow to his shoulder and sighted down the length.

"The bolts were already on the sash when I stole it," answered Raek. "I'm guessing it'll be standard issue. Fifteen feet or so. You'd know these things if you bothered to keep up your Grit licenses."

Ard sighted down the crossbow. "Seriously? We're riding in a stolen wagon, you're impersonating a Reggie, we're hauling five hundred Ashings we just swindled from a mobster...and you're lecturing me about licensure?"

"I'm a fan of the Grit licenses," Raek said. "If anyone could purchase Grit whenever and wherever they wanted, the islands would be a mess of anarchy."

"I'm not just anybody," Ard replied. "I'm Ardor Benn..."

"Yeah, yeah. I got it," Raek cut him off. "Ruse artist extraordinaire. Just shoot the blazing bolt already."

Ard barely had to aim, the goons were riding so close now. He leveled the crossbow and pulled the trigger. The bolt released with a twang, finding its mark at the foot of the leading horse. The clay ball shattered on impact, and the Slagstone chip sparked, igniting the powdered metallic Grit.

The blast was nearly large enough to span the road. The discolored cloud made an instant dome, a hardened shell trapping two of the horsemen inside it. Their momentum carried them forward, striking the inside perimeter of the Barrier cloud.

The two horses went down, throwing their riders and crumpling as though they had galloped directly into a brick wall. A third rider also collided with the outside of the barrier dome, unable to stop his horse in time to avoid the obstacle suddenly blocking the road.

The two men within the Barrier cloud wouldn't be going anywhere until the Grit's effect burned out. They were trapped, as though a giant overturned bowl had suddenly enclosed them. Although the Barrier cloud seemed like it had a tangible shell, it couldn't be moved. And this dirt road was compact, so they wouldn't have a prayer at burrowing under the edge of the dome.

Ard grinned at the successful shot. "Haha! That'll buy us some time to reach the docks. Teach those goons not to mess with Ardor Benn and the Short Fuse."

"Come on, Ard," Raek muttered. "You know how I feel about that name."

"It's a solid name for a criminal Mixer like you." Ard understood why Raek thought it was unfitting. Raekon Dorrel was neither short nor impatient. Several years ago, during a particularly sticky ruse, Ard had referred to his partner as the Short Fuse. It was meant as little more than a joke, but somehow, the Regulation ended up circulating it through the streets until it stuck.

"Still don't think that's a respectable weapon?" Raek changed the subject, pushing the exhausted horse as they moved out of the slums.

"I'll leave the Grit shots to you." Ard handed the crossbow back to the driver. "I'll stick with lead and smoke."

Here, the road opened to a few grassy knolls that led right up to the cliff-like shoreline. The steep path down to the harbor was just ahead, where the *Double Take* was moored and waiting. Ard could see flags waving atop several ship masts, but with the high shoreline, it was impossible to see the harbor clearly.

"Clear ride to the docks today," Raek said. Now that he mentioned it, Ard thought the thoroughfare, usually bustling with pedestrians and the occasional cart or carriage, seemed abnormally still for a summer's afternoon.

"Something doesn't feel right," Ard muttered.

"Now, that's what you get for eating oysters for breakfast."

"I think we should stop," Ard whispered.

"Definitely," Raek replied. "We wouldn't want to outdistance those goons…" Raek was cut off as the wagon wheels hit a shallow trench across the dirt road.

Ard saw the sparks as the wheels struck a buried piece of Slagstone. He didn't even have time to grip the side of the wagon as the mine detonated.

Drift Grit.

A lot of it.

The blast radius must have been at least twenty yards, the center of the detonation occurring directly beneath the wagon. The discolored air hung in a hazy dome as the Grit took effect.

Ard felt his stomach churn as a bizarre weightlessness overtook him. The jolt from hitting the mine sent the wagon floating lazily upward, straw drifting in every direction. The horse's hooves left the road, and the poor animal bucked and whinnied, legs continuing to gallop in the sudden weightless environment.

"What was that?" Raek shouted. He still held the horse's reins, though his body had drifted off the wagon bench, his long wool coattails floating around his huge form.

"We hit a mine!" Ard answered. And the fact that it was Drift Grit didn't give him much hope. Barrier Grit would have been an inescapable trap, but at least they would have been safe inside the detonation. Adrift as they were now, he and Raek would be easy targets to anyone with a firearm. "They were waiting for us."

"Remaught?" Raek asked. "Sparks, we didn't give that guy enough credit!"

They were probably ten feet off the ground, Ard's legs pumping as though trying to swim through the air. He'd forgotten how disorienting and frustrating it was to hang suspended without any hint of gravity.

Now upside down, facing west toward the harbor, Ard saw more than a dozen mounted figures cresting the steep trail and riding out to meet them. He didn't need to see them upright to recognize the wool uniforms and helmets.

"Remaught didn't plant the mine," Ard shouted to Raek. "The Regulators did it. They knew we were coming."

"Flames!" Raek twisted in the air to see the horsemen Ard had just announced.

A gunshot pealed, and Ard saw the ball enter the Drift cloud. The shot went wide, exiting the detonated area just above their heads.

"We're sitting ducks!" Raek called, sun beating down on his bald head, dark skin glistening. "We've got to get our feet back on the ground."

Even if they could, exiting the Drift cloud now would put them face-to-face with an armed Regulation patrol. Perhaps they could flee back into the slums. Nope. From his spot hovering above the road, Ard saw four of Remaught's goons riding toward them.

"I thought you said this ruse was going to be low risk," Raek said, also noticing the two groups closing on their position.

"Did I? You're putting words in my mouth," Ard said. "How long until this detonation burns out?" He knew there was no way to know exactly. A standard Drift Grit blast could last up to ten minutes, depending on the quality of the bones that the dragon had digested. Raek would make a more educated guess than him.

Raek sniffed the discolored air. "There was Prolonging Grit mixed in with that detonation," he said. "We could be adrift for a while."

There was another gunshot, this one passing below their feet. Ard didn't know which side had fired.

"What else have you got on that sash?" Ard asked.

"More Barrier Grit." Raek studied his chest to take stock. "And a couple of bolts of Drift Grit." He chuckled. Probably at the irony of being armed with the very type of detonation they were trying to escape.

More gunshots. One of the lead balls grazed the side of the bucking horse. Blood sprayed from the wound, the red liquid forming into spherical droplets as it drifted away from the panicking animal.

Raek drew a dagger from his belt. Using the reins to draw himself closer, he slashed through the leather straps that yoked the animal to the wagon. Placing one heavy boot against the horse's backside, he kicked. The action sent the horse drifting one direction, and Raek the other. The horse bucked hysterically, hooves contacting the wagon and sending it careening into Raek.

Ard caught Raek's foot as he spiraled past, but it barely slowed the big man, tugging Ard along instead.

Their trajectory was going to put them out of the cloud's perimeter about thirty feet aboveground. They would plummet to the road, a crippling landing even if they didn't manage to get shot.

"Any thoughts on how to get out of here?" Ard shouted.

"I think momentum is going to do that for us in a second or two!"

They were spinning quite rapidly and the view was making Ard sick. Road. Sky. Road. Sky. He looked at Raek's ammunition sash and made an impulsive decision. Reaching out, Ard seized one of the bolts whose clay head bore the blue marking of Barrier Grit. Ripping the bolt free, he gripped the shaft and brought the stout projectile against Raek's chest like a stabbing knife.

The clay arrowhead shattered, Slagstone sparking against Raek's broad torso. The Barrier Grit detonated, throwing a new cloud around them midflight.

The bolt contained far less Grit than the road mine, resulting in a cloud that was only a fraction of the size. Detonated midair, it formed a perfect sphere. It enveloped Ard, Raek, and the wagon, just as all three slammed against the hard Barrier perimeter. The impenetrable wall stopped their momentum, though they still floated weightlessly, pressed against the stationary Barrier.

"You detonated on my chest?" Raek cried.

"I needed a solid surface. You were available."

"What about the wagon? It was available!"

A lead ball pinged against the invisible Barrier. Without the protective Grit cloud, the shot would have taken Ard in the neck. But nothing could pass through the perimeter of a Barrier cloud.

"Would you look at that?" Raek muttered, glancing down.

The Regulators had momentarily turned their attention on Remaught's goons. Apparently, the Reggies had decided that an enemy of their enemy was not their friend.

"We've got about ten minutes before our Barrier cloud closes," Raek said.

Ard pushed off the invisible perimeter and drifted across the protected sphere. Since Prolonging Grit had been mixed into the mine detonation, their smaller Barrier cloud would fail before the Drift cloud.

"How do we survive this?" Raek pressed.

"Maybe the Reggies and goons will shoot each other and we'll have a free walk to the docks."

"We both know that's not happening," Raek said. "So we've got to be prepared to escape once these two clouds burn out on us."

"I plan to deliver you as a sacrifice," Ard announced. "Maybe I'll go clean. Become a Holy Isle."

"Right," Raek scoffed. "But they won't be able to call themselves 'holy' anymore."

"Just so we're clear, this isn't my fault," said Ard. "Nobody could have predicted that Suno would sell out his boss."

"Suno?" Raek asked. "Who the blazes is Suno?"

"Remaught's bodyguard," he answered. "The Trothian in need of a soak."

"How does he figure into this?"

Ard had worked the entire thing out as they drifted aimlessly in the cloud. That was his thing. Raek figured weights, trajectories, detonations. Ard figured people.

"Remaught wouldn't have double-crossed us like this," Ard began. "It would put too many of his goons in danger, sending them head-to-head with an armed Regulation patrol. Our ruse was solid. Remaught thought he got exactly what he wanted out of the transaction—a dirty Reggie in his pocket.

"Suno, on the other hand, wasn't getting what he wanted. The bodyguard recently had a kid. Must have decided to go clean—looking for a way to get off Dronodan and get his new child back to the Trothian islets. So Suno sold out Remaught for safe passage. He must have told the real Reggies that one of their own was meeting with his mob boss. Only, the Regulators checked their staffing, saw that everyone was accounted for, and determined..."

"That I was a fake." Raek finished the sentence.

Ard nodded. "And if you weren't an actual Reggie, then you wouldn't be heading back to the outpost. You'd be headed off the island as quickly as possible. Hence..." Ard motioned toward the patrol of Regulators just outside the Drift cloud.

"Flames, Ard," Raek muttered. "I wanted to wring somebody's neck for this setup. Now you tell me it's a brand-new dad? You know I've got a soft spot for babies. Can't be leaving fatherless children scattered throughout the Greater Chain. Guess I'll have to wring your neck instead."

"You already killed me once, Raek," Ard said. "Look how that turned out." He gestured at himself.

Ard knew Raek didn't really blame him for their current predicament. No more than Ard blamed Raek when one of his detonations misfired.

Every ruse presented a series of variables. It was Ard's job to control as many as possible, but sometimes things fell into the mix that Ard had no way of foreseeing. Ard couldn't have known that Suno would be the bodyguard present at the transaction. And even if he had known, he couldn't have predicted that Suno would turn against his boss.

Maybe it was time to close shop if they survived the day. Maybe seven years of successful rusing was more than he could ask for.

"There's no way we're walking out of this one, Ard," said Raek.

"Oh, come on," Ard answered. "We've been in worse situations before. Remember the Garin ruse, two years back? Nobody thought we could stay underwater that long."

"If I remember correctly, that wasn't really our choice. Someone was *holding* us underwater. Anyway, I said we aren't *walking* out of this one." Raek emphasized the word, gesturing down below. Their Drift cloud was surrounded. Goons on one side, Reggies on the other. But Raek had a conniving look on his face. "Take off your belt."

Ard tilted his head in question. "I don't think that's such a good idea, on account of us being in a Drift cloud and all. Unless your plan is to give the boys below a Moon Passing. You see, this belt happens to be the only thing currently holding up my trousers. Take it off, and my pants might just drift right off my hips. You know I've lost weight over this job, Raek."

"Oh really?" Raek scoffed. "And how much do you think you weigh?"

Ard scratched behind his ear. "Not a panweight over one sixty-five."

"Ha!" Raek replied. "Maybe back on Pekal. When you were with Tanalin."

"Do you have to bring her up right now?" Ard said. "These might be my final moments, Raek."

"Would you rather think about *me* in your final moments?" Raek asked.

"Ah! Homeland, no!" cried Ard. "I'd rather think about cream-filled pastries."

"Like the ones you used to eat whenever we came ashore from Pekal... with Tanalin."

"Raek!"

The big man chuckled. "Well, Ard, you're not usually the type to let go of things." He let out a fake cough, saying Tanalin's name at the same time. "But I have to say, you've really let yourself go. You're a hundred and seventy-eight panweights. Pushing closer to one eighty with every raspberry tart."

Raek had a gift for that. The man could size up a person, or heft an object and tell you exactly how much it weighed. Useful skill for a detonation Mixer.

"Still less than you," Ard muttered.

"Actually, given our current gravity-free surrounding, we both weigh exactly the same—*nothing*."

Ard rolled his eyes. "And you wonder why you don't have any friends."

"Don't mock the science," said Raek. "It's about to save our skins. Now give me your blazing belt!"

Ard had no idea what the man was planning, but nearly two decades of friendship had taught him that this was one of those moments when he should shut up and do whatever Raekon Dorrel said.

In a few moments, Ard's belt was off, a surprisingly awkward task to perform while floating with both hands shackled. A gentle toss sent the belt floating to where Raek caught it. He held the thin strap of leather between his teeth while digging inside his Reggie coat for the gun belt.

"How many balls do you have?" Raek asked.

Ard made a face. "I'd think someone so good at mathematics wouldn't have to ask that question."